# RUTHLESS
# SAINT

# RUTHLESS
# SAINT

*Ruthless Saint*

Published by DIRTY TALK PUBLISHING LTD
www.dirtytalkpublishing.com

Dirty Talk
PUBLISHING

# RUTHLESS
# SAINT

FOR THOSE LOST IN THE
SEARCH FOR SELF.
FAMILY ISN'T JUST BLOOD.
IT'S THE ONES WHO STAND
BY YOU

# PLAYLIST

EVERYBODY WANTS TO RULE THE WORLD – LORDE
TROUBLE IS COMING – ROYAL BLOOD
EXITS – FOALS
TIME – GEORGE RILEY
PLAY GOD – SAM FENDER
BAD INTENTIONS – NIYKEE HEATON
I WANT TO – ROSENFELD
NOT ENOUGH – ELVIS DREW
I'LL DIE ANYWAY – GIRL IN RED
BROKEN – LUND
BAD REPUTATION – JOAN JETT & THE BLACKHEARTS
DEVIL'S WORST NIGHTMARE – FJØRA
NIGHTMARE – HALSEY
SICK – DONNA MISSAL
GLORY BOX – PORTISHEAD
LOSE MY BREATH – RHEA ROBERTSON
NOTHING'S GONNA HURT YOU BABY
BAD IDEA! – GIRL IN RED

# IMPORTANT NOTE

Ruthless Saint is a dark-ish com, standalone mafia romance. It does contain content and situations that could be triggering for some readers.

This book is explicit and has explicit sexual content.

It is intended for readers 18+.

For a full list of triggers, please visit the author's website.

# AUTHOR'S NOTE

Hey there, awesome reader!

You made it, and I'm so excited for you to crack this book open, but... (there's always a but!) let's get one thing straight from the get-go—my spelling isn't wonky.

I roll with the UK-English vibe. You know, the one with extra 'u's. So, when you see 'colour' instead of 'color' or 'favourite' instead of 'favorite,' don't be alarmed.

And about the whole 's' and 'z' situation. In my world, it's 'apologise' and 'emphasise' rocking the scene.

Now that we have that out of the way, buckle up, grab your favourite snack, and let's dive into a story where mafia bosses flirt more dangerously than a cat with a laser pointer, and love is messier than my attempts at assembling IKEA furniture. We're in for a wild ride, my friend!

Love,

Jo Preston

AUTHORJOPRESTON.COM

# PROLOGUE
## DANTE

It is a rite of passage for every Santoro man to be initiated by blood. At fourteen, my time to be welcomed into the ranks of my father's men has finally come. My ticket to adulthood—an execution I'm to perform in the name of vengeance for crimes committed against the family.

Standing opposite my mark's house, my foot tapping impatiently and my palms growing sweaty, I count down the minutes, eager to spill enemy blood and taste the sweet, heady rush of power.

There is beauty in retribution. And Alessandro Carusso deserves every single thing that's coming his way.

"Dante?" Luigi, one of my father's trusted men, drops his cigarette to the ground, putting it out with the tip of his scuffed shoe. A billow of smoke surrounds us like a fog, mixing with the ever-present mist Blackwood is known for as he exhales his last puff.

Although by the coast, it's not exactly a holiday destination one would choose when seeking a place for a beach holiday. Dark pine woods that stretch out in all directions surround Blackwood, shrouding it in an eerie sense of isolation. With narrow streets winding down a steep slope, all pathways lead to the ocean. A sunset warming the horizon with a cast of oranges and yellows would be a beautiful sight, weren't it for the high rugged cliffs on either side, and a thick rolling fog present most of the year, ensuring that the only beachy thing about Blackwood is the sound of waves crashing against the rocky shore mixing with the creaks and groans of the old buildings, weathered by rain and salt in the air.

What you *do* get, though, is the best and purest drugs in Northern America, and the head of the Italian mafia who decided to make a home here.

"Let's go." I crack my knuckles, adrenaline coursing through my veins. "He should be asleep by now."

We usually wouldn't come in the night. Slaves to the Santoro code, we face our enemies head-on, giving them time to come to terms with their imminent death.

But this asshole doesn't deserve a warning, not Alessandro Carusso. He lost that privilege when he murdered his wife and child. And yet, even killing innocents wasn't enough to seal his fate. That would have cost him an arm. Maybe a bullet to the kneecap. Just a little reminder he's not in charge.

If it were up to me, he'd be tortured for his crimes. I would have relished the opportunity to subject him to unending agony for weeks, maybe even months, drawing out his sentence until death was a mercy. And as much as I'd like to take the matter into my own hands, tonight, I'm following my father's orders.

Go in, take out Carusso and his men, and get out.

At least he's going to pay for what he has done. Even if what sealed his fate was going after the man his wife had an affair with, Nico Nicolosi's son. And, despite his bad breath and questionable choices in women, Nico Nicolosi is Papa's dear old friend and a powerful enough capo residing in Blackriver for the death of his son to warrant retribution.

It wasn't going to be my job. It's not something a Santoro would usually get involved with at all, but since Carusso technically lives on our territory, I volunteered to come with Luigi and serve his sentence while Nicolosi's men got busy with ending the rest of the Carusso family line.

Even consumed by a need for revenge and a madness born of betrayal, Alessandro must have known it was going to end like this. Was his only goal to satisfy his own twisted sense of justice? He must have realised his actions—not driven by reason, but by a dark rage that knew no bounds—would bring on his demise. And all those around him would pay the price for his quest for vengeance.

With a grin, I scale the seven-foot fence, my heart pounding with excitement as I move stealthily through the undergrowth surrounding his house, carefully avoiding the spots that would trigger floodlights and give away my position.

Luigi and I move in silence, like predators stalking our prey. I watch as Luigi takes care of the guard stationed by the west wing, a quick, silent kill, and I can't help but feel a thrill of excitement as I creep up behind the unsuspecting guard leaning against a tree, absorbed in something on his phone. The knife slides through his throat with ease, and I watch with pleasure as the light fades from his eyes, his body collapsing to the ground with a gurgling sound as the annoying Angry Birds music continues to play from the phone clutched in his hand. I should feel something. Remorse, maybe? But he stood by a man who murdered his own wife and young daughter. He deserves his fate. The only thing I feel is the gratitude that it's dark enough for me to pretend the dark liquid seeping out of him is not blood. I kick the phone out of his hand and crush it under the heel of my boot before searching his body, trying not to gag at the smell of copper surrounding me. Choosing a knife as a weapon was a necessity. A calculated decision, one I had to make in order to be the person everyone thinks I already am. When my fingers wrap around a set of metal keys, I can't help but let out a low chuckle. This is too easy. Without a second glance, I continue my path around the house, dodging the manicured rose bushes and keeping my senses alert for any other guards, but the grounds are quiet. It's almost as if Carusso knows we're coming for him but doesn't care. Before I know it, I'm at the back of the house, slipping the keys into the lock and opening the set of glass doors with a satisfying click. The hunt is on.

Luigi steps behind me, panting. "Three on my side. You?"

"Just one," I reply, quietly inching the door open.

"There should be five more inside," he whispers.

I nod, then slide in through the cracked door and sneak behind a sofa.

"Let's split," I mouth to Luigi when he joins me.

He shakes his head.

I fight the urge to roll my eyes. Despite my age, I already hate when people underestimate me. "We split, or I'll knock you out and do it all myself," I seethe in a low, menacing tone, driving the message home.

With a shake of his head, he finally agrees, knowing better than to argue with me.

Hushed voices drift into the room from somewhere on the ground floor as Luigi motions for me to go upstairs to the bedrooms while he takes care of the men here.

When he sees my annoyance, he whispers, "Focus on Carusso. That's your target. No distractions, *Saint*." I never liked Luigi, but he's got a point.

With a reluctant nod, I hold back the sneer that's trying

to get loose at his use of the nickname—the wounds still too raw to bear its constant reminder of a tragic loss.

"Dante—" He stops me as I make my way from behind the sofa. "Don't forget. No witnesses. No one leaves here alive tonight. Got it?"

I nod once, not looking back at him. The fucker really needs a lesson in who he's speaking to. I don't need silly little reminders like that. I'm a fucking Santoro. The next in line to be the boss of the Italian mafia.

I'm so angry as I head up the stairs to the first floor, thinking of all the ways I can humiliate Luigi once I'm in charge, that I don't notice the huge guy standing on the landing.

Snarling, he lunges towards me, knocking the knife out of my hand before I can tighten my grip. Fuck. What a rookie mistake. I dodge the fist flying my way and roll to the ground, moving the fight away from the stairs and closer to the blade glinting on the carpet-covered floor in the pale moonlight. The fucker grunts in displeasure. He's huge. Like a Hulk on steroids. The vein in his neck is popping while he grins at me as I scramble backwards and away from him. He thinks he's got this fight won already, clearly having more muscles than brains. I may still be a kid, but I have a lifetime of training with the best of the best. I've learned to use my age and physique to my advantage, especially with fools like him who rely only on their physical strength.

He takes a step forward, his fists clenched, ready to rain down on me. But I'm not worried. He has yet to make a noise or raise an alarm, so it's me against him.

As he chuckles grimly and rushes at me, I move my hands up over my head as if trying to shield myself, but using the momentum to twist in the last moment, hooking my legs around his and throwing him off balance. I reach for my knife as Hulk tumbles to the ground with a grunt, his face connecting with the soft carpet. Within seconds, I'm on top of him, lifting his head by the hair and sliding my blade across his neck. The Hulk twitches underneath me as dark liquid gushes out from his wound, staining the plush cream carpet.

Once again, I manage to avoid the spray of blood, but this was close. Too close for my comfort. I look down, the darkness in the hallway making the stain look almost black. It will be a bitch to get out, but that's not my concern. Holding my breath, I wipe the blade of my knife on the dead man's shirt and get up.

My heart pumping in my chest from the thrill of being able to put my skills to real use, I make my way through the empty corridor, checking every room I pass. Unfortunately, they're all empty. I wouldn't mind another fight to get the adrenaline going before this is all over, but it seems that's not in the cards for me right now. My only goal is to make sure no one leaves alive.

The dark mahogany door of the master bedroom looms over me as I stand in front of it. I push the door handle down and crack it open, wondering if Alessandro knows tonight is the night he will take his last breath.

I contemplate if he has spent the last week living in terror. Or waiting for the inevitable. How would *I* spend my last week if I knew I had a death sentence? Not locked in my mansion, a prisoner to my own fear, that's for sure.

On light feet, I step to the bed where the man I came here to kill is snoring. I deliberate waking him, giving him a chance to fight, to say his last words. But as quickly as the thought crosses my mind, I discard it. He's a ruthless killer who deserves whatever death is dealt to him.

With a twisted smile, I press my blade to his neck. His eyes open, landing on mine instantly. His hand flies to my wrist, gripping it as I slide the knife across his skin, watching it part.

"I may be *Saint*, but I'm not your saviour," I say. "You should thank your lucky stars, because you deserve nothing less than a slow and painful death."

He opens his mouth, gasping for breath, or maybe trying to say something as I watch the life drain out of him and spill across his chest and pillow. His eyes leave mine and settle on a piece of furniture off to the side until, finally, they go blank.

"Was it all worth it?" I taunt the corpse.

He doesn't reply, not that I expected him to, but I can't help feeling that it was all his own fault.

Carusso's descent into madness was a tragic tale of love gone wrong. His obsession with his beautiful, younger wife was well known. And even though many believed he was one of the few mafia men who married for love instead of peace, the marriage he fought so hard for was his undoing. He fell prey to a woman, like the fool that he was. I guess it was inevitable that when shit went south, he'd go off the rails.

Love is nothing more than an illusion only fools believe in, a trap to ensnare the unsuspecting.

At fourteen, I already knew it would never be in the cards for me. My future was predetermined, my fate sealed the moment I was born. The first son of a powerful mafia Don, Massimo Santoro. Not that I minded. I've seen firsthand the destruction love can do to a person. I've watched my own mother hope and pray for my father's affection, only to be met with betrayal and heartbreak. But that's the life of a Don. A Don marries to sire an heir, to keep the lineage strong, and to keep the peace. After that, he does what he wants.

Papa never hurt her, not physically. But I saw the pain on

her face when he'd come back from a 'meeting' dishevelled and smelling of cheap perfume.

She never said a thing, though.

Not even on her deathbed after a year-long battle with cancer.

Even then, she believed.

*"Promise me you'll marry for love,* Dante," she asked me in her weak voice. I'd have promised her anything if it meant one more day with her.

But no matter the promise I made, I was never getting married for love. And I was definitely never falling in love. Love is a weakness.

I'll never put a woman through what my mama had to endure. Even if love wasn't on the table for me, I could promise my future wife faithfulness and companionship.

My eyes focus back on the still body in front of me and the ever-growing pool of blood beneath it. As quiet and quick as slicing somebody's throat open is, it's messy. And I don't do well with the mess. I like control. Plus, all the blood makes me want to vomit. I fucking hate blood. Unclenching Carusso's fingers from around my wrist, I wipe my knife on his pillow, then make my way to his en-suite.

I sneer at the splatters of red on my face. I fucking hate red. Blood is my worst nightmare. Not only does the smell disgust me, but it's also red. The same red Papa's mistresses like to smear on their lips. The same red he'd come home with on his shirt collar. Not caring that his wife or his sons could see it.

"Good job, Saint." Luigi walks in behind me, studying me in the mirror as I wash my face. "I'll do another sweep, make sure no one is left alive, and call in the cleaning crew."

"I'll do it," I say coldly, watching him step from foot to foot in the mirror. I can see the unease pouring off of him. "What is it?"

"It's okay to feel shit about your first kill..."

I chuckle darkly. "There is nothing to feel shit about. Carusso was an asshole. He deserved what came to him. Go home, Luigi."

"Okay, *boss*," he replies, leaving me in stunned silence. It's the first time anyone has referred to me as 'boss' instead of 'kid'. *About fucking time.*

I dry my wet face and hands on a fluffy towel monogrammed with Carusso's initials, then walk back into the bedroom.

It takes me twenty minutes to sweep the whole house and the grounds again, making sure we didn't miss anything. Tonight didn't happen. The Carussos didn't happen. Tomorrow, every single one of them, including all the men that stood by them, will be dead. Poof. Disappeared like they never existed in the first place.

Nicolosi is one fucked up motherfucker, but it's his revenge. And I'm still too young to intervene. Things will run differently when I'm in charge...

I make my way back into Alessandro's bedroom, giving it a quick once over before pulling my phone out and dialling the number for the cleaners.

As I'm giving them the details of the job, I keep coming back to the dead corpse on the bed, scrunching my brows as a thought crosses my mind.

I finish the call and follow his eyes to the piece of furniture he's blankly staring at. It's just a fucking antique wardrobe, nothing out of the ordinary, but there's a sick feeling in my stomach. Like something unpleasant is about to happen. He better not have a fucking decomposing body in there.

Fuck it.

In a few short strides, I'm right in front of it, turning the key in the lock and opening the door.

My heart stops beating.

What. The. Actual. Fuck?

"You," I whisper, going to my knees and trying to untie the ropes from around the scared three-year-old girl. Her whole body is shaking as tears are running down her cheeks, pulling around the duct tape covering her small mouth. "It's okay, I'm here," I murmur as I pull my knife out to cut her bindings off. My hands are shaking too much to try and untangle the stupid things. "This will hurt a little bit, okay?" I grip the edge of the tape, stroking her hair once she's free to move around. She nods, her huge green eyes so fucking trusting it nearly breaks my heart. I rip the tape off in one quick move, then pull her into my arms, shielding her from the corpse on the bed as she starts sobbing. "Shhh. It's okay. I've got you."

"Dantie?" Her watery eyes lift to mine. The last time I saw her cry was exactly one week ago when she fell over and scraped her knee. I put a bandaid on it even though she didn't break the skin, then played with her for an hour after, to the amusement of every soldier on our grounds. I didn't know that at the time, her father just found out about the affair. From what Papa told me, he came in, asking for help with retribution. Needless to say, it wasn't granted, so the fucker took matters into his own hands. But... *She* was supposed to be dead. Everyone thought she was dead.

"Why is Daddy angry at me?"

My blood boils again. How could he do this to an innocent child? How long has she been in there? Has she been here, tied up and alive all this time?

"Never mind that. You're safe now, and *he* won't be able to hurt you again."

"I want my mommy," her chin wobbles as her little fingers curl into fists around my shirt.

"I..." Fuck. What do I do? What can I do?

If I tell anyone that Carusso's daughter is still alive, Nicolosi will make it his mission to find her and kill her. I'll also be disobeying direct orders. Leave no witnesses.

Everyone in this house is supposed to be dead.

I pull her tight to my chest, stroking her matted hair as the need to protect her wars with the obligation to follow my papa's orders. I may be a Santoro, but I'm no saint.

"I'm sorry." I squeeze my eyes shut. "Mommy can't help you anymore."

*No one can.*

# 1

## ALESSA

*Nineteen years later*

Y ou'd think after years of having to wash myself with gas station soap and wet wipes, I'd be used to it by now. You'd be wrong.

The possibility of someone walking in on you as you try to dry yourself with toilet paper never gets old. But I like cheap thrills, so I always just roll with it. Hence why, with my duffel between my legs, I lean down, swinging my head under the hand dryer, hoping to god no one walks in on me. I swear they put those things specifically at hip level so they can have a good old laugh at idiots like me bending over backwards to try and dry their hair.

I try not to think about the thousand times I had no choice but to do this. Or about the thousand times I wasn't sure where I'd sleep that night or what I'd eat. I ignore the feeling that I'm back at the start. That, somehow, instead of going forward, I have taken a giant step back. I do all that because it's been years since the last time I was in this position. And deep down, I know I'm no longer the same girl who lived on the streets and almost gave up. I'm no longer in *that* place, and even though I still don't have much, I have enough.

Or, at least, I had before I decided to look for answers. I had a roof over my head, a fridge full of food, and a car. But I gave it all up to chase a dream. And it seems that chasing your dreams lands you square in the middle of a bus station bathroom, trying to wash off the stench of a day-long journey before rushing to a job interview.

To which I was late.

You see, the car I *had*? It broke down about a hundred miles away from my destination, and the bus that was going to take me the rest of the way was a five-hour wait.

So, a five-hour wait and a million stops later, I could no longer take my time to find a cheap motel and get ready. All I could do was stuff my luggage in one of the bus station lockers and hope that a sink bath would be enough.

With my hair dry and up in a bun, I quickly change into a white blouse, a grey pencil skirt that flares around my knees, accentuating my hips, and a pair of heels I stole the previous day.

Not having time for elaborate makeup, I swipe some concealer under my eyes, then finish up with mascara and some red lipstick.

*This will have to do.*

The security guy eyes me up as I rush past him to put the rest of my belongings in the locker. The way his eyes follow my every movement, I'm certain there's either a 'wanted' poster of me somewhere or a security camera in the bathroom, and he just got a show. Whichever it is, I don't have the time to dwell on it, so I shoot him a toothy grin before grabbing the piece of paper that will hopefully help me get settled in this town and hightailing it out of there.

As soon as I'm out of the station and following the map on my phone, I'm enveloped in a heavy fog I swear wasn't there when the bus drove into town. How on earth am I supposed to know where to go when I can barely even see my fingers?

For the first time since I listened to my gut and decided on this crazy adventure, I'm having doubts. Getting run over by a car because it couldn't see me in the fog would definitely put a damper on my plans. And was it really the right decision to leave everything behind and come here? What if this town doesn't have the answers I seek? What if I made a huge mistake? And let's be honest, this job sounds too good to be true. *Receptionist needed right away*? The guy I spoke to on the phone just a few days before sounded way too eager for me to come in.

Distracted with all these questions swirling in my head somehow, I arrive in front of the small building unscathed, slightly out of breath and only fifteen minutes late.

With my resume clutched in my sweaty hand, I step through the door, hoping they will not turn me away just because I'm a little late. And I'm greeted by... no one. There isn't a single person inside the small reception area. The place is eerily quiet.

Scrunching my face up, unsure of my next step, I spot a small chair in the corner and decide not to give up. If they're having another interview, I'll just wait until it's over and beg them to see me. I need this job. Well, I need *a* job if I'm to stay in Blackwood. The five hundred and fifty dollars in my bag will not last long if I don't add a steady stream of income.

It was luck, really, that just when I was researching the town on the Internet, I stumbled on a receptionist job offer. It was even luckier that they needed the position filled as soon as possible. Decision made and fake resume printed out, I packed up my whole life into two suitcases and a duffel bag, loaded up my car and set off on the nine-hour journey north. Then, an hour and a half left ahead, my car gave up on me, and the rest is a bus station sink-bath history. I'm almost ninety per cent sure there's actual footage.

But I'm here now, and I always land on my feet. This will be no exception. I scan the piece of paper in my hand once again. All the dates and fake companies I supposedly worked for were in my head the minute I typed them up. That's not what I'm anxious about. My story and resume are perfect. My acting skills—not so much.

But it will be fine. They won't find out I've never worked as a receptionist before. I'm a quick learner. Had to be, since I had to fend for myself from an early age. If I can learn how to make elaborate cocktails, pick a lock, cook and memorise the entire encyclopaedia, I can learn how to answer calls and smile at people. Surely.

I have my memory on my side. Ever since I was little, all I had to do was read or experience something once, and I'd remember it no matter what. I'm a fountain of useless information and bad memories I'd like to forget.

The one thing my memory ever failed me at is my parents. I can't remember a thing about them. Or why they'd abandon me.

But that's why I'm here.

To find the truth.

"What are you doing here?"

I whip my head to the side, my eyes meeting the icy glare of the most beautiful man I have ever seen. Tall, dark, wavy hair and eyes the colour of molten chocolate. His skin is golden like he's just come back from a month-long vacation on the French Riviera.

I scramble to my feet, taking a step toward him while my

eyes drink in his toned body hidden beneath his perfectly tailored suit.

"What are you doing here?" he growls at me. Holy shit. That growl. I'm pretty sure I've just experienced full-body shivers.

"I'm here for a job interview," I reply, somehow keeping my voice steady despite the clear disdain rolling off him. "Receptionist," I clarify, handing him my resume and plastering on a smile.

He takes the paper from me with two fingers—as if it offends him to hold the same thing I have touched—his eyes never leaving my face. A flicker of annoyance passes through them before, finally, he looks down and scans the document.

I breathe a silent sigh of relief, not realising how heavy his stare was until it is gone and I can move again.

Not even ten seconds pass before his knuckles whiten, and he crumples my resume in his fist, letting it fall to the floor.

"No, thank you."

I'm floored. "Excuse me?" Surely, I heard him wrong.

"Apology accepted." He smirks. The cold bastard smirks at me.

My blood boils in my veins, but I don't let it show. I have dealt with a million dickheads like him in my short lifetime. Slowly looking him up and down, I count back from ten. I need this job. I need something.

"May I ask why?" I finally say calmly.

"You may not," he replies curtly. What an absolute dick. *Ten. Nine.*

My fists clench as I focus on the collar of his white shirt. *Eight. Seven.*

There's a bright red spot on it, making him seem a bit

more human, and a bit less like a cold marble statue with a shit personality.

*Six. Five. Four.*

He looks me up and down with a bored expression on his face. I decide, right then and there, I hate him.

*Three. Two.*

Not like he's going to be my future employer, from the looks of it.

"You'll be missing out on the best employee you've ever had." I try one last time to persuade him, just so I can say I gave it my best shot.

"I doubt it."

What the fuck is his problem? Can he not at least be pleasant?

"Whatever," I mutter, turning around but stopping halfway through the motion, my eyes meeting his once more. His eyes are burning with anger. Anger that normally would have me stepping back for self-preservation. But, like I said, I like cheap thrills. And what is poking a bear if not a cheap thrill? He gives the appearance of someone who'd be bothered by anything out of place. "You've got something red on the collar of your shirt. Probably ketchup," I say, my eyes drifting down to the spot.

I can see the war in his eyes. Stay rooted like a cold dickhead statue, or look down at his collar.

As much as I want to see which side of him will win, I'm not sticking around in his highness's presence any longer.

"I hate red, and I don't eat ketchup." The disgust in his voice is clear as his eyes momentarily drop to my lips. My body instantly erupts into embarrassed flames, but like the pro that I am, I fake a sweet smile and turn away.

Then stop in my tracks.

"Are you shitting me?" The words are out of my mouth

before I have a chance to stop them. But in my defence, ketchup is life.

I'm pretty sure my mouth is wide open as I turn back to look at him once more.

And once more, I'm met full force with the absolute male perfection in front of me. For a second there I thought for once my brain played tricks on me, that maybe the image I had in my head was better than the reality, but no. He definitely is the most beautiful man I have ever seen. Pity about his rotten heart.

"I'm not *shitting* you."

"You're missing out." I shrug. "Just four tablespoons of the red stuff has as much nutrition as a tomato. Plus, ketchup on fries is legitimately to die for. "

"You'd die for ketchup?" He arches his brow, cocking his head to the side, studying my face.

"People have died for less. I once saw a guy stabbed to death because he looked at another guy wrong. If I had to die for something, I'd choose ketchup over a wrong look."

Instantly, his whole face shuts down as his whole body tenses. "I think this conversation is over, Miss Jones."

I look down to his feet where my crumpled resume lays. I guess at least he got my name in the split second he looked at it. I suppose that's something.

"I wasn't aware we were having a conversation." I smile once again. "More like you were trying to get rid of me from the moment you saw me."

"Goodbye, Miss Jones," he dismisses me with a flick of his wrist.

I turn around, seething at his rudeness, and stomp out the door, unwilling to be in his presence any longer, no matter how hot he is. I'm still fuming when I get to the bus station and retrieve my suitcases, ignoring the same security guard from before, still watching my every move.

It's only when I settle in the way over my budget hotel room I relax enough to see the positive in the situation. At least I don't have to work for the asshole. And surely there are other jobs in Blackwood. This place is big enough that I'll probably never see him again. Although, just in case, I should make a pact with myself to avoid that part of town.

That night, when I go to bed, I make a plan of action. The first thing on the agenda is to find a job. The second is to make my stupid eidetic memory forget the man who had me so riled up today.

It shouldn't be too hard.

But my brain is a beast of its own. And as I fall asleep, it keeps bringing up images of angry chocolate brown eyes, and full lips lifting into a sexy smirk.

# 2

## ALESSA

I don't know why it took me years to start searching for the truth. Lack of courage, maybe? Or maybe it's because I didn't want to find out I simply wasn't wanted.

I've struggled to fit in all my life, so finding out it's been like that since birth shouldn't really make that much of a difference. Except it wasn't since birth. For the first three years of my life, someone must have loved me. Or at least like me enough to take care of me. Because shortly after my third birthday, something changed.

My very first memory is waking up on a porch swing, a black bomber jacket over my body as I tried to make out where I was and why there was no one else with me. I remember feeling sad and scared, holding onto the material like it was my lifeline. I think I was waiting for someone to come back, so certain the owner of the jacket would be back at any moment, except no one ever showed up.

Well, the cops did.

Once a well-meaning neighbour called them, worried about a small child sitting in front of an empty house some lady died in a month before.

It's been foster home after foster home from that point on. Turns out not every three-year-old girl gets adopted. And the older I got, the more attention I started receiving.

Unwanted attention. Not the kind that gets you a happy family.

I was thirteen when the eighteen-year-old son of my then-foster parents came into my room and raped me for the first time. I ran away the next week when my foster parents tried to punish me for stabbing him with scissors, not believing I was just trying to defend myself, and never looked back.

Since then, I have been too busy staying alive to even think about my past. Survival was my goal, and trying to figure out who the owner of the black jacket was became second place to finding food and shelter for the night. The jacket stayed stashed away at the bottom of my backpack and at the back of my mind.

I'd take it out now and then, breathe in its scent, imagining the notes I smelled the first time I had it wrapped around me, the warm and rich woodsy scent wrapped in a citrusy undertone. As the smell faded over the years, so did my childish belief that the owner of the jacket would come back for me one day. I almost threw it out at least a dozen times, but could never quite get myself to follow through. It wasn't until I put it on a few months ago that I found *it*.

Instead of chucking the jacket, I decided to make use of it and put it on for once. Even after all these years, it felt huge on me. But unlike the first time, I wasn't drowning in it. I could make it work, make it look cool, except something was weighing it down. You can imagine my surprise when I ran my fingers over the soft material and found a small round object stuck between the material next to a breast pocket with a hole in it. After all the years of looking at it, the jacket delivered what I hoped was a clue to my past.

A small round pocket watch with intricate designs on the front and one word engraved on the inside.

Blackwood.

After the initial shock, I hid the pocket watch away, unsure if looking for answers was what I wanted. It took me longer than I'd like to admit to finally put on my big girl pants and google the one word that felt equally foreign yet familiar on my lips.

The minute I came across the isolated town, I had a gut feeling. For some reason, it never felt like it belonged to a person. But a town? One hidden away from the rest of the world? It just felt right.

So, on a spur of the moment, I packed all my belongings into my car and took the nine-hour journey north, hoping I'd find some answers *here*.

Except if I didn't find a job quickly, I'd be out on my ass and living that gas station life again.

"Do you have a printer I can use?" I ask the bored-looking receptionist at the hotel's help desk. You'd think with how much they charge for a room, their staff would be more approachable.

She blows a bubble with her gum into a big balloon until it pops as she looks me up and down. "No." Her tone is bored, too.

Jesus Christ, is this town full of assholes?

"Do you know where I could find a printer I'd be able to use?" I try again.

With a heavy sigh, she gets up from the chair she's been sitting in and walks around the counter to me.

"Phone." She extends her hand, chewing her gum loudly.

I hesitate for a second before placing my phone in her hand.

She rolls her eyes, handing it back. "Unlock."

I type in my code before passing it to her again. She opens the map app and types something in as I study her. She's not much younger than me. Eighteen, maybe seventeen? Was I this annoying three years ago?

"Here." She gives me my phone back.

I *definitely* spoke in more than just one-word sentences.

"Thank you," I murmur, looking down at the screen and finding directions to *The Tech Shop*. I swear to god, if she's expecting me to go out and buy a printer, I'm going to lose it.

The girl shrugs and walks back to her seat, resuming her previous blank stare into the black computer screen and loud gum-chewing position. Clearly, I've been dismissed.

I grab my bag and head outside. Might as well go now.

The day is much clearer today, the heavy fog from yesterday is all but a memory as I walk through the streets taking in the grey buildings that surround me.

The town of Blackwood is set on a slope, a jagged rocky coastline on one side and a thick pine forest on the other. I didn't pay it much attention yesterday, but since the fog has cleared, I can actually take in the view, and it's mesmerising.

Heavy dark clouds are floating above the town, casting shadows on the dark rooftops and streets, giving the whole place a mysterious vibe. It's breathtaking and gloomy at the same time. An odd combination, yet one perfectly fitting. I get the feeling the place has the same dark vibe whether or not the sun is out.

Within fifteen minutes of walking downhill, my calves are burning and the prospect of trudging it back up to the hotel is not one I'm looking forward to, but I have arrived at my destination. And thankfully, The Tech Shop looks more like a cyber cafe than an actual tech shop where one would go to purchase a printer.

I sigh, pulling out my red lipstick. If you don't ask - you don't get. Might as well have a little help when asking.

The doorbell jingles as I walk through the door, taking in rows of computers on one side and a repair desk on the other. It's dark inside since the large storefront window to the outside world is tinted, not allowing for much of the daylight to come through, but it's easy to spot the large heavy-duty printer in the corner, anyway. *Bingo!*

"Hello?" I call out to no one in particular. The place is empty. Maybe they need a receptionist, too? My eyes land on the prices. Holy shit, since when do they charge twenty bucks for an hour of internet? And is that two dollars to print a page? No way I can afford all of that.

There's a heavy sigh, then one of the chairs in the back corner moves, and I'm greeted by the sight of an annoyed teenager—a game controller in his hand and headphones around his neck as he reluctantly stands up.

"Yeah?"

What is it with kids in this town and one-word sentences?

"Hi." I smile sweetly at him, biting my lip.

He clears his throat and sets the controller down. *I love this part.*

"Wow, this place is amazing!" I twirl a strand of hair around my finger, taking a step towards him. "You must be the manager. I love what you've done here. It's modern but also *private*." I whisper the last word, taking another step forward.

The guy blushes, his whole face going red. "I mean my dad owns the place. I just work here. But, yeah. Kinda manage it, too."

"Wooow!" I slowly spin around, making sure he gets a good look at my butt before meeting his eyes again. Well, *meeting* is subjective. They're currently focused on my chest. "I can't believe you basically own the place! So impressive."

"It's nothing really," he shrugs his shoulder, getting a bit more cocky.

"You must be so good with computers." My eyes land on the repair counter. "You repair them too?" I say in awe.

"I can fix a few things." He puffs out his chest.

"Wow." I look at him with starry eyes. "I've never been good with computers," I pout. Absolute bullshit. "Never had anyone to show me stuff." My eyes cast down as I play with the hem of my t-shirt, lifting it just an inch to expose a little bit of my stomach. I should have worn a dress. Playing coy to get my way would have been much easier if my legs were on display.

"I can show you some stuff." He comes closer. His eyes focused on where my t-shirt meets my jeans.

"Really?" I gasp, clapping my hands. "Oh my god, that would be amazing! I'm Alessa."

"Matt." He grins. "Let's fire up this bad boy." He guides me to the closest computer. "And I can show you what's what."

"Oh, Matt. You're so amazing!" I say, but my heart is only half in it now that he's on the hook.

"No problem, *babe*. Here."

I try not to cringe at his use of babe, but the whole body shiver of disgust is obvious. Thankfully, Matt is not skilled at reading cues because he sidles up to me and switches the computer on.

I 'ooh' and 'aah' in all the right places before asking him to show me how to check my email. He doesn't question my ineptness. And when I pull up three different versions of my resume, asking him to show me how to print a document, he does so happily. Not even batting an eyelid when my finger slips, and I *accidentally* print eleven copies. Of each.

We're standing by the printer, waiting for it to finish, when I spot the gorgeous black Maserati outside. For a small, isolated town, this place sure has some nice cars and expensive gaming cafes. It probably has something to do with all the exclusive casinos they have here. From what I found online, which wasn't much, most of them are high-stakes clientele and invite only.

I longingly watch the Maserati outside as Matt places his hand on my hip. I pretend I don't notice. Just a few more pages, and I can tell him to fuck off. In a nice way, of course. Never burn a bridge if you think you might have to cross it again. I'm about to turn back around, sidestepping out of his hold, when the devil in disguise walks down the street and heads toward my dream car.

He looks even better today, his suit as black as his soul, impeccable on his toned body. His wavy, dark brown hair, despite all the humidity in the air, is styled to perfection, not a strand out of place. Now that the full force of his stare is not on me, I spot details I was too flabbergasted to pay attention to before. Like the dark, intricate designs peeking out from under his sleeves. This man is absolute visual perfection. There's no arguing about it. If only he weren't such a dick.

I take a small step toward the window, watching him as he unlocks his car and opens the door. But just before he's about to get inside, he stops, his eyes lifting and landing on the tinted window between us. My heart speeds up, and like a deer about to be shot, I suddenly have the urge to flee.

"Who's that?" I whisper, worried he might overhear me.

Matt stands behind me, his hand landing on my shoulder. I'd be annoyed at how touchy-feely he is, but I'm too engrossed in the man on the other side. The man whose jaw tightens as he stares intensely at the window, his eyes focused and angry.

Matt's hand disappears as he takes a step back behind me. "That's Saint. Fuck."

"Who?" My eyes drink in his perfect features as the man keeps his angry gaze on the tinted glass.

"Dante Santoro. As in *the* Saint," he replies shakily. "His family basically owns Blackwood. *He* basically owns Blackwood."

Dante *Santoro*. His eyes sweep the tinted window again before he slides into his Maserati and closes the door with a loud thud, making me flinch.

"Saint? He's more of a devil if anyone were to ask me," I mutter to myself, turning back to the printer and grabbing the papers. "Could he see us through the tinted window?"

"I hope not. You don't want his attention."

No, I definitely don't. But it's too late for that. He already hates my guts.

"Thanks for the computer lesson, Matty," I say, placing a kiss on his cheek. A car engine revs outside as I grab my things and head to the exit. "See you around."

"Wait!" Matt tries to stop me. "You're going already?"

"Bye!" I shout, my hand already pushing the door open, and slide outside.

The Maserati speeds down the street and away—tail-lights glinting red at me—before it turns down one of the side streets and disappears completely, leaving behind the smell of burnt rubber and something else, something familiar I can't quite put my finger on in the air. I start the walk back up the hill to the motel, but just a few yards later, my steps falter. On an inhale, I slowly turn back to look at The Tech Shop. But even before I do, I know what I'll see. I think I knew as soon as Dante's eyes landed on the tinted window and stared in my direction. The dark window does not obscure the view at all. I can clearly see Matt, with his headphones around his neck, as he watches me, standing in exactly the same spot I left him in.

With a resigned sigh, I turn around and start walking again.

This means Dante Santoro was shooting daggers at me yet again. One thing is clear. He does not want me here. But his intimidation tactics are not going to work on me. I know exactly what it feels like not to be wanted, and I have never let it stop me before. What's one more person added to the list?

He may run this town. Who cares? If he's so good at running, he might as well run circles around me. Because I'm not leaving Blackwood until I get some answers.

# 3

## ALESSA

It's been a few days of looking for a job and not being able to find a single place willing to hire me. I'd feel offended, but at this point, I'm not surprised. All the businesses around here seem to be family run. Hiring an outsider is most likely not on their priority list. Especially with all the expensive shops I keep walking past and cars worth more than a small island. I can't give up, though, because if things keep going the way they are, I'll end up having to sleep on a park bench soon. A prospect I'm not keen on.

Having exhausted the search in the town centre, today I'm heading to the port. They're bound to have bars or restaurants there that need help. One can only hope. And hope I do, because I'm desperate. Frankly, right now, I'd be willing to do almost anything for money. But before I even go *there*, I need to exhaust all my other options.

The closer I get to the port, the stronger the smell of the ocean and fish in the air becomes. I can almost taste the salt in the breeze, as the damp wind assaults my hair and clothes despite the buildings that should shield me. Since I'm not going to an actual interview, I opted for smart casual attire today. Black jeans, a white blouse and an oversized black suit jacket I lifted from a Zara store when I was driving through Massachusetts on my way here. My suede platform boots with chunky heels add four inches to my five-foot–seven height, completing the look and making me feel like a boss bitch, ready to take on the world. I spent most of the afternoon on my second day here in the local library reading management books to make sure I could pull off the lies I've painted on my resume. Now, my brain is full of policies, goal setting and communication strategies. Well, the first goal I'm setting is for myself—find a job. Because stealing is not something I'm willing to do in Blackwood. Not if there's a chance I could find my relatives living here.

However, the fulfilment of my goal is looking more and more bleak the closer I get to the actual port. There are no businesses around. Maybe they're hiding inside the large grey containers and weathered boats that have seen better days? Like pretentious speak-easies... There's a gleaming white yacht moored in the bay, sticking out like an odd duck. Who would come here on a yacht? Blackwood doesn't exactly seem like an exotic holiday destination. Unless you're looking for overpriced *everything* and people who don't seem too happy about a stranger on their street.

Ignoring my curiosity, I keep walking down the dock, hypnotised by the dark ocean as waves crash into the rocky shores of the bay. I've never seen anything so beautiful in my entire life. I thought seeing the ocean from the streets was breathtaking, but being so close, feeling the droplets of the salty water on my skin and hearing the wave's rhythmic song—is something else entirely.

My butt hits the stack of crates before I even register I'm sitting down. I can't look away, studying the vastness before me, feeling like a tiny little fish about to be swallowed by a big, great white shark. I've always lived inland, never swam or sailed before—I guess you don't know what you're missing if you've never experienced it before. But the water is calling to me now, just like it did the first time I'd seen it.

I remember driving next to Marion Reservoir a couple of years ago while on my way to Tennessee. After a five-hour drive, I needed to stretch my legs, so without a thought, I stopped at a small campground surrounded by a thicket of trees. There was no one else around, yet I could hear voices, children laughing and dogs barking. Curious, I started walking through the trees to where the sounds came from, only to stumble onto a lake. The sun gleamed in the calm water, blinding me as I got lost in the sight in front of me. I don't remember how long I stood there, but by the time I got back to the car—my thoughts still on the water—it was dark already.

I've seen more lakes since then, always making a point to stop if I drove near one, always losing myself in the shimmering blue. Maybe it's because I had a feeling how easy it would be to end it all this way. Just walk a few steps too far, and I'd be done for, never having learned to swim. Or, maybe it's because the water reminds me of the vast amount of possibilities still out there for me. Until I came to Blackwood, however, I hadn't seen the ocean.

The pull I felt when faced with the deep darkness of the Atlantic was tenfold when compared to the pull of the lakes.

"If you're looking for dolphins, you'll be looking for a while. They never come this close to the shore."

I blink, startled from my thoughts by a tall, handsome stranger blocking my sunshine.

"They don't?" I ask, peering sideways and trying to assess the danger. One thing I've learnt over the years is when a guy sneaks up on you, ninety per cent of the time his intentions aren't pure.

"No. You'd have to go ten, maybe twenty miles offshore.

But once you do, they're usually easy to come by." He smiles broadly, exposing his straight white teeth. He seems genuine, unthreatening even. The stubble gracing his tanned face makes him look around thirty. A thicket of lashes the colour of his black hair frames his dark brown eyes with laughter lines in their corners, designed to put you at ease, no doubt. But Ted Bundy was handsome, too. As was my foster brother and countless others who tried to take advantage of me while I was trying to survive.

My body tenses as my fingers wrap around the edges of the crate I'm sitting on, ready to push off and give me momentum the minute I decide to take off. My eyes dart to his heavy-duty boots, hoping they'd slow him down if he ran after me. I'm a pretty fast runner, so I'm hoping the odds are in my favour. The boots I'm wearing might cause a slight hiccup, but I've run in heels before, and it's doable.

"Sorry if I startled you," he says.

"You didn't," I reply, my head tilting to the side so I can covertly assess all my possible exit routes. There is a narrow street leading back to town just behind him, but I'm better off running the way I came. Everyone knows narrow side streets are made for hiding bodies...

"Good. I wouldn't want to start on the wrong foot. I'm Luca." He extends his hand to shake. It's calloused but clean.

Reluctantly, I take it, shaking it gently while trying to figure out his agenda. "Alessa."

"I swear I'm not a serial killer," he laughs.

God, he *really* is handsome. This close up, I can tell I was wrong about his age. He's younger than what I initially thought. And those lines around his eyes just add to his charm, especially when he's laughing so wholeheartedly. There is something familiar about him, like I've seen him before. Then again, I've been walking up and down the streets of this town for almost a week now, so it's not unlikely that I have. "It's exactly something a serial killer would say." I smile this time. Despite knowing that I should be on high alert, I can't help the feeling he means me no harm.

"So what brings you here, Alessa?"

Instantly, I'm aware of his watchful eyes, and something is not sitting right with me. "Why would you assume I'm not from Blackwood?" I chose my words carefully. It may be a small town. But it's not *that* small. Surely, he wouldn't know everyone here.

He shrugs, flashing those straight, white teeth again. "I wasn't. I meant the port. You don't see many women wearing heels around here. But now that you've mentioned it, I don't think I've seen you around before. And I would definitely remember." His whole body pivots until he is sitting askew on his crate, resting his calf on his thigh, man spreading as he turns around to face me.

I can't help but squirm under his gaze. "You got me. I'm new," I laugh awkwardly. "But I like this place so far and thought I'd look around for a job. I'd like to stay awhile."

"A job?" He rubs his chin with his fingers, looking back out to sea. "There aren't many places at the docks that need help unless you want to do crab fishing?" His face turns back to mine, an eyebrow raised in question.

I shake my head. With my luck, I'd be overboard and drowning before the fishing boat even left the port.

"The bar and restaurant district is a five-minute walk south from here. Have you tried there?"

Shaking my head again, the feeling of failure creeps up. I knew trying to look for an office-type job was ambitious, yet I still hoped I could get one. I should have started with bars and cafes. It's where I always end up, anyway. Besides, the flexible hours will be perfect once I can finally start digging for answers. As it stands, I didn't even know Blackwood has a 'bar district'. Not that I'd ever admit that to a stranger. "I was on my way there when I stumbled upon this view." I motion at the bay, trying to play off my ignorance as a distraction.

"Completely understandable," he smiles. "It's breathtaking here, isn't it?"

I nod. "Do you work around here?"

"Sometimes," he replies cryptically.

I brush off the feeling of unease and get up. "Well, I should really get going. Thanks for the tip." I smile at him, glancing at my wrist, trying not to look like an idiot as I realise I'm not even wearing a watch. I have no clue how long I sat staring at the ocean, lost in my thoughts, but judging by the hazy sun behind the thick clouds, it must have been at least a couple of hours.

"No worries. Good luck with your job search."

I'm a few paces away, brushing the wind-whipped hair out of my face and hoping I'm heading in the right direction when Luca shouts my name.

I turn back slowly, facing him once more. He's standing now. All six-foot-god-knows-how-tall, in a tight black henley hugging his broad shoulders and ripped chest, black denim jeans tucked into black boots and a smile spreading across his face. He is exactly what a good girl should avoid. The typical tall, dark and handsome bad boy vibe. I've always thought I was a bit of a brat, though. "Yeah?"

"Try *La Famiglia*. Tell them Luca sent you."

I nod, biting my lip, trying to stop myself from smiling. I should turn around and run, run as far away from him as possible because I can tell now—when we're face to pecs—that he's bad news. News I definitely want to avoid. But I can't help the feeling of curiosity and the undeniable intrigue. Enough of it to make me want to see him again.

"Thanks, Luca."

I wave at him awkwardly, because apparently that's just what I do these days, then turn back around, speeding away and blushing like crazy.

"See you around, Alessa." His words are almost swallowed by the sound of the waves crashing against the docks. Almost, but not quite.

My heart is still beating out of whack when I spot the first restaurant, then the next. This must be the place. Visions of other dark and dangerous eyes that have been haunting me since my first day in Blackwood are replaced by less threatening ones as my brain keeps replaying the conversation with Luca. Seems he has been useful in more ways than I expected.

The small restaurant isn't hard to find. *La Famiglia*, with its green sign, linen tablecloths and a deli counter, sits on a corner of the main street. My mouth waters just looking at the menu as I scan it while walking in. Once the smell of delicious, freshly made Italian food hits my nose, I'm certain I'll be coming back, even if the prices are higher than I expected.

"*Buongiorno.*[1] Would you like something to eat?"

I smile widely at the man greeting me because, heck, yes, I would, but first things first. "Actually, I'm here to see about a job. I was told you might be hiring?"

I fish out a resume from my bag and reach out to hand it to him, but before my arm is even halfway up, the piece of paper gets snatched from my grasp. What the hell?

I whip around, scandalised someone would do that, but I should have known better than to assume any civility from the man in front of me.

His suit is navy blue today, a colour that only accentuates his dark features and brown eyes. There are golden flecks in them I haven't noticed before. His cheekbones are sharp as he grinds his jaw, staring me down. For a moment, I am lost in the abyss framed by his lashes. How could I ever think Luca was even remotely as handsome as Dante Santoro? Then he brings me back to earth by tsking at me.

"*Perché sei ancora qui?*[2]" he seethes. And as much as I want to hate him, I can't help the way my body reacts to his voice and the foreign language slipping from his full lips.

There's only one way I can fight against the pull he seems to have on me. Words and anger. "I don't speak *asshole*, so unless it was a rhetorical question, ask again. In English."

His eyes narrow at me, and cold sweat gathers at the nape of my neck. I'm suddenly aware of the deafening silence surrounding us. No one moves, no one speaks, no one dares to breathe. I know I made a mistake as surely as I know I'd die if someone were to cut off my oxygen supply. And looking at the rage in his eyes, I'm quite sure he's considering a million ways to end my life. Ah, well, might as well go out with a bang.

"Shoot me," I whisper as his hand twitches.

His head tilts to the side. "Are you asking me to *kill* you? *La tua vita significa così poco per te?*[3]"

"You look like you'd like to snuff the life out of me," I shrug. "So, if I may be so bold as to choose the way to go, I'd like it to be by a bullet. Straight to the heart. Or brain. Either one. As long as it's quick." I reply, ignoring the way his gravelly voice affects me.

"Quick?" Dark amusement dances in his eyes.

"Well, by the way your hand twitches, I was worried you might want to choke me, and that just seems like a shit way to die. Choking, that is. Gasping for air, lungs burning and all that."

He's quiet as he studies me, and my brain takes that as a sign to continue its rambling.

"Asphyxiation just doesn't sound fun."

"Oh, but it can be. When done properly." In one step he is in front of me, his hand on my throat, his body inches from mine. "When done right." His fingers tighten around my neck, not stopping the airflow but tight enough for me to feel a surge of apprehension. I knew this man was dangerous the minute I met him, yet I didn't listen to my instincts and kept poking the bear. I should have known better than to make fun of him. Now the joke's on me. Seems the bear has had enough, and it's time to eat the mouse. My heart is beating so fast I almost miss his next words.

"For example, if I were to block your carotid arteries, depriving your brain of oxygenated blood." His thumb strokes my pulse point before increasing the pressure. Whatever he is doing, I'm pretty sure my brain is being deprived of oxygenated blood because as I stare into his angry dark brown eyes, all my blood whooshes south. My legs shake as I study the furious expression on his face, hyper aware of his hand on my throat and the proximity of his body. His enticing scent, expensive and masculine, renders me immobile. "The buildup of carbon dioxide as your brain loses oxygen could create a feeling of... euphoria," he continues, seemingly unaware of the effect he has on me—an overwhelming mix of loathing and desire. He leans down, his mouth next to my ear, his minty breath stirring the hair on the side of my neck. "Asphyxiation can be quite *pleasurable*, Miss Jones."

"Alessa," I breathe. I'm no longer afraid I'm going to die. In fact, if this is his way of wanting to torture me, I'm on board. Sign me up. My whole body shudders with excitement as his fingers tighten just a fraction.

He steps away from me instantly. "You need not be afraid. I'm not going to choke you. *Or* shoot you." His hand leaves my throat, leaving me feeling cold and disappointed. "Today..."

I'm scrambling for words. Preferably something witty, something to knock him off balance like he just did me. It's on the tip of my tongue to tell him I'm not afraid. Far from it, but thankfully, the arrogant bastard steps in before I have the chance to humiliate myself.

"You grew." He scans my body from top to toe, his eyes stopping on my boots, much higher than the small heels I had on the day we met. He licks his lips before gazing back up and smirking. "I miss the little *secretary* outfit you had going on last time, despite the hooker lipstick." His eyes drop to my lips, which once again are painted red. His comment should have made me feel self-conscious, but instead, the opposite happens.

I smile at him brightly. "I, unlike some, happen to like red. And if you liked my outfit so much, you should have given me the job then."

"I wasn't the one giving jobs. Besides, there *was* no job to give." He flicks an invisible piece of fluff off his sleeve.

The way he likes to dismiss me, like I'm nothing more than an annoying little fly who dares to buzz in his presence, infuriates me. "Like hell there wasn't. I spoke to the owner the day before. He was adamant they needed help straight away."

"There. Was. No. Job. No company anymore, and the owner went... on an extended vacation."

"Lucky him," I murmur. Clearly, he's not going to give me a straight answer. I sigh, looking around. I can't see the faces of the two guys standing behind him, partially obscured by his large frame. Or maybe it's because his presence demands my full attention, no matter how much I hate it.

"What are you doing *here*, Miss Jones?" He snaps at me as if the last few minutes between us never happened.

"It's Alessa. And I could ask you the same."

He chuckles darkly. "Are you stalking me?"

"I was here first," I scoff.

"*I* come here every day." Is he serious? What are we in kindergarten?

"Oh, wow. Good for you. Did you *lick* this place, too?" I can hear an amused cough from one of the men standing behind him. Goody, at least my humour is being appreciated.

"What. Are. *You*. Doing here, Miss Jones?" Dante repeats himself, his presence expanding and sucking in the air around us.

I know I should reply to him. Every bone in my body is screaming for me to, but my self-preservation has decided to take a vacation, much like the man Santoro must have scared into not giving me a job.

"None. Of. *Your* business," I reply sweetly, then start digging through my bag, looking for the right resume.

"Seems it is *my business* since you turn up everywhere I go."

"You should stay at home then," I quip, turning my back to him and smacking my resume on the counter with a satisfying sound. "Sorry about that," I say to the man, who is looking anything but amused. He doesn't move, his eyes not even looking at me or the piece of paper between us.

The air moves behind me as a suited arm reaches around me, and tattooed fingers pick my resume up. With a sigh, I turn around, then watch Dante scan the lies printed on the page he is holding. I'm pretty certain the resume he snatched from me when he walked in is different from the one I just whipped out. I blame the mishap on his infuriating presence. And his delicious cologne assaulting my senses and trying to render me all gooey.

He studies the two documents for what feels like an hour. I should be happy he's actually reading them this time, unlike the first time we met. But I'm not, because I've fucked up. His eyes lift to mine, an eyebrow arched in amusement as he smirks, pleased with himself for catching me in a lie.

I growl in frustration. Not wanting to be lectured by this cocky piece of shit.

"Sorry, Miss Jones. La Famiglia is not hiring at the moment."

I'm stumped as to why he's not mocking me, choosing to dismiss me once more instead, but I'm not about to look a gift horse in the mouth. "Whatever. There are other places around here. And my name is *Alessa*."

I try to push past him, but he stops me, his grip tight on my arm. Too tight. I slowly meet his eyes, the amusement from moments ago gone, anger burning bright in them instead.

"You don't belong here, *Miss Jones*. You're best going back to where you came from." Saint my ass, he's definitely the devil.

"Go to hell." I try to rip my arm out from his grip, to no avail. My heart speeds up again. My instincts kick in, sensing danger.

"I'm already in one. Ever since you decided to stalk me." With his other hand, he reaches for my bag, then finally lets go of my arm, only to open my bag and pull out the stack of papers inside. My jaw opens in shock as he hands me my now empty bag back, then smiles sweetly, flicking his wrist at me. "Run along now."

I'm done. I'm done with him, and with assholes like him. With men who think it's okay to treat anyone like that. I have no clue what I've done to him, but whatever it is, he can go fuck a splintery plank of wood for all I care. I turn back to the counter, pulling a note from my pocket and waving it at the guy in front of me.

"This is my last fifty," I tell him. "I was going to buy food with it, but it's yours as long as you promise to douse his food in ketchup." I point at the douche in the suit behind me.

The guy behind the counter shakes his head, his eyes still on Dante instead of on me.

"It was worth a try." I sigh, shrugging, then turn toward the door. "See you around, shitbag." I smile his way as I walk past Dante, finally seeing the two guys who were standing behind him. My eyes connect with a younger, less handsome version of Dante as he grins at me. What is with this town and the tall, dark and handsome gene? Is there something in the water here?

"*Lei mi piace*[4], Saint." The younger Dante chuckles as I reach the door.

It could be the doorbell jingle, but I swear I hear Dante bark, "Shut up." And that's enough to put a pep in my step all the way back to the hotel.

# 4

## ALESSA

Unfortunately for me, Dante Santoro may, in fact, run this town. And it's clear everyone around here either loves him to bits or is afraid of him because no matter where I go, as soon as they see my name, the position they had open is no longer available.

Since I'm fairly certain I don't smell, I can only see one reason this is happening. Whatever his motives may be, it seems like Dante made it his mission to make sure I leave Blackwood with my tail between my legs. Fighting against the man I know nothing about has been tiring. I've been to almost every single bar, restaurant and cafe I could find, and even the places advertising for help in their windows did not want to hire me once they glanced at my resume. I swear, if I want to stay in Blackwood, my only option is to change my name. And as big a pain as Dante Santoro is becoming, I *do* want to stay in Blackwood.

So I continue. My daily walks to the port are giving me buns of steel and the strength to persevere. But with every new place that turns me away, my heart grows heavier. Even if I don't get the chance to look for my family, it'll be hard to leave. Over the past week and a half, I've grown used to the overpriced shops, the steep streets, the amazing views and the smell of the ocean in the air. This town is unique and oddly familiar at the same time. I feel at home here. Like I belong, despite being blacklisted by a certain suited jerk.

For the first time in a very long time, the impulse to keep running, to keep moving, is gone. I wouldn't mind staying in Blackwood for longer, despite *someone* here making it their life's mission to get me to leave and go as far away as possible.

I don't get *him*. I don't get why he hates me so much when we've barely even spoken, and at this point, I'm no longer interested in finding out the reason. He's made his intentions clear, and now it's time to show him what I'm made of. Someone needs to knock him down a peg. Or two.

Will I be playing with fire? Undoubtedly. But I'm not afraid of getting burned if it means I'm staying true to myself. I'll have all the time in the world to find out more about Blackwood and how it is connected to my past once I take care of the thorn in my backside.

*It's time to up the stakes.*

Literally.

Armed with a stack of freshly printed resumes—courtesy of Matt from The Tech Shop—I walk through the double doors, my feet landing on a plush red carpet as soon as I cross the threshold. The smell of cigars and whiskey hangs heavy in the air as I look around, realising the stakes may be higher than I've gambled for. The Black Royale Casino is not like any other casino I've been to. There are no slot machines, no loud tourists in Hawaiian shirts gambling away their pocket money, and no smooth jazz flowing from the speakers.

This place is something else. The inside is lit with soft ambient lighting, casting a golden glow on the blackjack and roulette tables covered in black felt. There are high-end, comfortable-looking chairs around each table. Occupied by men wearing expensive suits, focused on the game they're playing. As soft, sensual music reaches my ears, my eyes draw up to the gilded golden cages hanging from the ceiling, each holding a dancer in a golden bikini, moving to the rhythm of the song. I take a step inside, looking for a bar, or servers milling around, but my eyes keep going back to the girls dancing in their cages. They are too high for anyone to pay them any notice from down here, and it isn't until I see the private rooms on the upper level, I understand their purpose. Each room has a glass wall facing the inside of the casino, giving it a perfect view of the dancers in their cages. These must be their high-stakes rooms. Possibly invite only. If I could get a job as a server, or a bartender here, I could probably make a living from tips alone.

With my resolve renewed, I stride through the casino, going straight for the gold bar with every type of liquor displayed on its glass shelves. I sense a theme—clearly, whoever designed this place likes gold.

"Hi," I smile at a server waiting for drinks by the bar, her tray balancing on her perfectly manicured hand. She's stunning. The blonde hair and smoky eyeliner bring out the blue in her eyes and highlight her delicate features. She's wearing a long-sleeved, short black dress paired with golden heels that sparkle each time the light hits them. As far as work attire goes, this one is not bad.

"Hi." She smiles back at me. "Do you need help?"

"I do, actually." I bite my lip. "Are you guys hiring?"

She looks me up and down. "You look young. Are you twenty-one? They're strict on age here."

"I am," I reply, trying to appear confident. I probably should have gone harder on the makeup.

"Benji," she calls out to one of the guys behind the long

bar busy pouring alcohol into tumblers. "Can you grab an application form?"

"I'm Mel. What's your name?"

"Stephanie," I reply. "But everyone calls me Stevie."

"Well, Stevie. If you fill out an application form with all your information, someone will be in touch." She turns back to the bar, placing tumblers filled with golden liquid on her tray. Sauntering off before I'm even able to say thanks.

"I'm Benji, and you are?" I'm met with a curious look as the guy behind the bar wipes his hands on his apron.

"Stephanie Nicks."

"Have you worked at a casino before, Stephanie?"

"Call me Stevie," I smile. "And no. Not at a casino, but I've worked in high-end bars both as a bartender and a server before." Technically, not a lie. I stayed in one after closing and let a bartender who was hoping to sleep with me teach me how to make cocktails. I had so much fun that night I stole a cocktail-making book from the library the next day and learned the ingredients for every single cocktail they had listed, hoping it would come in handy one day.

"Stevie Nicks?"

"Parents were big fans." I shrug. He doesn't need to know I belt out Rhiannon every morning in the shower.

"Alright, Stevie. We're big on whiskey here. Can you tell me your three favourite whiskey cocktails to make?"

I don't bat an eyelid. "Whiskey Sour, Old Fashioned and the Horsefeather."

"You mean The Godfather."

"No, The Horsefeather. Whiskey, ginger beer, Angostura bitter and lemon juice. Kind of like a Whiskey Mule. You should try it. It's delicious."

"Impressive." Benji nods his head, pulling a form from

46

beneath the bar. "Fill this out and let me know when you're done." He hands me a pen and gets back to work.

It takes me ten minutes to fill out the paperwork, with how much detail they require. It's all lies, down to the phone numbers I provided for my references. The people whose names I have given will come through for me like I've come through for them countless times before, but I still feel uneasy. This is exactly the reason I was aiming at cafes and restaurants—you can get away with giving them just the basics. My hands are shaking by the time I hand back the form. Maybe it'd be best if I could find a diner on the outskirts. Somewhere, Dante Santoro would never set his polished shoe-clad foot in.

Benji scans the information before beaming at me. "This is awesome, Stevie. I'm sure we'll be in touch once all the information checks out."

*Fuck.* "Great." I hop off the stool. "May I use your bathroom before I leave?"

Benji points me to a small corridor covered in mirrors, where I find what can only be called a lavatory fit for Buckingham Palace. Seriously, ever seen golden chairs upholstered in plush red velvet in a bathroom? Me neither. Until now.

I take advantage of it and plop myself in said chair, covering my face with my hands. I'm such an idiot. Why would I ever think I could pull this off? They'll have me sussed in no time. If I didn't have to put everything in writing, I could maybe con them into believing I have all the experience in the world, but even then, the jig would have been up the minute they wanted my ID. I may have paid good money for my fake Stephanie Nicks driver's license, but it's not good enough that a place like this would fall for it.

I get up and wash my hands with the luxurious soap,

drying them on the individual, plush hand towels softer than anything I have ever used on my body. I should take one with me. Have a bit of luxury before I'm out on the streets again, not even having my car to sleep in anymore.

Resigned, I leave the bathroom, my head down as I make my way toward the double door I came in through.

"Hey! Wait!"

I stop in my tracks.

Shit, I shouldn't have swiped that towel.

I thought I was in the clear when I didn't see any cameras in the bathroom. I'm about to take off at full speed, not ready to get my ass dragged into a casino jail or whatever they've got here for their towel thieves when I hear my name. Well, my fake name.

"Stevie, wait!" I turn my head to see Benji rushing to me, a woman in a pantsuit right behind him. I'm a curious creature by nature, and this situation is no different. And, I may be about to be thrown into a casino jail, but something tells me not to run.

"This is her, Martina. Stevie."

She looks me up and down, assessing me in my white blouse, skin tight black jeans, and heels.

"She's gorgeous," Martina says, making me blush. "Turn around, Stevie."

Confused, I listen, doing a small circle right where I'm standing.

"Okay." She puffs out a large breath, grabbing my hand and pulling me back towards the bar, Benji trailing behind us. "Thanks, Benji," she says, opening the door to a small office right beside the mirrored corridor. Benji nods and goes back behind the bar as I'm pulled inside and sat on a chair.

"This is unconventional," Martina starts.

I cock my head to the side, clutching my bag with the white hand towel inside to my chest, just in case.

"I'm Martina, the Head of Staff at the Black Royale," she explains, not easing my nerves at all. Have they already realised I'm a fraud and just want to rub it in now? "One of the dancers broke her leg today and is out of commission for the next six weeks," she continues. My ears perk up. "I know you're overqualified and were probably hoping to be a server or work behind the bar, and with your experience, I wouldn't hold it against you if you said no, but I had to ask."

"Ask?"

"Would you be interested in filling in for a dancer?"

"A dancer? In one of those gold cages?" I question.

"Yes. The dancers are all on a contract, so it works a bit differently. You'd mostly be paid cash in hand plus tips. And the clients playing cards in the rooms upstairs tip the entertainment *very* well. They're all high-stakes, invite-only tables. And, of course, when the other dancer comes back, we will place you in any role you'd like. If you wanted to, that is."

So, potentially, I could fly under the radar.

"When would you need me to start?"

Martina's eyes light up. "Tomorrow at five, then I can make sure you've got everything you need. Walk you through everything. Schedule, breaks, and get you fitted—" she breaks off. "I should have asked this before. The outfits aren't exactly *revealing*, but they cover only a little bit more than a bikini would. Are you okay with that?"

I hide my wince. Normally, I wouldn't be. Flaunting my body means bringing attention to it. *To me.* But these are extenuating circumstances. And as much as I want to say no, I need this job. "I'll be fine."

She smiles brightly. "Welcome aboard, Stevie."

# 5

# ALESSA

The gold choker around my neck reminds me of Dante's firm hand gripping my throat, whispering about pleasure in his deep voice. He is the last thing I want to think about, yet, consistently, he's there in my mind whenever I stop paying attention.

"You look gorgeous, Stevie," Mel says, changing into her black dress behind me.

Golden beads fan out from my choker in an intricate spider web design, stopping just above my belly button, covering the skin not hidden under the golden bikini. There is another set of beads nestled around my hips like a skirt designed to reveal yet obstruct the view. "It's much less than I like to wear," I mutter. "Still, more than I was expecting, I guess."

"Well. I think you look like a queen. The gold really suits your skin tone."

Looking at myself in the mirror, I have to agree. Martina did my makeup tonight, walking me through every step so I can replicate it next time. Somehow, the golden eye shadow she chose brings out the flecks of amber in the green of my irises, and the highlighter on my cheeks makes my skin look iridescent. Martina even added gold feathers in my hair to complete the look, attaching them to my wavy strands so that each time I move my head, a different feather would catch the light. I actually love the full effect. But I'd love it even more if I didn't have to go out in public and dance in front of a room full of strangers.

The one thing making me feel better about the situation is the fact they will all be behind glass, watching me from afar, not able to touch me. With little luck, they'll be more interested in their game than me.

"Honestly, Stevie. You'll be fine. They probably won't even look at you, too busy gambling to pay you any attention," Mel says, her hand reaching out to grasp mine and squeezing it in reassurance.

"Have you ever done it?" I ask.

"No. But then, I've never been offered," she shrugs. "I probably would, though. A week of dancing in one of the cages would pay a month's rent. Not that the tips on the ground floor are bad."

"Really?"

"I swear. Your shift will be over before you know it, and then you'll be walking home with a nice chunk of cash in your pocket."

"Hotel."

"Sorry?"

I sigh. "I don't have a place yet. I'm staying at this small hotel at the moment."

Mel leans against my vanity table. "How long are you planning to stay in Blackwood?"

"I'm not sure yet. Hopefully, for a while. That's why I needed a job."

"You've got one now." She winks at me. "Nothing stopping you from looking for a more permanent place."

I laugh. "I need to make some money first unless they

don't require a month's rent in advance in Blackwood."

Mel looks thoughtful as she studies me. "I might be able to help you," she says. "Let's go for a drink this weekend."

"I'd like that." It would be good to make some friends, especially since I want to stay here.

"Stevie, you ready?" Martina pops her head through the dressing room door.

*As I'll ever be.*

Thankfully, the staff dressing rooms and break-out space are all on the first floor, so I can go directly to where I'm supposed to be dancing without stumbling into any of the patrons here. The cages are fastened to the ceiling via a horizontal lift mechanism, so with one push of Martina's red-tipped finger, my place of work for the next four hours slowly moves toward me.

"Remember, there're water bottles at arm level hidden in all of the four thick bars. Make sure to drink throughout your shift. If you feel faint or something is wrong, press the buzzer on the door and we will get you back here," Martina rattles off as she helps me into the cage. "You good?" she asks, closing the door.

I nod, even though I'm not feeling *good,* at all.

"Outstanding. Have fun up there." With a wide smile stretching her lips she presses the lift button and I hold on to the bars as the cage goes back to its place.

Once there, I take a few steps, testing out how secure it is, and am pleasantly surprised when the whole thing doesn't move. I take a small sip of water, placing the bottle back in the thick corner bar, mindful that as much as I need to keep hydrated, I'm stuck here without a toilet for the fore-seeable future.

When the music starts, I'm surprised by how loud it

sounds, before noticing the speaker built into the top of the cage. Niykee Heaton's voice wraps around my body and before I know it, I'm moving my hips as she sings about Bad Intentions. I'm lost in the sensual music, my eyes closed and body swaying as one song changes into another, then another. The high-stakes poker room might as well not exist. I keep my eyes closed, not wanting to see the men inside. And I don't turn around when I feel the hair on my neck stand, certain I'm being watched from another angle, too. I just keep on dancing, feeling free in this gilded cage made to contain me for the viewing pleasure of wealthy men. Free like I've never felt before. And once my shift is over, the cage moving back to where Martina is waiting for me, there is a pang in my chest. My soul is already aching to feel the freedom again.

"You did great, Stevie." Martina helps me back onto the solid ground, then guides me back to the dressing room. Once I'm in my chair, unclasping the choker from around my neck, she places an envelope in front of me. "This is from tonight."

My hands stop as I stare at the bulky envelope.

"Your tips from the poker room," she explains.

"Thank you," I say.

Martina shuffles on her feet, waiting for me to move or say something else, but I'm unable to lift my gaze from what I hope will pay for at least a few more nights in the hotel. "So... I'll see you tomorrow?"

I tear my focus away from the dressing table and meet Martina's eyes. "Yes, I'll be here."

"Fantastic." She visibly relaxes. "I was about to have a heart attack! I'll text you your schedule for the week in the next hour. It's quite late, so let me know if you need me to order you a taxi home. Other than that, great job tonight."

"It's fine, Martina. I can make my own way, but thank you."

She laughs. "Oh, don't thank me. It's company policy to offer transport to staff who work late."

"I'll keep that in mind." I turn back to the mirror, hoping she'll take the hint and leave me alone to get changed. After a few beats, she does and I can finally breathe again. I take off my makeup, take the feathers out of my hair, and pull it up into a messy bun. Then I slip into a white t-shirt, ripped blue jeans and a pair of vans. Feeling like myself again, I grab the envelope and stuff it in my bag, not wanting to look inside just yet.

Mel stops me just before I leave, telling me how amazing I looked when I danced. I give her a hug and leave, the feeling of finally belonging somewhere spreading in my chest as I hike up the hill back to the hotel.

———

ALMOST A WEEK PASSES by without a hitch. Each night, I dance in the golden cage feeling free and like I can finally be myself. I ignore the people behind the glass in the high-stakes room, or the feeling that someone else is watching me from somewhere behind me. I dance for myself, letting the music flow through my body, letting myself feel like a woman for the first time in my life.

Last night, Mel and I went out for a drink after my shift, our friendship reaching a new level. For the first time, I opened up to another person, telling her about never knowing my parents and my nomadic life so far. Mel told me what it's like growing up in a small town. I've never laughed so much in my life. Feeling relaxed and happy wasn't something I was ever able to experience. Up until now.

"Did you think about it?" Mel strolls into the changing room, giving me a hug before dropping her bag on the floor.

Before we parted the night before, she told me she had a spare room in her apartment I could stay in since her roommate left to travel the world for a year. I was tempted to say yes straight away, but something stopped me.

I put the finishing touches to my golden eye shadow, then turn to face her.

"I did."

"And?" She stops unbuttoning her blouse, her eyes searching mine.

"Are you sure it's a good idea? We barely know each other, and what if this job doesn't work out for me?"

"Oh, please. That's the beauty of it. My roommate's rent is all paid up. So the money you'd pay would go to bills and food. And if the job doesn't work out, at least you'd have a roof over your head to figure out your next step without having to worry about where you're going to sleep." She shrugs, pushing a strand of her blonde hair behind her ear, like it's the most natural thing in the world to offer a practical stranger your house.

"You barely know me."

"I know enough."

"I could be a serial killer." I quip.

"Hopefully, you're a famous one. At least they'll remember my name."

I laugh.

"Seriously, though, *Stevie*. My place is yours if you want it."

And here is the reason why I haven't said yes. Because as much as I'd like to think of Mel as a friend, she doesn't even know my real name. "Okay, but I need to tell you something first. Then you can decide if you still want me around." The words rush out of my mouth. I could be shooting myself in the foot, because if anyone finds out my real name, I'll probably be back to being jobless thanks to Dante Santoro blacklisting me in this town.

"Oooh, intriguing. But I doubt it'll change my mind." She smiles as I fix the gold beads around my hips. "Honestly, I can't get over how hot you look in that gold bikini. If I swung that way, I'd be all over you like white on rice," she sighs, shaking her head. "It's unfair, really."

"If you keep this up, I'll move in just for the steady stream of compliments," I laugh.

"Whatever works," she giggles. "Hey, but since we're telling each other things, there's something you should probably know about Blackwood—"

"Steeevieee!" Martina shouts from behind the door. "Hurry up. You're on in five."

"Let's talk after my shift," I whisper to Mel as she ushers me out of the changing room and into the now familiar corridor. It feels so natural, walking barefoot on the plush carpet towards my golden cage. In a trance, I step onto the platform, pushing the lift button, and wait until I'm in position. When the music starts, I lift both my arms above my head and move my hips in a figure eight, slowly, while sliding my right hand down my left arm until it reaches my head. With my eyes closed, I drag my fingers down my face, neck, over my breast to my hips, my other arm joining with the first. For the first time in a week, I feel confident enough to open my eyes, and when the song changes, I sway to the music, lifting my eyelids.

Five men wearing expensive suits are sitting at the poker table behind the glass wall. A thick string of smoke lifts from an ashtray where one of them is resting his cigar, his eyes fixed on me. I move my gaze to the man next to him. He's in his late forties maybe, a mountain of poker chips sits by his left arm as he watches me move, a glass of whiskey lifted halfway to his lips. Their attention feels too much and suddenly I want to close my eyes again, no longer curious as to who is looking at me, wanting to be in my own world once again.

Then I see a flash of blonde hair, mixed with black and gold, and my eyes land on Mel, grinning at me from behind the table. I lift my lips into a barely perceptible smile then close my eyes once again, but the spell has been broken and I'm finding it hard to get back to that place where it was just me and the music. Frustrated, I lift the hair away from the nape of my neck, twisting it up, until I can feel the cool of the air conditioning hit my back. It's like the breeze from the ocean. As I keep dancing, I imagine the waves, the bay, the port. I can almost taste the salty air on my tongue. The third song kicks in, then the fourth as my anticipation grows. Will I feel that gaze on me again today?

Every night without fail, when the tenth song rolls around, it's always *I Want To* by Rosenfeld. And every time, without fail, as I dance to this song, I feel this prickling sensation on my back, like someone is watching me dance not from one of the poker rooms but from somewhere behind me. The song is short, and as soon as it's over, so is the sensation of being watched. I have never had enough courage to turn around and find out whose attention I captured, even for just a short time. But tonight I'm riding high from the expressions on the faces of the men watching me from behind the glass and from the possibility of moving in with Mel and staying in Blackwood for longer. So the moment the song starts, I turn around, opening my eyes.

The music still plays, but everything else comes to a screeching halt. Even the air doesn't move as I stand still and watch Dante Santoro drink me in. He must not realise who he's looking at as his eyes travel hungrily from my feet, over my stomach and breasts, until they finally land on my face. The hunger in his eyes turns into shock as he tries to comprehend what he's seeing. Sweat gathers at my temple for every single one of the ten seconds it takes for his shock to subside and turn into rage.

# 6

## DANTE

I'm not a nice person.

    Never been one and never pretended to be one. If you were to ask any of my men, they'd tell you I'm ruthless and I never hesitate to pull the trigger. They'd tell you I'm easy to anger and I don't tolerate insubordination.

It's in my blood. It would be in yours too, if you grew up being groomed to become the head of the mafia, a job I didn't want, yet had been given the moment my father's health started deteriorating. At seventeen, I had to work twice as hard and be twice as cruel as my father for his men to realise they had to answer to me. The road has not been easy and most people still think my father is pulling the strings. But it's me. It has been for well over a decade now.

People know not to mess with me, or the hard work I have put into Blackwood becoming the place it is now. So, you can imagine my surprise when two weeks ago I found a low-level accountant trying to steal money from me. He should have known better. Killing him wasn't just about setting an example and reminding everyone not to cross the Santoros. It was just as much about quenching the thirst for violence always brimming under my skin.

The moment I smashed his head into the black keyboard on his desk, breaking his nose and the letter 'h' in the process, I knew something was off. Normally, I like to hear the screams of those who wronged me. I like to draw out the punishment, inflict some pain, but this time, there was an urgency in me I hadn't felt in a long time. I needed him to be dealt with quickly and quietly. And as I watched the life seep out of his eyes, with my zip tie around his throat, I had a feeling of foreboding. Like something bad was about to happen, like I was missing something right in front of me.

And bad things don't happen to me; I see and know everything.

*I'm* the bad thing that happens to others. I'm the boogeyman that everyone is afraid of. Everyone except Alessandra "Jones" it seems.

When I saw her sitting on the small chair, in what I could only describe as a sad excuse for a reception area, I knew. I just *knew* shit was about to go terribly wrong. Something in my gut was telling me I should just get rid of her then and there, pull out my gun and stop the voice inside my head. Put my worries to rest.

But as I stood, watching her bite her red stained lip, her sad eyes unfocused as she stared at a framed picture of the ocean hanging on the wall, I found myself curious about her. And as a deep sigh left her plump lips, instead of shooting her, or retracing my steps and leaving through the back door, I stayed, wanting to see who she was and what she was doing there.

The minute I saw her name, everything clicked into place, and I knew I made a grave mistake not killing her on sight. I should have spotted it straight away. No wonder she looked so familiar, a carbon copy of her late mother. The woman in front of me had the power to ruin everything I worked so hard to build and there was little I could do about it, except get her to leave and go back to wherever she came from.

Unbeknownst to her, Alessandra Carusso came back to the one place she should have avoided. Because as soon as anyone recognises her, she'll have a price on her head. And with a face like hers, it's only a matter of time before others will figure it out.

I knew the decision to save the small girl I found in the antique wardrobe all those years ago would one day come back to haunt me. But I had a code, even back then, when I was trying to impress everyone around me.

Never hurt the innocent.

Handing her over to the Nicolosi family was not an option. So, after stuffing a few of Alessa's things in a bag, I drove her to a place his reach didn't extend to. Somewhere no one would think twice about an Italian girl. Somewhere no one would suspect she might have a connection to the mafia. There was only one person I knew of with no ties to Blackwood or the Family. I hoped to god that the kind woman I met at Mom's funeral the year before, who claimed to be her friend from college, was still at the address she gave me in case I ever needed anything. Because the time had come. I needed *something*. I needed her to take care of a little girl whose father's foolish actions had put her life in danger. I left her sleeping on a porch swing, covered in the jacket I was wearing. A note I scribbled giving her a fake name and explaining she has no family left and needs to be looked after, peeking out of a side pocket. That day, I gave Alessandra Carusso a new life. Life as Alessandra Jones, someone who did not have a past. Only the future.

I was stumped as to why the fuck she would want to

come to Blackwood, looking for a job as a receptionist, of all the professions, and threatening my empire. There's nothing here for her except pain and death. My only option is to make sure she leaves, going back to her mafia-free picture perfect life before Nicolosi discovers that there is a little long legged Carusso princess running around. If anyone finds out she's alive and that I am the one who helped her survive his wrath all those years ago, we could have a war on our hands.

Unfortunately, Carussos always had one thing in common. They couldn't take a fucking hint to save their lives.

Each time I saw her, my anger grew. Not only because, somehow, she knew exactly how to push my buttons, but also because her stupidity was endangering her life. And since I had already saved her from death once, I felt a responsibility to keep her alive, no matter how annoying and bratty she was and no matter how much it irked me.

So when I had to leave town for a few days, I was pleasantly surprised she was nowhere to be found upon my return.

With Alessa gone, I could finally go about my business without the constant rage clouding my judgment. I was in such a good mood I didn't even torture a guy we found card counting in one of my casinos. I let my men take care of him instead.

Things were looking up even more when I saw the new girl dancing in one of the entertainment boxes we had set up for our most exclusive rooms. There's nothing better than men with too much money distracted by a pretty girl while they're trying to make decisions.

Her back was to me as her hips swayed in rhythm to the music. There was something hypnotising about her body, about the way she moved. I watched her for at least twenty minutes that first night, imagining all the ways her skin would feel on mine, how her pert ass would fill my hands as I squeezed it. And when she arched her back, all I could think about was how I would wrap her hair in my hand as I pounded into her from behind. I had to snap myself out of it, reminding myself I wasn't a teenager seeing porn for the first time, but a grown ass man. The spell she had me under was just that—a spell, over as soon as it started. Or at least that's what I told myself when I finally tore my gaze away from her body and went back to my office where I decided it was a one-time thing, no need to ever go back.

But like heroin calls to a junkie, she called to me each night. And no matter how many times I told myself I wouldn't do it, I found myself walking down the corridor to watch her perform, hypnotised by her body. After that first time, I never stayed longer than one song, proving to myself that I'm still in control, despite the feral urge to run to the poker room facing her and stab every single motherfucker watching her with awe for being able to see her face before I ever did.

Since I need to feel in control, I turned it into a game. That way, I was the master. I held the power. I was able to look forward to these stolen moments she occupied every night.

I currently sit in my office listening to the clock and watching the hands move as minutes tick by. When the time comes, I stand up and go to my door, never rushing, always making a point to take slow and measured steps. I walk to the exact same spot I stood in the first time I saw her. Nothing but a short stop while I'm clearing my head, stretching my legs after a long day.

She is never the main attraction, just a distraction that lasts a song before I move on like she doesn't even exist.

Every fucking night for the past week.

Control.

Control is the only thing that's kept my beast in check. And I am not about to lose it for a pert piece of ass. Even if I've wondered more than once if her tits are equally as pert.

And as once again I find myself walking through the corridor to the glass wall where I'll allow myself to watch her for the duration of that one song, I'll tell myself she's just a faceless distraction. I'll tell myself this will be the last time, even if that means I'll never find out about those tits.

Just in time, the now familiar notes start again. It's the same song I've asked them to play at the same time each night this week. My measure of time. As soon as it ends, I'll be gone, my dick hard and my thoughts on her smooth body.

With my hands by my side, I stand, watching her back. But something is different tonight, because, unlike every other night, she starts turning around. My adrenaline spikes as I realise in a few seconds I'll be able to see exactly what she looks like, and I'll be damned if I'm not going to take my time with it.

Control.

I drop my gaze to her bare feet before she turns fully, her toes painted in a dark colour I wouldn't be able to name in the dim light, and slowly drag my gaze up. Up her long legs, her thighs obscured by the golden beads every dancer in my casino is required to wear. Over her hips, stopping on her belly button, pierced with a little stud that glints, reflecting the light each time she moves. Except she stopped moving. Her body is still, her fists clenched by her side, as she lets me drink her in. And when I get to her tits, I'm not sure if I should thank her for standing still or if I should order her to start jumping just so I can see them bounce. Reluctantly, I keep moving my eyes up, stopping on the choker placed on her slender neck. Fuck, that's hot.

It's like a collar I could use while I fuck her, making sure she knows who's in charge, who's in control. Then it's her lips. Even from this distance, I can see they're slightly parted, and glistening. My dick is getting harder by the second.

Until I get to her eyes. It's too dark to tell their colour, but I know they're fucking emerald green. My head is trying to process the bombshell in front of me that has had me so enthralled the past week and put her in the same category as the smart-mouthed pain in the ass I thought I got rid of.

Then it hits me. What the fuck is she doing in my casino, dancing in the entertainment box, her body barely covered by the skimpy outfit, for everyone to see? Come to think of it, who the fuck thought those outfits were a good idea in the first place? Rage fills me as I stare her straight in the eyes. My jaw ticks while, in my head, I imagine all the ways I could punish her for this. But first, I need to find who stepped out of line and hired the person I made sure every business in Blackwood knew to stay away from.

Her hands wrap around the golden bars, her body shaking as her huge eyes watch me. Good girl. She *should* be afraid.

Very fucking afraid.

I turn on my heel and walk down the corridor and down the stairs to where the person responsible for hiring her should be. I'm angry at myself for staring at Alessa's ass all week and thinking she was far away from here, safe, when she's been playing me all along. And in *my* fucking casino.

My control is slipping as I storm through the main floor. The struggle not to rip the door from its hinges as I enter Martina's office is overwhelming.

"New girl. The one dancing in cage three," I seethe.

Martina is no stranger to my moods, so instead of cowering like most men in my employment would, she smiles excitedly, knowing I would never hurt a woman unless she's begging me for it.

And they *do* beg me for it.

"Oh! Stevie." She beams. "Isn't she fantastic? We've had clients request the room directly opposite her box all week."

The knowledge men are lining up to ogle her body has my blood boiling. Stupid girl. She could have been recognised by someone who knew her mother. I want to scream at Martina for disobeying my orders when it clicks.

I blink.

"Who the fuck is Stevie?"

"The new girl in box three." Martina squints at me like I've lost my mind and honestly, I think I have, or I've lost my hearing because I swear I've just heard her call Alessa—Stevie. "Stephanie Nicks. But she goes by Stevie."

I rub my temple, a headache starting behind my eyes as rage turns to disbelief. For all the years Martina has worked for me, I've always been impressed with her work ethic and dedication. But it's fucking clear as day now—she's on drugs. Because there's just no way that Alessa convinced everyone she's called Stevie Nicks unless they were high. Martina reaches into a drawer and pulls out a small folder, where I find an application form and a photocopy of an ID with Alessa's picture on it and Stephanie Nicks written under it. The address—Seventeen Edge Way, Phoenix, Arizona. You've got to be fucking kidding me. Am I the only one who can see the obvious? Would they get it if she put her middle name as Rhiannon? I drop the folder on Martina's desk and head back into the casino, my eye twitching. I need to control my anger before I smash something valuable. But first I'm going to have to take care of *everything* myself. Just like fucking always. Can't anyone around me do their fucking job properly?

I know it's my fault when I walk into a man standing in

my path, looking up at the cage Alessa is dancing in. My vision blurs as the edges turn blood red.

"I don't think I've seen her before." Nico Nicolosi rubs his double chin. "Tell me, Dante. Are the girls for entertainment, too, or just for looking? I wouldn't mind a test drive."

As quick as a blink of an eye. I go from boiling hot to ice cold.

# 7

## ALESSA

I don't know how long I stand there, gripping the cold bars for balance and trying to calm myself down as the bitter taste of failure lingers on my tongue. But when the second song ends and still nothing happens, I turn back to the room filled with men playing poker and continue to dance. If you can call shaking like a leaf *dancing*. Whatever just happened is not good. I can't be a hundred per cent sure what Dante Santoro is doing at the Black Royale, but I'm smart enough to put two and two together. If it *was* him watching me every night this past week, he's either a regular or he's involved in running the place. And since I've been told he owns this town, my money is on the latter.

I could smack myself over the head. I should have known I had walked into the den of a dragon, offering myself up as a meal, like a sacrificial lamb. The only thing left to do is to convince the dragon himself I'm good for business. Martina said the spend in the room has increased since I started dancing and my tips have been *really* good. In the last week, I have earned more dancing in a bikini than I did in a month when I was serving tables at a diner in Texas.

Things were finally looking up for me—Mel wanted me to move in with her and I had a job that paid well.

Then in comes the angry Santoro, his face as red as Terence, the huge angry bird. Now I'm back to the start, in the same place I was two weeks ago, minus the bus station sink bath and with more money in my pocket.

The songs are changing one after another as I sway, considering my options. Speaking with Mel will need to be my priority. She needs to find out the truth about who I am before we take any next steps, but first I need to come clean about the possibility I no longer have a job. Maybe she'd be able to help me find something? There must be someone in this mist-covered town who is not under Dante's thumb.

With a sigh, I open my eyes, searching for Mel in the room in front of me, but I'm stunned to see it's now completely empty. The dim lights highlight the newly deserted space. One of the chairs slowly spins as thick tendrils of the half-smoked cigar resting in the ashtray float up to the ceiling. The chips are gone, but everything else is the same, including the crystal glasses with alcohol the men were drinking. Everything is there, minus the living, breathing humans.

The realisation that I'm trapped in a metal cage, hanging off the ceiling, with no means of escaping, sparks fear in my brain. The same brain that, with its eidetic memory, is most likely a top-notch zombie nosh. The scene in front of me is starting to make me feel like Jim in *28 Days Later*. Thing is, I've always had an overactive imagination. Ever since I was a kid, when things were dire, I'd make up stories in my head and pretend they were true, and that I was the main character. So it's only natural that when the cage groans and starts moving towards its dock, I let out a squeal, then drop to the floor. Not that a floor drop would save me in a zombie attack, but instincts die hard.

"You okay?" The younger version of Dante I first laid eyes on last week in *La Famiglia* smiles at me as he secures the cage to the dock, then opens the gate so I can step out.

I get up, dusting myself off like nothing's out of the ordinary, and let him take my hand as he helps me back into the corridor. My foot half over the threshold, I stop, my eyes on him, scanning his white button-up shirt with sleeves rolled up to his forearms for any marks. A thin black belt holds his suit pants on his narrow hips, as my eyes cast down to check his legs, trying not to pay attention that he looks positively edible. He'd be prime zombie real estate if *I* were a zombie. "Do you have any bites or scratch marks?"

His eyes widen, his Adam's apple bobbing as he swallows, then clears his throat. "Uh... What?"

I sigh. Why must everyone be so difficult? "Did anyone bite or scratch you?"

"I mean, I've got a few on my back." He shrugs, his lips lifting into a cocky half smile as he pulls me over the threshold and straight into his arms. "But I don't mind those. I like it when women get physical."

With my face plastered against his hard chest, the smell of expensive cologne and whiskey overwhelming my senses, I realise he has completely missed the mark.

"Good for you." I pat his pecs and push myself away, unwrapping his arm from around me. No matter how handsome and flirty he is, I need to keep my guard up, since he's more than likely related to Dante. You never know when the Terence gene wins out, even if that gene could come in handy when fighting brain-hungry monsters.

With my chin held high, I study his face. "The place looked deserted. I was just checking in case of a zombie apocalypse."

He leans past my shoulder, pointedly looking down at the ground floor. I follow his gaze and am greeted by a room filled with suited men playing cards. I didn't even think to look below when I started panicking about my impending doom in my cage. This is exactly why I should avoid stress. *And* Dante Santoro. Neither one is good for my sanity.

"No zombies here."

"Yup. Now that I've checked, I came to the same conclusion. Thank you for confirming," I reply, keeping my face straight because it is physically impossible for me to dig myself out of this hole I made, so I may as well lay in it and enjoy some stargazing. I've read Vega is particularly bright at this time of the year.

"I'm glad I could help."

"So, what's going on? My shift doesn't end for another two hours."

"There's been a slight change of plans."

I narrow my eyes at him again. "Where's Martina?"

"In her office. Now let's go."

"I'm not going anywhere with you." I cross my arms over my chest. "I don't know who you are. Haven't you ever heard of stranger danger?"

"Isn't that a warning for kids? I'm Angelo." He chuckles.

"I'm a kid at heart, *Angelo*," I explain.

"Aren't we all?"

"Except for Terence," I mutter, thinking about the way Dante's angry chocolate eyes stared me down like I was an annoying bug he was desperate to squish. "That one has a chip on his shoulder."

"Who's Terence?" he asks.

I'm not an idiot. I don't want to end up with a bullet in my skull because someone tattled to the angry bird himself about his pet name. Especially since we've already established my brain is prime real estate. "No one important. Angelo who?"

He's quiet for a beat, assessing me before he speaks. "Santoro."

My heart speeds up. I've hit the nail on the head in my assumptions. Now if I could only figure out how to make my escape. I'm in a narrow corridor, without places to hide. If I start running, he'll definitely catch me, especially since I'm not wearing any shoes. Or actual clothes. The only course of action I can see is to get him to trust me.

"Any relation to one Dante Santoro, perchance?" Maybe if I get him to lower his guard, he'll slip up.

"He's my brother."

"My condolences."

He laughs. "That's new."

"What is?"

"I'm not used to people reacting this way to my surname."

"How else would I react? It's not your fault you're related to the angriest and rudest man I've ever met."

He chuckles, shaking his head, before guiding me down the corridor. "Dante really did a number on you, didn't he? If it makes you feel any better, I'm pretty sure you get under his skin."

This time, I snort. "Not sure if that's a good thing."

"Yeah. I guess it's probably not," Angelo says quietly.

"Angelo?" I stop, turning to face him. "Where are you taking me?"

"To your dressing room, so you can get changed."

"And after that?"

He smiles. "You're a clever one, aren't you? After that, Dante wants to speak with you."

Dante.

Goosebumps rise on my arms as I try to fit the name and the soft way Angelo said it with the angry man I've met. Knowing that he is not *just* Dante gives me hope.

Maybe he'll see reason. Maybe this time, he'll be understanding.

And in the quiet staff room, with Angelo standing outside my door, as I change into my clothes and pull the golden leaves out of my hair, I try to stay positive.

The feeling gets crushed the moment I walk into Dante's office and am met by the man himself.

"Thank you, Angelo." Dante's voice is devoid of any emotion as he speaks.

Angelo, the traitor that he is, backs out of the room, closing the door behind him.

You can cut the tension with a knife—it's so thick. My body wants to cower under Dante's heavy stare as silence fills the room, but I stand my ground, waiting for him to speak first. Sun Tzu taught me that silence is a source of great strength. I've done nothing wrong. Except using a fake name to gain employment, that is. But if Dante Santoro thinks he can intimidate me that easily, he's got another think coming. He may believe he knows me. Or how to deal with me. But he's wrong.

Apart from cheap thrills, I also love playing games. And this is gearing up to be a delicious one. By trying to make me uncomfortable, he has inadvertently kicked my competitive side into gear. The fear of losing a job and not having any means to start the search about my past becomes all but a distant memory as recklessness drives me to show him just what I'm made of.

My eyes trained on Dante's, I stay silent, feet planted on the ground and my back straight. I take all the rage he's shooting my way. Absorb all the anger, letting it flow through me and disperse into thin air around me. And as the annoyance on his face grows with every second I don't break, I glow with determination. *If your enemy is quick to anger, seek to irritate him,* Sun Tzu said. And I can't think of

73

anything that will irritate Dante Santoro more than standing my ground. After all, he said himself that ever since I arrived in Blackwood, he's been in hell.

"Why are you still here, Miss Jones?" he grits through his teeth and I want to dance in the spot with glee at winning this small battle between us.

"I was told *you* wanted to speak with me," I reply innocently.

"Not here, in my office. What are you still doing in Blackwood?" His jaw ticks.

"Oh." I place my index finger on my lips as if I'm considering something. "I thought it was obvious—I'm working."

He slowly lets out a breath through his nose, trying to control himself, and my stomach flutters, thrilled that I'm getting under his skin.

"I thought I had been clear before. You're not welcome in this town. You need to leave."

I bristle. "*You* may not want me here, but there are others who do."

"Trust me, it's better for *everyone* if you leave."

"That's not going to happen."

His lips lift in a cruel smirk. "And how exactly are you planning to stay here with no job, or a roof over your head?"

"You can't fire me." My heart stutters. Could he really be this malicious?

"Oh, but I can, *Stevie*. I own this place, and *you're* fired."

Fuck. It's worse than I thought. "Martina said the spending in the room has increased since I started dancing."

His jaw ticks again, his fist clenching. "I'm not desperate for money, Miss Jones. The casino is doing great just on its own."

"Alessa," I snap, desperate for him to see me as a human being.

"In fact, *Alessa*. I'm thinking we'll stop the entertainment

74

for the private boxes altogether. This is a casino, after all. Not a strip club where desperate *girls* dance wearing next to nothing."

Hatred fills my heart as I watch his handsome face turn ruthless. "Leave the other dancers out of it," I whisper.

"I don't think so. I should probably tell them they lost their jobs because of you, too."

They will never forgive me. "They need the money." I try to plead with him.

"There are other jobs in Blackwood."

I shake my head, opening my mouth to protest, but he interrupts me.

"Just not for *you*."

My eyes start to sting. "Why?"

"Why what, *Alessa*?" He says my name like it offends him.

"Why are you doing this to me?"

"Because I can."

## 8

## ALESSA

I t takes everything in me not to let the tears fall and look strong in front of Dante. There's no point in arguing with him right now. So, without a word, I turn around and leave his office, passing Angelo along the way and ignoring his call.

I have no strength in me to talk to anyone. Not even Mel, whom by some miracle I manage to avoid as I make my way out of the casino. The streets are dark, the ever present mist settling on my cheeks and mixing with the one tear that sneaks out, before I quickly wipe it away and tell myself I'm stronger than some entitled asshole in a suit. I've dealt with thugs and dickheads who like to intimidate women all my life. I survived them—I'll survive him.

One way or another, I'm going to figure this out. He can't do anything else to me. I'm just back to square one. I need to get back to my room and regroup.

Except, when I get to the hotel I find out I was very wrong. There *was* one more thing he could have taken away from me. And he did.

*"And how exactly are you planning to stay here with no job, or a roof over your head?"* His words play on repeat as I watch

the receptionist, for once not looking bored, drag my suit-cases and my duffel bag from behind her desk.

My body deflates. I don't even argue about not being able to go to my room and check if they've left anything behind. I just grab my stuff and walk to the one place I can think of.

The bus station.

The same security guard greets me as I walk in—my vans squeaking on the tiled floor—sheltering me from the drizzle that's just started outside.

An hour ago my hair was blow dried to perfection. I had a job that paid good money and a place to stay. I started to make friends—something I never dared to do since I rarely stayed in one place long enough. And *he* ruined it all.

With unfocused eyes, I stare at the departure schedule.

"The next bus isn't until tomorrow," the security guy stands a little too close behind me. The scent of day old sweat fills my nostrils as I try to ignore his proximity.

"Great," I mutter, taking a step back and turning to face him. I came here for shelter, but faced with the option of just leaving this town and the douchebag who pulls the strings, I can't help feeling tempted. Maybe if I sleep on it... The dirty floor looks cold and uninviting, but I've spent nights in worse conditions.

"Sorry, darling." The guard shakes his head, his eyes studying me. He gives me the creeps. His narrow eyes and thin moustache really do not help his case. "Can't stay here. I need to close this place up for the night."

I sigh. Of course he does. "What time is the next bus?"

"Five. It would take you to Blackriver." He pauses, a small smile lifting his thin lips as he looks me up and down. Now I seriously want to get out. "I could take you there tonight after I lock up. It's where I live, so won't be out of my way."

Right, need to remember never to set foot in Blackriver. I thought security guards were supposed to make you feel safe. Whoever hired this guy didn't get the memo. My skin crawls as he keeps studying my features.

"That's okay," I smile, gripping the handles of my suitcases. "I'm going the other way, but thank you." I have no idea where 'the other way' is, but he doesn't have to know that.

He squints his eyes at me. "Have we met before?"

"Don't think so," I smile wider, my cheeks hurting from all the fakeness. "Anyway, I've got to go."

"You look familiar." He cocks his head to the side.

I laugh awkwardly as the phone in my pocket vibrates. "Pretty sure I'd remember a handsome fella like yourself if we ever met. Excuse me."

I pull my phone out, seeing Mel's name on the screen.

"Mel!" I say happily, pretending like I'm not creeped out of my mind. The guard is still watching me intently. His eyebrows scrunched in thought. I stick my phone between my ear and my shoulder and wave goodbye at him before awkwardly walking backwards, dragging my suitcases back to the entrance.

"Where are you?" she pouts. "I thought you were going to wait for me so we could talk."

"Haha," I laugh louder than I should. "You know me. Just missed the last bus."

"Why are you at the bus station?"

"Long story, babe." I step through the threshold. "Are you sure? You really don't need to come get me!"

Mel sucks in a breath. "Is there someone with you? Are you in danger? Never mind, not like you'd be able to answer. Stay on the line and keep talking to me," she pants, clearly running. "I'll be there in—" I can hear muffled sounds and then the roar of an engine. "Three minutes. Five minutes top."

Shit, five minutes is a long time if someone wants to do something sinister to you. I drag my suitcases down the sidewalk. I need to get rid of them for now or they'll slow me down. In panic, I look around for somewhere to hide, but aside from the large trash can next to a bush and the lamppost I'm currently standing under, there's nothing except the forest, which starts about three hundred feet north.

I can see the security guard still watching me through the glass as he slowly walks over to a switch on the wall, resting his hand on it, his eyes following my every move.

"Shit," I curse as he flicks it down, cutting off the light. The bus station goes dark, and with the lamp shining down on me, the only thing I can see is my own reflection in the glass. With one move, he's made himself invisible.

"What's going on?" Mel shouts into the phone.

I drag my stuff to the bush, stuffing them between the branches and the trash, then crouch behind the thick branches.

"My suitcases are by the trash can," I whisper.

"We're like two minutes away. What the fuck is going on?"

"The security guard—" I start replying, then stop when I hear the whoosh of automatic doors opening.

"Hurry," I whisper, then break into a run, heading for the trees.

The guard laughs behind me. Fucking enjoying himself as he gives chase. I get to the trees and, as soon as I'm behind the first few, I veer diagonally to the left. I can hear his heavy footsteps and heavy breathing behind me as I cut again, running parallel to the bus station, watching the glow of the lamppost.

"Little *Caaruusso*," the guard taunts from behind me. He

sounds like he's still running straight and didn't notice I've changed direction, so I slow down to a jog, getting closer to the edge of the trees. "Do you know how much money Nicolosi will reward me with if I bring him your head on a silver platter?" This time, his voice is closer. He must have figured out my move.

I stop, my heart racing as I search for the car Mel might be driving, and trying to figure out where the guard is.

A branch snaps thirty, maybe forty feet behind me, and I instantly spring into action. Headlights flash in the distance, making me want to cry with relief. Adrenaline propels my feet as I start running back to the bus station. The guard cackles behind me, not giving up, and clearly not noticing the approaching car. If I'm fast enough, I could just jump into the passenger seat and get Mel to keep going. I no longer care about my stuff. Even if it's everything I've ever owned. I can steal or buy new shit as long as I can escape the psycho behind me.

I get to the bus station just as a black Alfa Romeo screeches to a halt, and the driver's door opens. I don't have the time to contemplate how Mel can afford a car like this because I'm staring in shock at the driver as he jumps out, a gun in his hand, aiming it at someone behind me.

"Luca?" I ask in confusion.

"Get in." He stalks past me as the passenger door opens and Mel drags me inside.

The door shuts behind me as Mel pulls me into her arms, a phone still clutched in her hand.

"I was so worried," she mouths into my hair. "What happened?"

With the adrenaline leaving my bloodstream, I'm finding it hard to process it myself. Because what the hell actually happened?

"I'm not sure. But thank you for coming to get me." I

reply as the trunk of the car opens and the car moves under the weight of my suitcases. That means that the guard is dead, a thought that should revolt me but doesn't. He can rot in hell.

"Of course."

"How do you know Luca?"

She blushes. "He sometimes gives me a lift home."

I laugh. "Oh, really? Pray tell, what else does he give you?"

Mel hides her face in her hands, peeking out through her fingers as Luca closes the trunk of the car. "Things."

"I have a feeling those things are intangible." I grin. Happy the focus is no longer on me.

"Shhh." Mel pokes me in the ribs, causing a dirty cackle to escape my throat.

Luca's eyes are on me as he slides into the driver's seat, throwing the car key into the cup holder.

"You okay, Alessa?" he asks as he starts the engine and faces the road.

"Alessa?" Mel mouths at me.

I shake my head. "Later." Then meet Luca's eyes in the rearview mirror. "Is he dead?"

His eyes briefly leave mine as he watches the road. "Not yet."

Mel squeezes my hand as I try to figure out what he means by that. "You can just drop me off in the nearest town. Just not Blackriver."

His eyes meet mine again. "Why not?"

"That's where the psycho guard apparently is from and since he's not dead, I'd rather not go somewhere he lives."

"You don't have to worry about him. I doubt you'll ever see him again," he replies enigmatically.

"Fine," I sigh. "I guess Blackriver will do then."

Mel squeals, offended. "You're not going to Blackriver.

You're coming home with me!"

"I'm afraid we need to go somewhere else first."

"You trust this guy?" I whisper to Mel.

She nods her head. "He's a Saint," she whispers. Ugh, fine. So I guess he might be a good guy, but a saint? That's a bit much.

"Where are you thinking?" I ask the rearview mirror.

"My brother wants to speak to you."

Mel squeezes my hand again as I consider his answer. Trying to figure out what his *brother* might want from me.

"Okay, I'll bite. And who's your brother?" Mel's grip on my hand tightens.

Luca meets my eyes in the rearview mirror again. "Dante Santoro."

You've got to be fuckin kidding me.

# 9

## ALESSA

I can barely keep my eyes open by the time we drive all the way to the top of the mountain, where the town's edge meets the black forest. The gates open and we crawl up the dark driveway to a huge, sprawling mansion surrounded by a manicured lawn and trees. It's too dark outside for me to take in any details, but it's obvious the Santoros have money. Not that it wasn't obvious before, what with the expensive suits, the Maserati, and the casino.

"After this is over, you're coming home with me," Mel yawns, her head leaning on my shoulder.

I nod, not having the energy to argue. But really, there's nothing to argue about. I have nowhere else to go tonight. Dante has made sure of that.

I follow Luca up the stairs and through the front door, stopping in a spacious foyer where I'm greeted by my own reflection. The whole wall in front of me is covered in glass. If I squint hard enough, I can almost see past my bedraggled self and make out an outline of patio chairs and a light blue rectangular surface in the middle. It's hard to tell with the light reflecting on the glass wall, but I think it might be an outdoor courtyard with a pool in the middle. Fancy.

"Don't think so hard. You'll hurt yourself," the devil in disguise says, leaning against the wall. My skin erupts in goosebumps at the tone of his cold voice.

Luca takes Mel by the hand and guides her somewhere out of sight, leaving me alone with Terence. I should hate him. I *do* hate him. He's been nothing but cruel to me since the day we met. But a girl's got to take the time to appreciate a barefoot guy wearing a white t-shirt and dark jeans, his hair wet and tousled.

I'm a big fan of suits.

But clearly, I'm also a big fan of whatever Dante has going on tonight. And somehow, barefoot and clearly at ease in his own home, he still commands the room. His presence makes even the particles of dust cower, I'm sure. Although in my tired state, I haven't seen a spec of dust anywhere yet. Probably because it ran away screaming.

"Dante," I smile sweetly, like he hadn't reduced me to tears mere hours ago. Pushing off the wall, he walks toward me as I watch him. "I thought you wanted me to leave. A curious turn of events."

He doesn't speak when he stops right next to me, his dark eyes looking all over me, searching for god knows what. When his hand barely presses against my lower back, I let him guide me out of the foyer, through a narrow sitting room and into a spacious kitchen. I can feel the heat of his palm radiating onto my entire back, my body stiffening at first before relaxing under his touch. Too soon he moves away, gesturing to a row of chairs tucked under the kitchen island.

I guess he wants to play the silent game again. I already know I can win it, so with a smile, I walk over to the chairs, examining every single one before backtracking to the one smack dab in the middle and pulling it out, making sure it scrapes against the stone floor as I do so. Happy with my choice, I climb onto it and take a seat, wishing it was a swivel chair. It would definitely irritate Dante if I started to spin myself in circles in his kitchen.

I sigh, leaning my head against my hand, elbow on the cool marble, as I swipe one finger on the surface, lifting it to my eyes and inspecting it for dust. Like I thought, nothing.

"Up to your standards?" Dante asks, amused.

I whip my head to him so fast—shocked that he spoke first so quickly, and even more shocked he sounded amused —that my elbow slips and I nearly bash my chin against the kitchen island.

I clear my throat, righting myself as he opens the fridge and hands me a bottle of water.

"It's alright." I shrug. No need to let him know I'm impressed.

"Al-right," he repeats slowly. His chocolate brown eyes on me as he leans his forearms on the counter, clasping his hands together. "Tell me, *Alessa*. Why is it so hard for you to follow simple instructions?" His voice could freeze the Atlantic with how cold it is, the amusement in his eyes is gone as he appraises me.

I mirror his stance. "Well, Dante. I *was* following your simple instructions. Not my fault I had nowhere to go, since, imagine that,"—I widen my eyes,—"the hotel I was staying at suddenly had no rooms available." I gasp. "I wonder whose fault is that?"

His jaw ticks.

I continue. "And when I got to the bus station, which closes for the night, by the way. Who knew that? Definitely not the girl who's only ever been there once." I lift my hand in confusion. "Anyway, I get to the bus station to get out of this godforsaken town, only to discover that the last bus has long left." I shake my head, clicking my tongue. "If only I knew someone local. Someone who could have thought about it *before* they decided to make sure I didn't have a place to stay tonight."

"If only," Dante repeats. "What happened then?"

"Oh, you mean the security guard who wanted to kill me?" I smile brightly.

"Tell me exactly what happened, Alessa. Don't leave anything out." His tone is serious as he straightens.

For some reason, I don't make any more jokes, choosing to follow his direction instead. "I don't know," I sigh. "He was creepy. Kept saying I looked familiar. Then Mel called and said she'll get me, so I left the station and stashed my stuff next to the lamppost." I shudder.

Dante walks around the island until he's next to me. He moves the chair I'm on around. My back is to the counter-top, and he's right in front of me, caging me in. He's close. So close I can smell his minty breath. But for the first time, I don't feel threatened by this man. I can see the anger pouring off him, but for once it's not directed at me, and I'm able to take small comfort in that. "What happened after you hid your things, Alessa?"

"He switched off the light inside so that I couldn't see him anymore." I swallow loudly as I watch a vein in Dante's neck pulse.

"And then?" His mouth barely opens.

"I ran for the woods."

A curse leaves his mouth, drawing my eyes directly to his full lips.

"There was nowhere else to hide," I lick my lips as I watch his muscles tense. "I'm good at running. I was hoping I could outrun him before Mel showed up. So, as soon as I was certain he couldn't see me clearly, I started circling back until I saw the headlights."

"Did he say anything?" Dante asks.

I frown. "I guess? In the woods, he called me his little

'caruso', whatever that meant. And said Nicolas or Nicolos will reward him if he kills me."

Dante pushes away from me, swearing in Italian as he grabs the closest chair and throws it across the floor with such force one of its legs breaks. "*Cazzo!*" he roars.

"Look—" I touch his arm. I may get my arm bitten off, but I want to let him know he can just relax.

He whips around, caging my legs between his, as he cups my face in his hands. "You stupid, stupid girl," he whispers, but it doesn't feel like an insult at all, as his tormented gaze darts around my face. "Why couldn't you listen to me the first time I told you to run?" he swallows.

"I... I had my reasons to stay," I reply, not ready to tell him the truth—that I was desperately looking for someone to call my family. "I'll leave tomorrow." I close my eyes, resigned.

His thumb rubs my cheek gently, and I have to fight the urge to lean into his caress. What the hell is going on? Aren't we public enemies anymore? Fortunately, the fire in my stomach reminds me I still hate him. I lift my hands, wrapping them around his wrists and pull them away from my face. He sucks in a breath.

"No," he says, stepping back and out of my reach, taking his heat away.

"No?"

"There's been a change of plans. You're not leaving now."

My jaw opens. "What?"

"You're staying in Blackwood."

I'm about to laugh, psychotically, because this man, with his mood swings and mind changing, is causing me to lose all my senses. I don't, though. Instead, I hop off the chair and take a step forward, getting really pissed off. Is he for real? He spent the last few weeks making my life hell only to change his mind, and just like that, I'm supposed to stay?

My hands ball into fists, and I take another step forward. He takes one back.

"Did you forget?" I seethe, my jaw clenched as I take another step forward, one he matches as he retracts. "*You* made me unemployable. There are no jobs for me in Blackwood. And there's also the small matter of me being homeless now, too. *Also* thanks to you." I poke his chest.

"*I* have a job for you, as much as it pains me."

I close my eyes, breathing through my nose, needing to calm myself down. The last time he got me this angry was the day we met. And just like then, I have to count down from ten before I do or say something stupid that could cost me my life. Considering Luca, his brother, owns a gun, I'm pretty sure Dante has one as well. Not that he needs it. He could probably crush me with one hand if he wanted to.

"A job?" I finally breathe out.

"There are other jobs in the casino."

"*Other* jobs?" My lips form a thin line.

"Are you just going to repeat everything I say?"

Every single bone in my body is begging me to repeat what he's just said in a mocking tone. It's a fight I almost lose. "Maybe," I reply instead. "Why would I want to work for *you*?"

"If I remember correctly, you've been desperate to work for me from the beginning. And you actually did. The casino?"

"I was *not* desperate." I cross my arms, defiant.

"Mmm-hmm."

"Anyway, I still have nowhere to stay."

"You can stay here."

This time I do cackle. Hysterically. When his face remains stoic, I wipe the tears away and squash down the need to commit myself to an institution. "You're serious."

He shrugs.

"Yeah, buddy. I don't think so."

"It's a big place."

Why is he so insistent all of a sudden? Makes me want to see how far I can push this. "I think... I should probably just leave town, like you wanted me to in the first place."

"You can't."

"Why not?"

"It's complicated."

He's annoying me now. "Uncomplicate it for me, then."

"If you agree to stay and work for me."

I take a deep breath. I suppose I could stay with Mel. And what job does he want me to do? Server? Or maybe bartender...and, more importantly—"How much will you pay me?"

"More than you got dancing."

"How much more?" I cock my head to the side expectantly.

"Double."

I snort. "No."

"No?"

"I want triple."

"Fine." Holy shit, he agreed.

"And—"

"Don't push it, *Stevie*." His lips form a thin line.

"And I want all the dancers to get their jobs back."

"I can't do that."

"What? Why?"

"Because I meant it when I said I was getting rid of the entertainment for the private rooms. Black Royale no longer employs dancers."

"But—"

"*But* don't worry," he interrupts my plea. "Contrary to what you may think, I'm not a tyrant."

I snort.

"I'm not. I take care of my staff. All the dancers got placed in different jobs and promised training if they wanted it. They were also guaranteed equivalent pay."

"So..." I narrow my eyes. "What you're saying is, that you gave normal servers raises to match the pay, too?" He better not screw Mel over with this.

He sighs. "Fine. I'll do that."

I grin, excited to see Mel's face when I tell her the good news.

"You're very expensive, Alessa."

"That's because I'm just. So. Precious." I smile sweetly, batting my eyelashes at him.

He chuckles and my heart stops at the foreign sound escaping his lips. My eyes are glued to his mouth as his lips stretch into a half smile, making his whole face even more handsome. "Now that this is sorted, I'll get one of my men to get your stuff from the bus station and take it to your room."

"Umm. No, I'm not staying here. Also, what do you mean 'from' the bus station? Pretty sure Luca put my stuff in the car."

He laughs, his eyes crinkling at the side and I'm mesmerised. Why is he being so... human? I miss Terence. With Terence, at least I knew where I stood. Even if it was on very, very thin ice. Dante being all nice, has me all confused and angry.

"That wasn't *your* stuff." Meaning it was something of his. Considering all the comments Luca made about the guard who tried to kill me, I'm now almost certain it was him in the trunk. Who the hell are these people? Must be some sort of organised crime. It's the only thing that's making sense. And if that's the case, I probably would have been better off leaving town when Dante first told me to.

"Where will you stay if not here?" he asks.

"Umm. Mel's." I reply, my mind still racing.

"I don't like it."

I snort. "Well, that's too bad, buddy, because it's happening."

"Fine," he says like he's got any say in the matter. "But don't ever call me '*buddy*' again."

Little does he know, no one tells me what to do.

# 10

## ALESSA

Luca takes us to Mel's apartment. In a different car. One that has my actual suitcases in the trunk, which he kindly takes up the two flights of stairs and sets in my new room before awkwardly waving at us and leaving.

I drop my ass onto the sofa in the living room, looking out the window as the sky turns from dark to morning grey. Mel shuffles like a zombie before she, too, succumbs to the call of the sofa, grabbing a cushion and hugging it. We were both told to take the rest of the weekend off and come back to Black Royale on Monday.

"So," Mel says.

"I don't even know where to start." I rub my face with my hands.

"I'll get the wine then." She gets up, groaning like an old lady and making me chuckle.

"I'll get the glasses."

"How very bourgeoisie." Mel winks at me, pointing at a cupboard over the sink where I find wine glasses.

"It's a 'drink wine out of wine glasses' sort of a morning," I reply, yawning.

"That it is." Mel unscrews the bottle and pours a generous amount of white wine into each of our glasses. "Hungry?"

I shake my head.

"Let's go then. The sofa awaits."

We both let out a content sigh as soon as we're sitting, then giggle.

I sip the wine as she watches me. "Are you leaving town?"

I shake my head.

"I've got so many questions. I don't even know which one to ask first," she sighs.

"Dealers choice?"

"If you're not leaving, why were you at the bus station?"

I wince. "I *was* leaving."

Mel's eyes widen in shock. "What?"

"I didn't want to," I rush. "Dante basically made me."

Her eyes widen even more. "You call Mr Santoro —Dante?"

"Eeew. Mr Santoro? Makes him sound so old."

"He kinda is, I guess. Or at least older than us. I think he's in his mid-thirties."

"Really?"

"Mhhmmm." She nods her head. "Have you been thinking naughty thoughts about Mr Santoro?"

"More like *stabby* thoughts," I laugh.

Mel blinks. "So, why would he make you leave?"

I whine. "It's this whole thing. He's been an asshole to me from the day we met, telling me I should leave town and that no one wants me here. He blacklisted my name so that no one in town would hire me. I had to use a fake name and ID—"

"That's why Luca called you Alessa!" Mel exclaims.

"Yeah, my real name is Alessa Jones. I was going to tell

you tonight so you could decide if you still wanted me to move in with you, but I guess I live here now, so... Surprise?" I smile tentatively.

Mel chuckles. "Girl, I wouldn't have changed my mind. You have a place here for as long as you want. I'm a bit bummed, though. I was hoping you were going to tell me you're actually related to *the* Stevie Nicks."

"I wish."

"Don't we all?" she sighs, her eyes unfocused, as she stares out the window before shaking her head and looking back at me. "Anyway, Mr Santoro wanted you gone and..."

"Stop calling him that!" I shudder. "Just call him Dante, okay?"

"I'll try. But all my life I've known him as one of the Saints or a Santoro."

"What's up with the Saint nickname? He's more like a demon."

"The three Santoro brothers are all called Saints. It has to do with their surname, I think. I'm pretty sure Santoro means born on All Saint's Day. Or at least that's what I've heard."

"Huh. So definitely not a good guy. Anyway, tonight, or rather last night, he saw me dancing in the cage thing and saw my face. He was aaangry. Like with a capital 'A'. You know, steam from ears and everything. I was in deep trouble. He called me to his office, and then he told me I'm fired."

"He did *what*?"

"Yup. And get this. Not only was I fired. He'd also decided Black Royale would no longer have dancers at all. He made it sound like all the dancers were out of a job."

Mel's jaw drops.

"Asshole, right? Then he told me again to get lost and leave town. And when I said I wouldn't, he said he'd like to see me stay with no job and no *roof* over my head. A comment that I didn't put together until—"

"He did not!" Mel gasps.

"He totally did! He got the hotel to kick me out. So, I went to the only place I could think of. The bus station."

She playfully punches my arm, offended. "What about me, you whore?"

"Careful! Wine!" I take a long sip, hiding my smile. "And you kinda know what happened there. I don't think I want to get into it again right now."

"We can skip that part if it's too tough, okay?" Her eyes soften. "What happened when we got to Mr—I mean, Dante's?"

"He made me tell him everything that happened. Called me a stupid girl. Told me I should have left. Then, when I told him that I will, he said I'm not allowed to anymore."

Mel snorts.

"I know, right? Fucking whiplash. Then he offered me a job." I shake my head. "I told him I'll work for him as long as he gives me a raise and re-employs all the dancers."

"Did he?"

"Technically, yes, just not as dancers. And he already did before I even asked for it. He just made it sound like he kicked them to the curb to make me feel like shit. Dickwood move. Anyway, I made him swear they'll get paid the same as they would if they were still dancing."

"Seriously?"

"Uh-huh. I had your back, too." My lips stretch into a wide grin. "I told him he has to match the servers' pay or I will not work for him."

"You did?"

I nod. "And he agreed."

Mel squeals. "If I didn't love you already, I'd love you now—full on sister wives style. What's your new job?"

95

"I'm not sure. Probably a server like you or a bartender, maybe. Oh my god, but I forgot the best part, Mel!" I grab her hand theatrically. "He suggested I live with *him!*"

She drops her wine glass to the floor in shock. Thankfully, it's already empty. "I'm dead," she says, leaning to pick it up and refill it.

"If I'm honest, I thought I was, too."

"I gather you said 'no'."

"Obviously! Do you see me butt-imprinting *his* sofa right now?"

"Well, he *is* hot. You never know." She shrugs, then wags her eyebrows. "You might have wanted a bit of dick-a-dick-*ah,*" she singsongs the last bit like it's from that Spice Girls song. She's obviously crazy. And I love it.

"He's also got anger issues and half the time, he either wants to throttle me or kill me."

"*Or* sex you up." She moves her hips back and forth, making me spit the sip I just took all over my hoodie.

"Mel!" I wipe my mouth on my sleeve.

She chuckles. "Anyway. I was going to tell you something too, remember?"

I nod.

"I suppose it doesn't make much difference now since you're staying anyway, but it was about Blackwood. Blackwood and your beloved Dante."

"Shut up." I kick her with my foot as she giggles.

"Alright, alright! I'll stop. For now." She smirks. "Anyway, Blackwood is not exactly like any other town... How much do you know about the... mafia?"

My mouth dries, my brain already conjuring answers to where she's going with this. "I watched *The Godfather*. I'm basically an expert."

"Dante's dad is kind of like Don Vito Corleone. And

Dante is the next in line to take over. Except I'm pretty sure he's been running things for a while now."

"They're mafia?"

"The whole family, yes. And most of the town, with small exceptions, works for them. Dante is basically the boss that all the capos around report to. And it's not just around here. It's the whole country. They just made Blackwood their base."

I down the whole glass of wine Mel just refilled. "Fuck, Mel."

"Someone should. It's been a while," she sighs, lightening the mood.

"I'm sure Luca wouldn't mind."

She coughs. "Stop. He'd never. I'm like a younger sister to him."

"Step sister?" I tease.

She swats at me.

I didn't realise how much I needed this, her, a friend like Mel.

Somehow, by keeping to myself and not staying anywhere long enough, I deprived myself of the most basic thing humans need. A connection. They say you can't choose your family, but I'm pretty sure Mel and I have just chosen each other.

When we wake up, the bottle of wine is empty. The sun shines through the living room window, casting a golden glow on a new beginning. Because if surviving a psycho guard trying to kill you isn't a new beginning, then I don't know what is. And although I came to Blackwood looking for answers, I still didn't know the right questions to ask. I wasn't sure what to expect, definitely not a mafia boss first trying to run me out of town, then changing his mind and ensuring I wouldn't leave. This town, *his* town, with its grey sky, green forest and unruly shores, was feeling more like home than anywhere I've ever been before.

And for the first time in my life, I decided to just roll with it. See where the tide takes me.

For once, maybe I wasn't all alone.

# 11

## ALESSA

When Monday rolls around, I don't even remember that just a day-and-a-half ago I was running for my life through the woods.

Creepy guard who?

With Mel on the late shift today, I set off to the Black Royale on my own, finding my way up the winding streets of Blackwood. The apartment is less than a fifteen minute walk away, so when it starts to drizzle, I just lift my head up to the sky and let the rain do what it wants. I'm not worried about my clothes since everyone on the floor wears a uniform. My jeans and trainers will have enough time to dry out by the time my shift is over. And the old black jacket covering my white tee has been through much worse than a bit of rain. Since the day I was found in it, it has served me well. I've hidden stolen clothes and food inside, used it as a blanket, a pillow, a bag, you name it. Me and the jacket have been through things.

It's pouring by the time I arrive at the casino and find shelter under the golden awning. The wet strands of my hair are sticking to my face as rivulets of water drip down my front and splosh on the suede material of my Vans. Not that the extra drops of water make any difference. I'm quite certain if I were to take my trainers off, I'd have enough water in them to make a swimming pool for ants. You'd think I'd make it my priority to get an umbrella after deciding to set up shop in this place, but clearly, that has not been the case.

I could just walk in through the main entrance—since I'm already standing outside—looking like a drowned rat and hoping no one will pay attention to the squelching sounds my shoes will make or the trail of water I'll leave behind. But the question is, do I really want to risk doing that on my first day back and possibly jeopardise my shiny new position in the process? I'm pretty sure they wouldn't fire me for breaking the rule of employees not being allowed to use the main entrance, especially since Dante decided I can't leave town anymore, but I'd rather not risk it. Things are finally working out for me. I have a job that pays really well—even if I'm not sure what the job actually is. I have an apartment I can stay in, and a roommate that doesn't think clipping her toenails in the living room is acceptable. I'd say I'm winning at life.

And let's not forget the most important bit. I finally have the chance to start digging more into Blackwood and how I'm connected to it. Because it couldn't have been a coincidence that the same jacket I was found with had a pocket watch stuck in between a pocket and the lining. A watch that has the town's name engraved inside. I've lived through too many shit situations to believe in coincidences. Everything that happens—happens for a reason. Cause and effect.

Poking a finger through that one hole in my jacket pocket, I take a deep breath and ready myself for a sprint to the staff entrance.

"Alessa."

The skin on my body prickles as I turn to face the man with angry, chocolate-brown eyes.

"Dante," I exhale, resigned. Of course, he'd see me in *this* state. I was hoping to be able to change out of my wet clothes and at least partially dry my hair before I'd have to face him. But, as per usual, I should have known better than to have hope where Dante Santoro is involved. I swear, the guy's sole purpose of existence is to make my life difficult.

"You're... *Wet.*"

"Five points for observation." I squelch the urge to roll my eyes at him for stating the obvious.

"Don't you have an umbrella?"

How bratty can I be before the mafia boss with anger management issues decides to put a bullet between my eyes? I should stop right there. He carries a gun, after all, so the bullet-brain scenario is a definite possibility. Except... By now, we all know my stance on cheap thrills. Plus, where would he keep said gun? His tailored-to-perfection suit distracts me as I try to spot any gun-shaped bulges. My traitorous eyes cast to the one bulge I should not be drawn to. I can clearly see the outline of a thick, long—*What the fuck, Alessa? No, no, no.* I'd rather be shot between the eyes than admit I'm attracted to him. "Would I be *wet* if I had one?"

The smirk that graces his clean-shaven face is nothing short of predatory. He stays silent, letting his eyes slowly move up and down my body as the temperature all around me rises, igniting my nerve endings. It's a miracle the rain does not start evaporating off me in billows of steam under the heat of his stare.

"Right, anyway," I croak out. "I'd better get going before I'm late for my shift." Taking a step away from the entrance, I look past him at the hill I'll have to climb before having to turn and backtrack to the back of the building.

Dante stops me. Wrapping his warm hand around my

bicep, he pulls me back to face him. God, he's strong, and his hands are big, his fingers easily meeting around my arm.

"Come with me." He takes a step toward the door, making me stumble behind him.

"But, the staff entrance," I protest.

"Are you really arguing with me right now, Alessa?"

"It's the rules," I try again.

He stops, turning around to face me as the automatic door slides open. Cool air-conditioned air assaults my body, making me glad my jacket is zipped up because my nipples instantly stand to attention.

"*I* make the rules," he says in a cool tone of voice. A tone that should have me running for the hills with fear, but has my body warming instead. "You best remember that."

And even though my body is screaming, "*Yes, yes! Tell me all the rules!*" My mind is once again in the cheap thrills—poke the bear state. "Sure thing, boss man." I salute him.

His jaw ticks as those molten chocolate eyes bore into me. I want to run away from his scrutiny, from the full attention he is giving me. Not because it makes me squirm but because the more he gives, the more I crave.

And that's something I've never experienced before. Ever since I could, I ran from men, only offering them the bare minimum that ensured my survival. Men were always bad news for me. From that fateful night when I was thirteen, I didn't trust them. Their interest was never a good thing. After I ran away, more than once I have experienced a situation where a guy abused his power to further his agenda, where he lied and cheated just to get me on my own. Very quickly, I've learned that it's a man's world out there, but most of them are so far up their own asses they can be manipulated. Easily.

And I'm a quick study. Watching liars and cheaters in action, I picked up their tricks fairly swiftly, learned their tells, learned to spot their limits. I stole, I flirted, never getting close to one person and always running away before they had a chance to collect the *payment* they expected.

Standing in front of Dante and actually enjoying the attention he gives me feels...*exotic*. Even if at the back of my mind there is still that worry that he will want more. That for everything he's offering me right now, he'll expect something in return. Something I'm not sure I'm ready to give to anyone, and especially not *him*.

"To everyone inside," he says, his voice quiet as he pulls me out of my thoughts, "you're still Stevie."

I look at him quizzically. I was sure now that my ruse was up, I'd be back to Alessa, and he'd be Miss Jones-ing me at every opportune moment.

"It's safer that way. Just—don't tell anyone you're Alessa, okay?"

As soon as I nod, he drags me inside the still empty casino.

When he deposits me in front of the staff changing rooms, I stare at him.

"What?"

It would be nice if he told me which uniform I should go for, since I still don't know what my actual job is supposed to be. "What shall I change into?"

"Whatever is dry," he says dismissively, leaning against the wall, then looks down at the phone he just pulled out of his pocket.

My mouth opens. Is he just going to wait here while I change? And what the hell does he mean, whatever is dry? I swear if they had any of those feather showgirl outfits, I'd put that on just to see the expression on his permanently indignant face.

I giggle to myself, pushing the door open and imagining the fury in his eyes. My gut tells me that if he went through all the trouble of giving me a job and making sure I'd stay in town, the probability of him killing me is exponentially lower than what I thought at first. And with that knowledge, the thrill of poking Terence right in between his angry eyes is that much more delicious.

I take my time pulling off my wet clothes and stuffing them in the dryer. Then consider putting on the golden bikini outfit, but when I go to look for them, to my dismay, they're all gone. Dante must have executed his plan to get rid of the entertainment and everything connected to it pretty swiftly. Now that I think of it, I'm pretty sure when we walked through the main floor, the cages weren't hanging off the ceiling like they usually do.

Whatever, as long as everyone still has a job, I'm okay with them being gone. I dry and style my hair, not really caring that Dante is probably losing it outside because I'm taking so long, before walking barefoot back to the laundry room to look for a clean uniform to put on. With all my clothes still in the dryer, I'm only wearing my white panties and a small towel as I rummage through the cupboards, not finding anything clean. Monday must be laundry day because the clothes bins are full to the brim with discarded items waiting to be washed. I sigh, pottering back to the main room, looking around for something I could put on, my eyes landing on a white shirt with Benji's tag attached to it. I have no choice. The shirt will have to do until I can find Martina, who hopefully will have something stashed away.

Dropping the towel to the floor, I pull Benji's shirt on, starting to button it up before I take care of the tag.

"What the fuck is taking so lo—"

Facing the door, I have the perfect view of Dante storming in, looking down at his phone in his hand, his words cutting out as his eyes lift to search for me. His adam's apple bobs before his lips part as his gaze drops to my breasts. My nipples instantly pucker, poking at the thin material like beacons as he takes a step toward me, his tongue darting out to wet his full lips.

I fight the pull. It is absolutely imperative that I remember this man is a dickhead, and when his eyebrows draw into a frown, his face rearranging from curious to angry, it's enough to bring me back to a place where sanity regains control.

"What the hell do you think you're wearing?" He's staring at my left boob. I'd like to think he's looking at my nipple, but I have a feeling that's not what he's focused on.

"The only clean shirt I could find," I reply. "Must be laundry day."

"Take it off," he says through his teeth.

I blink at him in confusion. "What?"

"Take it the fuck off, or I'll do it for you. And I won't be gentle."

"There's nothing else—"

"Take. It. Off. Or I swear, Alessa." The absolute indignation in his voice makes me spring into action. My shaking fingers fly to the buttons of the shirt, undoing them one by one. When I'm down to the last one, I hesitate.

Dante's eyes are focused on mine, unwavering. I swallow, and undo the last one, then turn around, facing the lockers and slide the shirt down my back until it hits the floor.

My skin pebbles with anticipation as I stand there, my back to Dante, in nothing but my white panties. Although muffled, I can hear his footsteps as he walks from where he was and stands directly behind me. His hot breath on my shoulder. An involuntary shudder escapes me as something soft and silky hits my bare shoulders. I close my eyes as he drapes his suit jacket, still warm from his body, around me. Then, his hand touches my neck as he sweeps my hair to the side and out of the way. I need more air. I need more of his touch. More of the softness. More of everything that is happening because my body has never reacted like this before and I need to know what else it can do.

"That's better," he grumbles. "I'll get you something proper to wear. But this will do for now."

I nod, unable to turn around to face him, my chest rising and falling like I've just run a five-minute mile. I listen as he taps away on his phone before silence engulfs us.

"You can turn around now."

I ignore his words, not sure if turning around is such a good idea. His jacket is big enough that it covers most of my upper body, even with my arms not in the sleeves. Holding onto the lapels, I pull them together and take a big breath, trying to figure out my next step.

When I don't move, he clicks his tongue then walks around me until once again we face each other. I don't know what's more confusing, the smell of his oddly familiar cologne that surrounds me, or the outline of his perfectly sculpted chest, covered in black ink I can clearly see through the thin button down he's wearing. I take a step back as my eyes travel down and settle on the gun grip sticking out of a holster attached to his belt.

Dante sighs, shaking his head, before walking over to the vanity table I used when I was drying my hair and sitting down in front of the light up mirror. He's so big he barely fits in the chair as he starts investigating the golden eye shadows and highlighters. He picks up the bronzer, taking the top off and twisting the bottom until there's a large brown stick sticking out. As I watch him examine it, his eyebrows drawn as the stick pops up then disappears again each time he moves his hand, the whirl of the tumble dryer filling the otherwise silent room, I have this urge to walk over and crawl onto his lap. Curl into him, and just let his strong arms protect me. Because as ruthless and angry as he is, he is also trying really hard to make me feel at ease, and that's something. Plus, no matter how much I dislike him, I can't deny that he's *really* nice to look at.

Taking advantage of the temporary change from an angry douchebag to whatever he's trying to be at the moment, I walk up behind him and meet his eyes in the mirror.

"So, what's the plan, boss man? Am I just going to stand here in nothing but your jacket until someone comes to do the laundry?"

"We'll wait as long as we need to. I told you I'll sort something out for you."

"*We*? Don't you have like *mafia* stuff to get to?"

He stands up abruptly. The chair clattering to the floor as he whirls around to face me. "What did you say?"

I swallow as I watch the knuckles on his clenched fists whiten. "Uhm... Mafia?"

"What do you know, Alessa?" His voice is controlled, but I know better. I've seen how quickly he can switch from one mood to another, even if his control never slips. Anger and cruelty are his default settings.

"Just that... You run this town, I guess? You're some sort of a big mafia boss. Or you're going to be?" I take a step back.

"And how do you know this?"

"People talk," I say, biting my lip.

"Melissa," he says, rubbing his chin, his shoulders dropping down as he exhales. "She's too chatty for her own good."

"It's not like she told me anything I wouldn't have figured out by myself." I rush to her defense. "Come on, you drive a Maserati, carry a gun, own a casino and probably half this town, and you live in a high security mansion overlooking the whole thing. Let's not forget the tailored Italian suits and that most of the town is afraid of you enough to turn away a perfectly good potential employee because you told them to. If those aren't the signs of someone at the top of an organised crime food chain, then I'm the real Stevie Nicks. The only thing that's missing is tons of drugs."

"There are no drugs in Blackwood," he growls.

I open my mouth but at the same time the door opens and Angelo walks in, his eyes bouncing between Dante and me, his eyebrow arching as he assesses my current outfit.

"I've got what you asked for." He sounds pissed as he throws a bag at his brother's chest.

"Thanks." Dante catches it without an issue, then walks over to me.

When I raise my eyebrow, he holds the bag in front of him, waiting for me to take it. Holding his suit jacket together with one hand, I sneak the other out and grab it.

"Go change."

I'm on the verge of protesting, telling him he can't tell me what to do, but he's my boss and he totally can. Plus Angelo beats me to it.

"I'm not your *fattorino*[1], Saint."

"Of course you aren't my errand boy," Dante replies, as I push open the door to the laundry room, annoyed that neither one of them thought they should move their conversation outside so I can change in peace.

"I don't get it, Dante. What's so special about *her*?" The words reach me just as the door closes behind me. I have the biggest urge to press my face against the wood and see if I can make out the rest of that conversation because I'm in the exact same camp Angelo is. I'd give my pinky finger to find out why the hell Dante changed his mind about me so abruptly, especially since he was adamant he wanted me gone.

But I resist the urge, mostly because I wouldn't be able to make anything out over the noise the tumble dryer is making, and open the bag in my hand. I don't know what I was expecting to find in there. A clean uniform maybe? Definitely not black skinny jeans and a silk white blouse from Prada. And most definitely not a matching black lace bra and panties set from La Perla, all still with tags on. The prices on the tags are giving me heart palpitations. The lingerie alone is worth more than two months' rent at the last place I stayed in. This is too much. My survival instinct kicks in, making me wonder what I'll be required to do in return. Because they *always* want something.

I briefly consider taking my clothes out of the dryer and putting them back on even if they're still wet, but then think better of it. There were no female bartenders behind the bar, and Benji was wearing a white shirt and black trousers combo, so this, minus the bra and panties, might actually be the uniform. I decide not to look a gift horse in the mouth and just put everything on. When will I ever have a chance to wear anything this expensive again after all? Of course, the silk blouse is so thin you can clearly see the lacy black bra under. I'd take it off if I weren't certain without it, everyone would be able to see my nipples.

Dressed and barefoot, I take Dante's jacket and slip it on, rolling the sleeves up and pushing them to my elbows. His intoxicating cologne invades my senses and if I had any less control, I'd be lifting the collar to sniff it like a grade-A horn dog.

When I come back out, Angelo is gone while Dante is tapping away on his phone, probably playing Candy Crush and only pretending he's taking care of business.

"How did you know my size?" I ask the question that's been burning a hole in my mind.

He lifts his eyes, giving me a once over, a small smirk gracing his handsome face. "I guessed."

I narrow my eyes, wracking my brain. I don't believe

him. There's no chance he'd be able to guess a jeans size down to the leg length in inches. No one is *that* good. I want to punch his pretty face and wipe that smirk right off, because the look he has every time I see it, says he thinks he's way better than everyone else. Obviously, I'm not going to punch him, though. As much as he might be okay with having me around now, I'm pretty sure he wouldn't hesitate to rip my arm out for something like that.

"Doubtful."

He shrugs one shoulder, then turns around and walks out, throwing, "Come on," at me over his shoulder.

As we walk down the carpet covered corridors, it suddenly clicks. "You got all the measurements from my file!" I exclaim as he stops in front of his office door.

"I did?" He pushes the door open.

"It's the only reasonable explanation. I gave Martina all my measurements." I smile at my absolute genius as I cross the threshold and follow him inside. "All except for shoe size, because dancers are dancing barefoot."

"Were," he mutters, turning around, his gaze landing on my feet. "For fuck's sake, you're not wearing shoes."

"Observant, are we?"

"What's your shoe size, then?"

"Seven. Anyway, why are we here? Shouldn't I be getting ready for my shift?"

He stops the tapping on his phone, an eyebrow raised. "You are."

"Huh?" Maybe I got brain damage from all the excitement. "Shouldn't I go to the bar, then?"

"Why? I don't condone drinking on the job."

I clear my throat, tired of trying to figure him out. "And what exactly is the job I'm not supposed to be drinking on?" I ask.

"Why, *Stevie*," he says as the door behind me opens,

Angelo walking in with a pair of Prada trainers in his hand, handing them to me. What the fuck? Do they have a Prada store in the basement or something? "I thought with your deduction skills you're clearly so proud of, you'd have figured it out by now."

Angelo stands next to me as I look between him and his brother, trying to figure out what I'm missing. "I haven't." I finally give up.

"You're my new assistant," Dante says, all proud of himself.

My jaw goes slack. The fuck?

"*Ma che cazzo?*[2]" Angelo mutters, clearly as shocked as I am.

# 12

## ALESSA

Turns out, being an assistant to a mafia boss means doing a whole load of nothing. Dante arranges for a small desk and chair to be placed outside his office, tells me to get to work, then disappears behind his door.

I would have gladly done what he asked if only he remembered to tell me the password to log on to the laptop or at least told me what exactly he'd like me to do. But since he hasn't done either of those things, telling me he doesn't want to be interrupted instead, I pull out my phone and play Candy Crush before my lives run out and I decide to google how to break into a password protected laptop. I don't find anything useful unless I want to reset the whole thing, and I'd rather not, in case it's got something important on it. Not that I think Dante would trust me with anything important on my first day, the dick. He just shut himself in, and left me out here on my own to smile awkwardly at every Tom, Dick and Harry who passes by. So, instead of stewing in anger, I fall down the rabbit hole, reading about hacking. On a whim, I even join a couple of forums where @dirtyhackz tries to help me find a solution to my password protected laptop problem. I end up creating a new user account, and after hacking the internet password, I buy a couple of books on C++ and code breaking that came recommended by my new hacker friend.

I'm almost finished coding a program that makes my soul happy when the door behind me opens. I don't turn around, choosing to enter the last two lines of code before sighing with pleasure and cracking my knuckles when a white window appears with '*What can I help you with?*' flashing at the top.

I'm a regular Kevin Mitnick, I am.

"What are you doing?"

"Working," I reply. Because I might technically not be doing actual work at the moment, but I'm certainly working on my programming skills before I move onto hacking, and take down his network, so he can have a taste of how it feels to be locked out of everything.

"On what?" He steps closer, leaning over my shoulder as he looks at the white box on my screen. I can feel his body heat behind me.

"Just wrote a little program I think you might find interesting," I say innocently.

"You know how to code a program?" His breath fans my hair.

I take a deep breath, trying to calm down my racing heart. "I do now."

He doesn't question my response. Instead, he leans even closer. "What does it do?"

"Boy, am I glad you asked." I smile, then type. '*Tell me something about my new boss*' in the white box.

I hold my breath as three dots blink in and out before, finally, letters pop up under my question, forming a reply I coded to appear if that exact command is typed.

'Dante *Santoro* - *is a well-known douche nozzle. An heir to* the Santoro empire, he enjoys barefoot walks on morning dew-covered grass and giving his assistants laptops without the pass-words to log in.

*He is also known for his love of not giving instructions. He likes it if you try to figure out what it is exactly he wants you to do all by yourself, even if you have no damn clue.'*

Then *'Is there anything else?'* pops up.

I'm super aware of the stone statue next to me as he reads the words.

"Interesting," he finally says. "*Is* there anything else?"

A droplet of sweat slides down my neck as I consider my next move. It's just a bit of fun, after all. I type *'Tell me something everyone knows.'* Three dots appear then:

*'Everyone knows that ketchup is king.*

*Also,* Dante *Santoro smells like Italian merda*[1]*.'*

"I don't think Italian shit smells any different from American," he deadpans. "Curiously enough, you seem to be fond of the smell too, since you keep sniffing my jacket."

I huff. "I don't," I mutter. "I was just trying to figure out what it smells of."

"Let me guess, *Italian shit.*"

I turn in my chair, facing him, annoyed that he's trying to spoil my fun. "Is there anything I can help *you* with?"

I'm met with a cold stare. "Well, *Stevie*, since you're my assistant, you could do your actual job and assist me." He straightens, towering over me. I have to crane my neck up to speak to him.

"Sure thing, *boss man.* What can I do for you?"

"You can start by using my name."

"I like 'boss man' better at the moment. Makes me want to throttle you just a bit less." I cover my mouth with my hand, my eyes wide as I realise I've spoken that out loud. You see? This is what a day in solitude spent trying to enter-tain yourself does to a human.

His jaw ticks as he takes a breath and closes his eyes. I comfort myself with the knowledge that the annoyance he feels for me is mutual and that if he hasn't drawn his gun to shoot me yet, he might let my comment slide.

"Just—Go get me something to eat." He shakes his head then turns back to his door.

I clear my throat.

"What?" he asks without turning around.

I'm in a good mood. Probably because he hasn't killed me yet, so it comes to me as no surprise that my brain decides to ride the endorphins in style, like a turtle rides a dolphin. "What's the magic word?"

His shoulders tense. "You're on thin ice, Stevie." When I don't reply, his fists clench by his side. "Go get me something to eat. *Please*," he says through clenched teeth. See? That wasn't too hard.

"No problem. Anything in particular?"

"I don't care. Get something for yourself, and just get the same fucking thing for me. *Please*."

He puts his hand on the door, then stops and pulls a money clip out of his pocket, throwing it onto my desk without turning around, then stomps into his office.

I look down at the silver money clip that's so thick with one hundred-dollar bills there has to be a few thousand in it, at least. Who even carries that much cash on them? I pick it up, the clip heavy in my hand, and put it in the inside pocket of Dante's suit jacket before making my way out of the casino.

Now that I'm no longer busy being petty and learning to code just so I can make a silly little program where I insult my boss, I finally feel the hunger. In fact, when I see the time and realise all I've had all day was a slice of toast with peanut butter for breakfast, I'm positively ravenous. I rush outside and run down the street to the only place that won't make me feel like I'm a fish out of water pretending to be a seagull. Even if the fish is dressed head to toe in Prada.

I pass all the expensive-looking restaurants and walk into a bar, the smell of spicy wings making my mouth water.

"Can I have two portions of wings and cheesy fries to go, please?" I ask the bartender, my stomach already lamenting the wait we'll have to endure before eating.

"Any sauce with that?" he asks as he types the order into the till.

I grin. "Tell them to put ketchup all over one of the orders, and not to hold back. If they think there's too much ketchup, they probably need to add some more," I say. "And just a bit of ketchup on the side on the other order."

When he rattles off the amount to pay without blinking an eye at my request, I know I've found 'my' people. I take the money clip, pulling a hundred-dollar bill out and handing it to him when my eye catches something on the side.

I stare at the cursive engraving. My eyes blinking, unable to process what I'm looking at. When the guy behind the bar tries to hand me my change, I tell him to keep it as I flip the money clip around. One side is clear, but when I turn it around, the other has me all confused. Blackwood. The name engraved, a perfect twin to the engraving on *my* pocket watch. It's larger, but the font is exactly the same, down to the flourishes. Then there are the two curved lines on the side I thought were just scratches on my pocket watch, but can't be, since Dante's money clip has them in the exact same place. To anyone, they'd look like scratches since the lines are much thinner, almost looking like a mistake. But it would have to be one hell of a coincidence.

I've heard of jewellers leaving a signature mark on the pieces they create. Could this be one of those? And if that's the case, I could find whoever engraved it and see if they remember who bought the pocket watch I have. Maybe they have records of it. It could have been my father or mother. My heart flutters at the thought that I'm just a bit closer to finding my family.

I barely register when the bartender hands me the food or the older looking man who bumps into me as I walk back to the casino.

"Rosa?" he gasps.

I just shake my head and continue until I'm back inside, standing in front of Dante's office door, with the money clip still in his jacket. I put my food on my desk, then knock on his door.

He opens it, his phone pressed against his ear as he motions for me to put his food on the desk.

"You can head home," Dante says, covering the microphone on his phone. "Thanks for getting the food."

I smile, almost feeling bad, but I think better of it. I walk outside and grab my bag, deciding to leave my wet things in the staff room until tomorrow in case he opens his bag of food straight away.

I know I've done the right thing when I hear an angry roar as something crashes to the floor.

"Get back here, now!" he bellows after me.

I yelp. Taking off into a run. "See you tomorrow, boss man!" I shout, turning a corner.

"You'll pay for this!" Is the last thing I hear as I take the stairs two at a time, laughing. I only wish I could have seen his face when he opened the box containing his food and found it covered in ketchup.

I basically skip all the way back home. I most likely *will* pay for it tomorrow. But that's a future Alessa problem.

# 13

## ALESSA

I have a plan. I'm just going to tell him it was a mixup. It was *my* lunch I had left on his desk by mistake. I'll apologise, and that will be the end of it. He'll understand.

Maybe...

I pace in front of the staff entrance, trying to convince myself Dante won't kill me for what I pulled yesterday, but since the joy of annoying him had worn off within fifteen minutes of getting back home, I'm not so sure.

"Stalling, are we?"

I yelp, jumping in place and clutching my chest. "You scared me half to death!"

"Did I?" Dante's face is stoic as his chocolate brown eyes turn cold. I take a small step back.

"Look, about the food yesterday."

"What about it?" He moves closer to me.

"It was an honest mistake. I must have given you mine without realising."

"Hmmm."

I swallow. "Surely you won't *kill* me for one teeny tiny slip up?" I laugh awkwardly.

"Won't I?"

"You'd lose an excellent assistant. And good assistants are super hard to come by these days," I nod.

"I guess I'll hold off then," he says, then turns to open the door, leaving me stunned. Well, that was a lot easier than I thought. "You coming?"

I walk past him and up the stairs until we reach his office, where I stand confused once again.

"Something wrong, Stevie?" Dante says sweetly. The tone of his voice lets me know I'm well and truly fucked. Whatever he's got in store for me, I think I'd rather take death if it's still on the table.

"Am I fired?" I ask, trying to figure out if it was the little program I coded or the ketchup all over his food that sealed my fate.

"Now, why would you think that?" He crosses his arms in front of his chest.

"My desk?" I point at the empty space where my desk was just yesterday.

"Oh, that? I thought you might have been a bit cramped yesterday."

I bite my lip. The space was a little tight, but where the hell am I supposed to sit now?

"Nowhere to stretch your legs," he continues. "Walk off any silly ideas you might get." He pauses, making me blush. "I took the liberty of moving us to a bigger office."

"Oh. Okay."

When he keeps standing there like a statue, I clear my throat, finally gazing up into his eyes. The look he gives me is deadly. It's pure dominance and power, and I know I should be shaking in my brand new Prada trainers with fear, but my body has other ideas.

My heart beats wildly, pumping oxygen to all my nerve endings, causing my skin to feel ultra sensitive. I'm so on edge that if a feather were to float down from the ceiling and touch any part of my exposed skin, I'd explode. There's a charge in the air. And as much as I want to loathe it, I don't.

Dante Santoro doesn't scare me, *he excites me.* Even if I still struggle not to despise him whenever he opens his mouth.

Which he does, gracefully breaking the spell. "Are you going to stand there like Bambi, or shall we get going?"

I roll my eyes, then walk past him.

"The other way."

*Oh, for fuck's sake.* I turn around and ignore the smirk on his face. Or the overwhelming need to kick him in the shin for being a jackhole with perfect hair. Seriously, what's up with that? With the humidity in the air, my usually limp hair has a life of its own, creating a little halo of flyaways whenever I go outside.

Without a word, he starts walking, clearly expecting me to follow suit since he doesn't even look back once before disappearing around the corner. I dash after him, almost breaking into a run just to catch up. When I finally do, he doesn't even acknowledge my presence as I try my hardest to keep pace. For every step he makes, I have to take two, and I still fall behind. Wherever we are going, he's making me work for it, and if it weren't for the last few weeks of walking up and down the steep hill this town is on, I'd have been panting and out of breath, probably dreaming of getting a scooter just so I could catch up.

The image of me zooming around the casino on a scooter, like a millennial tech billionaire, has me so entertained that I fail to notice the lack of movement in front of me. It is only by pure luck I don't crash into Dante's back as he thoughtfully looks down the corridor. I turn my head, following his gaze until I see the crystal and gold chandelier from the entrance of the casino, glinting from behind the glass separating us and the main hall. I try to figure out in which part of the Black Royale we are, but I haven't got a clue. This first floor is a huge maze, and I've only ever been to the staff room, the dancing platform and, of course, Dante's office, so this area is completely new to me.

When I turn back to ask Dante why we stopped, he's a couple dozen feet away, his hand on a door handle as he looks at me with his brows drawn.

From this far away, he looks just like any other business executive, so handsome in his tailored suit it almost hurts. His thick, dark hair is styled, not a strand out of place. Come to think of it, I've never seen his hair messy. Even fresh out of the shower and still wet, it was perfect. A strange feeling comes over me, propelling my steps forward. What would his hair feel like between my fingers? What would his skin feel like? He's clean shaven this morning. Would I be able to feel the stubble if I traced his jaw?

"What are you doing?" His gravelly voice brings me back to Earth. I'm right in front of him, with my hand half stretched between us, his woodsy cologne surrounding me like a warm blanket, making me feel safe.

"You had lint on your suit." I save my dignity by flicking the nonexistent fluff off his lapel.

His hand is still on the doorknob, his arm between the now open door and me, blocking my way in. I don't let that deter me, though, leaning over and peering inside, my breath taken away by the window wall my eyes are instantly drawn to.

I push Dante's hand out of my way and walk in, taking in the view of the colourful houses and buildings below, their staggered rooftops looking polished, still drying after last night's showers. The day is clear, and I'm awestruck by the unobscured view of the waves crashing against the jagged rocks separating the bay from the wild ocean beyond.

My breath fogs the glass as I try to drink in the beauty in front of me, trying to comprehend why this room wouldn't be everyone's first choice for an office.

"If you get any closer to that window, you'll squash your little nose."

"Aww, you think my nose is cute," I murmur, still staring out.

"I said little, not cute," he scoffs. "It's too little for your face. Makes you look funny with your eyes being so large."

"Mhmm. Mhmmm. And now you think my eyes are big and beautiful? You better stop it, or I'll start to think you're in love with me," I quip.

His laugh is so loud it makes me turn around just so I can see his face light up one more time. "Fat chance of that."

My hand lands on my chest. "That's a bit hurtful. I'm very lovable," I say. But then my mirth dissipates. Clearly, he knows as well as I do that I'm not. After all, if I were, my parents wouldn't have abandoned me. Or at least someone would have adopted me. Instead, it's been a journey from one foster family to another, until the day I ran away. If that's not a sign of being unlovable, then I don't know what is.

"You could be the most lovable woman on earth. It wouldn't change a thing," he mutters.

"Whatever," I say, looking away to hide the hurt on my face and taking the opportunity to examine my new working space. It's bright with the natural light coming from the window behind me. The space is split into two rooms, partitioned by a glass wall. Each a mirror image of the other with desks facing each other, a filing cabinet, and a potted plant in the corner.

With Dante being able to watch my every move through the glass partition, it will be difficult to get up to anything mischievous. But having to try harder has never stopped me before, and it will certainly not do it now.

I walk over to what I assume is going to be my desk and sit down on the comfy chair with my back to the door. That's not very clever, is it? If I'm supposed to be his assistant, shouldn't I be facing the door so I can greet visitors before they go into his office? Be his gatekeeper? Not that it would make much difference. With his desk clearly visible, anyone would still be able to see whether he's busy or not.

I spin around in my chair, stopping after a full circle, the view beyond the window once again capturing my attention.

"Wow."

"Get to work, Alessa," Dante growls from behind. I can just imagine his crossed arms and pissed off expression.

"You mean Stevie," I whisper, not turning around.

He sighs, annoyed. "The password to your laptop is on a post-it note inside the top drawer."

"Mhmmm." I watch a seagull swoop down from mid air into the water before flying up with something in its beak. I jet out of the chair, running to the window with my jaw open as the seagull flies out of sight somewhere behind the rocks. "Did you see that?"

"Stevie," he says harshly.

"Yes, boss man?" I turn to face him.

"Get to work. I don't pay you to stare at the ocean."

I take a deep breath, reluctantly walking back to my desk before sitting down and opening the top drawer. True to Dante's words, there's a post-it note with a password on it. Pulling it out, I open the laptop then log in. When I look up to tell Dante that it worked, I find him next to a glass door separating our offices. Seriously, am I *that* unobservant or does he just move like a ninja?

"What am I supposed to do?"

He looks at me like I'm stupid.

I sigh. "What do *you* want me to do? You're the boss man."

"Middle drawer," he says, his eyes not leaving mine. There's a small upward tilt to his lips, like he's got a secret.

"Okay." I nod and watch him walk into his office, leaving the door ajar, then sit in front of his desk

He opens his laptop, and after a minute starts typing away. I look between him, my laptop and the drawer. I just need to figure out what a normal assistant to a mafia boss would do, and I'll be fine. Am I like his 'second' in a duel? If there's a fight, I'm the one to hand him his gun and count to ten?

Let's be honest—if there's a gunfight, I want to be as far from it as possible, so if that's what he expects from me, I'm out. I forgo opening the drawer for now and quickly google what an assistant does. Something I would have done yesterday had I not been locked out of my laptop and then hellbent on creating my lovely little program as revenge.

One of the first things that pops up is managing emails and calendars. So, like the best assistant Dante's ever had, I open the email client and look through the completely empty calendar. Do I even have access to his? I dig around and find his email address in the address book, and request for him to share his calendar with me, then wait, watching his face. I can pinpoint the exact moment he sees my request, his eyes briefly flying to meet mine before ducking down to his screen. He clicks something, then smirks to himself. I don't even have to check my screen to know that the request has been denied.

Annoyed at him, I go back to my calendar and start creating meetings, adding his email address.

'Anger Management Classes at *Goosfraba Institute*' at lunchtime today. Then 'Kill all my enemies so I can rule over the world like I've always dreamed of,' scheduled for

Friday at three in the afternoon. And my personal favourite —a recurring meeting on the first Tuesday of each month at nine in the morning—'Back, sack and crack waxing appointment for Mr Santoro at *We Love Shiny Balls in Blackwood*'.

A message dings and a messenger box pops up on my screen. I knew that the last one was a winner.

I quickly go into the settings and change my screen name in the app.

**Dante Santoro:** Get to work.

**The best assistant in the mafia:** I'm working. One of my assistantly duties is to schedule your appointments.

**Dante Santoro:** Don't test me.

**Dante Santoro:** Middle drawer.

I roll my eyes, then open the middle drawer of my desk, a large white box in it. I carefully lift it up and set it next to my laptop, hoping there are cupcakes inside, but knowing better than to aim that high where Dante is involved. There's a small sticker on the side, 'Wood cased HB pencils, unsharpened,' and a stamped number below. I slowly lift the lid open, praying it's a factory number or something, but once again, I should have known better. There are at least three hundred unsharpened pencils inside.

The messenger dings again. I close my eyes and count to five before looking up at my screen.

**Dante Santoro:** Looks like you're going to be busy for a while. Shhhr shhr shhr.

**Dante Santoro:** I need them sharp enough to stab a person.

*Motherfucker.*

I look back in the drawer, and sure enough, there's a small, green handheld pencil sharpener in there. Sighing, I take it out, setting it next to the box with pencils, then pull the trash can from under my desk. *I best get to work.*

The first five are quite therapeutic. After that, it goes downhill. At pencil number thirty, I imagine it's me who stabs Dante with one of those pencils. At pencil one hundred, I gauge his eyes using pencils like chopsticks. After that, I try to imagine a new inventive way to kill my new boss with each new pencil. It's hard to kill a man with a pencil if your name is not John Wick, so after a while, I settle for pencil torture techniques. Imagining where I'd stick those pencils to show him just how much I'm enjoying the task he has set for me.

It seems to work because by the time I run out of ideas, I'm almost done, and the trash is filled with pencil shreds. As I place the last pencil back in the box, I'm pretty proud of myself. My fingers might be cramping, but the asshole can't say I didn't do what he asked for, even if I imagined stuffing a pencil up his nostril and walking out of his office at least twenty times while I tried not to curse at the small sharpener slipping out of my grip. But perseverance is my middle name. So, with the box full of my hard labour, I walk into Dante's office, then drop the pencils on his desk.

He ignores me as I stand above him, my arms crossed in front of my chest. I clear my throat.

"Yes?"

"I did what you asked."

"Lovely." He continues to type.

"Aren't you going to check them?"

He sighs heavily, like he's dealing with a petulant child, then looks over to the box, lifting a pencil and pressing a sharp tip against the pad of his index finger. "Hmmm," he says, dropping it back into the box before grabbing the whole thing and chucking it into his trash can.

My jaw drops open. Seriously? What the hell is wrong with him? I'm so exasperated I want to scream, but the douchebox just ignores me, opening his top drawer and pulling out a small stack of papers, then handing them to me. It's only because of an automatic reaction that I take them instead of smacking him over the head like I wanted to. God, I hate the asshole. Even if he smells delicious.

"The font is all wrong on these," he says, looking at his screen. "Retype them. *Please.*"

I narrow my eyes at him, sticking my tongue out, then turn around and walk back to my desk. Once I'm sitting behind my laptop, I flip him a double bird concealed by my screen, but there nonetheless, then open a new sheet in a word processor.

I don't even count the pages I'll have to go through. I just sit there typing away, not really paying attention to what I'm typing or what's in the papers. *If there are typos, he can stuff it.* I'm about five pages in when a dark figure blocks the light from the window.

"Could you go get us some food, please?"

I look up, smiling. "Sure."

"There's a sandwich place next door. I'll have the mortadella one. Get something for yourself, too."

I smile even wider.

"You still have my money, right? Or have you spent it already?"

Was that even an option? If I knew, I'd have gone shopping last night. I pat my jacket, the one I 'borrowed' yesterday, where the inside pocket is.

"Of course." His lips form a thin line, drawing my eyes. "*My* money is in *my* jacket. Anything else of mine you'd like to commandeer?"

I look him up and down. "I'm good, thanks. And I do *love* my new jacket. Thank you, by the way."

He looks up to the sky. "Of course. It's only a two thousand dollar Ferragamo, anyway."

My mouth dries, because honestly, who spends this

much on clothes? Hasn't he heard of Nordstrom or Macy's? What's wrong with a two hundred dollar suit? But I'm not about to ask. As I walk down to the sandwich shop, mulling over the last couple of days, I realise there's a pattern. Prada, La Perla, Ferragamo, La Famiglia, the sandwich shop and even his Maserati are all Italian. I wonder if everything he owns is Italian, or Italian made. It's highly likely considering how much money he has. And is it just him feeling so patriotic or is this something every Italian mafioso does?

And most importantly, does that mean that his money clip is from an Italian owned jeweller? It would hopefully narrow down my search quite a bit. Because when I looked up all the jewellers in Blackwood last night, I was surprised to find over twenty in a small town like this, and another fifty in the neighbouring towns. I guess the mafia is big on jewellery.

And as I squirt a big dollop of ketchup between the slices of his bread, I decide I might as well ask him where he got his clip from. The worst thing he can do is tell me to go do my work and ignore me. With my resolve renewed, I walk back to the Black Royale, swinging the sandwich bag back and forth. The hair at the back of my neck stands as I turn the corner, making my overactive imagination run wild. *Someone probably just glanced my way*, I tell myself as I rush through the main door, not wanting to walk to the staff entrance alone. My paranoia is in full swing though, and as I wave to Mel, passing her by, I try to reason with myself that the only person who gave me the creeps, the guard from the bus station, is most likely sleeping with the fishes by now—as Mario Puzo has aptly called it.

By the time I'm back in the office and placing the bag with Dante's sandwich on his desk, I'm almost certain I made the whole thing up. He mutters a thank you without looking up from the spreadsheet he's studying. I look at it for a couple of seconds, trying to gather the courage to interrupt him.

He makes it easier by reaching for his sandwich bag. I pull the money clip and put it on the desk right in front of him, pulling his attention from the bag.

"I like your clip," I say.

"You can't have it." His eyes lift to mine.

I laugh nervously. "I was just going to ask where you bought it. I really like the engraving. It's very unusual."

He studies my face for a beat. I'm glad he can't see my back, because a large droplet of nervous sweat is sliding down between my shoulder blades. "It was a gift," he finally says.

"Oh." My face falls. Well, that's a dead end. "Okay." I hang my head resigned and walk to my desk.

"Stevie?" he says, stopping me as I'm halfway there.

I look over my shoulder.

"I might be able to find out where it was purchased. Is there anything in particular you'd like engraved?"

"A vase." I'm usually able to think quickly on my feet, but the way he's looking at me has me all flustered.

"A vase?"

"A silver one," I nod. "A family heirloom," I add.

His brows scrunch up, causing an adorable line to form in between, one I have an urge to smooth with my finger while sitting in his lap. *Stop it, Alessa!*

"Okay. I'll have a look."

I nod again, then walk back to my desk, unwrapping my sandwich and taking a bite. I put the same amount of ketchup on both of them this time. It's hard to admit, but even as much as I love the red stuff, I'm struggling with bite number two. I don't know if it's the mortadella or what. But it just doesn't go together.

"Oh, for fuck's sake!" There's a clutter in the other room. "Stevie!" Dante shouts.

I smile behind the screen, trying not to giggle.

"Yes, boss?"

"Can you come here, please?"

Swallowing my chuckle, I get up and walk over to the door that separates us.

"You know what would be good in here?" I say, looking around. "A couch, and maybe a small table with some chairs. It's a bit *bare*, don't you think? It could use some colour too. Didn't you say red was your favourite colour? Red would look nice here, too."

His jaw is clenched so tight I can hear his teeth grinding from where I'm standing. "I'd tell you I hate red, but I'm afraid you'd just use it as ammunition," he says, and boy, is he right. "What the hell is this?"

"What?" I ask innocently.

"This," he points at his sandwich.

"Your sandwich. The one you asked for."

He closes his eyes slowly. His eyelids fluttering like he's trying to compose himself. "Inside."

"Mortadella," I say.

"The fucking ketchup, Stevie. What the fuck is ketchup doing in there?"

My eyes go huge. "It's not supposed to be inside? I was wondering why they'd put it in the sandwich. It tastes a bit weird, doesn't it?"

"Get out," he grits through his teeth.

Having done my bit, I go back to my desk and pick up my sandwich, taking a bite. I wasn't lying. We really could use a table with chairs in here. It can't be healthy eating at your desk. As I continue to eat my lunch, I can feel Dante's angry stare on me, studying me.

I look up, meeting his dark brown eyes and lifting my

sandwich in a 'cheers' motion. To my surprise, he lifts his sandwich to his mouth and rips a savage bite out of it, his eyes never leaving mine.

A shiver runs down my spine as he eats his food like he's a starved animal ripping into my throat. And what's confusing is, in that moment, as I watch him devour his food, a drop of ketchup dripping down his chin, rage filling his features, I'm not sure if I'm more scared or turned on.

Dante Santoro never let his control slip like this before, and as I watch him, I can't help but wish he would let this beast out more often. Because as scary as he is, he's also raw, and passionate, and so damn sexy my panties are soaked.

As he licks his lips, then the sauce of his fingers one by one, I clear my throat and look down, unable to take any more of it. If he continues this charade, I'll have no option but to get up, walk over to his desk and hump his lap. Consequences be damned.

So, to save myself the embarrassment, I put my sandwich down and shuffle through the papers I'm still to transcribe. There are two pages filled with numbers, dates and names, the title on them the same as the one on Dante's spreadsheet he was going through earlier. I doubt he wanted me to see them. They probably got mixed up when he grabbed the stack for me. I'm about to set them aside when something catches my eye. The name the bus guard used when telling me he's planning to kill me. I scan the documents again. Something doesn't add up. I study the pages closer, the feeling that I'm missing something so potent I can almost taste it. I think the numbers are off. If only I could see the spreadsheet Dante had on his laptop and compare it to these two. Maybe I'd see it?

Dante's phone pings, making my head snap up. I watch him read the text, his whole body tensing up right in front of my eyes. I thought I knew what he looks like when he's angry, but I was wrong.

I've never seen him like this before.

The face, a mask of stone, the eyes with an ice cold expression, his rigid stature—if the anger was aimed at me, I'd cower.

His eyes focus on the door behind me.

"I'll be back soon. Do not leave this room, Alessa. Do you understand?" he says as he stops by my desk.

I know better than to argue. Nodding, I watch as he walks through the door, leaving me alone.

Alone with his laptop. And I never waste an opportune moment.

# 14

# DANTE

"Why is he here? *Again*." I ask Angelo as soon as the door behind me closes.

He looks pointedly over my shoulder. "Is *she* there all by herself?"

"She's safe." I cut him off. No one apart from my brothers knows I've moved into a new office space.

"I *meant*, is she there all alone with your stuff, Dante?" Angelo growls.

I shrug.

"*Cazzo*[1]! What the fuck is wrong with you? She could get into your emails. Or our business files! What if she's a snitch? She could take it to the cops."

"She won't." I start walking, brushing past my younger brother and doing a hell of a good job of ignoring him.

"You've been fucking pussy whipped, haven't you?" He laughs bitterly. "Never thought I'd see the day, but it's finally upon us. Dante Santoro, taken down by pussy. And all it took was some out-of-town cunt," he spits out.

I whirl around, pushing him against the wall and press my forearm against his neck. "Never," I say cooly. "Ever." I press my arm harder. "Call. Her. A. Cunt. Again. *Capisci*[2]?"

133

Angelo nods, his hands pulling at my sleeve. I breathe out through my nose, my eyes shooting daggers into his, then finally, when the anger is no longer the driving force, I take a step back, straighten my jacket, then lead the way down the corridor, pretending I didn't just use force against my younger brother just because he called Alessa a name. I've never hurt my younger siblings. I vowed to always take care of them. I was the one who'd separate my brothers when they fought. I was the voice of reason. And now that voice of reason was gone. I saw the shock on Angelo's face the moment my arm was against his throat, pushing him against the wall. He hadn't expected the outburst. Neither had I.

It's all because of *her*.

My fists clench. It would have been so much easier if she just didn't exist. If that day, all those years ago, I never found her. Then everything would have been fine. Nico wouldn't be sniffing around, threatening everything I've built. I wouldn't feel this sick obligation to protect her, like she's my responsibility. And I wouldn't have attacked my brother just now.

Of course I'm on edge. Anyone would have been with all this hanging in the balance.

"It's okay, Dante." Angelo touches my arm. "You like her. It's fine."

"I don't *like* her," I seethe. But deep down, I know she intrigues me. And I. Fucking. Hate. It.

"Okay, whatever," he says softly. "You don't like her. You just like to fuck her. We've all been there, brother."

I exhale through my nose. "I haven't fucked her. *And* before you say it, I'm not going to." Nevermind how much my dick thinks it would be a good idea to.

"Maybe that's your problem," he mutters under his nose as we walk down the stairs.

I scoff in a reply. This conversation needs to be over. It needed to be over before it started. But, as we walk through the staff door and step onto the plush covered carpet of Black Royale's main floor, I can't help thinking his words might ring true. Not because I haven't fucked *her*, but because I haven't fucked *anybody* in forever. How long has it been now? A month? Longer?

If I'm being honest, I can't even remember the last time I actually had sex. There have been a few blow jobs here and there—to take the edge off—but even those were over a month ago. I've been too preoccupied with Nicolosi requesting more port access than usual, then the fucking accountant screwing with me, and let's not forget the queen of not being able to stay the fuck away herself. And keeping her alive seems to be a full-time job in itself.

She's a magnet for trouble. First, she comes back to a town where everyone thinks she's dead, then almost gets killed by one of Nicolosi's groupies. Needless to say, I have not had time for extracurricular activities. Even if, with everything going on, you'd think a release would do me some good.

I spot Nico instantly. It's hard not to notice an aging gangster flanked by two of his soldiers. The trio makes quite the sight, in pin-striped suits, with two-tone spectator shoes and slicked back hair. I can just imagine the overbearing smell of their cologne from here. They look like they walked off the set of an Al Capone movie.

I should be used to this by now. Nicolosi has always been fond of making sure everyone in the room knows he's a made man. I've often wondered if it was a way of making up for his five-foot-five height. After all, no one makes fun of a capo, even if he's short and fat and resembles Oswald Cobblepot–the Batman Returns version. Not to his face at least. And those that do—don't live to tell the tale. I like to think of it as his little Napoleon complex.

"Dante, my dear boy!" he booms when he spots Angelo and I, droplets of saliva flying out of his mouth and hitting the black felt of the poker table nearby. I swear every time Nicolosi calls me 'boy', I have the biggest urge to shoot him between the eyes. I've put up with him for far too long now, letting his blatant disrespect fly, only because he used to be close with my father back in the day and because of that fucking contract they signed.

"Nico, always a pleasure." I nod and guide him into one of the secluded meeting rooms.

"How is your father? I haven't seen Massimo in far too long," he probes for information, groaning as his heavy frame fills the chair he collapses on.

"He's good." Angelo closes the door behind us. "Busy, of course, with important business. He sends his regards."

I want to laugh, because everyone in this room knows full well my father wouldn't wipe the shit off his shoe on Nico's face these days, let alone send his regards.

Nicolosi's face sours, probably annoyed at the reminder of his past indiscretions. He should kiss the floor with gratitude that he's still alive, thanks only to the bond he and my father once had. At one time, they were like brothers. They grew up together, played together, killed together. They have probably done many despicable things together. But Nico always had a chip on his shoulder. I've seen the way he used to look at my father. Like he thought he'd be better placed heading up the Family as the Don, not just the little arm he got when Father named him the capo of Blackriver. Nico does not consider himself a fool, but in my life, I've learned only fools forget that things are given easily and can just as easily be taken away.

I'm surprised my father didn't take care of the 'situation'

when Nico decided the best way to replace his dead son was siring another. Maybe my father still felt bad for him, like terminating the entire family line wasn't retribution enough, or maybe it was the sickness already taking over his mind. But he agreed to hand over my second cousin's hand in marriage so that a forty-six-year-old, widowed Nicolosi could have a family once more. Giana was only nineteen. By the time she got pregnant, we all saw the signs of physical abuse. I even tried to talk her into leaving him, despite everyone around me saying, '*Tra moglie e marito non mettere il dito*[3]'. Don't intervene in someone else's marriage.

When Giana gave birth to a girl, somehow Nicolosi convinced my father to sign a marriage contract, promising a Nicolosi daughter to a Santoro, once she came of age. Natalia's future was determined the moment she drew her first breath—ensuring the Santoro-Nicolosi ties would never be broken. And when four years later Giana, failing to get pregnant again, died in a 'car accident', he didn't expect for us to find out that the vehicle had been tampered with. By that time my father had isolated himself from everyone, leaving me to run his empire, Nicolosi's hold on Blackriver and its residents was too strong to tamper with and the iron-clad marriage contract was the only thing that kept him alive.

"What brings you to my casino today?" I ask. "Poker? Fine whiskey?"

He squints his eyes at me, a plump drop of sweat rolling down his temple to his cheek, where he catches it with a monogrammed handkerchief. "As fine as your whiskey is, I prefer your entertainment. Word on the street is you let them go. What a shame that is. Those girls were nice to look at indeed."

He studies my face, looking for a reaction he clearly doesn't get since he continues. "You know, if any of them want a job, they're always welcome in one of my clubs." The smile he gives me, as he taps his gold rings on the table, makes the eyes on his round little face look porcine.

I stifle the urge to grab the hand tapping on *my* table and squeeze his fat fingers until the bones inside start to crack for even thinking I'd let any of *my* female employees go anywhere near his strip clubs.

"I'll let them know," I say cooly, letting the rage percolate underneath my skin.

"The new girl in particular," he continues, unaware that his life is hanging by a thread, his only saving grace being the rule I have about no blood shed in the casino. The glint in his eyes lets me know Nico might have more information than he's letting on. "What's her name again?"

"I don't have the time to learn the names of all my employees," I say, crossing my arms impatiently.

"Ah. What a shame. But you're a busy man, so I understand."

"Good."

"Well, I'll get to it quickly then." He lets out a little cough. "We have a shipment scheduled to come in on Thursday. There's been a bit of a problem."

"Oh?"

"Well." A new bead of sweat rolls down the side of his face and makes it to his collar this time. "It won't get here until Friday now."

"That's it?" I ask.

"Indeed." He nods. "It would be so much easier if you just let me take over the port, Dante. You barely use it anyway."

I don't miss the fact he doesn't ask me to ask my father, but rather appeals to me directly. I guess the ruse about Massimo still being in charge is truly up.

"I don't think so."

"Well, it was worth a try." His chuckle turns into a fit of coughing. "Thank you for your time, Dante. I'll let you get back to work. Casinos don't run themselves after all." He knows as well as I do that the casinos I run in Blackwood take a fraction of my time and attention.

One of his men opens the door, the sound of sultry music from the main hall, almost drowning his parting words. "Give my regards to Massimo, *boy*. Oh, and Natalia's eighteenth birthday is coming up. You should come over for dinner soon. Your bride should get to know you before the wedding night."

I kick the chair next to me as soon as the door closes behind him.

"Motherfucker!"

More than once I wanted to tell Nico to go fuck himself over the past years, but business is business. And Nico pays good money for each shipment, even if he does so with disdain. He's always been jealous of Blackwood's location. Blackwood's coastline, both north and south, is too jagged and rocky to allow for another port, and with the forest and mountains surrounding us, there's only one private airstrip. One that belongs to the Saints. Nicolosi is stuck with our port, which means we're stuck with him and his shady dealings.

"I don't get it. Why would he come here just to tell us his cargo is late?"

And that's the other side of the coin.

I sigh, sitting down on the meeting room table, my feet carelessly propped up on the upturned chair, and bury my face in my hands. The weight of everything that's happened in the last month is pressing down on me, making it hard to breathe.

"There's more to it. Somehow, he must have found out. Most likely, he just wanted to see for himself."

"See what?" Angelo prompts.

"Stevie," I whisper with resignation. The secret I've kept for the last nineteen years aching to be let out.

"Your assistant? He wanted to see if you really have an assistant?" Angelo asks, confusion clear in his voice.

I inhale, lifting my head to meet his gaze. "Not quite."

"Quit being cryptic, Dante. What's so special about Stevie?" he demands, growing impatient as Luca opens the door and strolls inside. I motion for both of them to sit down. It's time they found out how deep the hole I've dug for myself is.

The words stick in my throat as I clench my jaw. "Well, I guess one thing is that her name is not exactly Stevie." I look at Angelo then at Luca who already knew that part. "I fucked up, brothers. I really fucked up," I admit.

"You've always had our back," Angelo says, placing a hand on my shoulder and squeezing it with reassurance. "How about you let us have yours for once?"

I take a deep breath, steeling myself for the truth. One I've been hiding for far too long. "How much do you remember about the Carussos?"

# 15

## ALESSA

I t's good to have friends in high places.

Or at least deep dark web sort of places. Wherever @dirtyhackz and their fellow hacker friends reside. Probably in a penthouse somewhere, surrounded by at least six high-resolution screens and riding a scooter to get from the kitchen to their bedroom. Lucky bastards.

One thing is clear—I really need to get myself a scooter because I can't seem to let this scooting around thing go. I have a thing for things on wheels, and evidently, scooters are not excluded from that category.

I also have a thing for hacker friends who help me send innocent looking emails to one Nico Nicolosi titled 'Oh my god! Look at the tits on her!', and an attachment comprising a lovely picture of a well-endowed brunette that has an itty-bitty bikini on and a lovely itty-bitty string of code encrypted into said lovely picture.

As soon as Nico opens the email on his computer, that little code will open a door for me to get inside and have a look around his files, hopefully helping me make sense of the data I've found on Dante's port log spreadsheet, which of course I have emailed myself already.

@dirtyhackz said they will walk me through how to get into Nico's computer this evening, provided Nico is old school enough not to open his emails on his phone. Until then, it will be a waiting game. I sigh with frustration and make sure Dante's chair is in the same position as he left it in. He just strikes me as a bit of a control freak, you know, the sort of person who can tell if their stapler has been moved one inch to the left.

Just to see if I'm right, I decide to fuck with Dante by tilting the fountain pen on his desk forty-five degrees. I'm giddy, anticipating his return, checking the door every few minutes. But the anticipation slowly ebbs away as the hours tick by and I'm still all alone.

Out of boredom, I end up finishing the task Dante left me with, typing up all his boring documents. I'd have gone back to his laptop to get digital copies of those files, something I'm almost certain he has, but with him due any minute, I chickened out. So, like the good assistant that I am, I painstakingly type up all the documents, adding an almost invisible watermark—'My gun is bigger than my dick'—on every page. I email the files over, then dump the originals on top of his stupid fountain pen, not caring anymore if he even notices it's been moved.

Being efficient is a curse, trust me. With nothing else left to do, I spend the next half an hour playing Solitaire on my laptop, then getting bored with that, I decide to rearrange my part of the office. I rotate my desk until it faces the window, then feeling like I need a bit more zhuzh I go to Dante's office in search of treasures. No longer caring that he might get pissed off, I rummage through his things, coming out with a stapler, a paperweight and a sharp-looking letter opener that will come in handy as soon as Dante notices I stole his shit and tries to kill me. A girl's gotta have the means to defend herself.

After a short deliberation, I also decide his big leafy green plant would be more at home by my desk, obscuring his view. The blasted thing is a lot heavier than it looks though, and by the time I'm done dragging it over, I'm out of breath and feeling like I've just done a cross fit session. Happy with the new look, I take a much deserved break, staring at the ocean and imagining the calm whooshing sound the waves are making.

It's hard to believe I've been in Blackwood for almost a month now. No thanks to Dante, who is definitely going to run me out of town as soon as he notices I've been pilfering through his things. Not that it's going to happen anytime soon at this rate. Dante has been gone for hours now, and I'm actually starting to worry, which is ridiculous because why would I worry about a mafia boss? He obviously can take care of himself. Except... I just can't forget the expression on his face when he received his text. Like something really angered him. Like something was wrong.

Trying to shake away the feeling, I check in with @dirty-hackz about the capo-email-infiltration-mission situation. I might be stupid for trusting a hacker I met a day ago with potentially incriminating data, but in the words of Kip Dynamite, *we chat online every day, so I guess things are gettin' pretty serious.* Basically, @dirtyhackz is the La Fawnduh to my Kip. Ok, fine. So maybe it's not exactly a love story, but we clearly hit it off from the start. They are clever, funny, compassionate, helpful, and fluent in sarcasm, which makes them legend material in my books.

Plus, it's not like I'm sharing any information about Dante or his businesses. All I want is access to Nico's files to compare the data and see if I can find out why the hell the bus station dude even mentioned his name. And if @dirty-hackz turns out to have their own agenda, hopefully the capo and his shady business dealings will be enough to keep him busy.

"What if I'm an actual idiot and @dirtyhackz works for the government?" I groan, banging my head against the desk. And why the hell am I even feeling bad about the possibility I might be betraying Dante? It's not like he's been nice to me. Come to think of it, he's been the ultimate douchebag all this time. Well, except giving me a well-paid job where I barely do anything of substance... And making sure I was okay after the bus station guard attacked me. Still, he's a dick. A *hot* dick, I wouldn't mind giving a lick. *Gah! Focus!*

A message alert coming from my laptop has me lifting my head up to scan the screen, only to be greeted by a joke about hackers and anal that makes me snort and has my mood lifting. Biting my lip, I hover my fingers over the keyboard and wiggle them before replying with a dirty joke about a toaster. I get a laughing gif in reply followed by a message that Nico hasn't opened the email yet. I scrunch my face in disappointment.

Well, fuck. Did he just delete it? @dirtyhackz tries to convince me it's still early and he could just be out and about, then distracts me with questions about Blackwood and the view from my office. Apparently, they have an ocean view too, except they're somewhere in California. After a while of me hinting at it, they finally admit they do in fact own a scooter, but haven't ridden it in years. I'm appalled, which just makes them laugh. It honestly feels like we've known each other our whole life, and when, just before we say goodbye, they tell me their name, I can't wipe the smile off my face.

*Arrow.* I suppose knowing it makes it that much more real. Like we really are starting a friendship. Maybe, at some point in the near future, I could even ask them to help with *my* search. Track down my family, or dig out information about me and how I'm connected to this town... Maybe. But for now, the thought alone has my stomach in knots, so I push it away and pick up the two printed pages with the port data on them.

It wasn't hard figuring out what the headings and abbreviations mean, well except the two I'm still trying to decode. The DI and DO. For the life of me, I can't figure out what they could be, and neither does Google. It just doesn't make sense. There are dates, vessel's name and number, cargo weight declared—all abbreviated or in code. It's not surprising, since it's all probably relating to drugs or guns or whatever it is mafia deals in these days. Poker chips? Whatever it is, the two columns I've been unable to decode are giving me a headache. There's nothing I can make sense of. I'm just about to google example spreadsheets of shipping port logs when the door to the office opens.

I squeak, jumping in my seat like I've just been caught doing something naughty. I clear my throat, trying to calm my racing heart and turn my head to give Dante the stink eye for scaring me.

"Hey, Alessa," Luca smiles at me from the doorway. "Or is it Stevie? Which one do you go by these days?"

I smile back, swivelling my chair around to face him and crossing my legs. "That depends on who's asking. Most often I'm just known as Enigma."

He chuckles. "Funny, coming from someone so transparent."

I gasp in shock. Transparent? "You must have me confused with someone else. My poker face has won more awards than Lady Gaga's."

He just raises his eyebrow, his eyes sweeping around the place. "Done some rearranging?"

I feign ignorance. "It was like this when I got here this morning."

His lips thin as he tries to suppress a smile. "I like it," he finally says. "But Dante will probably get ma—"

"He'd have to get back here first," I interrupt, narrowing my eyes. "And where exactly is *El Enojado*?" I ask, definitely butchering the language.

"El who?"

"*Enojado*. It means angry in Spanish." I should know. I googled how to say angry in every single language.

"You know we're Italian, right?"

"A leopard doesn't change his spots, no matter the language. Besides, *arrabbiato*[1] makes him sound like a delicious pasta dish, and he's definitely not delicious." *Lies. All lies.*

Luca scratches the back of his head before shaking it slowly. "Not sure I want to argue with that," he mutters. "Anyway, Dante asked me to give you a lift back home."

*He's not coming back?*

"Not today. He's got business to take care of."

*Shit, did I say it out loud?* Never mind, I won't turn down a free lift home. "Do you think we could go down to the port first?" I ask, turning around and stuffing the logs into my bag.

"Probably not a good idea. I'm supposed to take you straight back home."

"No worries. I'll just walk there after you drop me off then." I smile sweetly before turning back to close my laptop.

"Ah, fuck. Fine. We'll go to the port first." He shakes his head.

*You see?*

Poker face is my middle name.

# 16

# ALESSA

"Y ou really need to stop stroking the car." Luca laughs when my hand darts out for the millionth time, fingers grazing the shiny console.

I sigh. He's right. Even though the inside of this particular Alfa Romeo is calling for me to pet it. The last time I was inside, I was too shocked and too tired to truly appreciate its beauty. But like always, there's a time and a place. "I miss my car."

Luca looks at me sideways. "What was it?"

"Bibi," I say wistfully, thinking of my red companion. "She was a good girl." Or a sneaky little whore if I count the way she abandoned me, condemning me to that bus ride from hell. But who's holding grudges?

I can feel Luca roll his eyes, probably thinking I'm 'such a girl'. "Never heard of a *Bibi* car. Is that a model or a make?" Awww, look at him, trying to be all nice like he's not secretly thinking I'm a ditsy female.

"It's her name." I roll my eyes for added measure. Oh, how I love it when the opposite sex underestimates me.

"Right, of course. And what type of car is Bibi?"

I nearly fail at suppressing my smirk, so turn my head to look out the window just in case. "A red one."

The grunt that leaves him has me biting my lip.

"And red Bibi is a..." he trails off. You've got to love a trier. This guy will make someone a fantastic sexual partner, if he applies this method in bed.

"A very old car." I sigh. "I should have known she was on her last legs. A journey like ours is not for the faint engined."

From the corner of my eye, I can see his fingers tighten around the steering wheel. Why is he so damned curious about my car, anyway? Whatever the reason, I could be nice enough and throw him a bone. Or I could drag it out as long as possible and see how far I can take it. Decisions, decisions.

"Alessaaa," he groans, parking his beauty of a car by the boardwalk leading to the port.

"Yes, Luca?" I turn to him, my eyes huge.

"Just tell me the damned make and model of your old car, so I can send someone to retrieve it."

Swinging open the passenger door and jumping outside, I burst out laughing. The hum of ocean waves and the cacophony of squawks coming from the low-flying seagulls assault my ears. Taking a deep lungful of the fresh air, I turn around, facing Luca over the hood of his car.

"I didn't take you as someone who collects scrap metal."

He closes his eyes as his mouth moves in a silent prayer. Or maybe he's counting down from ten, just like I do when something annoys me to no end.

I smile, closing the passenger door and making my way to the same place I first met Luca all those weeks ago.

"How come you weren't wearing a suit back then?" I ask when he catches up to me.

"I'll tell you when you tell me the make and model of your car."

"What about the location? Don't you need that?"

"Mel already told me."

Makes sense. She's the only one who knows about my journey here and I never told her it was a secret, so...

"Why do you want to get the car, really?"

He's silent as he walks alongside me, watching the waves crash against the dock.

"If you tell me," I say, slipping my hand around his elbow and looking up at him, "I'll tell you everything I know about that little, old red car called Bibi."

His eyes focus on my hand, gripping his bicep. It's a nice bicep, so I squeeze it for encouragement.

"Dante—" of course, I should have known the master and commander was behind this. "—wants to make sure no one else finds it."

"Why?" I prod.

"Beats me," he grumbles.

I narrow my eyes. "Why, Luca?"

"To keep you safe, apparently."

I stop in my tracks. Whoa. Why is he so concerned with my safety? And where the hell does Bibi fit into that equation? "I don't get it," I whisper.

"Neither do I. Your turn."

I resume walking, my head spinning as I rattle off the main stats. "Seat Ibiza, five door hatchback. Made in nineteen-ninety-nine. One point four litre engine. One hundred and one horsepower that will take you from naught to one hundred in ten point seven seconds." She was a fast little thing.

This time, it's Luca who stops, pulling me to face him. His eyes narrowed as his lips thin. "Bibi? A red old car?"

I show him my teeth. "All true."

"Why, then?"

"Why, what?" I ask innocently.

"Why put me through all that misery?"

I pat his cheek gently. "Information for information, my friend. And it's much easier to convince someone to give up their secrets if they're frustrated."

"Dante is going to have his hands full with you," he grumbles.

"He already does, Luca." I grin up at him.

"Yeah, I don't doubt that," he chuckles, all the frustration gone from his face. "So, why did you want to come here?"

"I just..." I turn away from him, facing the ocean. The waters are choppier than the last time I was here, probably because of the dark clouds in the sky. A sprinkling of salty ocean drops lands on my face each time the waves collide with the dock. I lick my lips, tasting the brine. "I just love it here," I whisper.

"Do you swim?"

"No."

"I could teach you."

I whip my head. "You could?"

"If you want." He rubs the back of his neck, a blush creeping up onto his tanned cheeks.

"I'd love that."

"Cool, I'll see what I can do. So, Alessa," he says as we resume walking, my arm sliding back into its place between his body and the crook of his elbow. "Why a Seat and not, let's say... a Fiat?"

I burst out laughing. "God, you guys are so predictable."

"*Us*, guys?"

"You know." I gesture, swooping my hand around like it's a good enough explanation. When he doesn't look any more clued in, I whisper, "The *mafia*."

This time, he's the one bursting into laughter. "Are you worried someone will overhear you?"

"I don't know. Are we supposed to say it out loud? Isn't it like Rumplestiltskin or Bloody Mary? Say it three times and they show up? Except, it would be the FBI showing up."

He stops, his body tensing as he looks around. "Shit. You're right. We need to find cover! They'll be here any minute." I might have believed him if his shoulders weren't shaking up and down in silent laughter.

"You fucker." I roll my eyes and kick him half heartedly on his calf. "I don't know what the mafia etiquette is, do I? Unlike you, I wasn't born into it," I huff.

He stops laughing. "You're safe with me. You're safe with Angelo. And you're safe with Dante. People around here know we're in charge. And even though we don't advertise it, they know who we are. Whether you were *born* into the mafia or not, you're under our protection now. And despite the small town we live in, Santoro is a powerful name."

"I know, I know. You guys are the Saints, blah, blah," I mumble, unsure what else to say.

"So, tell me. What about mafiosos is so predictable," he teases, the mood shifting instantly.

"Say Seat Ibiza again."

"Seat Ibiza," he repeats, his face screwing in distaste.

"There it is."

"What."

"You hated even saying it."

"I did not," he protests.

"It's because it's Spanish, isn't it? It could be the fastest, the most awesome car on earth, but if it's not Italian..."

"You little shit." He shakes his head in awe. "How?"

I laugh. "I'm just observant. The clothes, the furniture, the cars. Everything is Italian. It's very patriotic of you."

"We just know who makes the best shit."

"Well, I won't argue about the cars. And my new clothes are pretty good, too—Is that a delivery?" I take off towards a large boat moored to the dock. An old guy with a clipboard chatting with another guy who just hopped off.

"Alessa," Luca hisses from behind me. "What the fuck are you doing?"

But I'm too focused on my target to reply. I have no clue what boats that ship Mafia's stuff look like, but this clearly ain't it. This one is more of a fishing boat. As tired and scruffy looking as the owner who's watching the clipboard guy measure something, then note it on his clipboard. Once that's done, the owner hops back on and begins unloading. I can smell it from here. It's fish. But that doesn't deter me one bit. I'll bathe my brand new Prada trainers in fish juice if it means getting answers.

"Howdy!" I say to the clipboard guy the minute I stop in front of him. I'm not sure where the 'howdy' came from, but whatever. He looks over my shoulder at Luca, nodding at him in a greeting then back to me. His dark eyes assess me as I step from foot to foot. This up close to him I can tell he's a lot older than I thought, in his sixties, seventies, maybe? Or maybe it's the exposure to constant elements that aged him.

"Good catch?"

"I ain't the one fishin'," he replies, looking at me like I'm slow.

Luca stops right behind me, his hand landing on my shoulder as I watch the boat owner unload the fish boxes. Once all of them are out, he gets off the boat again.

"What is he doing to the boat?" I whisper to Luca as the clipboard guy taps a line on the side of the boat, then notes something on the clipboard.

"He's checking its displacement."

"Why?" I ask, hoping it doesn't show. I have no clue what displacement is. I can google it later.

"Don't know. It's just something Dante has the man do to every boat. I think it's something to do with safety."

I nod, like it all makes sense, while the thoughts in my head swirl at warp speed.

"Can we go now?" Luca asks.

I nod and follow him away from my new best mate, *Santiago*, my brain working overtime, trying to connect the dots. Neither one of us speaks on the way back to the car, or the ride to Mel's apartment.

"Thanks for the ride," I say, breaking the silence when he parks on a double yellow line right outside our front door.

"I'll walk you in."

"I'll be fine. I'm sure you have other things you need to be taking care of. I've kept you long enough."

He sighs, nodding. "Alright. I'll see you tomorrow."

I wave at him as he speeds down the street and out of sight, then turn to unlock the front door.

A door which I find to be ajar already. Unusual, but I haven't lived here long enough to know how forgetful the neighbours can be. Nevertheless, I walk up the stairs as quietly as possible, keeping close to the wall in case anyone is watching the handrail. Paranoia? Maybe. But I've been on the run for far too long to just take the open door at face value.

Paranoia is a funny thing. It can be crippling, making you unable to ever truly taste life. Or it could save it.

When I hear hushed tones coming from the top floor where Mel's apartment is, I know my paranoia may have just saved me. There's no missing the tattooed fingers wrapped around a handrail above me. With a bated breath, slowly and as quietly as I can, I retract my steps down the stairs. I know in my gut these are not Dante's men. Luca would have known they were here. He would have told me.

Shit. Luca. He wanted to come up with me. Suddenly, I'm glad I told him to go take care of business. Whoever these guys are could have killed him. I have this sick feeling they're not waiting in our apartment just to borrow a cup of sugar. I honestly don't know what it is about people in Blackwood having it in for me, and I'm not in a mood to find out.

I'm almost at the bottom of the stairs, my ears straining to make sure the hushed conversation upstairs is still ongoing when the front door swings open. With heart in my throat, I watch the light spill into the corridor as one of the neighbours walks inside, confusion etched on his face as he looks between the door and the key in his hand.

"Hey, did you forget to lock the door?" he asks before I even have a chance to lift a finger to my lips.

Shit. The loud thumping in my chest is deafening. I shake my head and try to calm my suddenly shallow breaths.

"Never mind," the guy smiles. Oh god, someone please tell him to shut the fuck up. "I'm Josh, by the way. I live just below you."

When I take a step toward him, or toward the door rather, his smile stretches wider.

"You just moved in with Mel, right?"

I close my eyes for a split second, contemplating punching him square in the face, but a split second is all I have before I hear a thunder of footsteps down the stairs and decide punching Josh in the face will have to wait. I need to make sure he lives first.

I push past him, grabbing his hand and pulling him through the still open door.

"Someone broke in," I say as I run towards the cafe

down the street, dragging my confused neighbour behind me. Saving him might cost me my life but I can't have *his* on my conscience.

"Go hide in the cafe and call the police."

"What about you?" Josh asks. Ah, sweet, sweet Josh, trying to appear chivalrous but endangering us both.

"I am the police, numbnuts," I hiss. Surely, he won't argue with that.

To his credit, he doesn't. As soon as Josh is inside the cafe, I duck into a side street, praying we were quick enough the intruders didn't see us. I've done everything I could have for Josh.

Now it's time to do what I do best.

Run.

# 17

## ALESSA

I'm a fast runner when properly incentivised. Not Usain Bolt fast, but still pretty damn fast. So, I'm not surprised by how quickly I make it back to the Black Royale. The streets are dark by now and the smell of ozone permeates the air, threatening thunder and rain.

Not caring for the rules, I bolt through the main entrance and speed walk toward the bar, where I can see Benji chatting with Mel. As soon as I get to them, I dive behind the counter. No, no. I don't jog, walk or run. I vault. Full on nosedive with a belly slide at the end.

Mel tries to stifle a laugh.

"Did anyone follow me in?" I manage to ask through lungfuls of air. I was running so fast I didn't even bother to check if I was being followed all the way here. They could have lost my trail back at the apartment. But it's better to be safe than sorry. And I speak from experience. The night my foster brother, Casper, walked into my room was the night I learned to always lock your door no matter how tired you are.

"I don't think so." Mel's eyebrows draw together as worry

replaces her ever-present smile. "Why would anyone follow you?"

"Just keep watching the door and pretend like I'm not here until I tell you to."

She nods.

Huh. Who knew hiding from one's pursuers is much easier when there's someone willing to cooperate with you instead of flagging said pursuers down to give away your location? Benji tries to ignore me, too, but he's extremely bad at it, shooting me looks every few beats. When ten minutes pass and both my coworkers confirm no one suspicious looking has walked through the door, I finally exhale in relief.

"What's going on?" Mel asks after dragging me all the way to the staff room. I walk into the laundry room, happy to see my things are still there, nice and dry.

"So," I say, picking up my clothes and shoes and stuffing them into a bag when I hear her shuffle into the small space behind me. "Do you have any relatives in Blackwood?"

I wait, peeking into the corners and behind the shelves, like I've lost something, just to avoid looking back at her.

"Of course. I was born here," she says. Her hands are on her hips when I finally turn around. Her eyes studying my every move.

"Okay. That's good." I exhale, taking her hand in mine and guiding her back into the main area, before sitting her down on a chair. "Can you stay with them? After work tonight?"

"What? Why?"

"I think someone broke into our apartment." I squeeze her hand. "Like ninety per cent certain it was ours. Someone was waiting on our floor and considering the front door was unlocked, I doubt they had difficulty unlocking the apartment door. I mean, they could have been waiting for the neighbour across the hall—"

"That apartment is empty," Mel cuts in, white as a sheet. "Why do you think they were there and what did they want? Was it me? You?"

"Honestly, Mel? I have no clue. Maybe they were the bus station guard's friends? Whatever it is, the apartment is not safe, and I need you to stay somewhere else."

"Okay. We could go to my parents tonight, then figure something out later."

I squeeze her hand, my heart filling with a sensation I've never felt before. Someone wants me to be safe. Someone needs me.

"Not tonight, babe. I've got somewhere safe I can stay and if they're after me, I don't want you anywhere near me."

"You're right. I don't want you to be in danger, either. Maybe instead of my parents, I should call my cheating ex," she muses, making me laugh.

"That's the spirit. We'll touch base tomorrow and figure out our next step. For now, it's probably best if you say you've got a headache and need to leave early, then get someone to drive you to your parents. Or your ex," I add with a smile while inwardly cringing at the fact I've become *that* person. The one who says things like 'touch base' and 'circle back to this topic at a later date'.

"Cheating scumbag." She nods. "Maybe we should tell Luca, or Dante?"

"No!" I exclaim.

"Okay, I got it." She grins. "No hot boss involvement."

"He's not..." I don't like to lie, so I roll my eyes instead.

"A boss?" Mel burst into laughter.

"Fine, so he's a ten, but his personality makes him a two."

She purses her lips, trying to control herself. "Oh, you

mean, the brooding, the charm and the way his eyes follow you hungrily?"

"Yup, like a bear stalking the prey it's about to pounce on and eat."

She falls over laughing, holding onto her stomach as she giggles uncontrollably. It's a sight—the snorts, the flushed face, the delirious look in her eyes and the mascara running down her cheeks. At this point, I doubt anyone will question whether she should go home. She gulps in a lungful of air. "I bet." *Laugh, laugh.* "He wants to pounce on you." *Laugh, laugh, laugh.* "And eat your puss—"

"Mel!" I cover her mouth with my hand, my eyes huge.

"Meow!" she screeches from behind my hand, still giggling.

"He does not!"

She starts making purring noises that come out more like a moped that gave up on life, but I know her game.

"I'm gonna tell Luca you have a crush on him." I resort to the only blackmail I have in my arsenal.

She instantly freezes as her eyes narrow to slits. "I'll tell Dante you said his abs were lickable."

I gasp. "I was drunk!"

She wipes at her cheeks and smiles. "Don't mess with your best friend, then."

*Best friend?* My chest expands. "You started it," I grumble.

"Because you guys are one angry argument away from fucking. There is a thin line between love and hate."

"More like hate and oh, look, he's got tattoo covered abs and not a bad-looking face."

She rolls her eyes. "You're going to eat your words, lady. Now help me fix this, so I can go talk to Martina." She gestures at her face.

Once Mel is out of the staff room, I try to figure out my next step. I could go to a hotel, provided Dante remembered to tell them I'm no longer blacklisted, or... I could go to our office and sleep there. I'd be away from prying eyes, and out of everyone's way, and I could use the facilities here to shower and get ready in the morning before Dante even got in.

Exhaustion outweighs my growling stomach, so I decide to go straight there and crash. I don't even remember the last time I ate. Breakfast was it? But it's not the first time I've not eaten all day. I've gone much longer than that on nothing but water and crumbs.

The office is locked, but with the key I swiped from Dante's desk earlier today, I should hopefully be able to get in. If not, I'll have to go looking for help, and there will be more questions and more lies I'll have to come up with. Thankfully, in no time, I'm pushing the door open and stepping inside.

I don't turn the lights on, gazing out the large window instead at the colourful lights below me and the ocean not too far away. It feels like light years away when I stepped through the door for the first time, but it's only been this morning. Maybe it's because I spent most of the day by myself, or maybe it's the feeling of belonging. I have this weird feeling like I'm living through one long déjà vu. Walking through streets I've seen before. Seeing houses that look familiar. And then there's the ocean. Its waves greeting me like a long-lost friend, calling my name in their hushed whispers.

I'm clearly overtired. With a heavy sigh, I pull the stuff I took from the laundry room out and bundle it up into a makeshift pillow. First, the freshly washed uniforms, then I neatly fold my clean and dry clothes on top. Lastly, I cover myself with the black jacket and lie down on the floor, gazing out at the lights. I try not to think about how many times the jacket served as my blanket. And I try not to think about the first time it did, when they found me as a toddler. I held onto this jacket for so long it's honestly a miracle it survived this long. But apart from the pocket watch, it was the only thing I owned, tying me to my past.

Sometimes, I wish I could recall what exactly happened the day they found me. Or the events preceding it. But then I remind myself that some things are better left forgotten.

I yawn and close my eyes, my fingers digging into the familiar material. Just for a second.

# 18

## DANTE

Even after three strong espressos, exhaustion is dripping down my body like a two-hour gym-induced sweat. There's nothing I'd like better than to turn the car around and go back home. Take a few hours to myself and not care about all the shit that's falling apart around me. But, instead, I'm sitting here in my designated parking space. The engine turned off as I watch the stars disappear and the sky turn from black to dark grey on the horizon.

Last night was a shit show.

The minute I got home, I had a phone call.

One of my men was found dead by the docks. Not just any man, either.

Fuck.

Someone shot one of my father's longest standing soldiers, one who worked for the family for as long as I can remember. The same man who was with me during my first mission.

It wasn't a clean kill, either. Whoever was involved had a sick sense of humour. The wounds and abrasions all over his body made it clear Luigi suffered greatly in the last few hours of his life. Then, his body was dumped by the docks without a care.

Did Luigi stumble onto something he shouldn't have, or was this a message addressed to me?

Discarding his body in my port sure as hell felt like a personal affront. And I have a sick feeling there's more to Luigi's death, something obvious I am missing.

Someone is threatening the peace the Santoros have had in Northern America for years. Someone is threatening the peace I have worked so damn hard for. And there's no way in hell I will stand by and watch everything unravel without a fucking fight.

My most trusted men are combing through Luigi's house as we speak, looking for anything out of place, any information that could shed light on his very recent demise. It's a waiting game, and time is not on my side. With Nico constantly striving to undermine me, clearly making plans to take control over my port, and let's not forget sniffing around the casino for god knows what reason, I have enough on my plate to be dealing with. And that's just from one disgruntled capo who's on a power trip.

Then there's Alessa, the annoying bane of my existence. Although, I have to admit, fucking with her yesterday made my shit show of a day much better. Her outraged expression when I dropped all the pencils she painstakingly sharpened in the trash was the highlight of my day. Come to think of it, the prospect of making today difficult for her is the only thing still keeping me in the parking lot instead of firing the engine up and driving back home.

With a sigh, I open my door, letting the fog that came out of nowhere into the tight space around me. The damp air I used to hate so much as a kid, now a welcome reminder of where I came from and what I've built. I can taste the salt on my tongue as I inhale a lungful of air, making my way across the lot and into the familiar building. Black Royale is my baby. It was the first building my father entrusted me with, the first business he gave me free rein over. I don't think anyone thought the casino would become as big of a hit as it did. Definitely not when I closed it and gutted the whole thing. But I was determined, and I had a vision.

A vision for a business that would surpass even the best casinos in Vegas. A vision for the town that would become a mecca for those under our protection. And a vision of what I wanted the future of the family to look like. I was met with an uproar when I first banned drugs from being sold on the streets of Blackwood and legitimised all mafia owned businesses. Then, with confusion when I provided jobs, houses and education for the citizens who were left with nothing. Those who tried to defy me ended up either leaving or dead. It was the easiest way of getting what I wanted.

Trust.

And people in Blackwood trust me. They fear me, but they trust me more. That's why I need to figure out what the hell is going on and who's behind it and make sure no one finds out about Alessa. Just how the fuck does one hide a five-foot-seven bombshell with legs for days? I have no clue. But I'll figure it out. I always do. There's a lot at stake here. If anyone finds out for certain who she really is, it could give Nico just the ammunition he is looking for to use against me. To ruin me, and everything I have achieved up until now. After all, I didn't follow the explicit instructions of my initiation. In the mafia world, that means *failure*.

A technicality?

Yes.

But it's one that could cost me my place as the head of the Santoro family. The head of the mafia. Not that I'm worried about losing the power. It's losing the trust of those around me that bothers me.

The reaction from Angelo and Luca once I told them the truth was enough of a cold shower. At first, they didn't believe me. I can't blame them. I never keep secrets from them. One for all, and all for one. Or so they thought until they found out that for the past nineteen years, they believed a lie. I lost their unwavering trust. The one thing that made us unbreakable.

And now I need to answer the question I've been avoiding for the past week. Was saving Alessa's life all those years ago worth it? Or would she have been better off if I had never found her? Because once again she's got a target on her back, a walking beacon for death that follows her around as long as she's in Blackwood.

I suppose at least she's had a good nineteen years of safe life with a nice, loving family. What on earth would make her want to leave that behind? I'll never know.

But then again, I never understood women. Never had the time or the urge to try. And I never needed to.

Besides fucking, I had nothing to give them. I didn't want love, didn't want a relationship. But even if I did, it's not like I had a choice. Despite my penchant for ruthlessness, I could never make one of my brothers follow through with the marriage contract our father agreed to. It was always going to be me. In a few short months, once she comes of age, Natalia, Nico's first-born daughter, will walk down the aisle and become my wife, whether either of us wants it or not.

That's why getting to know women has never been on my agenda. Until Alessa strutted into Blackwood in her high heels, wearing a pencil skirt, and almost see-through blouse, her lips red, making the blood in my veins boil with rage the minute I recognised her.

The anger in me has not simmered down as the days have gone by. I hate her for coming back. I want her and her affinity for messing shit up for me gone. And, at the same time, I have no other choice but to protect her. But it doesn't mean I have to make it pleasant for her. The to-do list of meaningless tasks I'm going to give her is growing longer and longer as I walk down the empty corridor to the office we now share, my footsteps the only sound keeping me company. Although I can catch glimpses of the main floor, crowded with people too amped up to sleep, it's like a different world up here. Silent, cold and dim.

The office is dark as I step through the threshold, and it takes my eyes a few seconds to adjust to the lack of artificial light. But once I can see, a smile spreads across my face. Alessa has been busy. Good. The punishment will taste that much sweeter. I can't wait to see the expression on her face as I make her pay for her bratty mouth and blatant disobedience. My gaze sweeps over the room as I take in the changes she has made—the moved desk, the big green plant right next to it—I suppose she at least kept herself busy and out of trouble. That's something I should be grateful for, I guess.

Without turning the light on, I walk over to her desk and open her laptop. If she hasn't changed her password yet, I'm about to make her life a hell of a lot more difficult. There is a rustle next to a window as the laptop screen comes on, bathing me in a bluish glow. Instantly, I freeze, my eyes snapping to where the noise came from. My vision is blotchy from the bright screen, but I can still make out something long and dark lying on the floor. Is this another one of Alessa's pranks, or am I starting to see things, delusional from the lack of sleep?

With my eyes trained on the dark object, I watch it, waiting for it to move or do something, but it stays still. I can feel the tension coiling in my body, as with one hand I close the laptop, bathing the room in the dark, and reaching for my gun with the other. Whatever this thing is, it sure could use a few bullet holes in it. I don't like to be disturbed or startled in my own space, and the best way to teach Alessa to never do this again is to destroy whatever she had planned.

Safety unlocked, I lift the gun up, training it on the object on the floor as my eyesight adjusts to the darkness. There's a small thrill in my chest—there always is before I pull the trigger. The anticipation of power that I'm about to wield makes the action so much sweeter. My finger wraps around the trigger, pressing against the cool metal as I scan the object with the barrel, trying to decide where best to aim. I increase the pressure on the trigger just as the thing moves, turning around to face me.

"What the fuck, Alessa?" I roar, my gun arm dropping to my side.

She sighs, her eyes slowly opening and taking in the space around us, before landing on the gun in my hand.

"Dante?" She sits up. Her voice is croaky and confused as she tries to comprehend what's going on.

My hand is shaking as I look down at it. The gun I was holding clutters to the floor.

The gun I nearly used a second ago.

The gun that, had it been fired, could have killed Alessa.

I try and fail to calm my pounding heart as my eyes stay glued to the gun.

"Is everything okay?" she asks, her voice close, but I can't tear my gaze from the floor. "Dante?" Her warm hand cups my cheek as she lifts my head to face her. We're both kneeling on the floor. When the fuck did I drop to my knees? I don't know and I don't care as Alessa's green eyes search mine. "What happened?"

"I almost fucking killed you," I whisper, shame, guilt and something else, something that tastes an awful lot like fear, filling my lungs as I inhale.

"What—Why—?"

I shake my head, clearing my jumbled thoughts. "What are you doing here, Alessa?"

Her thumb strokes my cheek, a soft scraping sound filling the silent room as she just continues to watch me. She's so close I can smell her flowery scent. I can feel her body heat as the tips of her knees touch mine. My fists clench and unclench, still shaking a little as I try to come to terms with the emotions inside me. The terror is new. I've never been this shaken up by the possibility of taking a life. Of doing something irreversible. And I don't understand why this time I feel so different.

"It's okay, *kızgın*," she mumbles. "You didn't hurt me. It's okay."

*Inhale. Exhale. Inhale. Exhale.* It's all I can do as her dark green eyes keep me ensnared while her thumb rhythmically strokes my skin to the cadence of my breaths.

"*Kızgın?*"

Her eyes twinkle in the dark, and I have to remind myself that I nearly shot her to stop myself from pulling her onto my lap and kissing her just to see if they turn dark when she's aroused.

"Just a silly word in Turkish, never mind that." She bites her lip, turning my thoughts to her mouth again.

"Why were you on the floor?"

Her eyes flutter closed as a deep sigh escapes her. Her hesitance infuriates me, and in one swoop I push away her arm, losing her soft touch in an instant. Good. The further away she is from me, the better. Clearly, I feel this sick protectiveness over her. I saved her once, so now it's on me to keep her alive.

"Why?" I growl.

"I was sleeping," she finally replies, rolling her eyes.

"Alessa," I growl, barely stopping myself from taking her over the knee and spanking her ass raw for that display of insolence.

She moves back, putting a small distance between us, her instincts warning her from the predator inside me. Clever girl. Although those few measly inches will not save her if she keeps acting like a brat. "I—" She wraps the jacket she has on tight around her body as if it's somehow going to protect her. A jacket I left covering her small fragile body the night I saved her life.

"Spit it out." My heart speeds up in my chest, the images that haunted my subconscious from the moment I found her bound in the antique wardrobe punching me in the gut.

"I had nowhere else to go," she finally blurts out.

The anger I felt focuses on a new target as the urge to storm to the main floor in search of Mel and find out why the fuck she'd kick Alessa out for the night, after they both insisted they wanted to live together, takes over. I don't realise my whole body is shaking with indignation until a small, warm hand wraps around my forearm. Maybe that's why, for the first time in my life, I don't let anger guide my actions.

And instead of basking in the feeling of cool control brought on by the calm in the centre of the rage that consumes me, I let Alessa's touch pacify me. I let her green eyes stare into my soul and read me like an open book. I let go of everything. For a few short seconds, none of my problems exist. I'm just an average man. No one relies on me. My life's path hasn't been written since the day I was born. And my family and friends are not in danger.

For a few short seconds, as I drown in the depths of

emerald eyes, I can breathe again. Until Alessa opens her mouth and cracks the ice in my chest with one word.

"Someone broke into our apartment. This was the only place I could think of that felt safe."

*Safe.*

# 19

## ALESSA

The front door quietly shuts behind us as we make our way through the house, stopping only when we get to the kitchen. I go to sit on the same bar stool I sat on the first time I was here as Dante walks behind the kitchen island and flicks the coffee machine on, the whirring sound permeating the silence between us.

It's funny, actually. Both times I've been to Dante's house, it was because someone tried to kill me. I'm assuming whoever was up in Mel's apartment didn't want to just pop in for a cup of tea. I don't know if it's me or this town, but clearly, Dante was right—it seems I'm not welcome in Blackwood. I can't shake off the feeling it would have been better if I left when he first told me to. I'm not one to easily admit I'm wrong, but two attempts on a girl's life will change her outlook on *that* fairly quickly. It's hard enough being the new girl in town without someone chasing you once a week, making everything seem hostile.

The thing is, I didn't lie to Dante when I said the casino was the only place I could think of that felt safe. I just omitted the *real* reason behind it. Maybe it's because I'm not quite ready to admit *it* to myself. My boss, after all, is one of the scariest men I've ever met. He clearly has anger issues and from the moment he laid eyes on me, he wanted me gone, making sure I knew how he felt about the matter. And yet... The only time I feel like I can breathe without looking over my shoulder is when he's around.

He still terrifies me at times, but there's also this under-lying thrill and, most of all, the certainty that nothing can hurt me when he's around. I don't understand how one man can bring out two such opposing emotions in me, but despite the fact I've known Dante for less than a month, he feels... Oddly familiar.

I groan, my forehead hitting the cool counter. Why does it always have to be me? Why, for once, can't I be the person who has a normal life, a normal job, normal friends? I'm exhausted. I can't even remember the last time I wasn't running. The last time I didn't have to lie, steal, cheat, gamble. All that, just to get by. One day to the next. One foot after another. At what point does it stop? At what point do I get to just sit down and relax?

I thought Blackwood was the answer, but clearly, this small town is not quaint and welcoming. Maybe I should forget about finding my answers and come to terms with the fact I'll never know where I came from, or who my parents are. The thought shouldn't hurt. I've lived without the knowledge all my life. And really, there's nothing wrong with the status quo. In fact, am I really prepared to gamble my life away just to get some answers?

The dampness on my cheeks and the tightness in my chest says it all as a coffee mug scrapes across the island toward me.

"Thanks," I mutter, lifting my head and feigning a smile. But I'm not fooling anyone. Not myself and definitely not Dante.

"Alessa." His molten eyes bore into me as I try to pretend

I'm absolutely fine, and the events of the past twelve hours have not impacted me at all. I pretend I haven't just basically given up.

I take the coffee in both my hands, then slide off the chair, turning around until my back is to him. I want to leave, go somewhere where he can't see the anguish in my eyes. Where he won't be able to read me like a book. But my knees are weak and my body feels so heavy, too heavy to move. So, instead, I lean my back against the counter and hang my head, trying to steady my shaky breaths.

I'm usually stronger than this—the girl with a tough skin many have tried to break. The one that can take anything life throws at her and gives back twice as hard. But as the sound of footsteps approaching breaks the silence, for the first time in my life, I feel weak.

Everything from the past few weeks, everything I had to face before I arrived in Blackwood is suddenly weighing me down, threatening to pull me into the uncharted depths of emotions I've always been able to avoid before.

"I'm not giving up." My voice shakes as I try to convince myself I'm stronger than the overwhelming feeling of failure.

The smell of Dante's cologne hits me before I see the tips of his shoes in front of mine. He takes the cup away from me and puts it down somewhere behind me. I still can't lift my gaze to meet his, even when he gets closer and places his hands on the counter, caging me in between his arms.

With the way he's towering over me, I should feel threatened. I should try to escape, get myself out of his stronghold and get as far away as possible from this confusing man. But I stay immobile, like a rabbit startled by a loud noise, letting Dante's heat warm my shaking body. His proximity calming the storm inside my head.

"Giving up on what?"

"I'm not," I repeat, shaking my head as I finally look into his brown eyes, unable to tear my gaze away the second our eyes meet. For once, I don't see anger inside them. Instead, as his brows draw together, I try to decipher the emotion inside them.

"Will you—Will you tell me, please?" he asks, his tone barely above a whisper.

I'm caught in a trap. A snare, his tentative words and caring actions set for me, making me forget about the angry man who's been making my life a living hell from the moment I met him. But I can't seem to get away, and the more my instincts are telling me to run, the tighter the noose of his chocolate eyes gets. I don't realise I'm nodding my head in reply until his long, callused fingers wrap around my hand, squeezing it in comfort. For some reason, I didn't expect his fingers to be rough. His polished image and expensive tastes are so at odds with the man I'm seeing right now, standing in front of me.

"I—" My voice is raspy as I try to formulate my reply. If he had asked me the same question a few days ago, I'd have laughed in his face. A few days ago I'd flip him the bird, steal his money clip and walk away, cursing his audacity. A few days ago, I didn't trust him as far as I could throw him. So what changed? "I'm going to find out what ties me to Blackwood. I think I'm from here. I think... maybe my parents are still here." I whisper the last part, having spoken the one thing I have not dared to even think of.

The grip on my hand tightens.

"Why?"

"Wouldn't you want to know?"

Dante clenches his jaw together, an angry muscle ticking just below his cheekbone. "I wouldn't. I'd have stayed with the person who took care of me. I'd have stayed in my perfect little life."

My mouth opens, all sense of trust I fooled myself into believing I felt evaporating. "Perfect?" I half-choke, my mind reeling. As if transferred through his touch, anger pulsates in my veins, directly to the tightening of my chest. Swallowing hard, I grapple for self-control, but there is none. "If foster care was so perfect, why would I have fled at thirteen? You think the streets are any kinder to a young girl with no hope of survival?"

He doesn't respond. At least not in the way I expected. Those brown depths lighten, his grip on my hand loosening as he takes a step back, shock and disbelief on his face as if I just slapped him.

"What do you mean?" he finally says, his posture rigid, his eyes searching mine trying to catch me in a... lie?

"Exactly what I said, Dante." I turn away from him.

"But—" He's back in front of me in an instant, his rough hand on my chin, tilting it until our gazes meet once more.

"But what?" I grit through my teeth. "Not everyone gets to grow up with a family. Some of us have to fend for ourselves. Some of us have no one to take care of them."

His grip on my chin lightens, his thumb stroking my bottom lip as his eyes cast downwards, focusing on them.

"You're under my protection now, Alessa."

"I don't need your protection," I snap back. "I've taken care of myself all this time and I can keep doing it just fine. I'm not some damsel in distress waiting for a knight on a white horse to show up and save her from the cruel world."

He chuckles darkly. "I'm not a knight in shining armour, Alessa. I'm the stuff of nightmares."

"You don't scare me," I say defiantly.

He licks his lip, his thumb making his way up, tracing the outline of my top lip. The gentle touch making my lips part, as an unfamiliar ache starts deep in the pit of my stomach. I want to lean into him, grab his shirt, and pull him closer. I want to feel more of him than just the pad of his thumb on my mouth.

"You *should* be scared," he says, his voice gravelly.

And maybe I should be, but at this moment, all I can focus on is how close he is to me, and how enticing his lips look.

The air between us thickens, stealing the breath from my lungs. I don't see his head dip, but rather sense it. The scent of his cologne fills my airways, as the shadow of his face falls over me, blocking the morning light. My hand lifts of its own volition, needing to touch him. Needing the reassurance that he is real. This is real.

"You should be scared, Alessa," he says, his forehead touching mine, his words stopping my hand midair. I can taste the coffee on his breath, feel the air move between our lips as he speaks. I have to fight the urge to grab his shirt and pull him to me to close the distance between us. "Because you may have survived foster care, you may have survived living on the streets," he continues, closing his eyes for a second as he takes a deep breath. "But I am one thing you will not survive."

# 20

## ALESSA

As quickly as the words leave Dante's mouth, he's gone, leaving me leaning against the cold marble of the kitchen island with my hand suspended in midair. I watch his back as he storms out, his fists clenching and unclenching in anger.

Rolling my eyes, I drop my hand to my side. What even was that? He's clearly unhinged, teetering on the edge of a scorching hot and angry killer. And just because I find the jackhole alright looking, doesn't mean I should be throwing myself at him. Although, if he stormed back into this room, all furious and demanding, I know exactly what my response would be. Apparently, after years of avoiding having one, I have now developed a type. Tall, dark, handsome and disturbed.

I grab my coffee mug and take a long drink, trying to figure out what I am supposed to do now. If Dante thinks he can intimidate me with his angry personality into staying in the kitchen while he goes off God knows where, he is deeply mistaken.

First things first, I haven't eaten since yesterday, so I start my exploration by raiding his cupboards. Once satisfied and with a half eaten granola bar sticking out of my mouth, I step through the threshold and into a long corridor with a glass wall on one side and a door at the end. I'm just about to turn around when Dante comes out into the courtyard, clearly visible through the glass panels. It is only by a miracle I manage to catch the granola bar as it falls out of my mouth, which is now hanging open.

Dante is wearing nothing but a pair of swimming shorts.

In my twenty-two years, I have never been interested in men. Not in *that* way. Men were always a means to an end. Never something that had my body tightening and my breath speed up. Until Dante Santoro.

I watch him in all his tanned, ink-covered and sculpted glory as he walks over to the edge of the swimming pool, his calf muscles swallowed by the billows of steam rising off the warm water, and dives disappearing under the surface. My eyes trace the dark shadow as it moves gracefully from one end of the pool to the other. When he comes up for air, a swarm of butterflies sets off in my belly. He is looking straight at me. His chocolate brown eyes instantly trap me in my place. Not that I would move. I'm too mesmerised by the rivulets of water tracing down his sharp jaw and neck before drenching the tip of the wings tattooed on his chest and merging with the pool water.

I fight the urge to press myself against the glass, just so I can be closer to him, imagining what the water on his chest would taste like if it were on my tongue. He crooks a finger at me, beckoning me over, his burning gaze never leaving mine.

I'm at war. One part of me wants to walk down that corridor and join him, despite the fact I have no clue how to swim, nor do I own a bathing suit. The other wants to run for the hills, as far away as I can get from this confusing man.

The chicken shit side wins over as I turn on my heel and pretty much run in the opposite direction. As alluring as Dante dripping in water may be, I'm not about to go into the lion's den. I don't want him getting any ideas, even if said ideas might be somewhat reciprocated. I'm here only because he insisted this was the safest place for me. But how safe can it actually be? Because, at this point, I'm not sure what scares me more. The men who are trying to attack me or Dante Santoro.

I walk down another corridor until I get to a set of double doors leading into a brightly lit large room. Covered wall to wall in bookshelves, every single one is filled with books of all shapes and sizes. Gasping, I turn in circles, trying to take it all in. Like a kid in the candy shop, my eyes are drawn to the colourful spines, unable to decide where to start first. This is heaven and hell at the same time because as I'm trying to discern the titles on some of the books I'm already mourning the moment I'll have to part with this room. In a daze, I walk over to the closest wall, letting my finger trace the spines of old books. Pushkin, Tolstoy, Bulgakov, Gogol, Chekhov, Nabokov and many more, all in perfect condition. Curious, I pull a thick tome out, Doctor Zhivago, and nearly drop it when I flip it open and find it's a first edition, signed by Boris Pasternak himself. I hastily put it back in its place and move to the next shelf, where I find books on American history. There's so much knowledge contained in this room I find it hard to breathe. My heart is beating loudly in my chest as I move around from one bookshelf to the next, taking in all the titles.

"Rosa? What are you doing here?"

I squeak, jumping in place as a book about Roman aqueducts I was flipping through slips from my grip and lands on the floor. With my hand on my heart, I turn around, coming face to face with an older man wearing a pair of pyjamas and a long burgundy velvet robe tied around his waist.

"I'm so sorry," I stutter. "I didn't know someone else was here." I could have sworn the library was empty when I first walked in, but then again, I have been completely besotted by all the books contained within these walls. I probably would have missed an elephant if it was right there in the middle of the room when I entered.

"Don't be silly, *Rosalita*. You're always welcome here." The man smiles at me.

I take a tentative step back, matching his step forward as he tries to close the distance between us. This whole thing is creepy. The Hugh Hefner bathrobe, him calling me Rosa, like I'm Belle in the Beast's library. With the next step he takes forward, I turn around and run back the way I came.

*Safest place for me, my* ass.

I run through the corridor and back to the kitchen, hoping the old man is nowhere near agile enough to follow me. In my head, I run through all the ways I want to tell Dante to stuff this huge *safe* mansion and all the creepy old men living here up his perfectly pert ass when I smack against a wall, bouncing off and falling on my butt.

Except I never land, since the wall's hands shoot out and wrap around my arms, steadying me.

"You okay?" Angelo's gaze rakes me over, looking for injury while I stare at his tank top covered chest. Seriously though, this man is pure muscle. No wonder I mistook him for a wall.

"I'm fine." I pull my arm away from his grasp and rub my forehead where it bounced off of his pecs, eyeing him from underneath my hand. He's wearing fitness gear. Black shorts and a loose tank, that do little to cover his bulging muscles. "Where are you going?"

Angelo looks me up and down like I'm slow.

I huff. "I'm not dumb. I can see you're about to work out."

"Dante's gym."

Huh. Of course he has a gym. Figures. I should probably make my acquaintance with the room, considering I've had two attempts at my life already. Three, if I count Dante saying he almost shot me last night. "Can I come?"

Angelo shrugs, walking past me to the fridge and grabbing a bottle of water. "Suit yourself. I don't mind the audience."

I follow him down the corridor I drooled over Dante's body in. My eyes focus on the crumbs of the granola bar by the spot where I stood. Pretending I don't care if Dante is still in the swimming pool or not, I make a point to keep my gaze away from the glass covered wall, even though my insides are screaming at me to peer to the side and check as we near the door. But I stay strong. And as we walk into a small changing room, then through another set of doors and into a spacious room with equipment even the best gyms would be envious of, I mentally pat myself on the back for keeping my resolve about ignoring Dante's existence.

Angelo makes his way to the mat in the middle, stretching his muscles as I sit down on a weightlifting bench, trying not to look like I'm ogling him. Once he's satisfied, he walks over to the side and wraps his hands in white long cloth bandages before walking over to a punching bag and starting his training session.

My jaw hanging open, I watch his footwork and quick jabs as he gracefully dances around the bag. *This.* This is exactly what I need to learn.

Without even noticing, I'm up and walking over to him, unable to tear my gaze away. "Can you teach me?" I ask standing next to him.

He hugs the bag, stilling it as his eyes dart to mine. "Teach you what?"

"How to do this?" I point at the punching bag.

"You want to learn how to punch?"

"And fight."

"Why?" He steps away, crossing his arms in front of his chest, which does nothing for my resolve to stop eyeballing his delicious biceps.

"I've been here for a month and I've already been chased twice. I'd like to be able to defend myself if someone finally catches up to me."

"I suppose your luck is bound to run out at some point." He smirks.

"Exactly." The joke's on him, though. My luck ran out the minute I stepped foot in Blackwood and met his over-bearing older brother.

"Fighting and defending yourself are two different things." He cocks his head to the side.

"I know. I just don't want to be powerless."

"Fine. But you can't fight in this." He gestures at my jeans and t-shirt. "Dante should have some spare clothes in the changing room. Go find something to wear and come back. Then we'll see what you're made of."

I don't bother nodding, retracing my steps and walking into the adjacent room instead. Ignoring the door leading into the courtyard, I rummage through drawers, finding a pair of grey sweatpants I could swim in, a pair of boxer shorts and a tee. I change out of my clothes quickly, pulling the drawstrings on the sweatpants taut and tying them together with a double knot in hopes they'll stay on my ass while Angelo teaches me how to fight. I forgo a bra, not having found anything that I could use instead of the expensive La Perla one I had on, then tie my hair into a high ponytail. Barefoot, I walk through the door into the gym, instantly finding Angelo. I haven't been gone long, but his tan skin glistens with perspiration as he attacks the punching bag, uppercutting it. The force with which he moves lets me know that if it was a real life opponent on the receiving end instead of an inanimate object, he would probably be lying on the floor, knocked out.

"Ready?" Angelo exhales rapidly, his shoulders moving up and down. "Let's see what you're made of," he continues as I walk over to where he's standing, my feet pressing against the soft mat underneath.

Without warning, he lunges at me, his arms shooting out to grab my waist, but I'm not as defenceless as either one of us thinks. Years of having to dodge unwanted hands and running away made me agile enough that I manage to slip past him as he barrels through. This is not too bad at all. I swing to the side, thinking I'm in the clear, but, like an idiot, I underestimate my opponent. Angelo whirls around, kicking his leg out from under him and cutting me down. I crash land on the mat with a thud as he lands on top of me, his hands pushing my arms over my head, locking them as he renders me immobile. My breathing speeds up as I kick and buck underneath him, to no avail. My mind conjures images of the last time someone was on top of me like that. I'm seconds away from a full-blown panic attack.

"What the fuck?" A cold voice rings through the quiet gym. But instead of sounding threatening, it grounds me. I close my eyes, letting the feeling of calmness and safety wash over me.

"Your little secret wanted to learn how to defend herself." Angelo gets off me, releasing my wrists.

I stay on the floor with my eyes closed as Dante and Angelo argue in hushed tones, letting my ragged breath normalise. Maybe this wasn't such a great idea if my reaction to being pinned down is anything to go by.

"What are you wearing?" Dante towers above me.

I lazily open my eyes, meeting his gaze. "Clothes."

"One day, Alessandra." His voice is low and rumbly. "I'm going to spank the brat out of you."

I swallow, unable to look away.

"And you're going to beg me for more," he finishes, dropping to his knees beside me. He's wearing a pair of grey sweatpants just like the ones I have on and nothing else. His beautiful tattoos are in my direct line of sight and this time I can't help but study them. The avenging angel with a crown on his head and a gun in his hand, hovering over a graveyard made out of skulls as its unfurled wings span the entirety of Dante's chest. The Latin words strewn across the side of his abdominals. *In Nomine Familiae* on one side and *Sanguis Super Omnia* on the other.

"Had your fill?" Dante asks as I lick my lips, lifting onto my elbows.

"Where is Angelo?" I look around.

"He had to leave."

I sigh, annoyed. "He was teaching me how to defend myself."

"He's not a very good teacher, Alessa."

"Oh, and you are?" I mock.

"As a matter of fact, I am."

I burst out laughing. God, he's cocky. And handsome. Would licking his abs really be such a bad idea?

"If anyone is going to teach you how to fight, it's going to be me," he says confidently, reaching his hand out and wrapping it around my arm before pulling me up to a sitting position.

"Fine." I glance about the room, giving him a half shoulder shrug while in all actuality my body is on high alert. "Not like I have a choice."

"You don't," he confirms.

# 21

# ALESSA

D ante is relentless, shouting at me to get up and fight back the minute I'm down on the mat, reminding me if it were anyone else, I'd be dead by now. I know he's speaking the truth, but it doesn't make me resent him any less. I'm sweaty, tired and out of breath.

"That's enough," I pant as he circles me, having barely broken a sweat.

"Tell that to the guy who wants you dead."

I look him straight in the eye, remembering the hatred, the anger and all the times I felt like he was ready to kill me just for my mere existence.

"That's enough, Dante."

He chuckles darkly, pouncing on me. The movement throws my tired body off balance. I have no more fight left as we land on the mats one more time, with him on top of me. "You think *I* want you dead, Alessandra?"

I bite my lip.

"You think I'd be wasting my time trying to keep you safe and teaching you how to fight back if I wanted you gone?" His sharp gaze snaps to my lips, then back to my eyes. "You think I'd keep you around instead of snuffing the life out of you the minute we were alone?" His face scrunches up in agony, as if the words just spoken pain him, as if he's fighting against the urge to wrap his fingers around my throat and squeeze until I can no longer breathe.

"I wouldn't put it past you to play with your food," I whisper, gasping for air, knowing it would probably take him less than ten seconds to end me. Pinned like I am beneath him, I wouldn't be able to fight back. I wiggle, testing how much space I have to manoeuvre, but all I achieve is feeling every inch of his deliciously hard body pressing against mine. My breaths quicken as his eyes move to my lips. My tongue darts out, wetting them as I'm rendered immobile once again. But this time is different. His dark amber eyes have me enthralled. There's no threat in the air, no fear. Instead, all I feel is anticipation as his face slowly but deliberately inches towards mine. My body ignites underneath his, every nerve ending begging to feel his touch.

"Fuck," he curses almost inaudibly, his lips just a whisper above mine. His cock grows hard, pressing against my thigh as his hand traces the side of my face until his fingers are cupping my jaw and lifting my chin.

I feel so helpless caged beneath this mountain of pure muscle, yet so cherished at the same time. It's such a mind-fuck—this hot and cold he's putting me through. I'm torn between pulling him to me and pushing him away.

"Dante," I whisper, my breath mingling with his. But the whisper comes out as more of a moan.

He shudders above me, driving his hips against mine as liquid heat pools in my lower belly. Our lips touch, but neither one of us dares to move. "You will be my undoing."

For half a second, I'm not sure if I imagined those words,

but then he dives in, his tongue licking my lips, then slipping inside and nothing else matters. Moaning against his mouth, my thighs open of their own accord as he grinds into me, causing a delicious ache to build in my core. I nip and tug and kiss him back, my hands in his hair as he lifts my t-shirt exposing my breasts. I'm in flames, consumed by the fire he has ignited within. I don't recognise the person I'm becoming when Dante is holding me, kissing me, pinching my nipple between his fingers. My body moves against his as his mouth becomes rougher, his touches more demanding. I'm equally terrified and yearning for more. For all of him.

His hand slides down the side of my body, leaving my breasts cold and aching for his attention. But he doesn't leave me wanting for long, moving his mouth away from my needy lips, biting and licking down my neck until his mouth is over my pert nipple, sucking it in so hard the sensation teeters between pleasurable and painful.

"You should only wear my clothes," he murmurs as he undoes the tie on my sweatpants, pushing them down and seeing his boxer shorts underneath. He bites the side of my breast, then moves back up, his mouth on mine before I can even reply. His fingers move beneath the waistband of the boxers as his lips skilfully turn me into liquid. I have never felt a desire like this before. Never wanted for things to go any further than meaningless flirtation. Never let anyone get this close to me. To my body. And, as Dante's masterful hands continue their exploration, my impulse to avoid physical contact with the opposite sex at all costs is silent, letting things unfold as they may. It is only when his fingers slide against my slick entrance and he groans—"Fuck. You're so wet for me, Alessa."—that I still, the full realisation of what's happening dawning on me.

*What the fuck am I doing?*

His fingers move rhythmically, circling my clit and I squeeze my eyes shut, lost between the feeling of horror and overwhelming pleasure. I want to close my legs and spread them open to give him access at the same time. The urge to push him away is consuming me, but god, he's making me feel so good I don't think I can do it. I'm oscillating between ecstasy and the sour taste of hate still lingering in my mouth. Heat prickles behind my eyes as my hands drop from his neck and land by my side, curling into fists.

"Alessa." He stills above me, his fingers poised against my entrance, where no one has touched me before except— "What's wrong? Do you want me to stop?"

*This.* This is exactly the reason I'm so torn up. How can he go from being the angry man I'm trying my hardest to hate to this caring person, worried about my feelings at the same time? The Dante with concern in his dark brown eyes, is not the same man I met on my first day in Blackwood who made it his job to make me feel unwelcome. He can't be. I shake my head, my eyes still closed as I try to steady my shaky breaths. The feelings he has ignited in me are foreign. The closest I've ever felt to wanting something *more* from a man. The closest to feeling like I can trust someone with my body, and I—as terrifying as it feels—I don't want it to end. I want to feel all the things Dante Santoro is making me feel and more. I don't want to be this broken girl, always running away. From men, from authorities. From memories.

"Are you—are you a virgin?"

My eyes snap open as once again I shake my head. Somehow, through all the turmoil I'm feeling, I still manage a smile as I lift my hand and smooth the wrinkles of confusion between his eyebrows. "No. Not technically." The words slip out and as soon as they do, I want to take them back.

Questions I'm not ready to answer mar his features. Memories I don't want to dredge up, swimming up to the surface, but I push them down. Drowning them in the pits of my soul where darkness clings to my trauma like tar. A self-defence mechanism I've mastered in order to survive.

"Keep going, Dante," I whisper, moving my hand to the side of his face. Focusing on the way this man is making me feel.

He hesitates, his eyes searching mine, making sure I'm not deflecting. And that's more reason for me to urge him to keep going. I don't want my sudden change of heart scrutinised. I just want to stay in this bubble with him, where we're not trying to insult or annoy each other. Where the scariest man I have ever known makes me feel alive.

I thread my fingers through his silky hair. "Make me feel good," I whisper, pulling his face down to mine and kissing him again, deeply and demanding, until he groans against my lips and kisses me back like he means it, his hand digging into my waist.

"I'm not gentle," he says between kisses, and I almost sigh with relief.

"I don't want you to be. I won't break," I reply. And it's true. I don't want him to treat me like I'm fragile, I want him to take what he wants and I want to enjoy every second of it. I need him to demand the parts of me I would never give freely. I need to feel like he's in control, otherwise, I actually might break. But if I let him take charge, I can let go of the control I've been trying to hold on to since I was a child and maybe, just maybe, I can enjoy myself.

His thumb circles my clit again as his index finger teases my entrance before slipping in. Our moans meet as he shudders on top of me. I focus on the way the weight of his body feels on mine, the way his fingers ignite my skin. I focus on the here and now and let go of my fear, letting Dante take me wherever he desires.

"Holy fuck, Alessa. You're so tight. Jesus, I can't—Fuck, I can't even imagine what it's going to feel like having this tight pussy wrapped around my cock," he groans against my lips, the deep, rumbly baritone of his voice making me shiver with need.

Each movement of his finger against my soaked pussy, every word that leaves his mouth, lets me know I've made the right decision, trusting him with this part of me I have not given to anyone willingly before.

He moves his finger in and out, curling it against my inner walls, adding another when my hips start to move in rhythm with his. My body gets hotter, a burning ache building in my spine and threatening to set us both ablaze.

"Fuck, you feel so good." He trails kisses down my neck, sucking and nibbling at it like it's the most delicious feast, the sensation sending my senses into overdrive. I'm no longer able to think. I'm all feelings—hot frenzy and burning desire as Dante's fingers pump into me while he keeps telling me in his deep, sexy voice how good I feel around his fingers and how wet I am for him.

"I want you so bad, Alessa," he admits. "The minute I saw you, I wanted to fuck you. You are exactly what I should avoid," he continues. "But can't. You have me under a fucking spell, *la mia Fata*[1], and I'm disintegrating, no longer able to think straight. I need your taste, Alessa," he growls. "I'm fucking dying. *Sono malato e tu sei la mia medicina. Il tuo gusto, il tuo corpo, è l'unica cosa che può riportarmi indietro da questa follia*[2]. Please, Alessa," he groans, nuzzling his face into my neck, "bring me back from this insanity."

The speed of his fingers picks up as he bites my skin, marking my throat, before leaving a trail down to my breast. I crave the sting. Wanting more, wanting it harder. His thumb rubs against my clit as he finger fucks me like it's the only thing that will bring him peace. And when he bites my nipple hard, I scream, shattering around him, the pain and pleasure mixing in the most delicious feeling I have ever experienced.

"Look at me," he demands when my eyelids flutter closed mid orgasm. Instantly, they snap open, meeting his chocolate eyes, full of desire and fervour. He watches me reach the crescendo, drinking in my every sound as a blush spreads across my body.

"Fucking stunning," he croaks out, pulling his fingers out of my pussy and licking them one by one. "And delicious."

My eyes trained on him, I try to steady my breathing, let the calm wash over me, but I can feel his swollen cock against my thigh as he leans over me, and the sudden need to have every inch of him paralyses me. The inexplicable desire to let him do with me as he pleases, see his perfect face overcome by ecstasy as he drives into me. Am I crazy, wanting the one man that should terrify me? Probably, but at the same time, this is the only man who has ever made me feel safe.

A yawn escapes my lips. The break-in, the restless night, the training that Dante put me through and the mind blowing climax finally catching up with me.

"Let's get you to your room, *Fata*," he says, pushing off me and leaving me alone on the floor. All the warm and fuzzy post orgasm feelings threaten to leave me as he stands up and surveys me, basically spread eagle on the floor. But then he smiles and leans down. "You're a mess." His lips tilt up once more, as he picks me up with no effort, then carries me out of the gym, through the corridor and up the stairs. The gentle rocking, his warm body and his delicious scent relaxing me enough that I let my head fall on his shoulder, and bury my face in his neck, pushing away any worries to the back of my mind.

The magnitude of what just happened can go fuck right off. I will let it swallow me whole tomorrow. After Dante makes good on his promise on seeing how his cock feels inside me.

# 22

## DANTE

"**I**s this my room?" Alessa asks on a yawn as I drop her on my bed. She makes a half-ass attempt to cover herself while I make no effort to help. Covering her breasts, albeit with my t-shirt, should be a crime. So, instead of offering assistance, like the gentleman my mother raised me to be, I turn away, grunting something noncommittal before heading to my bathroom. I need space. Space to cool down. Space to think straight without her intoxicating scent and her big green eyes muddling my senses and rendering me unable to make decisions that do not involve her being naked.

Torn between following my instincts to fuck the living daylight out of her and needing to make sure she's taken care of, I shove my hands through my hair—much like she just did on the floor of the gym. A foreign feeling wars within, wanting to look after someone other than my brothers. Don't get me wrong, I always take 'care of' the women I fuck, making sure they're satisfied. Somehow, this is different. *Alessa* is different.

I splash my face with icy water, then look at myself in the mirror. *Man the fuck up.* My wet fingers dig into the cool ceramic of the double sink as cold sweat gathers at the nape of my neck. I need to face Alessa head on. Get this shit over with. Once I've had her, maybe this innate need to make her come will dissipate. Fuck, even that little taste of her sweet pussy on my fingers had me so on edge, I could barely stop myself from ripping her clothes off right there on the mat where anyone could have walked in.

My brow furrows as my heart speeds up in my chest. I'm oddly aroused at the thought of taking what's mine in front of everyone. Claiming her pussy and making sure everyone can hear how hard I can make her come. The elation of ensuring no one will dare to touch her is mixed with red hot rage brimming underneath my skin. Rage at someone else seeing that tight little body of hers. Her creamy skin, flushed and covered in goosebumps from my touch. That perfectly round ass, red from the spanking I give her for always being such a brat.

My cock strains against the thin material of my sweatpants once again. At this rate, I'll need to haul an ice freezer upstairs and just have my balls take up residence in it whenever I think of Alessa. Which, with the way she came on my fingers, makes me think might be a lot.

But she's not mine. Not mine to pleasure and definitely not mine to keep. I need to—

Fuck.

"Dante?"

My eyes snap up to the mirror as they meet her tentative expression. Her long fingers are white with the force she's holding onto the door. Like it's the only thing keeping her up. At once I want to go to her, pick her up and take her back to bed. But I stay where I am. Not moving a muscle. Just watching her, waiting for her next move. I wish I could pretend I was strong enough to deny her if she were to drop to her knees and offer to suck my dick on the tiled floor of the bathroom, but now she's in my space, her cheeks still red from the orgasm I've just given her...Well, I'm only human.

"Dante?" She bites her bottom lip this time. Reminding me of the way she bit it when my fingers were inside her. Fuck, I need to nip this in the bud or I'll go insane from constantly thinking of her.

"What is it, *Miss Jones*?" I grit out, using her last name as a way to put up a barrier between us. Hoping to distance myself from her. It's this, or I'll lose the last shred of control and fuck her into oblivion. The simple taste I've had is proof enough. One instance won't be enough. She's in my home, my clothes, my fucking bedroom. My scent is all over her and the predator in me won't be satisfied until she's been ruined by my hand. My tongue. My cock.

Yet by the dim light of the bedside lamp glowing behind her, I see her face crumple. How the wall I'm building confuses and humiliates her. A sigh rocks through my chest as I scrub a hand through my hair again and shuffle her aside.

There's no whimper, no sobbing. No. Alessa is fucking strong. No matter how hard life hits her, she hits back. I could see that the minute she opened her mouth.

I could see that in the way she fought back every step of the way. I could see that today, when even exhausted, she gave everything as I was teaching her how to protect herself. And damn it, I find it admirable.

An unease starts in my chest, words she spoke niggling in my unconscious mind, but I push them aside for now.

Instead, I turn back to her, crooking my finger and beckoning her over. She watches me, her big green eyes narrowing at my gesture. I can see the indignation on her face warring with the desire to listen to my silent instruction and see what I have in store for her.

The curiosity triumphs as she takes one step after another until she's standing right in front of me, her head tilted up, her eyes storming. Still a brat, even when obedient.

"Good girl," I whisper, grazing my thumb across her cheek. Her eyes flutter closed as she leans into my touch, responding to my praise. My cock strains at the idea of her submissiveness. "Sit." I gently guide her until the backs of her knees hit the bed, and she falls, sitting down.

I suck in a breath, trying to calm the blood racing through my veins. This woman, yielding to my commands, no matter how small, is making me dizzy with need. Especially when her pouty lips are at dick level.

Thoughts of fucking her mouth hard and fast overwhelm me as she stares at my growing bulge.

"What now?" she whispers, her pink tongue darting out, wetting her lips as her eyes meet mine. There's apprehension in them, maybe even a little fear. She's playing cool, but I can see the truth behind her straight back. I see her fingers digging into the bedsheet.

I grab her by the waist and throw her into the middle of the bed before crawling on top of her. She goes rigid, her eyes closing as her body shivers beneath mine.

Thoughts swirl in my head. As much as I want to fuck her right now, get her out of my system, something isn't right. I'm not one to force my dick on someone. Unless they want to play pretend. But we are not role-playing and Alessa does not look like someone who wants to be fucked. She looks terrified. She looks like she's in pain. Before I can think better of it, my hand strokes her cheek, and I roll us over until she's on top. Releasing control to make the woman in my arms feel more at ease.

Her eyes snap open.

"I—I," she starts, sucking in her bottom lip before shaking her head.

"What is it?"

"Shouldn't I be on the bottom?"

I chuckle. "You can be anywhere you want to, *Fata*. On the bottom, on the side, upside down. However you want to be fucked—I'll fuck you. As long as you *want* me to fuck you."

Her jaw clenches. I watch her face for a second, my skin on fire as her thighs clench around me.

"Do you, Alessa?"

"Do I, what?"

"Want me to fuck you."

She hesitates before nodding her head almost imperceptibly. But the hesitation is enough to stop me in my tracks, words she spoke earlier invade my thoughts once again, putting breaks on all the plans my dick has drawn up.

I sit up, until we're face to face, her legs shaking as she straddles me, undoubtedly feeling the evidence of my arousal. She's wary, but not even the million thoughts crossing her mind right now can stop the way her body melts into mine. It takes every ounce of control I have in me not to grab her by the hips and drive against the heat pressed against my length.

"Earlier on—you said something."

"I talk too much," she mutters, her cheeks flushing as her pussy moves against my hard cock with each breath she takes.

"Alessa," I growl, on the verge of sanity. I'm two seconds away from ripping my clothes off of her and sinking myself balls deep into her tight cunt. But the predator in me needs to know the truth.

Alessa whimpers, her movements becoming bolder as she grinds against me. Sweat is pouring off me from the exertion of keeping myself still.

"Tell me, Alessa." I close my eyes, her name tasting on

my tongue like a sin. She is a sin to me, one I should never have allowed myself to become this familiar with.

"Tell you, what?" Her voice is raspy as she wraps her fingers behind my neck, her forehead landing on mine. Fuck, she feels so good. All soft and ready in my arms. Just one little taste. One taste, and I can get back to questioning her. Her lips move closer to mine, our breaths mingling and I'm on the verge of giving in to this beautiful witch, my *Fata*. Forsaking the control I'm trying to cling onto and letting Alessa rip me to shreds.

And just like that, with her body against mine, our lips mere inches away, I have the sinking feeling that one taste, one fuck, will not be enough. Will never be enough.

Not with her.

I push her off me, needing a reprieve from this overwhelming realisation. What the fuck am I getting myself into? Even if I wanted to believe that the feelings she's stirring up in me are possible, I belong to someone else. I could never ask either of my brothers to give up on finding true love and marrying Natalia Nicolosi just because a piece of paper requires it. I'm the jaded one. The one who doesn't believe in love. The ruthless one. One without scruples. I'm the eldest Saint. Marrying to keep the peace is my responsibility as the future Don.

But... if I just—If I could have Alessa for now. Have a taste of what it feels like to be with her. Then maybe I can live the rest of my life as a pawn in Mafia games.

"You want to come?" I pull the sweats she's wearing down and over her feet, leaving her in just my boxers. She nods, gasping, as my knuckle grazes the damp spot between her legs. "Words, Alessa," I demand.

"Y-yes."

"Then you'll play my game." I press my palm against her entrance, rubbing it through the thin material. A moan escapes her as she starts panting, moving her hips against my hand. "Good girl." I flick her nipple.

Our eyes meet and it takes all my focus not to take her right then.

"Earlier on." I push the shorts she's wearing aside, finding her hot and slippery. "You said something I didn't quite understand. I want you to tell me what it meant." I circle her clit with my thumb as my index finger starts playing with her lips, stroking up and down her entrance, coating it in her own arousal. "I'll keep making you feel good as long as you talk, Alessa. When you stop,"—I move my hand away, leaving her panting and exposed—"I stop, too."

"Don't!" she whimpers, her eyes wide. "What do you want to know?"

"You said you were 'not technically' a virgin. What did you mean?" My hand goes back to her folds, gently stroking them as her body goes rigid underneath. Despite my earlier words, I don't stop, needing her to overcome whatever it is that has her on edge. Slowly, her body becomes relaxed again. Her eyes meet mine, darkened with sadness and fear. But the fear is not directed at me.

"Tell me," my command is quiet but stern.

She sinks her teeth into her bottom lip, and I use my thumb to drag it free, giving her a warning glare, all the while my fingers keep working her.

The same expression contorts her face as it did in the gym, and now, a slither of dread trickles through my being.

"It's not something I like to talk about..." her voice quivers. I sink my index finger inside her, curling it up and stroking rhythmically as Alessa gathers her courage. "Promise you won't stop if I tell you," she gasps as I assault her g-spot and her clit at the same time.

"I don't make promises," I grit out, annoyed that she's stalling again.

"Just this once. Please." Her hips move against my hand as she's getting closer to a climax. The dread I could feel creeping up a second ago comes back full force. If she's asking me to make a promise, whatever she's about to tell me can't be good.

"You have my word."

"I just—I want to override my memories. They won't have control over me anymore."

"Alessa," I all but bark.

Her gaze snaps to mine as my fingers continue their explorations, becoming the only part of my body moving as the rest of me goes rigid in anticipation.

"The only experience I've had with...*intimacy*...wasn't consensual."

My muscles tense even more. Alessa feels the sudden change, snapping her eyes shut, taking with it the only thing that's keeping me tethered to reality.

"Open your eyes, Alessa," I say, my jaw as hard as a rock. I want to pull her to me. I want to protect her. Make her feel safe. Wrap my arms around her. But I made a fucking promise, so no matter how wrong it feels right now, I continue fingering her sweet pussy as rage bubbles under my skin.

She moans softly, her eyes still closed as she throws her head back, riding my hand.

"He will no longer have this hold over me, Dante" she whimpers, her face determined as a tear slips past her closed eyelids. "I'm taking control."

I want to smash things to pieces. I want to break the bed, destroy this room. But most of all, I want to kill the motherfucker who has touched Alessa without her consent.

"How old were you?" I manage in a strained voice, something huge lodging in my throat as I try to swallow.

"Thirteen," she gasps as I increase the speed, my fingers moving inside her frantically. I nearly stop right alongside my heart. Jesus Christ, she was only thirteen. "Don't stop," she moans, her pussy tightening around me. She's so close. But I need to know more. Pulling her close, my hand climbs up her back, finding her nape, before twisting around her throat, pinning her in place. Her eyes snap open in shock as my grip tightens. I can barely control the rage and anguish inside me as she continues to move. She should not be so trusting. She should be running for her life, as far away from me as possible. Although even running wouldn't help her anymore. I'm a possessive motherfucker.

"How many times, baby?" I look away as the words leave my mouth.

Her hand lands on my shoulder and taps. Once. Twice. Three times. Each tap sending me into a frenzy I have not felt before, my hand tightening around her throat as my fingers assault her pussy.

"Breathe," I say, releasing the pressure on her neck. She blinks, gasping for air, before my grip tightens once more and my thumb rubs her clit with renewed vigour. I can see in her eyes she needs this. See the need to be in control as much as to give the control away. She could tell me to stop anytime. Grab my hand around my wrist and pull, but she doesn't. She lets me hold her life in my tight grasp as I finger fuck her to orgasm. Her whole body shakes as the impending climax builds. All that's keeping her upright at the moment is my hand around her neck. There'll be bruises there tomorrow, but the thought gives me pleasure. I want to mark her whole body, make sure that every inch of her skin knows who it belongs to. I lean over, sucking her nipple into my mouth and biting down on it as Alessa screams out my name, her body convulsing on top of mine.

Releasing the death grip on her throat I bury my face

against it, grasping her tightly to me as she melts against my body. I should be the one comforting her. Asking her if she's okay. But I can't stop the feeling of dread and shame inside my chest. It's my fault. It's all my fault. I was the one who abandoned her, never making sure she was okay. How the fuck could I have let this happen to her?

"Dante?" she croaks out, her cool fingers stroking the side of my face.

"I need a name, baby," I say, barely above a whisper.

She stiffens, but her fingers continue their calming motion. Not that it helps.

"The fucking name, Alessa." My voice breaks as red curtains my vision.

"Please, Dante, don't—" I flip us over before she can finish her sentence. Crushing her into the mattress underneath me I search her eyes, hoping she can see the torment inside despite my entire body radiating with deadly intent. I don't want to hurt her. I never fucking want to hurt her again. All I need are two simple words and the longer the silence continues, the more unhinged I'm becoming.

"Please," I choke out in a voice I don't recognise. Or maybe it was she who spoke the words, her eyes filling with fear once more as she studies my face.

"C-Casper...Lockwood," Alessa finally croaks out, and just like that, I'm standing beside the bed, her body still splayed out in my bed as she reaches out to grasp my hand, stop me from what she must know I'm about to do. "Please, don't leave," she sheds a tear. I lean over her and kiss it, tasting the salt on my tongue.

"I will make this right, Alessa." I will make this right if it's the last thing I do on this fucking Earth.

# 23

## ALESSA

The rain doesn't fall. The thunder doesn't strike. And the sky doesn't turn red as I watch the bedroom door with my heart in my throat, feeling like the world is ending. It's the confusion at what just happened that has me immobile. My head hurts from the mixture of emotions I'm feeling. I'm spent, yet on edge. Elated but afraid. Hurting and feeling safe at the same time.

Slowly, I lift myself into a sitting position, my eyes still trained on the door despite the fact I know there's no chance of him coming back anytime soon. A part of me knows exactly where he went, even if I can't quite believe it. I could see the intentions behind his eyes. And goddamn it, I should feel something. Anything. But I'm numb.

He gave me my power back. Made me cherish being in control and giving that control away. He made those awful memories disappear and replaced them with his fingers, with his lips and then... he just left. Shrouded in a cloud of what felt like guilt. Yet, he had nothing to be guilty of. He didn't take anything I wasn't willing to give freely.

My stomach rumbles, reminding me that it's been hours since my last proper meal. Come to think of it, I don't even know what time it is. It feels like weeks have passed since I woke up on the floor of our office with Dante standing above me. My mind is racing from the events of the past twenty-four hours. The goons in my apartment, the restless sleep. Dante's vulnerability when he realised he nearly shot me. His insistence I stay in his house where I'd be the safest. The strange man in the library who kept calling me Rosa. The training session in the gym with Dante, followed by what we did on the mats and later in this very bedroom. And then his swift exit.

I'm emotionally and physically exhausted. And I'm hungry. Plus, all my stuff, including my phone, is still down-stairs, somewhere in the kitchen. I should really check in with Mel, make sure she found somewhere to stay overnight, and that she was safe. My brain feels overloaded with the amount of stuff I should be doing, but at this moment in time, all I can think about is stuffing my face.

I should probably have a shower after the workout I've had, maybe even try to find a change of clothes, but I'm too tired. So, with my hair a mess, and still in Dante's oversized and now wrinkled workout clothes, I pad barefoot down the stairs and make my way into the empty kitchen.

Except it's not empty.

"Hello." The beautiful woman behind the kitchen counter smiles at me. Instantly, my hand flies to my hair, trying to smooth the rat's nest atop my head. There are pots and pans on the stove in front of her steaming away, yet she looks like she just walked off a catwalk.

"Ummm, hi?" I take a tentative step forward. Her black hair is pulled into a tight ponytail and her makeup is flaw-less. As are her nails, I notice when she moves to grab a huge knife and starts chopping a bunch of herbs, not taking her eyes off me. I swallow, feeling oddly out of place.

"Is *Saint* upstairs?" she asks, her eyes dragging up and

down my body, assessing me. My skin crawls uncomfortably, and I wish I had that shower I dismissed so nonchalantly earlier. I must look a right state.

I shake my head, not liking the way she almost moans his nickname. "He left a while ago," I say, then go over to my bag, which is sitting in the corner of the room, exactly where I left it. After some rummaging, I find my phone, the black screen of death greeting me when I try to unlock it. *Great.*

Hoping there's a charger around somewhere, I look around the room. When my gaze glances past the woman cooking, I stop. Her hands are crossed in front of her chest, annoyance painted on her face as she motions with her head to the end of the kitchen island, where I spot a built-in wireless charging dock blending into the marble counter.

"Thanks," I mutter, walking over and placing my phone on the top. Biting my lip, I turn back to face her and lean against the counter, my senses intrigued by the smells coming from around her. Whatever she's cooking smells incredible.

She narrows her eyes at me. "I can call a car service for you."

"That's nice," I reply, pulling out a bar stool and placing my butt squarely in it. "But you don't need to."

"Look, I'm sure you've had a great time and all, but you should learn to take a hint. If a guy leaves, so should you."

She's really trying to get rid of me, isn't she? "What are you doing here, then?"

"I'm his... chef." She lifts her chin up. "I take care of *all* of Saint's needs."

A zing of jealousy shoots through me. "Like scraps, don't we?" I glance at my phone, which has started powering up. Finally! Don't know how long I can pretend to be social. Especially to someone who wants me gone. No matter how delicious the food she's cooking smells.

"Listen, cheap slut, I was here before he had you, and I'll be here when he's bored of you. He always comes back to me. *Always*."

"Lorena!" A sharp voice startles us both. I turn to see a pissed off Angelo standing in the doorway. "Know your place," he hisses at her before smiling at me and saying, "How did the training go?"

I grin back. "I got in a jab. Pretty sure it rearranged his kidneys, though. It was very powerful."

Angelo snorts. "Zombies beware."

"Preach it, brother."

"Oh, you're family?" Lorena asks sheepishly.

Angelo snorts again. "She's definitely like an annoying little sister."

I gasp. "I'll have you know I'd be your favourite sister."

"Favourite or not, still annoying, Alessa."

"Has Stevie been made?" I pout

"She went her own way," Angelo shrugs, making me burst out laughing and forget all about the rude chef looking all confused at our exchange. As if on cue, my stomach growls.

"You're hungry," Angelo's expression morphs into concern. "Lorena, can we have two of whatever you're making?"

Her mouth opens and closes like she's debating saying something, but the working brain cells must win over, because she stays silent. I watch her like a hawk as she dishes up two portions of risotto, making sure she doesn't spit in mine. It's what I would have done. As soon as the plate is in front of me, I waste no time, digging like the starved heathen I am and moaning at the burst of flavours in my mouth. Wow! Wow, wow, wow. Bitchy or not, Lorena can cook.

"Thanks, Lorena. You may leave now. We'll put away the rest."

"But—"

"I said you may leave. You won't be needed for a while."

She nods, her lips a thin line, then shoots me an evil glare before taking off her apron and storming out on what must be a pair of six-inch heels. How the hell did she cook in those?

"What's her deal?" I ask as soon as she leaves, pretending I'm not jealous of her amazing cooking skills or the fact she's apparently slept with Dante.

"She's the chef. Comes in three times a week and cooks for Dante and—" he stops abruptly.

"And?"

"Luca and I, whenever we're here," he finishes, but I know he's withholding information.

"Who cooks for the old dude I met in the library?" I ask innocently.

Angelo's sharp gaze snaps to me. I'd feel intimidated, but I went through a 'sharp gaze' school courtesy of his brother, Terence the Angry Bird himself. Nothing can phase me now.

"Fuck."

"Who is he, Angelo?"

"That's, uhmmm, Massimo. Our father," he blurts out. "Shit, Dante's gonna lose it. You can't tell anyone you've met him."

"Why?" My eyebrows draw together.

"That's a story for another day. Just promise me you won't tell anyone else about him."

"What about Dante and Luca?" I ask.

"Well, you can tell them, but no one outside *la famiglia*[1], okay?"

I nod. He seems serious enough for me to take notice.

"Going back to Lorena..." I pause, waiting for him to elaborate on his previous explanation.

"She's a chef."

"A very territorial one."

He winces. "Dante slept with her once. Pretty sure she thinks they're going to get married."

I scrunch my face, the idea really not sitting well with me at all.

"She can dream on," Angelo continues, oblivious to my discomfort. "Unless her last name is Nicolosi, it's never going to happen."

The skin on the back of my neck prickles. "What do you mean?"

Angelo clears his throat. "You probably should ask Dante."

My blood boils. "Angelo, I swear to God, I—"

"Fine. Fine. Jesus, Dante is really rubbing off on you, isn't he?"

Probably in more ways than he thinks.

"Tell me."

"Father signed a marriage contract when we were kids. One of us has to marry a Nicolosi."

Excuse me? Is he serious?

My face must show my emotions because Angelo scratches his neck then shrugs. "It's a done thing, Alessa. It's how the Mafia works. Strengthening bloodlines. Ensuring peace."

"It's barbaric," I reply, a heavy stone settling in my stomach as I think of what Dante and I have done all the while he was promised to another. A heady mix of anger at him failing to mention the detail and apathy at the situation coils within me as my nails dig into my palms. "What about...love?"

"It's not something that matters in cases like that. But

even if it did, it wouldn't make a difference. My brother doesn't believe in love."

I suck in a breath, feeling like I've just been punched in the stomach. I shouldn't care. I really shouldn't, but I can't help the feeling of disappointment. It's like I've had this small spark of hope that maybe he cares about me. A spark he's helped me nurture into a tiny flame. One that Angelo just brutally snuffed out with his honest words.

"Cool, cool, cool," I say, turning away from him and grabbing my phone pushing away the hurt. "I better check in with Mel." I yawn. The tiredness hitting me full force.

"She's fine. Luca dropped her off at her parent's house last night, and she's had someone watching her house overnight. She's safe, Alessa."

I bite my lip, still not moving, my eyes stinging for some odd reason.

"One of the guys has put your clothes in your room upstairs."

"You got my stuff back?" I whip around to face him.

"Not exactly."

# 24

# ALESSA

**D**ante is still gone the next morning. As is pretty much all my stuff. 'My clothes' Angelo was referring to is a walk-in wardrobe full of designer things Dante has arranged to be delivered and deposited in one of the bedrooms upstairs. Not the one we were in yesterday. But I have already figured out it was his, anyway.

Despite my exhaustion, I tossed and turned most of the night in my new bed, until I finally gave up and wandered across the hall to Dante's room. As soon as my head hit the pillow, the scent of his cologne surrounding me like a warm hug, I drifted off, sleeping soundly until the morning light woke me up.

I'm not proud of myself for spraying his cologne on myself, just so I can bask in his addictive smell while he's away. No one is here to judge me except me. And trust me, I shit talked myself in the mirror for a good five minutes after *that* loss of sanity.

Alone, bored out of my mind and wearing an outfit that most likely costs way more than five Bibis put together, may she rest in peace, I decide to go on a little exploration. With Angelo having slipped and spilling the beans about their dad being the guy I met yesterday, I am decidedly less creeped out. Although I probably shouldn't be. If Massimo is Dante's father, then he's the actual head of the Mafia. I should be quaking in my brand new Gucci boots.

But instead, like the cheap thrills whore that I am, I grab my phone and laptop then head downstairs. Having caught up with both Mel and Arrow last night, I can focus on digging up some dirt on Mr Angry Bird himself. Maybe his dad will have some good stories?

I tentatively walk into the library, looking around for any traces of the man I saw yesterday. But the room is empty, so I sit down in one of the plush chairs and fire up my laptop, before dialling Arrow, who helps me crack the wi-fi code.

"Nice digs," they whistle as I wait for my browser to load. If I can't find out more about Dante, I may as well start digging into the numbers that weren't adding up for me.

"You're such a stalker," I laugh. "Are you on Google Earth spying on my IP?"

"Something like that," they murmur.

"Satellite? Drone?"

"Warmer." I can hear the smile in their voice. "But at least I know where you are, and that you're safe. I still can't believe you didn't tell me straight away someone was in your apartment."

"It's cute that you think you'd have been able to help me when you live all the way in California."

"It's cute that you think otherwise, Alessa. I have access to...things."

I swallow. A lump forming in my throat. "Government things?"

The silence that follows has me sweating in my seat. I'm on the verge of a nervous breakdown when they finally speak again.

"Not quite."

"Okaaay."

"Don't worry, babe, your secrets are safe with me."

A jolt shoots through my heart, stunning me into silence. It shouldn't come as a surprise that Arrow dug into me or the people I have talked about—with the skills they clearly have, it would be silly for me to assume they haven't. Yet the fear that they may be working for a government operation hell bent on taking down the Santoros makes me unable to breathe for a few seconds. And then there's the question: how many secrets are they referring to? Have they looked into me? Into my past? I dismiss that thought and decide to focus on the mafia aspect. "You're not just friends with me to take *them* down?"

Arrow doesn't reply straight away. Each long second of silence between us making my anxiety about walking into a big pile of shit skyrocket.

"No. It's insulting you'd think that, but on some level, I understand, I guess," they finally huff.

"It's just that—"

"You know that phrase 'when you know—you know'?" they interrupt.

"Yes."

After another long exhale, Arrow continues, "From the minute we connected, Alessa, I knew. You and I just clicked on a different level. I see so much disgusting shit on a daily basis. And you...you were just a breath of fresh air. As stupid as it sounds for someone who doesn't trust anyone for a living, I felt like...I could trust you from the beginning. I knew I found a kindred spirit in you."

"I felt the same." I smile at the receiver.

"So, you see, as crazy as this sounds from someone you have not met face to face, you can trust me. We're more similar than you think. Except my IQ is one hundred and sixty, I'm a tech prodigy, I have a huge dick and am a billionaire."

"Tiny differences," I laugh before adopting a serious tone. "Arrow, I love you. But if you're lying and you screw me over, I swear to god, billionaire or not, I'm going to poltergeist the shit out of you."

"As much as I'd love that, I'm not screwing you over. Once you're under my protection, nothing can touch you." A shiver runs down my spine at the cold tone in their voice and for the first time since I met them, I feel like maybe I have underestimated the hacker I have so easily made friends with. "In fact, I have some good news," Arrow continues. "You want to help that grumpy Mafia boyfriend of yours?"

"He's not my boyfriend," I grumble, forgetting all about the uneasiness I felt mere seconds before.

"Sure, sure, keep telling yourself that," they chuckle. "Anyway, I didn't feel like waiting any longer, so I sent Nicolosi a little present he wouldn't be able to resist. The asshole just took the bait. We're in."

———

THE EXCITEMENT of hacking into Nicolosi's system quickly ebbs into disappointment when Arrow has to go attend to some national level crisis.

I mean, priorities.

We barely scratch the surface before they get an alert and leave with a promise to look through Nico's hard drive and email as soon as they can. I wish they'd just leave it with me, my skin itching to get to the bottom of the scum bucket Nicolosi is, but I don't say a thing. Instead, I wish them good luck with the crisis and log off. But not before I hear a dark chuckle and a, "I don't need luck. The Albanians will need it once I'm done with them."

What the hell is Arrow entangled with? I shudder, unsure I even want to know and decide it's better if I just leave them to do their hackery magical juju.

All that's left for me to do is to wait and hope Arrow will have some free time sooner rather than later. To be honest, I'm a little pissed off I didn't insist on going through the files myself, but Arrow was adamant they want to be there as we go through the stuff. Nicolosi is a dangerous man, who deals with dangerous things. I guess my danger meter is a bit off because I really don't care about anything other than trying to figure out why everyone is so sure he's got it out for me. I can appreciate Arrow trying to keep me safe, though. Because we both know I'm the 'no plan with all guns blazing' sorta girl.

On a huff, I stuff a granola bar in my mouth and bring up the spreadsheets I swiped from Dante's laptop. Might as well do something less illegal and try to help him in the process. After all, he did give me a safe house to live in and two orgasms—the latter outweighing the former, if I'm totally honest. Even if he left straight after on a fool's errand.

I shouldn't be meddling in Mafia business but I also can't let it go. My brain despises anomalies, things that don't add up, things that seem odd or strange. So to quiet it down, it's best if I figure this thing out.

It's got nothing to do with my innate need to prove myself. Nothing. Not like Dante ever made me feel less than...who am I kidding? I still feel annoyed when I think of how he treated me in those first weeks. Still feel rage about not getting that receptionist job. Even if the current job he gave me pays a lot more for doing pretty much the same thing. Except, technically I'm not doing any work holed up in his mansion all by myself.

So now, I'm set on showing him I not only can look after myself but also that I'm an asset. One he'd be stupid to let go of. Dante Santoro might have Blackwood in the palm of his hand. He might be the head of the Mafia. But he's never gone head to head with someone like me before. And by the time I'm done, he'll be begging me to stay. Only thing is, with the lines blurring more and more each day, I'm no longer certain I should...

With a sigh, I skim through the numbers, my fingers playing with the chain around my neck. A glaring reminder.

I'm stalling.

Stalling from what I should *really* be doing. The one sole reason I came to this town. The only reason I should want to stay.

The pocket watch I threaded the chain through and placed around my neck is burning against the skin of my chest, hinting at its existence. Reminding me my family could be somewhere in Blackwood. I pull it out and look at it, turning it in my hand, tracing the pattern and the engraving on the casing before flipping it open to look at the unmoving hands taunting me about the time that stood still the day I was abandoned. Two thirty-eight. I don't know how many times I thought about winding it up, or moving the hands, but each time I stopped myself. I needed the reminder that once there was a time someone cared for me, no matter how abruptly it stopped.

"You better give that back to him before he realises it's missing."

# 25

# ALESSA

M y eyes snap up, meeting Massimo's face. His eyes, hidden behind a pair of glasses, are focused on *my* pocket watch.

"Who?" I ask, my gaze trained on him, as my hands begin to shake.

"Elena will be heartbroken if she thinks he's lost it again."

"Who did she give it to?" My voice comes out as a whisper, as my heartbeat picks up in my chest, an inkling of hope sprouting in the darkest part of my soul. I push it back, too fearful of the potential wreckage it could cause if it gets crushed again.

"Dante of course. She gives everything to that boy." My heart stops. "Where is she? It's not like the two of you to be separated. You're usually joined at the hip."

I swallow. "She went to grab something to drink." My voice sounds odd, like I'm under water, as my brain is trying to process Massimo's words. He must be mistaken. This pocket watch can't be Dante's, there's just no way.

Massimo laughs. "Of course, it's Margarita Monday. You love your Margarita Mondays..." He finally tears his gaze away from me, his eyes losing focus as he takes in the library.

Shit, shit, shit. When Angelo mentioned Massimo was unwell, I didn't ask what sort of unwell, but from the way his father is acting I have a feeling it's dementia. The only person giving me any information is technically senile. Just my fucking luck.

I laugh awkwardly. "You know us. Elena and I. We love Margaritas." God, where am I even going with this?

"You almost missed your high school prom, because of them. Must have heard the story a thousand times."

"We went to high school together?" The question slips out, but now that's it out, I have a million more and I can't stop them.

His eyes snap back to me.

"The pocket watch. Elena gave it to Dante?" I change the topic.

He nods. I try not to squirm under his gaze. "Just another thing for the boy to lose."

"Is Elena your sister? Daughter?"

His face tilts, his eyes sharp as he assesses me. "Who are you?" His voice turns ice cold, just like Dante's does when he's pissed off.

"Me?" My voice quivers as he squares his shoulders, towering over me, menacing.

"Who the hell are you and what the fuck are you doing in my house? Elena!" he booms, patting his dressing gown, probably for a gun. Any signs of the feeble old man from yesterday gone.

"I—I—"

"Massimo! Stop!" A nurse rushes into the library, grabbing Massimo by his arm, trying to move him away.

"Don't touch me!" He turns on her, but she's quick,

pulling a syringe out of her uniform and stabbing him. Almost instantly, his posture relaxes.

"I'm so sorry. I didn't know you'd be here, otherwise I'd have not let him go in by himself."

"It's fine," I reply shakily, despite not feeling fine at all.

She guides him through the open door and out of the library, just as she's about to leave she turns back to me. "Please tell Mr. Santoro this will not happen again."

I nod, confused as hell and a little scared, if I'm honest with myself. My heart thumps wildly in my chest, threatening to break through my ribcage as, with trembling hands, I pick up my things and leave the room.

My head is a jumble of information and uncertainties. He could be wrong. He may have been mistaken. For all I know, Massimo could be a madman. But...something in me tells me he's the first person who's been totally honest with me. All this time, like a fool, I've been four moves behind, running in the dark whilst trying to catch up, while he's been playing games with me. It's clear as day now that he knows a lot more than he's been letting on. What Dante doesn't know, though, is that I'm a worthy adversary. And let's not forget the bomb Angelo dropped on me. If Dante think he can just fuck around with me and forgt to mention he's promised to marry another he's sorely mistaken.

He wants to play games? Let's fucking play.

# 26

# ALESSA

They say money can't buy you happiness, but it sure as shit can be used as a weapon against Dante Santoro. Especially when it's his own.

It takes Arrow exactly five minutes to come through and earn the title of *my hero*. They were fully on board once I told them I'd like to make Dante's life miserable until he fessed up the information he'd been withholding from me. And even whilst dealing with their hacking crisis, they still take the time to send me Dante's black Amex details and wish me happy shopping.

The plan is simple. Be a pain in Dante Santoro's ass. Use every trick in my handbook to make him think twice about keeping shit from me. Make him miserable. Well, miserable might be a bit of a strong word, but knowledge is power, and in the last month, I have learned the likes and dislikes of one Mafia boss, my brain storing every little tidbit. I'm fully intending to take advantage of said knowledge and annoy the crap out of Dante every chance I get. Maybe it's the wrong approach—I mean, the saying goes, '*you catch more flies with honey*', but it's the only approach I know.

I need to know how on earth a three-year-old girl he's

never met before ended up with *his* pocket watch in her jacket. I need to know if somehow Dante and I are connected. And I highly doubt he'd offer that information freely.

A plan forms in my head while I stuff my face with yet another amazing meal courtesy of Lorena, the chef. With a grin on my face, I get to work, and four and a half Bibis later, I am satisfied with my life choices enough to call it a day. God bless next day delivery and credit cards with no limits.

It is not until I go to sleep that dread fills my veins. Lying in Dante's huge bed, my eyes snap open as the realisation dawns on me.

Technically, I am stealing from the Mafia.

If Dante were Don Corleone, I'd be facing repercussions. My limbs would be in danger of being cut off by a pissed off Mafia boss. Gruesome scenarios of what he could do to me once he finds out I stole his card details and went on a shopping spree keep running through my head. It takes hours for my racing heart to calm down and a few more to fall asleep.

Now, after a shitty night of sleep and a morning shower, I decide to just fuck it. *It is what it is.* And what it is, is me fighting for myself. Just like I have always done. My whole life, the lesson to not trust anyone but myself has been taught to me over and over again. Why should this be any different? Just because I got two orgasms and somewhat feel safe in his presence doesn't mean he's not *the 'big bad'*. Maybe I'm taking the wrong approach, putting myself in a position where the angry bear could come out and end my life with one swipe of his big, angry paw. Then again, poking the bear is my go to cheap thrill after all.

Just in case, I spend the morning looking over the spreadsheets I stole from Dante's computer. You know, to placate the grizzly in case limb removal is in the cards. Still unable to find answers to my DI-DO dilemma, I decide to take a different approach. If the letters won't speak to me, the numbers might. They usually do.

I go through each column, trying to spot trends, and finally stumble on something that makes a modicum of sense. There is a correlation between the numbers and cargo being received. On the dates that goods are being delivered, DI is larger than DO, and the opposite happens when things are going out. I try a few things, but it isn't until I subtract the smaller number from the larger that things start clicking into place. The number I get is similar to the weight of whatever the cargo is. Goods in and out - that's what the 'I' and 'O' must stand for. My brain finally lets go of its obsession with finding out what the acronyms stand for, and I focus on comparing the actuals instead. Everything seems fine until I start clicking through the tabs and notice a couple of the weight numbers logged differ from those on the main sheet. I go through each entry, comparing the two columns and find two others that are off.

I note the dates and shipping numbers, plus any other information I might need. The dates are two to three months apart, spread over the last year. Each time the cargo is listed as 'club equipment' and signed by the same guy.

*M. Conti.*

I look over my notes, the picture forming clear in my head. M. Conti and I have one thing in common it seems.

We're both swindling the head of the Mafia.

My next move should be to find the delivery tracking files or to get Arrow involved so we can find out more about those shipments tampered with. But Arrow is busy and there isn't much more I can do until I can get into Dante's laptop. So, instead of worrying, I push the thought to the back of my mind, stretch my arms above my head and finally go to the one place that has been calling to me ever since I stepped through the front door of this mansion.

THERE IS a slight breeze as my bare feet touch the cool stone of the courtyard. Misty tendrils hover above the calm surface of the heated pool as I think back to when I saw Dante's perfect body glide through the blue water. The day is clear but cold, the ozone in the air mixed with the smell of pine trees, foretelling a change in the weather. A thunderstorm is coming.

Disregarding the voice in my head telling me to turn back around and go inside, I take a deep breath and sit down at the edge of the pool. My legs are trembling as I tentatively stretch them out and ease my feet into the water, dipping my toes in. It takes a couple of minutes of being still, but my body finally relaxes. Soon, I'm swirling the water around, watching the ripples grow then disappear, getting used to the sensation of my feet feeling weightless.

In all my years of running, I never let myself experience this before. Never felt the lake water on my legs, never even had a real bath, always opting for the shower, rushing to get away or get somewhere. It feels odd and comforting at the same time, how my feet float on the surface, pushed out by the water around them.

Before I know it, I'm up, stripping down to my brand new La Perla underwear and walking down the steps until the warm water touches my chin, my eyes focused on the other end of the pool, still a few meters away. It would be so easy to take another step. Then another until my toes could no longer reach the bottom. Let the water consume me. No matter how many times I have thought of this before, I can no longer imagine myself doing it, at least not right now, with answers so close I can almost see them.

"Pools are for swimming, not just standing in them."

## 27

## ALESSA

I squeak, jumping in place and swallowing a mouthful of salty water in the process. I'd be impressed at the fancy saltwater pool if I wasn't currently hacking up a lung and trying to stay alive. Finally, after I'm sure drowning is no longer in my immediate future, I tread to the edge of the pool and, holding onto the ledge, I look up at Angelo.

"I'd totally be swimming if I knew how to, but never learned, so..."

"Get out of the pool," Angelo orders, his jaw tighter than a pair of spandex shorts. Silly, silly Mafia boy. Doesn't he already know that I don't take well to orders? Dante should have warned him. But I suppose it's not really Angelo's fault his brother has the communication skills of a toddler.

Smiling, I let go of the ledge and slip my hands back under water before taking a few steps away. I'm careful, but fast enough for him not to realise what I'm doing until I'm out of reach. "For fuck's sake, Alessa. Saint is going to kill me if you drown in his pool on my watch."

I cock my head to the side. My curiosity piqued. "Why did you refer to him as Saint? I don't get it." From my observations, he's as far from a saint as one can be so the nick-name really doesn't work.

"I'll tell you if you get out of the pool," he rebuts.

"Tell me *and* I will get out of the pool." I arch my eyebrow and take a step in the direction of the deep end.

"Jesus, she's got a death wish, and she's going to drag me with her... Fine. Fine!" he shouts as I take another step, enjoying the desperation in his voice. "Just go back to where you were first before I have a heart attack. Please." He adds the last bit while I try to hold in my triumphant grin.

Since he asked so nicely, I decide to not stress him out further and with a sigh, I finally move a couple of steps toward the shallow end of the pool.

"Dante is going to have his hands full with you," Angelo murmurs.

I don't tell him he already does. I wait for his explana-tion instead, like the good girl that I am.

"We're all *Saints*," he starts, placing his thumb and index fingers on his temples, rubbing them in a circular motion.

"Like the whole Mafia? Or more like we're all saints walking this earth every day churchy propaganda?"

He sniggers. I'd take a step back, but he's quick to continue. "No. *We* as in Dante, Luca and I. Santoro roughly translates to 'born on All Saints' Day'."

"So it's just your surname?" I know I sound disap-pointed, but I was hoping there was a bit more to that. "I was hoping there was more to it," I say just that.

"We all had blonde hair when we were kids, and our mum used to call us her little Saints. It stuck. Except we're no longer blonde, and no one would dare to call us little."

"Oh?"

"They wouldn't want to lose their life for disrespect."

I roll my eyes at the typical Mafia macho man talk and make my way to the steps. A deal is a deal.

Angelo groans. "What the fuck are you wearing?"

"I didn't have a swimming suit." I turn to him, only to discover his back is to me. "Are you okay?"

"Just—Just put something on before my brother finds out and loses his shit."

I huff, forcing my jeans and top over my wet body. Whatever.

"So, your mum used to call you Saint?" I ask.

"Yup."

"You can turn around now," I say, grabbing my shoes from the floor and walking barefoot back to the house, leaving wet footprints with each step. "What's her name?"

"Her name was Elena." His voice is distant and sad. But I can't stop the thrill that runs through me at another puzzle piece fitting neatly. It must be the same Elena Massimo was referring to.

"I'm sorry, did she pass away recently?"

"When we were kids. Let's get something to eat." He changes the topic.

I follow after him, disregarding the uncomfortable feel of the wet underwear under my clothes. I should really go change out of them, but I'm too excited about Angelo's sharing mood. "So how does anyone know which Saint someone is referring to when they mention your nickname? Is it like the Royal first, second, and third?"

Angelo chuckles, rounding the corner to the kitchen and going straight to the fridge. I sit in my now usual chair at the kitchen island, waiting for him to explain.

"Well,"—he turns to me, holding out a Tupperware with pasta in it, to which I nod eagerly—"if they're trembling and look ready to pass out with fear when saying Saint, they most likely are talking about Dante. If they're terrified, it's probably me. And if they're just a little scared, then it's Luca."

"Full of yourself much?" I chuckle.

A hand slams on the countertop, making me jump in my seat. Angelo's frame looms over me as he sneers, "You just haven't seen what we're capable of. Just because I'm nice to my brother's newest play thing does not mean I'm nice to everyone else. You should remember that."

I clear my throat, blinking, well aware of who I'm dealing with. "So, what—"

"No more questions." Angelo turns his back to me, ending the conversation abruptly. I follow his movements as he pops the pasta and sauce into the microwave. His voice is back to his usual cheery one, and his posture relaxes as he sets the timer on the microwave, whistling to himself. My mouth opens as I watch him. Seriously, one of the Santoro brothers is bound to give me a whiplash from all these mood changes.

"Angelo."

I spin in my seat, curious to see who the owner of the smooth baritone is. In the short time I've been here, Angelo, Dante, Massimo and his carer are the only people I've seen, so my spidey senses are full on tingling from excitement.

"Hello." I grin at the man standing in the entrance. His black suit covered back ramrod straight as he ignores me completely, waiting for Angelo to answer.

"What is it, Fred?" Angelo sounds bored as he leans down, watching the spinning plate in the microwave.

Fred clears his throat, his eyes darting to me for a split second. I'd have missed it if I wasn't paying attention to him. I wonder what Fred is short for.

"Manfred? Frederick? Alfred?" I mutter, my eyes narrowing. Fred just doesn't suit him. "Want some pasta, Wilfred?" I watch his face for clues. No, that doesn't sound right either. Belfred's eyes crinkle almost imperceptibly.

"Seriously?" Angelo sighs. I can feel his eye roll on my

back, but I choose to ignore it, because I'm gracious like that.

Freddie clears his throat once more, his eyes momentarily moving to me before landing on the man standing behind me. "There—uhm—" he clears his throat again, eyes moving to me once more before moving up to the ceiling then back to Angelo.

A few things happen.

The microwave pings. Angelo swears, most likely burning his fingers on the hot plate. I decide to investigate our guest up close and hop off my stool, walking to him before circling him like a little shark.

"So, which one is it?" I ask at the same time Angelo growls, "Spit it out, Fred."

*Fred* ignores me and looks straight at Angelo. Despite his bad judgement in top priorities, I have to admit he smells nice. He's also very handsome. Tall and muscly, filling his suit up to perfection. His jaw is smooth, like he's just shaved, full lips sitting atop a square chin, shadowed by a straight nose. He doesn't look like a Fred. He should be called Augustus, David or maybe Caesar. Something strong and Roman, definitely not Fred.

"Packages." Fred finally speaks, his eyes bouncing to me as I make another circle around him.

At his words I straighten, excitement building in my stomach.

"Packages?" Angelo and I ask in unison, albeit my voice is an octave higher from excitement.

"They're here!" I jump in place and skip past Fred, all but forgetting about my investigation into his proper name.

"What the fuck now?" Angelo sighs as I run out of the room.

Well, Angelo, the fun is about to begin.

# 28

# ALESSA

F red never divulges what his name is short for. Despite me nagging him as he lugs all my deliveries to the spare bedroom I'm supposed to be sleeping in. And I would sleep in there if I wasn't a big wet blanket and choosing to sleep in Dante's bedroom instead.

I *do* find out, however, Fred is one of *fifteen* guards who patrol the grounds surrounding the property. Fifteen! I'd feel safe with all these people protecting the mansion if I wasn't too busy beating myself up over not even checking out the place properly and being totally oblivious to their presence. *Very* unlike me. Usually, I'd be all vigilant, checking out all plausible routes of escape, but apparently, two out-of-this-world orgasms render a girl incapable of coherent thoughts since, like a blissed out dumdum, I've been wandering around happy as a clam, not caring one bit that there might be other people around.

Once Fredster is gone, I get busy opening the parcels and... 'sprucing' up Dante's house. I start with his bedroom, adding the red cashmere sweaters and ties into his wardrobe. All Italian brands, of course. Then I arrange a crimson bedspread and cushions on his bed. After that, I move through each room, adding red accents everywhere. Vases, throws, cushions, a rug for the living room, a standing mixer and a set of utensils for the kitchen. I even got a bunch of red sports bottles and towels for the gym. I'm nothing if not thorough.

Finally, happy with the results, I get back into the kitchen and start on part two of my plan. Honest moment here—I'm not a skilled cook. I mean, what I make is edible, but by no means is it Micheline chef standard. I cook to survive, not to impress. So you can imagine, with that ethos, baking was never a skill I dabbled with. Something I truly regret now as I look at the complicated recipe for red velvet cupcakes. Am I going overboard with all things red? Probably. But like I said, I'm very thorough.

Two hours later, the kitchen looks like a flour massacre took place in it, and I was the main victim, if the red food dye splotches are anything to go by.

Nevertheless, I remain positive as I grab the tray of red looking blobs, vaguely resembling cupcakes and head out of the kitchen.

"Oh, Freeeddyyy," I call out cheerily, poking my head out the front door.

Not even thirty seconds go by before Fred jogs over, smiling, no doubt smelling the delightful homemade goods. "Hey, Alessa."

"I baked some cupcakes, want some?" I push the tray in front of him.

"Cupcakes?" He looks sceptically between my face and the shapeless things on the tray before plucking one out and bringing it to his mouth. Just before it touches his lips, he hesitates. "You're not trying to poison me, are you?"

I gasp, aghast. "Why, Frednando! How could you even think that? We're practically best friends, you and I." Thing is, I'm actually trying to make him love me. In a platonic way. And if there's one thing I have learned from daytime TV, is that the way to a man's heart is through his stomach. Once Dante gets home and sees all the changes I have made, and all the money I've spent, I'll need as many people in my corner as possible. Not that one person, or even a crowd, would be able to stop him from ending my life if he was so inclined. But maybe, just maybe, they could convince him to let me explain first.

Fred reluctantly takes a small bite of the cupcake. His eyes flutter closed as he stuffs the rest in his mouth, moaning appreciatively. "So good," he murmurs, his mouth full.

Not gonna lie, I feel pride and a sense of accomplishment as I watch him reach for another cake. It's most likely the sugar content in them. If we're being all nitpicky, I'll admit I might have misread the amount required in the recipe, but it's all good.

"Something smells good. What do you have in there?"

I whip my head to the side from which the deep baritone came from and am met with yet another smiling, tanned, suited and way too handsome man.

"Why thank you." I smile back. "It's Chanel. Would you like a flatcake?" I'm not going to pretend that the things on the tray can be called anything else at this point. Bake Off material they are not.

He snorts, but unlike Freddyteddy, does not comment on my bake and just puts the whole thing in his mouth, humming with delight as he chews. This guy is quickly becoming my favourite. Fredkins better watch out.

Shortly, I'm surrounded by a group of tall and gorgeous looking men, all excited and fawning over my cupcake disaster. Seriously, have I been missing something? Are all of these guys Italian? Because I've clearly been living in the wrong country all these years.

"These are amazing, Alessa," Antonio mumbles, blushing, as he snatches the last one of the tray.

"They look awful, though." I bite my lip, squeezing my fingers around the tray. If I'm to paint Dante's life red, I want to do it in style, not with flat as pancakes, sad excuses for red velvet cupcakes that contain ten times your daily allowance of sugar.

"Maybe you need to start with something easier?" Fred pipes up. "Chocolate chip cookies?" he adds hopefully.

All the faces around me nod enthusiastically.

"It's got to be red, though," I mumble.

"How about a cherry pie?" Mario asks.

"That could work," I reply in thought. It would be a red surprise once he cuts into it. It could totally work. And I remember a recipe I saw when I was browsing for ideas.

"We could taste test." Fred smiles.

I laugh. Of course they're up for eating sweet food.

"Totally, just let us know, and we'll be right here," Mario says.

"It doesn't even have to be dessert," my sweet best friend Antonio adds. "We're just a growing bunch of men, constantly hungry."

"Growing sideways," Lorenzo laughs.

"Don't you all worry. I've got you. Can't believe you have to stand around the property for hours on end and don't get fed. Absolute disgrace. I'll be sure to tell Dante what I think about it when he gets back." I scowl.

About ten puppy dog eyes meet my eyes. Seriously. Whoever said guns are the worst weapon has yet to stand in front of ten handsome Italians while they make puppy dog eyes at you. Honestly. These guys know exactly how to make their good looks work to their advantage. My brain, which was all 'Dante this' and 'Dante that', is currently going 'Dante who? I want to lick one of these tasty men, please'.

"I better get back, though. Gotta clean that kitchen."

"Do you need help?" good old Freddy asks. He clearly has no clue about the state the kitchen is in.

"That would be wonderful," I exclaim eagerly, startling some of the puppy dog eyes away.

I can tell from the expressions on their faces as soon as they walk in, they all regret their decision. But no take backs. I put them all to work faster than they can say 'Dante Santoro is the worst boss we've ever had'. Their impeccable work ethic has the kitchen spick and span in under ten minutes, and before I know it, I'm alone again, standing in front of a bunch of ingredients which, with a little luck, will resemble a cherry pie once I'm done with them.

When the pie is in the oven and I'm almost done with the kitchen cleanup, Fred pops his head in again.

"Another delivery."

I look up, confused. I thought everything I ordered had arrived already, but I must have missed something. Racking my brain for what I could have possibly forgotten, I follow Fred to the main entrance, where I'm met with a large brown box.

Now, before I continue, I'd like to insert a caveat here. In all my years on this earth, I have not received presents. Not on birthdays. Not Christmases. No 'just because gifts'. Nothing. Zilch. Nada.

So excuse my excitement as I tear into a package I have not expected. With the delivery box shredded into tiny pieces, I freeze, gazing upon the most beautiful thing I could ever imagine.

My phone buzzes in my pocket, and I pull it out, answering without taking my eyes off the thing I most definitely didn't order.

"By the panting coming through the phone, I can safely assume my gift has arrived."

"Arrow," I whisper, my free hand reaching out to stroke the shiny red surface of the handlebar.

They clear their throat. "It's nothing, really. You've just been so obsessed with the idea of a scooter I figured someone ought to get you one. Just to shut you up."

"It's red." My fingers stroke down the column to the wheel, then the porous deck.

"Might as well go with the colour scheme you had in mind. What's one more thing?" they chuckle. "Well, actually, a few more things. There's a red helmet and elbow and knee pads, too, and a little bracelet."

"Arrow..." My voice comes out choked up as tears well in my eyes. "It's perfect. Thank you so much. And I'm putting the bracelet on right now. The scooter charm is perfect."

"Oh my god. Stop it. It's nothing."

"It's *not* nothing. It's the first gift I have ever received."

There's a sharp intake of breath, and my eyes lift briefly to meet with Fred's. He looks confused, his eyebrows drawn, so I smile at him reassuringly before looking back at the beautiful scooter in front of me.

"I'll be like all these techy billionaires now," I bite my lip.

"If you wanted to be just like me, you should have said. I'd have gotten you some abandonment issues and dubious morals."

I laugh. "I've got those all on my own, but thank you for the offer."

"Well, take the Red Devil for a spin. I've got places to be, computers to hack."

"Arrow?"

"What's up, sausage?"

"You're the best friend I could ever wish for. Thank you for being you."

"Back at you, sister."

I rest my phone in my lap as I reach for the shiny red helmet, my fingers shaking.

Fred's warm hands envelop mine as he takes the helmet away from me. He gently places it on top of my head before locking the strap in place.

"What did you mean you've never got a gift before?" The fingers under my chin lift it up until my eyes meet his.

I swallow, my bottom lip trembling as my heart beats in grief for the life I could have had. "Exactly that."

"What about Christmas? Your birthday?"

My eyes flutter shut as my head shakes from side to side, almost imperceptibly.

"How?" Fred sounds confused, his fingers dropping from my chin and wrapping around my hands, enveloping them in his warmth.

Sucking in a large breath, I open my eyes and look up, meeting his gaze. "I'm a stray, Freddy." I shrug.

His lip twitches. "A stray?"

"I was abandoned as a toddler, in foster care since then until I ran away at thirteen."

All signs of mirth leave his features as my words penetrate. "What about your foster families?"

"They never were real families. I'd have been better off living on the streets." I shrug again. "I don't even know what a family should feel like." My nose tingles.

Fred swoops me in one motion onto his lap and cradles me in his arms.

"Alessa," he murmurs into my hair, rocking me. A tear slides down my cheek. It's stupid, really. I've never cried because of my situation. But here, in Fred's arms, I feel so vulnerable. Yet free at the same time. Like it's okay to be sad for what has been. What should have been. "No matter what happens, you have a family now. I'll be your family. Pretty

234

sure the boys would agree with me, too. Fifteen minutes in your presence is all it took for them to love you."

"Bullshit," I chuckle.

"It's true. You're amazing, and don't you dare deny it."

"I'd never deny the truth," I chuckle, wiping my eyes on my sleeve.

"Good. Now, let's see your scooting skills. Just let me take a photo first." Fred grins before getting up.

I pose like the big nerd that I am. Dressed in the whole getup before taking my new toy for a spin around Dante's property.

# 29

## ALESSA

Having fun and making friends is exhausting. In fact, by the time the evening comes and the skies darken, I'm so tired I basically crawl into Dante's comfy bed and burrow under his warm blanket.

Surrounded by his fading scent, I toss and turn, trying not to think about where the hell he is and why whatever he's doing is taking him so long. The worry that something has happened to him is a constant throbbing pain behind my rib cage. And despite the fiery anger lit by the discovery of his deceit, I find myself caring more than I'd ever expect. It's a feeling I've never experienced before, a combination of a raw ache in my chest, a tightness in my throat and a heaviness in my stomach.

Normally, I'd be all over Google trying to figure out what I am dying of, but this time, I have an inkling of what's happening and am pretty sure only one thing can cure this. Or person, I should say.

I think...

Gah! This is harder than I thought.

I think... I miss Dante.

I miss teasing him. His heated stares. His angry

demeanour. The ticks in his jaw when I say something aggravating. But most of all, I miss the way his whole body melts when he holds me against him.

God, I miss the way he touches me. And how he knows the exact amount of pressure with which to stroke my skin to make me feel like I'm on fire. How even when he's angry, he's the only person who makes me feel safe. And, as hard as it is for me to admit it, I miss the feeling he elicits in me when his fingers are inside me.

I've never given much thought to what sex could be like. Not after having my virginity so brutally taken away from me at such a young age. Since then, I've never felt the desire to explore that part of me. Never felt attracted to anyone in that way. Don't get me wrong, I could appreciate a fine male specimen, but no one has ever made me feel... *empty*. Like I needed to be naked, skin to skin. Taken. Filled. Craving the feeling of the other person inside me.

Until *him*.

Until his angry eyes made my heart stutter, and my pulse race.

I used to think I was not meant for any of that. Destined to end up alone, and to never experience that sort of closeness with anyone. I didn't think it could feel good, and I was definitely not eager to find out how bad it could be. In fact, before coming to Blackwood I was sure I was asexual. I wasn't even that bothered about exploring myself. Until *he* touched me. Until today.

Before I know it, my hands travel south, brushing my exposed skin, while my brain conjures up images of Dante, bare chested, coming out of the swimming pool. I stroke my breasts, thinking back to when he made my world explode into a thousand little pieces. Touching the skin just above my panties and skimming the line, I imagine his calloused fingers doing it.

My breaths are coming fast as the temperature in the bedroom skyrockets. My body tingling with anticipation, waiting for the fireworks. Droplets of sweat gather at the nape of my back, and with a crazed growl, I kick off the blanket. I need more. More control. More freedom.

Dante's t-shirt is next. The same one I fished out of his closet just so I could feel a small part of him around me. So I could feel safe while asleep. I'm about to toss it to the side, but then I think better of it and put it right next to my face, inhaling the heady scent of Dante's cologne.

For a second, I feel like a weirdo. Almost naked, lying on a bed belonging to a man I was sure hated me while sniffing his t-shirt. But despite the sudden awkwardness, I don't stop my explorations. Instead, I finally slide my fingers under the cotton material and circle my clit, all the while thinking of the confusing gorgeous Mafia boss who acts like he hates me one moment, then treats me like I'm precious the next. Like, I'm worth savouring. Worth saving.

My hips rock against my fingers as I slide them over my wet slit before teasing my clit again, thinking back to when Dante's fingers were inside me. What would it feel like to have him again? But not just his fingers. I want to do everything. I want him to show me that sex could feel good.

I am desperate for the euphoria he brought me to. I'd give anything to feel his body against mine right now. No clothes, no barriers. Feel his weight on top of me. Feel his cock pressing against me. Inside me.

My fingers pick up speed, so does my breathing. I'm close. So close. I can feel my whole body tingling, the orgasm I'm craving just within reach. But every time I think I'm *there*, it evades me, the jumble of thoughts swirling in my head, not allowing me to let go.

With an angry growl, I rip my underwear down my legs and sink my fingers inside my pussy, trying to mimic the way Dante touched me. Trying and failing to jump over the ledge.

Tears spring to my eyes as, frustrated, I circle my clit over and over again. Why isn't this working?

Why did it work when he did it and not now? Is it because I'm doing it wrong? Is it because I gave over control to him? Let him put his hand around my throat while he finger fucked my pussy? I was the one holding the power, my foot hovering over the brakes, but he was the one in charge of steering my body.

I try. I try so hard my brows are creased in concentration as fever engulfs my body. I think of everything Dante has done. I think of the way he smells. I think of how his mouth tasted when he kissed me.

But I must be broken because, despite my efforts, nothing happens. Could Dante have ruined me for all future orgasms?

Frustrated, I groan before swinging my legs off the bed and naked as the day I was born, head outside of the bedroom, down the stairs and into the dark courtyard. Not caring one bit that someone could see me. I'm too far gone for *that*. My body heated to the point ice caps would melt, craving the weightlessness of the water. Maybe if I'm deprived of my senses, I can forget about the dull ache inside me.

As soon as I open the patio door, the chilled air assaults me, causing goosebumps to erupt all over my skin.

"Jesus wept," I hiss, jumping towards the lit up pool, steam rising up in misty billows. Maybe this naked walk was not one of my best ideas. I briefly consider turning around and going back inside, but then my toes reach the steps, and before I know it, I'm submerged up to my neck in the warmth. My heated skin tingling as the current from a nearby jet brushes against my mound. An involuntary moan escapes my lips as I tilt my body so I can feel more. Once again, I spread my legs, reaching down with my fingers to brush against my clit. But the release I've been craving is still out of reach. I'm so hot, so frustrated I could cry. With my bottom lip wobbling, I let my legs fold and kneel on the bottom of the pool, holding my breath until my lungs burn.

A flash of genius strikes me as I get back to the surface. Is this it? The missing ingredient?

Without a thought, I dive back under water, my fingers pressing against my swollen clit.

# 30

## DANTE

The gravel crunches beneath the wheels of my car as I pull into the faintly lit driveway. It's only been a few days, but I'm already feeling uneasy. I need to make sure she's safe.

Not because I care.

I fucked up once already, leaving her to be swallowed by the system. So now I need to repent. Make sure I fix what I've done wrong.

Definitely not because I care...

Jumping out of the car, I rush through the front door and into the house in less than a minute. It takes me no time to run up the stairs and reach her bedroom. With my hand on the doorknob, I lean my forehead against the cold wood and take a deep breath. I know I'm being unreasonable with my need to see her, the need to make sure she's unharmed. I can't explain it. This feeling is messing with my head so much I'm starting to lose myself. Just to prove to myself I'm not completely crazy, I should turn away. Go to my bedroom instead. But then I might be assaulted by her scent on my sheets. With that, my mind snaps back to a few nights ago when my fingers were buried deep inside Alessa's pussy as I made her come.

"Fuck," I growl, my fisted palm tapping against the wall —when all it wants to do is punch a hole through it—in hopes of trying to shake myself from the memories. From this obsession I have developed.

I can't lose it like that—at the mere thought of her pussy. I'm a grown ass man, for fuck's sake. My dick has other ideas, though, as it strains against the thin material of my sweats.

Resigned, I twist the knob and quietly open the door, my heart pumping fast for no apparent reason. It's only when I see the room is empty that I realise I'm holding my breath. Hesitant, I take a step inside, taking in the space around me. It feels cold, unlived in. Has Alessa decided to sleep in a different guest room? I know she's been staying in my house and hasn't left, because I've been getting regular updates from Angelo and my men.

I check the other rooms nearby, but every single one looks the same—cold, empty and untouched except for the red coloured knick knacks added. I fight the smile trying to break through despite my annoyance; she sure has been busy. There's only one room left. My bedroom. My heart picks up speed again as my feet take me closer. This time I don't hesitate when I push the door open and step in. Her scent instantly surrounds me, and my dick wakes up once again, hoping for playtime. Has she been sleeping here? Her clothes are on the floor near the bed, which looks like someone had a fight with the sheets in it, and lost. I press my hand against the mattress, only to find it cold. She's not here, but she has been.

The smirk on my face feels odd, almost like a smile, as I walk out of the bedroom and head back downstairs to find her. I can play hide and seek, but when I find her, she'll have to pay. And I might just have a few ideas in my mind how she could do it.

Just as I'm about to head to the kitchen, something catches my eye. Frowning, I turn around, trying to make sense of the feeling of unease pulsing through my veins. Something is wrong, but I can't quite put my finger on it.

Just to ease my mind, I turn around once more. When everything seems fine, I shake my head and start for the kitchen again only to stop dead in my tracks, my head slowly swivelling to the glass pane between the entry hall and the courtyard.

The lit up pool looks still and quiet, steam rising off the surface, unbroken by movements, despite the dark blob in the middle. The blob with dark hair strands floating around it.

"No," I gasp, choking on the lump in my throat. "No, no, no, no, no! Don't you fucking dare!"

I run straight through the glass pane. My mind having made the decision to get to the pool as fast as possible and calculating the way around and through the gym, not being optimal.

Because Alessa is in the pool. Not moving.

Alessa, who can't swim.

*My* Alessa.

I can't even feel the shards of glass clinging to my skin or the cuts on my arms and face as I dive straight into the pool and swim to where Alessa's lifeless body is crumpled on the bottom of the pool.

Like an arrow, I shoot through the water until I'm behind her. My arms reach around her waist and lift her up as I bounce off the bottom and push us both to the surface.

But then Alessa grasps my arms, digging her nails into my skin as she starts to wriggle against my grip.

"What the fuck?" she spatters as we break the surface.

"I could ask you the same. I thought you were dead."

She wriggles again, and I loosen my grip only to allow her enough room so she could face me.

"Dante," she whispers, her eyes searching mine, roaming over my face. "You're back. Where were you? What happened to your face?"

"I thought you drowned, Alessa," I grit through my teeth. "Why the fuck were you in the pool? I know you can't swim."

"Angelo is such a tattletale," she grumbles before rolling her eyes, and I want to spank her until her ass is red. My arms tighten around her body, pulling her closer as I tread the water towards the steps out. Her legs instantly wrap around my middle, and I shift her up, one hand supporting her backside.

That's when I realise. Or rather, my dick does.

Alessa is completely naked.

# 31

## ALESSA

I can't believe he's here. Holding me so close it's hard to tell where I end, and he begins. I try to remember why I was angry with him in the first place, but he's covered in bleeding cuts, and there's a small piece of glass coming out of his shoulder. It's all I can focus on. He's here. And he's hurt. I gently place my fingers against his cheek, right below a gash that's seeping blood, frowning at the amount of abrasions on his face, neck and arms.

"Why are you naked?" His growl is quiet, but despite the tornado of thoughts in my head, I hear him just fine. My cheeks burn hot because I just remembered what I was doing the moment he pulled me from underwater and scared the living daylight out of me. When I don't reply, his arm tightens around me, and the hand holding up my butt digs into my wet flesh. My skin erupts in goose pimples, the emptiness in my core pulsating full force—stronger than ever, now that Dante is back—and it takes immense power not to rock against him and moan with neediness.

Because that's what it is. I need him. I want him. But I also want to know what the hell happened to him.

"Why are you covered in cuts?"

His eyes close, irritation raising his nostrils as he inhales. "I thought you were dead, Alessa. I saw your body on the bottom of the pool and... I thought you were fucking d—ead." His voice breaks on the last word.

"I'm okay." I hold on to him tighter, hoping my touch reassures him. "I was just holding my breath."

"Why? Why would you—"

"It's stupid," I interrupt, hiding my head in the crook of his neck.

"Tell me." His fingers dig into my bum harder, almost breaking the skin. But the pain actually feels good. So good the butterflies in my stomach take off again, and I have to hold back a moan.

"Let me clean your wounds first, then I'll tell you," I soothe in a raspy voice, hoping it'll distract him from wanting answers.

Dante nods curtly, then turns to walk back home. A glint of something catches my eye, causing a gasp to escape my lungs.

"What happened to the glass? It's all broken."

My question is met with silence.

"Dante?"

"I thought you were dead." He grits, his jaw tight.

I'm confused.

Dante sighs as we walk inside the house, our wet bodies stuck to each other. "It was the fastest way I could get to you."

I nearly choke on the squeak that's trying to tear out of my chest. My heart is hammering as a swarm of butterflies takes off in my tummy. He broke through the window to get to me. He's hurt because he was worried about me. Heat prickles behind my eyes. No one has ever cared for me. No one would have cared if I was dead. But he does. Enough to injure himself.

246

I lean my head against his shoulder and inhale his intoxicating scent. Despite diving underwater to get me, he still smells exactly like the cologne I've been spritzing on myself and all over his room at night. On him, though, it smells a million times better.

"Thank you," I murmur. My lips against his throat. He shivers as he takes me up the stairs, not letting go until we're in his bathroom. Slowly, he puts me on the ground, sliding me down his body inch by inch. Instantly, I miss the feeling of being wrapped in him. His warmth.

His back is to the mirror as he stands in front of me, his fists clenching and unclenching, his gaze focused on the pool of water gathering at our feet.

Without thinking, I reach behind him, opening the cabinet and taking out tweezers and alcohol wipes before reaching out and lifting his chin to face me.

"Let me take care of you," I whisper.

His eyelids flutter closed again, but he nods slightly. I smile a small smile and turn to grab a towel to wrap around myself, but just as my fingers reach the soft cotton, his hand wraps around my wrist, pulling it back.

"No," he says firmly. "Like this."

I blush, hesitating. While my body was right against his, I forgot I was even naked. Now, though, with the first-row seat to the 'Get an eyeful of Alessa's boobs and ass' show, things seem a bit more exposed. But when I look at him, he's not ogling my body, probably sensing my unease. He's looking at my face, studying it. I bite my lip before taking a step back to him, resolute about what to do next.

Two can play this game.

Not breaking contact from his eyes, I step to him, then lift his wet t-shirt up his torso and over his head, losing his gaze just for a second before we're staring at each other once again. Then I move down, kneeling on the floor as I take his sweatpants off. He's not wearing socks, and he must have kicked off his shoes before he jumped through the window because the pool of water beside us is mixed with red. Once Dante is naked, I stand up again and break eye contact, reaching for the tweezers and sterilising them before looking back at his face. There are small pieces of glass lodged in his wounds, and I get to work, gently taking them out and dropping them into his empty water glass. Each time there's a clink of glass against glass, Dante blinks. That's the only emotion coming from him, apart from his undivided focus on my face. I move from his face to his shoulders and arms. Still, he doesn't wince or sharply intakes a breath despite the larger glass shards.

When I get to his feet, I'm the one sucking in the air. Several of his cuts are bleeding, the red liquid flowing freely.

"This might hurt," I say as I lift his foot to look at his sole and finding a piece of glass stuck in there. "Please don't kick my face. I happen to like how it looks."

A small smile greets me back. "I won't. I happen to like how it looks, too," he hesitates. "I'm going to close my eyes, Alessa."

"Okaaay."

I pull the piece of glass out and check his other foot.

"I—" he starts, then stops. His tattooed knuckles grip the countertop, and I briefly wonder if it's because my face is currently at dick level or because I'm hurting him. As soon as my mind utters the word 'dick', my eyes glance at the appendage I have been avoiding looking at with all my powers, and Jesus Christ, I nearly scatter back. Because I'm face to face with a one-eyed monster. At half mast, his penis is thick and long, with small veins running up and down the sides. He's uncut, and the head is peeping out from behind his foreskin. I have the biggest urge to touch it. See if it's as smooth as it looks. Like velvet. "I don't like blood."

I nearly squeak and jump on the floor as Dante brings me back to the ground and away from his beautiful dick. My eyebrows scrunch, trying to process what he's saying. "You —you don't like bl—but you're mafia..."

"So?"

"I mean, you have a gun. You seem like you know how to use it. Isn't blood like a daily thing for you?"

"There are many creative ways to kill a person." I can hear the smile in his voice as my heart picks up. "Many of them don't involve blood."

I bite my lip, adding another piece to the puzzle that is Dante Santoro, and trying to pretend he didn't just allude to killing people on the daily, albeit creatively. It's curious, though—the head of the mafia disliking blood.

"Is it just your own, or others too?" The question slips past my lips before I can stop it. I put his foot down and get back up, making sure his one-eyed monster is not within poking distance, just in case my libido decides I should let it poke one of my holes. Vagina. I mean the vagina.

"All blood. It..." he trails off, opening his eyes.

"Shower or wipes?" I lift the wipes in front of his face, smiling.

"Shower."

I nod, then step away from him until I'm in his walk-in shower, turning the knob to lukewarm water. "It what?" I prompt him from behind the glass panel.

Firm hands land on my hips as the one-eyed monster presses firmly against my buttocks, and his face lands in the crook of my neck, his stubble tickling me. My body ignites as my palm slaps the tile in front of me, holding on for dear life.

"It's a secret, *la Fata*. Are you trying to bewitch me to give you all my secrets?" he whispers, peppering small kisses on my shoulder while his roaming hands move from my hips to my belly, his index fingers flicking my belly ring. Every touch of his calloused fingers makes me feel weak.

"If it works." I shrug, pretending the close proximity doesn't affect me. My wobbly knees say differently.

"Have you been sleeping in my bed?" He pulls my hips flush against him, causing a gasp to escape my throat, my body arching into him.

"You first."

"Are we keeping score?"

"Yes."

"You're cheating then. You still haven't told me why you were naked in my pool."

I shiver as his warm fingers trace circles over my lower belly, then up my body, before pinching my nipple and spinning me around. I no longer have control over my body as he manoeuvres me around the shower until we're both under the warm spray of water. Rivulets of blood make their way down his neck to the avenging angel on his chest, making it look like it's raining blood over the desolate graveyard.

"I haven't finished cleaning you up."

"Blood always made me nauseous. I just—I don't like the way it smells, the colour—I just don't like it."

"Is this why you asked if I was a virgin? You were worried about the blood?"

He stills, his eyes two stormy whirlpools as he looks down on me.

"Never. With you... it's never about me, Alessa. Fuck. I—I lose my mind around you. For you. What the fuck are you doing to me?" Anguish replaces the storm like the simple act of admitting he cares for me causes him great pain.

"I'm sorry," I apologise, sneaking my arms around his waist and pressing my face against the avenging angel. "You don't have to look at the blood. I'll make it all go away."

Understanding about his reactions while I was taking the glass out of his cuts dawns on me. Little nuances I've picked up on since we met suddenly make sense and for the first time since my brilliant idea of turning Dante's house into an oasis filled with red things, I question myself if I've done the right thing. If maybe, I've crossed a line I wasn't aware of.

"Alessa," he rasps into my hair, his heart galloping so hard I can feel it against my cheek.

"I'll take care of you." I sneak my hands around his midsection and press myself against him, closing my eyes. The feelings in my chest foreign and overwhelming.

He stills in my embrace, his body becoming rigid. "No."

I stiffen at the sound of his voice. No?

He unwraps my arms from around me and takes a small step back as a feeling of utter shame and rejection comes over me.

Then he drops to his knees in front of me. Blood mixed with water pooling around him.

"I'll take care of *you*." He lifts my leg and places it around his shoulder as his face dives between my legs.

# 32

## ALESSA

The first stroke of his tongue against my pussy has me throwing my head back and nearly choking on the shower water. But nothing matters except Dante's languid strokes against my slick entrance. He hums in delight as his tongue breaks through the seam and dives into my wet channel. My hands tangle in the wet strands of his hair, and I fight the urge to either pull his face against me hard and hump it like there's no tomorrow or push it away because it's too much. And it is. The stubble on his face—rough against my thighs. His nose rubbing my clit each time he moves his tongue. I've never felt anything like it. My legs begin to shake as his hands land on my bum, massaging and spreading my cheeks. I've got nothing to hold on to except the hair strands on his head. I moan as pleasure builds in the pit of my stomach, the steam in the shower becoming unbearable to breathe through. If this man ends up with no hair by the end of this, it'll be all his fault. A damn shame, but he'll have no one but himself to blame for it.

Dante attacks, eating my pussy like a man starved, and with each noise I make, he's more determined, more focused, and more attuned. It's clear as fucking day this man knows what he's doing, but what's unbelievable about this whole thing is that he listens. Each time I squirm, he eases off the pressure. When I moan, he relentlessly focuses on the spot over and over again until I see stars and can't take anymore. The feeling of emptiness overwhelms me once more, and I want to cry, teetering at the edge of what feels could be the absolute end of me.

Then Dante slips a finger inside me, his mouth moving onto my clit and sucking it hard as his finger rubs against a spot I didn't know existed.

Fireworks explode around me as I scream his name, my head falling back and cracking against the cold tile. But who cares about a potential brain injury when they're in the midst of the best orgasm of their life? Not this girl.

I'm still panting, trying to catch my breath, when he unwraps my leg from around his neck and sets it down on the ground before slowly getting back up, trailing kisses up my body as he stands until his forehead is pressed against mine.

Water cascades down his hair and face, joining at his chin and streaming down between us. I focus on the little cuts on his face, on a small scar just beside his nose. Anything but his enticing lips.

"I've been fighting this since the day you came back into my life, Alessa." His lips move, but the words don't quite register because somehow his face is even closer to mine, our breaths mingling with each other. "I should fight it still." He lifts his hand, his fingers holding up my chin. "It's the wise thing to do."

"Why?"

His eyes close for a few seconds, then open, ensnaring mine in some sort of a spell, rendering me unable to look away. "Because every time we do this, I want you to stay. I want to keep you. And I can't keep you, Alessa."

"Why?" I probe, needing to hear the truth from his lips.

"My life has never been mine. My path has been written before I was able to walk, my freedom taken from me with my father's signature."

"I don't understand."

"It's for the best. As much as I want you. Want this. I can never have you. It would be a dick move to try and take things from you, knowing I can't give you anything in return."

"What if I don't want anything in return? What if I want you to take things? What if I just give them to you?"

Dante sucks in a breath, the fingers around my chin tightening. "I could listen to you scream my name in pleasure infinitely—it's what I think heaven sounds like."

My lips lift in a smile. "You're confusing."

He smiles back.

"So, you don't want anything from me." It's more of a statement than a question.

His smile drops, his eyes narrowing. "I want *everything* from you, Alessa. That's the problem. I shouldn't, but I do. And I'm slowly losing the battle. I know what's the right thing to do."

"But?" My breathing speeds up.

"But... Just one taste, baby. Then I'll stay away." His mouth is pressed to mine as he whispers the words against my lips.

"Just one," I confirm. But I already know it's too late. One taste will never be enough. At least not for me.

He kisses my top lip, then the bottom one, before moving to each corner of my mouth and pressing his lips firmly against mine. I sigh because this feels so right, being this close to him. The lack of clothing or the fact he's just gone down on me is not even registering with me. He's a contradiction I can't get enough of. The hot and the cold. The anger and the blatant care he shows me in all his actions. All his hard ridges and the gentleness with which he holds me. The scruff of his beard against my skin and the soft, velvety feel of his mouth.

My arms wrap around him as he strokes his tongue against the seam of my lips, making them open instantly for him. I can vaguely taste myself as he kisses me, his tongue pressing against mine, gently probing. Taking his lead, I match his moves, then nip at his bottom lip. I have no clue what I'm doing, having never let anyone get this close to me before, but the anguished moan that escapes him, full of longing and desire, tells me I must be doing things right.

Then, as quickly as his lips were on mine, he steps away from me, leaving me cold and lonely without his embrace.

"Thank you," he says before turning away and walking out of the shower, then out of the bathroom.

"Fuck," I curse under my nose. Because this was one hell of a kiss. And despite me saying I want nothing in return from him. Despite me pretending I'm okay with him marrying someone he's been promised to most of his life and being so sure I've been in charge of this situation, it is clear I am lying.

## 33

---

## ALESSA

I take the red bathrobe I bought during the 'get everything you see in red to annoy Dante Santoro' shopping spree and wrap it around my wet body, then clean all the blood in the bathroom. It's stupid, but I hesitate with my hand on the door handle before walking out. I'm not sure if I'm more relieved or disappointed that Dante is not in the room when I walk out. In fact, he's gone altogether. Again.

I know because I take great care to wipe away the blood trail he left in the house and clean the glass away from where he Hulked through the window to get to me. With a sigh, I go back to his bedroom and curl up on his bed. The guest bedroom I'm supposed to be sleeping in feels just a bit too cold and empty. I'll sleep in there tomorrow. Tonight, I'll give myself one last time to soak in the faint scent he left behind.

When I wake up, it's bright, and I'm still alone in Dante's bed. Wearing nothing but the red bathrobe, which undid itself at some point in the night. The spot next to me is cold, but the smell of fresh pine and citrus is strong on his pillow. Did Dante sleep next to me but left before I awoke? Were his arms wrapped around me? I try not to imagine him cuddling up to me during the night because I know better. Dante Santoro is not a cuddling sort of man. He's cold, demanding and ruthless.

So how come when he's near, I feel safe and warm?

The guest bedroom is dark when I walk in, so I open all the curtains before heading into the attached bathroom to take a quick shower. Once sparkling clean, I mull over my choice of what to wear today. Despite what we shared last night and my hesitance after finding out his aversion to blood, which may be fuelling his dislike of the colour red, I still go with my initial plan, putting on a red bikini and a red wrap-around dress on top of it. Operation 'Find the truth' begins now.

Barefoot, I tip-toe downstairs and into the kitchen, stopping by where the shattered glass panel should be. I have no clue if Santoros have house elves or magical skills, but there's a fresh pane of glass where there was a Dante-shaped hole in the window.

With a shrug, I keep walking until I'm in the kitchen, rifling through the shelves in search of something sugary for breakfast. Apparently, shark week is upon us. What kind of monster would I be to deny my body sacred nutrients that keep womankind tolerable during those turbulent times?

"Good morning."

I squeal-jump, turning around to face Fred and Lorenzo standing on the other side of the kitchen island. A half-eaten chocolate bar is hanging out of my mouth as I take them in, in all their suited glory.

"Morning," I grumble, my mouth still otherwise occupied. "Coffee?"

They both nod, exchanging glances. I turn my back to them, pulling three cups and press way too many buttons on the complicated coffee machine, making it hiss and grumble in return.

Lorenzo sidles up to me and thankfully takes over as I growl, plopping my face on the cool marble of the kitchen counter.

"Rough night?" Fred asks, coming to my other side. I shrug my shoulders, not ready to speak full sentences yet, as a steaming cup of coffee lands in front of my forehead. Just the glorious smell has me perking up enough to smile in gratitude.

"Thank you," I sigh before inhaling the hot drink in four long gulps. "Hit me." I place the cup next to the coffee machine expectantly. Lorenzo bursts into laughter as Fred spins me around to face him.

"We've got something for you."

"Me?" My lips turn up, excitement making my heart speed up. "Really?"

"Yes, you." He lifts his hand, palm up, drawing my attention to a small object atop it. Curious, I step closer, reaching out to take the stone he's holding in his hand and examining it. "It's nothing special. But we were patrolling this morning, and Lorenzo spotted the red stone, and with all the red stuff delivered yesterday, we instantly thought of you and—" The words tumble out of his mouth at warp speed as my mouth stretches into a huge grin.

"You got me a stone?"

"It's stupid."

"It's a gift?"

"You know what? Just give it back. We'll chuck it."

I pull my hand to my chest. "Don't you dare! I love it!"

"You do?" Fredster's eyes look hopeful. "It's just you said you never get gifts and the boys and I..."

"You got me a gift." I throw my arms around him, placing a kiss on his cheek. "It's perfect, thank you."

"And you." I turn to Lorenzo. "Don't think I didn't hear you spotted this beauty." I skip over to him, smacking a loud kiss on his cheek and making him chuckle.

"Next time, it'll be something better, not a stupid stone. It's just we haven't left since yesterday and—"

"Stop it, you goof!" I exclaim, throwing my arms around him. "It's absolutely perfect, thank you."

A throat clears behind me. It's an angry sounding kind of throat clear. One that sends shivers up and down my spine and makes my thighs clench. I slowly peel myself away from Lorenzo and turn to face the music.

Or the angel of darkness. One and the same, really. Especially since he's wearing yet another tailored-to-perfection suit and a pissed-off expression to match. His neck is red, a vein pulsing underneath his ear, fists clenched tightly.

"Good morning." I take a step forward as Dante's eyes roam over my body. A slow perusal that starts at my toes and ends with a piercing stare right into my soul. Everything else disappears as he takes a step forward and reaches for the bow on my dress.

"Leave," he growls, his other hand landing on my hip.

I can't look away from him, but just because I'm under some sort of a spell doesn't mean I can't sass. "Don't worry about him. He's just grumpy because he didn't get *any* last night." Not that I wasn't going to offer. He just left before I had a chance to reciprocate, but no one needs to know that detail.

"You're lucky they already left, Alessa. Undermining me like that in front of my men is a cause for punishment."

I swallow hard. "Punishment?"

"Severe punishment." The fingers on my hip grip me tighter.

"Oh?" I reply breathlessly as the other hand traces up

my body and in between my breasts until it wraps around my throat, pushing me against the counter.

"Spanking."

My thighs clench at his words.

"Behaviour like that will earn you a spanking."

I'm not sure if I'm mortified or aroused. I'm not a child to be disciplined. But something about his dark tone and the way he's looking at me like I'm the tastiest dish he's ever sampled has my skin burning.

A needy whimper escapes my mouth, making Dante's lips twitch into a smirk.

"You like the idea, don't you, *Fata*?"

My eyes flutter shut, but I nod.

"God. *Perchè sei così perfetta*?"

That's it. I'm done. If he wants a puddle on the floor, he should just keep speaking Italian to me.

"What am I to do with you?"

"Teach me to swim?" I reach for the bow on the side of my dress and pull on the string, untying it in the process. My dress falls open, revealing my red bikini.

Dante sucks in a breath. His hand leaves my throat and rakes through his hair as he takes a step back. Muttering something illegible. He turns away from me, holding onto the kitchen island and drawing my attention to the healing cuts on his hands.

"Unless it's going to hurt your cuts. I just—"

"Five minutes."

I bite my lip. "Are you sure?"

He doesn't answer. Instead, he reaches for his tie and loosens it. I don't question him, too worried he might change his mind if I do. Slowly, I walk towards the gym and through the door onto the courtyard. It's been getting colder with every day that passes, and today is no exception. My nipples pebble as a gust of icy wind assaults me, whipping my open dress about. I shrug it off, dropping it onto the cold stone beneath my feet, and walk down the steps into the warm water of the pool until I'm submerged up to my shoulders.

Dante walks out in nothing but his swimming shorts and dives into the pool at the deep end, swimming beneath the surface like he's Aquaman, the show-off, until he reaches me.

This has not been my best idea. I'm a period fuelled, horny mess of hormones, and this man is like catnip for my pussy. All droplets of water on tanned skin, muscles and tattoos. Despite being thoroughly satisfied last night, I'm desperate to feel him close to me again.

And when his strong hands wrap around my waist, I'm not disappointed.

# 34

## ALESSA

I am disappointed, *actually*.

As sexy as Dante teaching me how to swim was in my head, the reality turned out to be more of a choke on water and look like a wet dog situation.

Each day, after an hour of torturing me with his hotness in the swimming pool, Dante insists on a two-hour gruelling session in the gym. He's hell-bent on making sure I'm prepared for every eventuality. I'm hell-bent on having a repeat of what happened the first time he was with me in the gym, but to my dismay, he stays aloof and keeps himself at a distance, disappearing for hours every time I think we're about to get closer.

The boys bring me gifts every day. Little trinkets that are priceless to me. A fridge magnet, a book to read, a red scrunchy since they think I'm obsessed with red.

On a Friday, after an hour of being pinned by Dante to the training mat and fighting my horned-up brain from thinking of how it felt to ride Dante's fingers, I decide enough is enough. I'm no longer sure If I'm more annoyed that he's not trying to make a move or impressed.

Whatever it is, I'll have to bring out the big guns if I want a chance at getting some answers. Most importantly, despite the undeniable pull between us, I'm still pissed off he's been withholding information from me all this time, and I'm determined to make him pay. At least a little. I know he's noticed all the red items around the house, especially since I keep placing more of them everywhere—replacing his boring old things—but he has yet to comment on it.

Sweaty, on shaky legs and looking like I've been just put through the ringer, I make my way back into the guest room. I need an ice bath, painkillers and probably a nap, but all those things will have to wait.

"I was thinking I could make dinner for us tonight," I say, wringing my hands.

Dante halts in front of his door, his head tilting towards me. I don't know if he's surprised I've not been back to his bedroom, but I've been intent on staying by myself ever since he got back in hopes he'll break first. Obviously, it hasn't worked. In fact, I'm pretty sure he's relieved I'm not in his face all the time since he's been so adamant he's not the right person for me. "You want to cook?"

"Sure." I shrug, my eyes darting to his chin, avoiding the two pools of molten chocolate like wildfire. There's only so much heated eye contact a woman can take before turning into a gooey mess. "I could make pasta. I take it you like Italian food?"

His eyes drop to my lips. "I can't get enough of *it*." The deep rumble of his voice has my knees trembling. I could pretend it's from the intense workout, but I don't like lying, especially to myself.

With the willpower of San Tzu, I say, "See you at seven, then," and walk into the guest room, praying for inner strength where Dante is concerned.

After a particularly cold shower, I dress in yet another red ensemble and head downstairs. I usually don't wear dresses—ever—so I'm still trying to get used to the feel of all that floaty material around me. But the pain will be worth the prize, I hope. For tonight's mission, I chose a floor-length number with a side slit that goes all the way up to my red lace panties. No bra as the sleeveless dress has a deep v on both front and back, a more slutty take on a Grecian style. It's a red lipstick and strappy heels kind of outfit, and if Dante isn't completely bamboozled into giving me what I want by the end of the night, I'm clearly barking up the wrong tree. My dirty mind conjures images of the things *it* wants from Dante, but I shake my head and pretend all I want is answers about my past.

I'm just taking the cherry pie, which I baked and managed not to screw up, out of the oven when Dante comes into the kitchen.

"Hi." I smile at him, putting the pie on the counter and taking off the oven mitts.

"You look—" he swallows.

"Nice?" I rub my hands on the red material of my dress, suddenly aware of how much exposed skin I'm actually showing.

"No."

"Oh." I take a step back, taking my eyes off him, my shoulders dropping. "Right. Well—"

He's in front of me before I even notice him move, his fingers lifting my chin to face him. I keep my eyes averted as a blush spreads across my cheeks. I'm so stupid. Of course, he'd hate my dress. It's red after all.

"You don't look nice, Alessa." His body is against mine. "You look like a vision."

"Really?" I mutter, biting my bottom lip.

"Look at me," he orders, gripping my chin harder until I relent. "So fucking beautiful, you took my breath away when I walked in."

"Oh." I think I blush even harder.

"Mhmmm," he hums, stroking my cheek with his thumb before pressing it to his lips and licking it. "You take my breath away every time you walk into a room. Your beauty is unfair to everything else around you. Art, nature, people. They all pale in comparison to you."

I'm breathless by the time he's finished. Caught off guard by his words. Does he really think this?

"Thank you," I whisper, licking my lips, my body buzzing with excitement.

He steps away nonchalantly, giving me whiplash as he looks around, totally oblivious he's just tilted my world on its axis.

"What's for dinner?"

I narrow my eyes, glad I didn't waver from my food choices despite having second thoughts since he's been putting all that time into teaching me to fight and swim.

"Have a seat." With a sweet smile, I gesture at the table I set up earlier. A red tablecloth and a lit red candle atop it.

Dante's eyebrow lifts, but he silently follows my direction, flinging a red napkin onto his lap. As I bring a bottle of red wine to the table, I almost stumble with horror, connecting the dots on how this all looks. Like I'm a psycho who's trying to seduce him. I mean, I *am* trying to seduce information *out of* him, but I'm not a psycho. I just want to make things as uncomfortable for him as possible. Hoping it would help him sing like a canary. At no stage of my master plan did I consider I might come off like a bunny boiler.

"Hope you're hungry," I laugh awkwardly, pouring the wine into his wine glass.

Dante clears his throat, then reaches for the glass and takes a sip before looking up, his gaze following my moves as I turn around to plate the food. The silence between us is deafening, so I quickly press shuffle on my Spotify playlist, hoping to ease the tension in the room. As soon as the first beat comes through the speakers, I lunge for the phone, knocking it off the island and under the table as Khia asks all the ladies to *pop their pussy like this*...

For fuck's sake.

I round the kitchen island and dive under the red tablecloth in search of the blasted device as the song continues, sending a message to Dante that I'd like him to lick my neck, my back, my pussy and my crack. Kill. Me. Now.

The phone has fucked off to god knows where because it sure as hell is not under this table with me. I should just stay here and pretend I don't exist. Except my face is inches from Dante's crotch, which surely adds a cherry on top of the clusterfuck I've gotten myself into.

"Alessa." His strained voice barely reaches me in my little den.

Mortification is not something I feel too often. By now, you might have noticed my penchant for cheap thrills. And let's be honest, with that comes thick skin and a low embarrassment threshold. But with my cheeks burning so hot I could fry eggs on them, I come to terms with finding said threshold.

I decide I might as well move in under the table. It's nice and cosy down here. Throw in some cushions and a blanket, and you've got yourself a palace. Bonus points, it's in the kitchen—easy food access.

"Hi." Dante slides under the tablecloth.

"Hi." I blush even further as he sits opposite me. His eyes are so intense I can't take it anymore, so I bury my face behind my hands.

"What's going on, Alessa?" His large fingers wrap around mine and pull them off my face.

"You must think I'm desperate, but this came out all wrong," I mumble, trying and failing to explain my horror.

266

"What do you mean?"

"I mean, it looks like I'm trying to seduce you!" I throw my hands up, banging them on the underside of the table in the process. "Ouch." My face crumbles in pain.

"You're not trying to seduce me?" He takes my hands into his, cradling them before placing a gentle kiss on each. I shake my head. "Well, it's a bit of a blow to my ego, then. I was hoping you were."

"You were?"

"I've been walking around with my cock rock hard for you ever since I saw you in your pencil skirt and your lips painted red, Alessa. It's been the toughest month of my life, staying away from you. The only thing keeping me from giving in was the knowledge that I don't deserve you and that I can't give you everything you deserve."

I bite my lip, my heart hammering in my chest. "Oh."

"Indeed," he sighs. "Shall we have dinner?"

I nod, scrambling from under the table.

"So if seduction wasn't your plan, what was?" Dante asks once we're standing up. I move to grab the plates off the counter and place them on the table, my lips thin. "Ah, I think I get it," he chuckles.

"You do?" I sit down, my gaze on my lap as he takes a seat opposite me, replacing the red napkin on his lap.

He grabs a fork from beside his plate and mixes the spaghetti around cautiously. "Do you really think I'm that stupid?" His piercing brown eyes look right into my soul, blazing hot with... amusement?

# 35

# DANTE

The stench of ketchup-based sauce wafts up to my nostrils as I move the pasta around my plate. Alessa bites her lip, her cheeks flushing hot pink, making me think of all the other pink places on her body. My dick stirs in approval.

This past week has been hell. It's been more and more difficult to keep myself away from her and not give in to every single dirty thought I have when she's around. I spent as much time away from her as possible. Mostly in the basement, torturing the piece of shit I brought home in the trunk of my Maserati. Today my patience snapped, and after cutting off his dick, I briefly considered raping him with it, just so that he could taste his own medicine, start repenting for everything he has done to Alessa, but also to any other girls his family fostered. And I'm sure there were many others. Sick fucks like him don't stop at one when they can get away with it. But, unfortunately, the fucker died on me. A shame since I had so many wonderful plans for him. Alas, his heart gave out from the shock of losing his useless, tiny cock, no doubt.

There was blood everywhere, and normally, I'd be feeling the overwhelming urge to vomit up my insides, but this time was different. This time, I couldn't care less. All I could see when looking at him was red anyway. The absolute rage because he touched *my* girl, hurt her, blinded me to everything but the need to make him pay. To make him suffer.

"What do you mean?"

I chuckle. She's so fucking cute, pretending like she hasn't filled my house with my least favourite colour. I have to admit at first, I was confused. The new cushions, paintings, trinkets. I thought maybe she wanted to make my house feel more homely. More comfortable. Make it hers. I thought I'd shrug it off and let her get on with it. But that same night, I found my toothbrush had been swapped to a new one, a shiny red one... As were my towels, which were now fluffy red and monogrammed with my initials.

I was almost able to hold back the chuckle. The little spitfire has balls.

"Well, either you have lost your mind, *or* you're toying with me."

She blinks innocently. "Me? Toying with the biggest bad in town?"

"I'm definitely the biggest in town," I look down at my crotch with a smirk, "but am I really the *baddest*?" I look back up, my eyebrow lifted.

Alessa swallows, then licks her lips. "You get very angry."

"That's true. But usually, there's a good reason."

"You can also be very scary."

"You don't seem to be scared of me, Alessa. Do I scare you?"

"Not right now." Pink stains her cheeks at the affirmation.

"But sometimes...I do?"

"Not quite—" she trails off, sucking in her bottom lip.

"Elaborate," I demand.

"I think—I think when you get all angry and scary," she takes a big breath, "you excite me," she mumbles.

A corner of my lip lifts up as my cock stirs in my pants.

"I excite you," I repeat, my voice muffled by my fingers rubbing the sides of my face, trying to hide the smile behind them.

She nods.

"So, you putting red shit all over *my* house—knowing full well I hate the colour—was just...you trying to get excited?" I'm finding it really hard not to grin now, but I do my best to keep the unimpressed look on my face, playing the game she so obviously wants to play.

Alessa releases her lip from its prison, drawing my eyes to how plump and enticing it looks. "I was just trying to gain the upper hand."

"An upper hand?" She has my interest.

"You're always so...so in control—" she stops, her eyes casting downward. "It's stupid."

I get up and walk around the table, kneeling before her until she's towering over me, looking down into my eyes. "Alessa," I whisper, clenching my fists. "Don't you realise you're the one in control? You've had a hold on me for weeks now. I'm under your spell, *Fata*. I can't help myself when it comes to you. You," my voice breaks, "fucking *own* me."

She sucks in a breath, her small hands holding tightly onto the flowy material of her dress.

"I used your credit card to buy all these things," she whispers.

"Good, " I say—this wasn't news to me. In fact, when the Amex representative called me about potential fraudulent activity, I laughed at her resourcefulness. She only needed to ask anyway. Finding the smooth skin of her calf with my hand, I gently glide it up, marvelling at the softness of her skin beneath my fingertips.

"Good? Aren't you furious? I must have spent thousands of dollars!"

I smile, my hand skimming over her knee. "You can have whatever you want, Alessa. I'll give you anything. You want this whole fucking house red? I'll call the decorators tomorrow to get the walls painted," I snort. "What you fail to realise, baby, is that I don't hate red. Not anymore. Not since it's the colour of the lipstick you wore the first day back in Blackwood. Not since the dress you're wearing," I finger the material, pulling it aside and exposing her toned legs, "makes you look like a goddess. Makes my mind go to the dirtiest of places. I'll happily live in a house filled with red if I get to see you in it. Preferably naked."

"I don't get it." She shakes her head, not put off by my confession one bit. "You've been avoiding me, pushing me away all this time. What changed?"

"I can't fight it anymore," I sigh, resigned. I don't want to. Not when she makes me want to kill anyone who looks at her the wrong way. Not when all I can think of is her. I don't understand what's happening to me, but I'm done trying to stop it. "I've got something for you." I stand up, walking over to where I placed the gift box. Picking it up, I hesitate, considering if it's the right move. Showing Alessa just how obsessed with her I am. How fucked up. And how possessive and vengeful I can be.

"What is it?" she asks from behind me. Her curiosity is enough to make the decision for me. She needs to know what she's signing up for now that I've decided she's mine.

Her emerald eyes trace my steps as I make my way back

to her, handing her the box. Her fingers tentatively play with the satin bow tightly binding the box—a subtle reminder of the rage and overwhelming need for vengeance that engulfed me when I wrapped it.

"Open it," I order, watching her every move.

She follows my instruction, untying the bow, pushing the ribbon aside, and then lifting the lid. My eyes are glued to the object in her hands, so I don't see the expression on her face, but I hear the sharp intake of breath just fine.

"Is this a joke, Dante? What is this?" A hint of panic in her voice.

"It's what you make me do, Alessa," I murmur, not daring to lift my gaze and see the disgust on her face.

Her hands shake. "What?"

"You make me crazy. You make me want to kill every last motherfucker who ever laid a finger on you. You make me want to hurt anyone who has ever hurt you."

"So this is..."

"A dick," I shrug. "Freshly severed from the body of a rapist, who took what belonged to me," I growl, not able to hide the distaste in my words. "I wish I could hurt him more, but sadly he died from shock."

She pushes the box away, the chair scraping against the floor as she stands up abruptly. A surge of panic courses through me, the realisation hitting hard that I might be on the brink of losing her. The mere thought is unbearable, and I can't fathom letting her slip away any longer. Closing my eyes, I brace myself for the impending heartache. If she can't accept me for who I am...

I'm left grappling with the urgency to either temper my wild instincts or devise a way to make her stay, even if it means pushing the boundaries of reason. The temptation to bind her to me, to keep her from escaping, whispers in the recesses of my mind like a forbidden desire. It's a dangerous thought, yet the desperation to claim her as my own intensifies.

Just as the shadows of doubt threaten to engulf me, a warm and comforting presence envelops my senses. The chill around me is replaced by the soft press of her body against mine, and her arms encircle me with a gentle force. The alluring scent of fresh soap, a familiar fragrance that now feels like home, wraps around me.

In that moment, the realisation strikes with profound clarity—I can't let her go. The fear of losing her is eclipsed by the inescapable truth that I need her like I need air. As she nestles her head into the curve of my neck, seamlessly melding with me, I find solace in her presence. Without hesitation, I reciprocate, enfolding her in a tight embrace as if to anchor her to my very essence.

"Thank you," she mumbles into my shirt. "Thank you so much."

"No one will ever hurt you again," I vow. The words punching a hole in my chest with how true they strike. I can't wrap my confused mind around why she evokes those emotions in me. I don't understand it, and I'm done trying. I want her, and I will deal with the consequences whenever they come.

"I don't need your protection," she says, lifting her head to meet my eyes. I stiffen. If she's about to reject me, I'm going to—"I just need your truth." She smiles. "I don't want any more lies. Just the truth."

Her eyes are shining as she says it, and I already know I will have to break the promise I'm about to make. If she ever found out what I've done, who I am, and what role I played in her family's demise, she'd never forgive me. She'd leave me. I'm a selfish bastard. Once I find something I want, I hold onto it. And I want her.

At any price.

Be it deceit *or* war with Nicolosi over a fucking marriage contract.

"I promise."

She smiles. "Dante?"

"Yes?"

"Remember when you asked me what I was doing in the pool?"

Just the memory of what her body looked like beneath the surface of the water has me tightening my grip on her. "You never told me."

"I was embarrassed."

I scrunch my eyebrows in confusion.

"But since we've agreed to tell each other the truth..." A blush spreads over her cheeks, and suddenly, I'm more curious than terrified.

"What were you doing in the pool, *Fata*?" I trace my finger over her jaw until the pad reaches her soft lips. She shivers as her pink tongue darts out, giving me a little lick. My cock strains, trying to rip through my pants and desperately get to her. But there are too many layers between us, too many clothes it would have to tear through to get to her soft body.

"I was trying to...Oh, god. I can't believe I'm about to tell you—"

"No secrets, remember?" A flash of impatience runs through my body.

"This applies to you too, Terence." She shoots me a narrowed look, making me want her even more. Always bargaining.

"Terence?"

"You wouldn't understand," she sighs.

"Your brain—" I say in awe.

"What about it?" She stiffens in my arms, defensive.

"No, *Fata*," I say softly. "Your brain is fucking fantastic. I

274

can't keep up with you sometimes. It's quick, sharp, witty, and fuck me, the sexiest thing you've got. And that's saying something 'cause you're a fucking vision, Alessa." I chuckle as her mouth falls open.

"You like my brain?"

"I do." I place a soft kiss on her forehead.

"Terence is a bird," she mumbles.

"A bird?" I laugh. "You see what I mean? And why, pray tell, do you call me Terence?"

"He's the biggest and scariest looking of all the Angry Birds," she mutters into the lapel of my jacket.

I burst out laughing. "So, now I'm a big, scary Angry Bird?"

"He's also red," she narrows her eyes. "The same colour your whole face goes when you get into a hissy fit."

The fuck? "I don't do *hissy fits*." I unwrap my arms from around her and cross them in front of my chest.

She cocks her hip, placing her hand atop it. "Point proven." She motions her finger in the air.

"Alessa," I growl. "Don't push me. This is not a hissy fit. This is a man defending his manhood."

"Potato-patatho." She rolls her eyes. "Anyway, I was in the pool because I was trying to get off and couldn't, so I figured if I can't breathe underwater, it will feel like when you had your hand around my neck." She shrugs nonchalantly as the world around me comes into a lust filled focus.

"You what?" I lick my lips, my arms no longer crossed in front of my chest but by my side, fists clenching and unclenching.

She sucks in her bottom lip as I take a step forward, closing the space between us. "You want me to repeat all that?" she squeaks.

I nod. "Preferably with very graphic details on where

your fingers were, what they were doing, and what that beautiful brain of yours was thinking about."

"You," she whispers. Her mouth now inches from mine. "I was thinking of you."

"Fuck," I growl.

## 36

## ALESSA

**D**ante's hands dig into my hips as he effortlessly lifts me up. My legs instinctively circle his midsection, locking at his back.

"Alessa." His forehead touches mine. There is a strain in his voice. "I want to do bad things to you."

"Do them," I urge, rolling my hips against the erection I can feel pressing between my thighs.

"I'm trying to restrain myself, baby. I don't want to hurt you."

"Do them all." I grind against him once more, needing his heat, his body. Needing something to connect us. "Please." My voice breaks.

"Fuuuck." His breathing is shallow. "How can I deny you when you beg me so nicely."

"Please, Dante. I need you. I want you."

It is only when we're by the stairs I realise we've been moving. He stops at the bottom of the staircase, fists the flowy material of my red dress and rips the bottom off in one quick move. I gasp, because, holy hell, that was hot, but also because that's over a thousand dollars now lying on the floor.

"I'll buy you another one. I'll buy you ten more like it. But this one was getting in my way. It had to go," he says as he carries me up the stairs and into his bedroom.

Fuck, yes! His bedroom again. The land where good things happen to my pussy and everything smells like Dante Santoro. This time, I'm not going to hesitate. I'm not going to stop him. There's no denying I want him, and if this past week of him being distant was meant to put me off, well, then it failed. It fuelled the fire, and it made me want him even more.

I briefly berate myself for not sticking to my guns and getting information out of him, but all the plans I've had go out the window as soon as our lips connect.

Dante's fingers are in my hair, and we're falling back, back. I should be scared. Feel off balance, maybe. But his strong presence and the heat of his body make me believe nothing bad will ever happen to me. Just like he said. There's time to ask questions. Not now, though. Not when he nestles himself between my thighs, my red thong and his trousers the only thing between my centre and his hard length.

His tongue invades my mouth, his strokes hurried and hungry. Like he's been waiting a long time to kiss me. We both have because it feels like eons since the last time his lips were on mine. For all the things he's done to me, all the places he touched and cherished. All the things he said— this is only the second time he kissed me. And boy, was it worth all that wait, tension and frustration.

I moan under him, the gravity of what's happening between us knocking down my walls.

"Alessa," his lips separate from mine in a whisper before he dives back for more. "Fuck, baby," he moans in between fevered kisses. And I know exactly what he means. Somehow, this feels like everything. Like the whole world could collapse right now but we'd stay like this, suspended in this perfect moment of need and despair. A precipice right before something unsure turns into more. Dante's hands roam over the bare skin of my legs. Up and down, up and down, leaving a hot trail where our skin touched. For a second, he plays with the side of my thong, but instead of pulling it off, he skims past it, up the side of my body before he rips the scrap of the dress material that was still covering my boobs.

He pushes himself up, hovering above me as his eyes take in my body. He shakes his head as if out of a stupor. "*Perfetta. Così dannatamente perfetta.*[1]" The Italian words making goosebumps erupt all over my skin. He could be reciting his shopping list for all I know, and I'd still be melting into a puddle.

"Dante," I whimper. Feeling exposed under him. Once again, I'm almost naked, and he's fully clothed. If it wasn't for the heat in his dark eyes I'd feel unsure, embarrassed. But the expression on his face, full of awe and need, has me reeling for the feel of his skin on mine.

"*Cosa, mia bellissima Fata?*[2]" he replies.

I reach for his face, pulling it down to mine and kissing him until I'm breathless, until his hips start moving against me, eliciting a languid moan when he hits just the right spot.

"I don't know what you just said," I gasp into his mouth. "But I need your clothes off, Dante. I want to feel you," I mumble as he kisses the side of my lips, my jaw and down my neck, licking a path just beneath my ear that makes my toes curl, and my whole body shiver with pleasure.

Then he's gone, my body cold and needy as I try to catch my breath. I keep my eyes closed for a second longer, terrified that, once again, he changed his mind and is about to leave me alone in his bedroom.

"Alessa." His deep voice doesn't sound like it's by the door, ready to bid me goodbye, so I crack one eye open. He's sitting on the edge of the bed, still fully clothed except for his feet, which are now bare, his shoes and socks kicked off next to them on the floor.

"Mmm?" My gaze is glued to his perfectly pedicured toes.

"If you want me naked, then undress me," he orders. And the command in his voice makes my nipples tighten.

Dante hums in approval. "You like it when I tell you what to do, don't you?"

I nod eagerly, not feeling any shame in letting this man take control. In fact, when Dante does it, it makes me feel safe. It makes me feel cherished and taken care of. "Come here," he says firmly, extending his hand towards me. Placing my hand in his, I slide off the bed and stand in between his open legs in nothing but my red thong. He licks his lips, his eyes glazing over as he hungrily stares at my boobs. "Undress me."

I let go of his hand and stroke his face, letting my fingers trail down his neck onto his chest before pushing them in between his shirt and jacket and leaning my torso into his face as I slide his jacket off. The groan that leaves his mouth as my nipple brushes his cheek has my thighs clenching at the rush of desire between my legs.

"Wait," he says as I reach for the top button of his shirt, having discarded his expensive jacket to the floor.

I freeze, waiting to see if he changed his mind as he leans down to where the jacket lays on the floor and rummages for something in the inner pocket. Once he's got it, he places a kiss on my hip and straightens back up. The phone in his hand lights up as he taps away for a few seconds before throwing it back on the floor. Tensing, I'm about to ask what the hell was that about when a thrum of a bass guitar comes through hidden speakers in the room, the beat filling the space around us. "Continue," Dante orders, putting my hands back on his chest before placing his on my hips, stroking circles round my exposed skin.

My breathing picks up as my shaking fingers fight with the buttons on his shirt, the task much harder since his hands are on me and his breath teases my aching nipples.

When I get to the bottom one, I have no patience for it any more and just yank it open, needy to see his sculpted chest and the angel tattoo once more.

"Impatient, are we?" he breathes as my fingers stroke up his chest before pulling the white shirt off and chucking it somewhere behind me.

"Very." I lick my lips, going down to my knees in front of him, My fingers eagerly reaching for his belt.

"Fuck, baby," his raspy voice propels my movements. Off. Those trousers need to be off. "You, on your knees in front of me. Licking your lips, just. Like. That." His finger brushes against my mouth before dipping inside. I swirl my tongue around it, moaning at the taste, imagining I'm licking something else entirely, something I'm currently busy trying to free from his stupid trousers. "Jesus," he growls. "Will you put those pretty lips around my cock, Alessa? Will you let me fuck your mouth?" I nod eagerly, turned on at the prospect of making him feel as good as he made me feel. His finger leaves my lips and grips the back of my head.

"I've never done it before," I whisper, finally undoing the belt buckle, sliding the belt out of the loops and chucking it behind me, then eagerly reaching for the button on his trousers.

"Jesus fuck, Alessa," he groans. "Will my cock be the first you've ever sucked?"

I bite my bottom lip, undoing the zipper and trying to yank his trousers off, to no avail. Dante lifts his hips, letting me pull them down his legs until they're pooled around his ankles.

"We're on even keel now," he says, motioning to his underwear, his cock straining to get out.

I reach for his boxers, but he grabs my wrist just as I'm about to pull at his waistband. My eyes snap to his.

"Not tonight, baby. Okay?"

My body freezes. Is he for real? What does he mean 'not tonight'? Anger, frustration, and belligerence cause my eyes to prickle with wetness.

"Tonight is about making *you* feel good," he continues. "Tonight is about you claiming back control."

"So, you don't want to stop?" I ask, hopefulness filling my voice as the hold on my wrist loosens.

"Fuck, no. I just meant we take care of you tonight. You can suck my dick every night after if that's what you want," he chuckles, "just not tonight."

I pout because I was looking forward to tasting him, to finally knowing what it feels like to have power over someone in that way.

"As much as I want to wipe that pout away with my cock, Alessa," he guides my hand back to his waistband, "I want to taste you first. I want to feel you shudder around my tongue as I make you come. I want your pussy sopping wet for me before I fuck you so thoroughly you'll be chanting my name in prayer." Jesus Christ, doesn't he know I'm already dripping for him?

"Saint..." my fingers dip beneath his waistband.

"I'll give that nickname a whole new meaning, baby," he continues in his seductively deep voice, "I will worship your body. Every inch of you will be claimed tonight. Your body is my offering. Your pleasure will be my reward."

"Shouldn't it be *my* reward?" I ask, pulling his boxers down and revealing his huge cock, hard and smooth, his foreskin barely there as it stretches proudly in front of me, a droplet of precum glistening on top. Just one lick wouldn't hurt. Surely.

"No, Alessa." He lifts my chin with his index finger until our eyes meet. "Any man worth his salt will tell you that making his woman come over and over again is his biggest privilege," he says as his boxers join the rest of his clothes on the floor.

*His* woman. I try not to purr like a kitten at him calling me his woman. But before I can even berate myself, he pulls me roughly back up and onto his lap until I'm straddling him, and then his fingers press against my centre through my panties.

"Jesus, you're so wet for me," he groans. "*Questa sarà la tortura più dolce, non è vero?*[3]"

"Wh-at?" I stumble over the word as he circles his thumb against my clit.

"My torture. You'll be my sweetest torture. But I'll repent," he chants feverishly before his lips capture mine, and his index finger slides my thong to the side and pushes inside me.

# 37

## DANTE

"Ooooh," Alessa moans into my mouth as I push my finger inside her tight, wet pussy. She's so responsive, so fucking perfect for me, I nearly weep with the need to be inside her. But I have to make sure she's ready first. Both in her body and in her mind. I don't want her doubting what's about to happen between us. I need her mind focused on the pleasure I'm about to give her. No one else but us matters tonight. Not ever.

My sole purpose is to chase away all her bad memories and create new ones in their stead. When Angelo called me pussy whipped a few weeks ago, I didn't know his words were prophetic. But they were. In a few short months, Alessa became the sole focus of my brain. Thoughts of her invade my every waking moment, every dream, too. At first, I was certain it was because of the threat she posed. An unwitting reminder of what I had done so many years prior, fuelling my rage and disdain. Then, I thought it was intrigue, the need to find out why she was so hell-bent on staying in this town, despite my many attempts to make her leave. Some-where along the way, I realised I was impressed by the sheer determination in her. By her wit and her sharp mind. And now? Now I know this thing between us was inevitable. Written in the books the moment her green eyes looked into mine when she was a little girl. I knew back then I had to protect her at all costs. I just didn't know why.

Now I do.

She was destined to be mine, and I will destroy everything and everyone that will try to get in our way. Marriage contracts be damned.

"Dante," she gasps, her head throwing back as I add another finger, making sure to stretch her in preparation for my cock. "Yes. Dante, yes," she exclaims, rocking in my lap as I stroke her g-spot, my dick rubbing against her thigh and leaking precum. I want to hear her gasp my name like that every day. Every fucking minute of every single day. With a growl, I stand up, throwing her on the bed and crawling onto it behind her until I'm right between her thighs, her sweet scent rendering me speechless. The need to taste her, to feel her perfect cunt beneath my tongue overwhelms me. It's a feeling akin to the rage that always comes over me. All consuming and unbearable. And like the rage, I let it take over, listening to my instincts as I dive in, feasting on her like she's the best meal I've ever had.

Alessa moans my name, making me dizzy with need, her fingers digging into my hair, pulling on my strands as she pushes against my mouth, my tongue spearing inside her. When I feel her legs tremble around me, her body convulsing with uncontrollable shakes, I move my mouth, my lips sucking in her clit. She screams, her body coming off the bed and into the air as she comes on my mouth, liquid gushing against my face.

Jesus fucking Christ. She's going to be the end of me. I lick every last drop, delighting in her confused moans as my tongue strokes her sensitive bud while I lick her clean before moving over to her thighs.

"Did I—" her voice is croaky, "did I just pee?" her arm lands over her face, hiding it from me.

I climb over her body, settling my weight on top of her, before pulling the arm off, revealing her embarrassed face.

"No, baby."

"It was incredible, and then—I feel like I just peed myself." Her lower lip trembles.

"You didn't. You just came all over my face in the best possible way." I nuzzle into her neck licking a path up to her ear, before nibbling her perfect little lobe.

She hums in pleasure. "You liked it?"

"Loved it."

"I made a mess. You hate mess."

"You can make this sort of mess every single time."

She chuckles as I nip her jaw, trailing kisses until my lips hover over hers.

"Dante?"

"Yes, baby?"

"You smell like me."

"Do you want me to go wash my face before I kiss you?"

"No, I like it. It's sort of sexy."

"You're sort of sexy."

She laughs. "Who are you, and where is the angry man I met my first day in Blackwood?"

"He's still in there. He's just focused," I trace my fingers over her pert breast, "on making you come as many times as possible before he can't hold back any longer and fucks you."

"A very important task indeed."

"You see? You get him."

"Dante?"

"Yes, baby?"

"Even back then, I knew."

286

"You knew what?" I ask distracted, playing with her nipple.

Her back arches into my touch.

"I knew you were never that angry."

"Mmmm." My lips close over the pert bud. I suck it, then lick a circle around it, before blowing cool air on it, watching it harden even more. "What was I then?"

"I'm still trying to figure it out," she sighs as I move my mouth to her other breast, my hand stoking down her body until my fingers reach her soaked pussy.

"Maybe I was just lonely," I say, the truth of that statement hitting me straight in the chest. I freeze, trying to process the words I just spoke. Pushing onto her elbows, Alessa reaches out to cradle the side of my face. Unable to stop myself, I lean into her touch. "What are you doing to me, *Fata*?"

"I don't know," she whispers.

"I don't understand this—this turmoil inside me. I've never felt—I don't feel, Alessa." I close my eyes as her thumb strokes my cheek.

"Me, too."

My eyes snap open, finding her shining ones, glistening with emotions neither one of us is ready to name.

"I need you to say my name," I plead.

"Dante," she croaks as my fingers begin stroking her pussy.

"More." I slip two fingers inside then pull them out.

"Dante, please," she moans when I add a third finger.

"Please what?"

"I want you."

"Not good enough." I pump all three fingers steadily as her legs begin to shake around me.

"Dante," she gasps as my cock brushes dangerously close to where my fingers pump inside her.

"Say it, Alessa."

"Please."

"Please, what?" I demand, my body on fire from the sheer need to be inside her.

She whips her head from side to side, breathing shallowly.

"I need you. I need you inside me," she gasps as her walls clench around my fingers. With my dick I rub her clit, precum seeping straight onto her swollen nub.

With just a few strokes of my aching cock she moans my name, convulsing around my fingers.

Her mouth parts in a silent scream as a blush spreads across her chest, up her neck and onto her cheeks. Now that I can see her come, my face no longer between her legs, I'm mesmerised by how beautiful she looks. All spent and satisfied.

I never really took the time before to watch the women I've been with, and I never really cared enough, except for making sure they left me satisfied. But with Alessa, I don't want to miss a thing. Every single second counts, every little twitch of her fingers, every gasp, every moan, every arch of her body, every tremble beneath mine.

It's like something tells me to take notice, to make sure I remember everything. A sense of urgency comes over me. I cannot wait. I don't want to wait anymore. I need to be—

"I need you inside me." Alessa's whisper brings me back to her. Pulling my fingers out of her, I swallow, moving my body, shaking with need, over her. The need to be inside her blurring my vision. Her small hand brushes against my hair, shaking slightly.

I try to hold myself back, knowing the gravity of what we're about to do. Knowing that I'm the first man she willingly lets claim her. The first. The last. And the only. I'll make it my mission to erase anyone else from her mind.

When her legs spread wider, opening up for me, I align myself with her entrance, a drop of sweat making a trail down the side of my face from the exertion of stopping myself from just slamming into her.

"Are you sure?" I ask, the head of my cock pressing against her heat.

"More than anything," she replies, pulling the strands of my hair until my face is inches from hers. "Kiss me while you do it," she pleads quietly. I'd do anything for her in this moment, anything she'd ask me to. And kissing? That's no hardship.

Pressing my lips against hers, I let her guide me in the kiss, opening when her tongue licks at the seam, meeting her slow stroke for slow stroke as she nips at my lower lip and then kisses the sting away. Her arms and legs lock around my body, pulling me closer, and I have to strain not to push inside her.

My arms are shaking, muscles strain, when I feel her ankles press against my back. The pressure gentle but firm. I could drop to my knees and pray in gratitude if I wasn't about to sheath myself inside her. I press firmer against her opening, her pussy resisting the intrusion despite how wet and ready she is.

Moving my tongue faster, I speed up the rhythm, no longer letting her dictate the kiss. Her arms tighten on a moan and finally, I push inside her, groaning at the feel of her around me.

"*Cristo, così stretta*[1]. So tight, baby. So fucking tight," I moan in between kisses as I push further in. She tenses around me. Her legs shaking. "It's okay. Relax." I stop halfway inside. "Just listen to the song," I whisper against her lips as the song that's been playing on repeat reaches the chorus. "Do you hear it?"

"Yes," she says, her breaths shallow.

"Listen carefully."

She closes her eyes, unmoving.

"Nothing's gonna hurt you, baby," I whisper into her hair. "It'll all be alright."

She swallows before her eyes open and meet mine full force, the emotion in them making my heart flutter in my chest. I try to say everything I'm feeling with mine, trying to make sense of the jumble inside my head, my heart. Then her lips lift into a small smile, and the jumble becomes clear. Clear as a fucking sunny day in the Bahamas. How could I have been so blind all this time? If my mother were still alive, she'd have laughed at how blind I have been to my feelings. And she would have loved her.

Alessa bites her bottom lip and presses her heels against my back, pushing me all the way in. And just like that, all thoughts disappear. It's just me and her, connected. Gasping for air at the feeling of absolute bliss. How could I miss something I've never experienced before? How is it possible that all my life I have missed this? Being inside her, feeling her body pressed to mine.

Her eyes never leave mine as she whispers, "Do you feel it?"

I nod, unable to speak. I know exactly what she means. As my hips start to move, our gazes never waver from each other. The spell she has on me unfolding, whirling until it consumes me and I'm no longer my own man. I'm hers. All hers. And she is—

"Mine," I growl as I thrust into her, pulling back out almost all the way.

"Yours," she gasps, biting her lip.

I push back in. "Yo-urs." My voice breaks, the word coming out gravelly. Like an ancient truth coming into light for the first time. "Nobody elses, *Fata*." Fuck what is expected of me, I'll die before I let her go.

"Mine." Her lips part as a tear wells up in her eye.

I stop, leaning down and catching the tear with my lips just as it escapes. "I've got you," I croak as her arms wrap around my neck, and she pulls me tighter, burying her face under my jaw. This is not me. Not how I usually am, dominant, unforgiving, demanding. But there's time for that. Right now, she is the one in charge. This time, it needs to be on her terms. We'll have a lifetime to play my games, I'll make sure.

Alessa moves her hips against mine sliding up and down my length, more and more sure of her actions. I try to hold still, let her guide this, but there's only so much restraint I possess, and within seconds I'm moving against her, meeting her push for push.

# 38

## ALESSA

My whole body trembles with pleasure as Dante moves against me. The moans escaping me increase in volume the deeper the strokes. Nothing gets past him since straight away his hand wraps around my knee and pushes my leg up, the angle of his thrusts changing and making my eyes roll back with pleasure. He feels so good. But it's not just his incredible cock, that fills me up so thoroughly I can barely breathe.

It's everything. It's the restraint I clearly saw on his face. The rapture when he slid inside me, and the care he showed me at every single step. This is not fucking. It's not just sex. What's happening between us is...lovemaking.

When I realised the depth of my feelings for him, I almost cried, partly from fear and partly from elation. Then Dante kissed my tears away, and I knew. I knew deep down he feels the same. It was the assurance I needed to keep going. The reason this feeling of pleasure is overwhelming me right now. There's not an ounce of dread in me, no hesitation. This thing between us is right.

Dante speeds up, his hips moving faster, punctuated with a grind each time he bottoms out. I'm no longer able to hide in his neck as he pushes onto his arm and changes the angle once more, this time hitting a spot so deep inside me the moan which escapes me sounds foreign to my own ears.

"You like that, baby?" He does it again, and once again, I moan loudly, unable to control myself.

It's all the confirmation he needs as he continues his strokes, not changing a thing about them, while my body grows hotter and hotter, sweat pooling between my breasts.

"Open your eyes, Alessa," he demands, and I instantly follow his instruction, meeting his hooded eyes. "Good girl," he rasps, pressing his lips together, the muscles on his neck straining as he moves in, out, in, out, the dark brown of his irises burning with unspoken words.

"Dante," I cry out as unbelievable heat centres in my abdomen, all my muscles tensing, before shivers wrack my whole body as he hits a spot deep within me again and again. "Dante, Dante, Dante," I chant as wave after wave of pleasure hits me. I can't stop.

*It* won't stop, because Dante isn't stopping. In fact, he speeds up. Grinding against my clit with every push and making me come over and over again until I can see stars.

"Jesus fuck, Alessa," he roars, his cock becoming even harder, if that's possible. By the time his release comes, I'm pretty sure I am dead. Or passed out, my body still convulsing in ecstasy as he falls on top of me, breathing shallowly.

The last tremors of my climax wreck through me as Dante moves his hips one last time, before nuzzling his head next to mine.

I'm blind. And breathless. Alessandra Jones has checked out of this building—this body. There's no chance in hell I'm moving my limp body any time soon, so having a Dante-shaped blanket on top of me is not such a bad thing.

"Wow," I breathe after a minute, once I can finally speak

again. Dante hums in affirmation. "Is it always like this?" I ask, a hot blush creeping into my cheeks as I flaunt my inexperience.

Lifting up onto his arms and looking straight into my eyes, he chuckles, "Never, baby. It's never been like this."

Well, shit.

His gaze roams over my face and then down my body until he looks at where we're joined. Instantly, he hardens again. Biting his lip, he watches himself slide out to the tip, then back in again. The coating of both of our climaxes making the movements slick.

"Shit," I gasp when realisation dawns on me.

"Is everything okay, Alessa?" He stops, his eyes back on my face.

I bite my lip, unsure how to broach the subject.

"What is it?" he pushes.

"Condom," I mumble. "We didn't use one."

He blinks. Once. Twice. "Well, hell. You're right."

My blood boils at how flippant he is about it. "Dante," I growl, trying to push him off me. He doesn't budge.

"I'm clean. I've never *not* used a condom before, plus I've just had a physical. It's fine."

"It's fine?" My voice comes out way more high-pitched than expected. "What about, you know...a pregnancy?"

He stiffens, his eyes growing cold. "Would it be such a terrible thing to have a baby with me?"

I don't even have the time to contemplate an answer before he moves his hips away from me. On instinct, I wrap my legs around him and lock us in place. "Don't," I whisper, biting my lip.

"Well?"

"It wouldn't, Dante. I just...I never even considered bringing children into this world. I'd never wish for anyone to go through what I did. Plus, I'm only twenty-two..." I trail off. Why am I even defending myself? We've barely known each other for a few months, and despite how intense those months were, it is way too early to be thinking about having babies with Dante Santoro. Even if the thought does not repel me. Not one little bit.

"Right," he says. But it sounds off. Is he—is he hurt?

"Dante," I say softly, placing both my hands on his cheeks. "Where is this coming from?"

"I don't know." His eyes close as he jerks his head to the side. "Earlier, you asked me for my truth, Alessa. So here it is. It's like, now that I've got you, I can't let you go. I'm not going to. And if that means tying you to me with a baby," he looks back at me, "I'm okay with that."

I shiver under his intense gaze.

"Normal people would get engaged first," I gasp as his hips begin to move again.

He smirks. "Consider yourself engaged."

My lips lift into a half smile. "Don't I have a say in this?"

"No, baby. Not with this. You said you're mine. That's as much of an agreement as I needed."

"You're psychotic and aren't you engaged to someone else already?"

"We'll get you a ring tomorrow." He grinds into me, shrugging, while I turn into a puddle. "And I don't want anyone else but you. That contract might as well have been ripped up the minute my cock made home in your sweet, little cunt."

"What—about—condoms?" I ask in between thrusts as they pick up speed. Although, at this point, I no longer care. He can put triplets in me if he just continues fucking me like this.

"I'll get my vasectomy reversed when you're ready."

My heart sinks into the mattress below me as I freeze, disappointed. "Oh."

"I never wanted to bring children into this world either, *Fata*. Not until a few months ago. I had a vasectomy when I turned eighteen. I wasn't going to leave things to chance, even if I always used a condom."

"What changed your mind? You turned forty and suddenly got a hankering for a family?" I pout.

He roughly pinches my nipple. Moaning, I arch my back off the mattress as he continues pounding into me.

"I'm thirty-three, you little brat. And you know exactly what happened."

"What was it?" I gasp as he leans down, licking my earlobe.

"Not 'what' but 'who'," he whispers, then nibbles the skin on my neck.

"Who-o-oooh." My question turns into a long moan as his thumb finds my clit, while the thrusts pick up speed.

"Don't play coy, *Fata*. You know it was you."

# 39

## ALESSA

I've lost count of how many orgasms I had in the last twenty-four hours. Not that I'm complaining.

After the first few times, Dante carried me to the shower where he washed me thoroughly before giving me another exquisite orgasm with his mouth. Then we continued all night, falling asleep wrapped around each other, then waking up making love.

It's no wonder I'm sore now, but it's a good kind of sore. One that I welcome and cherish. Despite having the title of the ruthless Saint, Dante has cared for me, watched me and made sure I was okay every single time, all the while whispering how hard he wants to fuck me, how he wants to spank me and put his hands around my throat. The big tease. I think it's time to tell him I have been thoroughly acclimated to his body and to sex. I'm ready to bring out the big guns. The truth is, I'm ready to try anything he throws my way. Not only ready, but also eager.

"What are you thinking about?" Dante asks, his laptop screen reflected in his black-rimmed glasses as he watches me from behind his desk.

We're in his office, a room I haven't discovered previously. Stretching in the large wingback chair in the corner, I cover myself tighter with a blanket.

Feigning a yawn, I say, "Just tired."

"Come here," he orders, and my pussy instantly throbs with need at the tone of his voice.

I get up and walk over to where he's sitting, in just his boxers. Moving the chair back he indicates his lap. "Sit."

Like the good girl that I am, I smile and straddle him, the blanket slipping off my shoulders, exposing my naked breasts.

"I thought we promised each other the truth," he growls, his mouth moving closer and closer to my nipple.

I sigh. "I was thinking you're all talk and no follow through."

"*Che cazzo*?" He sits back.

I wriggle in his lap. Despite his obvious shock, his hard dick still wants to play, pressing through his boxers onto my already wet, bare pussy.

"You're all big words," I roll my eyes, "but you don't actually practice what you preach." I move my fingers up and down his torso, letting the blanket fall off my body as I dip my finger below his waistband.

"You said you were sore," he pants, no longer bothered by the words I'm saying.

"Oh, I am. But I still have a promise to collect on." I bite my lip as my hand connects with his erection.

"A promise?" he groans, confused.

"A promise." I kiss his neck, then slide down off his body until I'm in between his legs.

"*Cazzo*," he mumbles. I've noticed when he's turned on he tends to switch between English and Italian, and my pussy loves it. "What promise, baby? I wouldn't want to let you down."

I lick my lips. "Let me taste you, Dante. Show me what you like."

His eyes snap to mine as his thumb brushes my lips. "I like it rough, Alessa. I'm worried—I—"

"Let me worry about that. If it's too much, I'll tap your leg, or we can have a safe word," I look around, "'yearbook'." My eyes focus on the yearbook on one of his shelves. "Hey, you went to high school in Blackwood?"

Swallowing, he nods. "I grew up in Blackwood. We've been here for three generations." He slips his thumb inside my mouth and I forget why this information should be filed away in my brain for later. All I can focus on is Dante's thumb as I suck it. On a groan, he pulls it out roughly.

Whimpering with need, I grab his boxer shorts and pull them down, revealing his beautiful cock. It's hard, smooth, and already glistening at the top.

Licking my lips, I reach out to stroke it.

"*Fata*," Dante growls.

"I want you to fuck my mouth, Saint. Let me worship your cock."

"*Cristo, Fata*[1]. Do you even know what you're saying?"

I don't reply though, because I'm too busy leaning down and licking his length from the bottom to the very top, tasting his saltiness for the first time. I was worried it would be unpleasant, but I like it. In fact, I want more of it.

I wrap my lips around the head and suck, swirling my tongue around the little hole, licking off every last drop of what he's giving me. His hips buck, as his hand lands on the back of my head, fisting my hair before pulling my head off.

"Tap my thigh three times if it's too much," he growls as he leans down to kiss me roughly. When he pulls away, I nod, assuring him I understand. "Good girl," he says, causing a shiver of pleasure to run down my body. "Now, open your mouth and take my cock like the needy little slut you are for me."

My cunt instantly floods with arousal at his words, and I open my mouth, eager to taste him again.

He pushes the head past my lips, stretching my mouth wide around him as I try to swirl my tongue around. Wrapping my hand around the base of his cock, I lean closer, desperate to take him in deeper. Desperate to taste more of him.

"Relax, Alessa," he says as I tense, straining to accommodate his thick length. "Your mouth is perfect. Just like your tight little cunt."

Once again, his words make me groan with arousal, the action making his cock jerk inside my mouth. The movement releasing something primal in me. My left hand goes to his balls, while with my right, I find my clit, circling it round and round, already on the verge of climax. I moan around him again, taking him in as deep as I can.

"Are you touching yourself, baby?" His voice sounds strained. Opening my eyes, I look up, taking him into the back of my throat. With my eyes on his hooded ones, I hum my response, my finger slipping past his balls and stroking the skin between them and his ass. His hips jerk up into me, hitting the back of my throat and making my eyes water.

"Fuck, baby," he rasps as I pull off to catch a breath.

"Fuck my mouth," I plead, my finger assaulting my swollen clit, before I take him in all the way. He still hesitates, so with a groan of frustration, I dip my fingers inside me, then swap hands. My right going straight for his asshole. The slick finger, pressing against his hole, slips in past the knuckle easily. Dante roars, jerking into me, the grip of his hand on the back of my hair tightening as he furiously thrusts into my mouth.

Elation, pleasure, pride. Those are the emotions I'm feeling as I watch the rapture on his face.

"Baby, I'm gonna come. If you don't want—"

I swirl my finger inside his ass, then reach for my soaked pussy, pinching my clit, then rubbing it feverishly as Dante's cock assaults my mouth. My brain is going fuzzy from lack of oxygen, my vision going dark, tainted with white spots. My aching pussy clenches around the fingers I have slipped in, and I come around them just as Dante pulls out enough to let me catch a breath and shoots hot cum down my throat. I swallow every last drop, then lick his dick clean, still shaking from my own climax.

He pulls me onto his lap and covers us with the blanket I discarded onto the floor. Wiping away the wet tears from my cheeks, he kisses my forehead, each of my eyes, then my mouth. Slowly, greedily.

The words are at the back of my throat. I want to say them, but I can't, a fear I haven't felt before stopping me before I can even open my mouth.

*Ping.* The sound from his laptop startles us both. With a sigh, he wakes the computer up, his eyes scanning the screen. I move to slip off his lap, but his arm around me tightens.

"Stay," he murmurs into my hair.

Tensing, he curses under his breath, the grip he has on me becoming strained.

"What is it?" I ask.

My body sags as he shakes his head. Of course, he wouldn't share anything of importance with me, but then he surprises me when he speaks. "It's just a feeling."

I don't probe for more, not wanting to spook him.

"It's nothing, really," he trails off, taking a deep breath. "Just a capo who's being a dick. I normally would put him straight back in line, but he's an old family friend and—" he doesn't finish. "He wants to take over the port for something shady. I just know it."

I gasp. The port.

"Who is it?" I ask. Dante stiffens around me.

"No one you need to know about," his voice is cold, the same ice I heard from him the first time he spoke to me.

I brush it off. "Is it M. Conti?" I ask eagerly.

Dante's fingers dig into my skin. "How do you know Marco?"

"I don't!" I exclaim, bouncing excitedly in his lap. "You know, when you made me rewrite all those useless documents, I put a penis watermark on?"

His lip twitches. "Penis watermark?"

Ugh. I'll have to change that too, because the watermark is a blatant lie. Either way, that's not important right now. Disregarding his playful question, I continue, "Well, there was a spreadsheet amongst them. One you were working on when I was by your desk, except the printout didn't have all the numbers, and I remembered seeing something off on the screen and—"

"Slow down." His grip on me eases. "What do you mean you remember something was off. You were by my desk for less than a minute."

"Yes, yes. It's my eidetic memory. I saw it for less than a minute, but my brain registered the numbers."

"Your what?"

"Eidetic. I kinda remember everything I see."

He stiffens again. "What do you mean, *everything*?"

"If I read something once, I can recall the whole book, tell you what page a passage was on," I shrug, eager to get back to the topic.

"And events?"

"That's hyperthymesia. I don't have that." I wish I did,

though. Maybe then I'd remember my parents and what happened to them.

Stroking my hip, Dante says, "So, you saw a spreadsheet on my laptop and remembered something was off?"

"Yes, so because the printout didn't look like it had the same numbers, I kinda took the liberty to get the file from your laptop," I bite my lip, "and compare the two, and I found something."

# 40

## ALESSA

"Y ou have eidetic memory." He rubs his temples once I'm done relaying to him everything I have uncovered.

"I guess," I reply with an unsure shrug.

"One in a million." He shakes his head, a hint of amusement lifting the right corner of his mouth.

"One hundred million," I mumble.

"What?"

"Well, up to ten per cent of children under twelve have eidetic memory, so that would be one in one hundred million."

"You're twenty-two."

I clear my throat.

"Alessa."

"There aren't actually any adults recorded with eidetic memory. I'm a freak of nature."

He chuckles. "You are phenomenal, is what you are. So fucking incredible, clever, resilient, and Jesus Christ, have you even seen your body? If I didn't have to run this town, I'd be fucking you twenty-four-seven."

I laugh. "Anyway. Hopefully, that information will come in useful."

"Don't do that."

"Do what?"

"Brush off how incredible you are."

I blush, not sure what he wants me to say. "Thank you?"

He chuckles. "That will do for today, but we'll work on you."

"So you *do* run this town."

"For all intents and purposes. Yes. I've been doing it for over a decade."

"And your dad?" I bite my lip, remembering my last encounter with Massimo.

"He has dementia. Only a few people know about it, but I've been planning to officially take over for the better part of this year. It's time," he says matter of factly.

"How will that work? Will you have a meeting with all the bosses around?"

"I'll probably just send an email once everything is in place," he says, holding back a smile when he catches my shocked expression.

"An email?" I ask incredulous, arching back to meet his gaze.

"Everyone knows who I am and that I've been running things around here anyway. At this point, it's just a formality, especially for the older generation."

"So there won't be like a mafia boss convention, where they crown you?"

He laughs. "You watch too many movies. It doesn't work like this in real life."

"I read books, thank you very much," I scoff.

"Well, it's too dangerous to have everyone in the same room at the same time. Even if precautions are taken, the risk is too great. Not only because many of the families are warring, but also because the FBI would have a field day if they ever found us all in one place."

"I guess." Might not be the best time to tell him I made friends with a hacker who threatened to take the entire operation down if Dante hurts me.

"We'll probably have a Zoom call at some point."

My jaw drops.

"What? Don Vito Corleone would turn over in his grave."

"Considering Mario Puzo wrote that book in the sixties, probably on a typewriter, I reckon you're onto something."

"Do you think he'd even have written The Godfather if he had access to the internet?"

Dante shrugs.

"I bet he'd spend most of his day watching porn, The Godfather the last thing on his mind." I grin. "So, you're like the boss of Blackwood?"

"Something like that." He nuzzles my neck, pulling me closer into his embrace.

"What do you mean?"

Dante sighs, "My family is the oldest one in America. We have been at the helm of things for a long time, ensuring things don't get out of place. I guess you can say the families govern themselves but ultimately answer to us. To me."

I bite my lip, "So they come to you if anything is wrong?"

"Yes."

"And you have to go deal with that?"

"Sometimes. Sometimes, I send others."

"Has anyone ever tried to...take over?" My heart speeds up.

"Every day, *Fata*. Being a Don is a constant battle. I cannot step out of line. I have to be ruthless; otherwise, others will think me weak."

"So you're in danger?"

"Are you scared for your life? I'll protect y—"

"No, I'm—" I interrupt, chewing on my finger, my brain working overtime. "I don't want anything to happen to you."

His arms tightened around me. "I promised you the truth, so I won't tell you that nothing ever will. But I can promise you that I'm a tough motherfucker."

"So full of yourself," I giggle, my eyes landing on the yearbook once again. "I bet you were voted 'most likely to take over the world' in high school."

He shrugs.

"Oh my god, you were!" I exclaim.

"There wasn't really a need to vote me anything. I was already in charge of this town by the time I left high school."

"Of course," I laugh. "You said your parents also went to the local high school?"

"My mum did. My father went to Sicily. The only reason I didn't follow in his footsteps was because my mother died when I was twelve."

"I'm so sorry," I mumble, my chest feeling tight all of a sudden. "Why didn't you go to Sicily?"

"Angelo and Luca, I didn't want to leave them on their own...they were too young when it happened. Angelo was eight, and Luca was five. Sometimes—" he trails off, his fingers stroking my hair, "I think I'm the only one who remembers her."

"I'm so sorry, Dante. How old was she?"

"Thirty-four," he says so quietly I can barely hear him.

"Your dad," I start, the burning desire to find out the truth making me stumble over my own words. "He said she gave you a pocket watch."

Dante stiffens beneath me.

"Elena. He said her name was Elena and that she gave it to you."

"What pocket watch."

"I—I found one a long time ago. He said it was yours."

"He's a senile old man. He must have been mistaken."

Feeling the lie between us, I chew on my bottom lip. "The engraving is the same as the one on your money clip. I thought—" I rush.

"That's why you asked me to find out where it was from."

I can feel the chasm opening up between us and growing with every word he utters, despite him holding onto me like I'm his life raft.

"I thought I'd be able to find out where it was from and how it got to me."

"I didn't," he interrupts me. "I'd tell you if I knew anything."

"Right," I say in a small voice, fighting the heat behind my eyes.

"Alessa," he soothes. "Trust me, baby."

The thing is, I *did* trust him. If you asked me a minute ago, I'd say I trusted him wholeheartedly.

But right now?

Not so much.

# 41

## ALESSA

All throughout the rest of the day I can't stop thinking about Dante's words. *Trust me.*

I want to. I'd give anything to go back to the moment before he lied to me, where I was willing to believe anything he'd tell me. And maybe I could if I knew why he's withholding information.

Sun Tzu once said, '*The whole secret lies in confusing the enemy, so that he cannot fathom our real intent*'. And that's exactly what Dante has done. He's drip-dropped bits and pieces of information shrouded in deceit and unsaid truths until I no longer could tell what made sense and what didn't, putting things together where they don't belong.

My mind is in utter chaos right now, trying to figure out the next steps. But in the midst of chaos, there is always opportunity.

Here's what I know:

Dante's mum was friends with someone who looked like me.

They went to the same high school together.

The same high school Dante went to.

Dante has a money clip with the same engraving as the pocket watch I was left with when I was abandoned.

Dante got his money clip from his mum.

The pocket watch might be Dante's.

Except for the life of me, I can't figure out why he would lie about the last one. Could he somehow be involved in how I was left as a toddler? I always thought the black jacket I was found in belonged to my father or another adult, but it could have been Dante's.

Unable to sleep, I slip from under Dante's arm and slide out of bed. Watching him for what feels like a minute, I try to memorise his features. He looks so peaceful as he sleeps, the angry line between his brows smooth as his eyes flutter beneath his eyelids. There's only one thing I can do—find out the truth for myself, and there are crumbs now. Crumbs I can follow.

Tiptoeing into the spare bedroom, I make sure not to make a sound as I get dressed in black jeans, a black hoodie and black lace-up boots, swinging on the black jacket that has been on my mind as an afterthought.

Like I said, even in the midst of chaos, there's always an opportunity. And right now, my opportunity is to go figure out who Elena's best friend was and why the hell everyone is mistaking me for her.

As silently as possible, I creep down the stairs and out the front door. Jogging down the gravel and taking great care to avoid the floodlights scattered around the front of the property, I creep down to the edge of the driveway while trying to figure out how the hell I'm going to scale the ten-foot wall surrounding the property. I should have really thought this through.

An idea forms in my head as I slow to a walk and then stop altogether. Turning on my heel, I run back to the mansion and stand in front of the large garage door.

"What are you doing out at this time of the night?"

I whip my head to meet Freddie's suspicious gaze. I put on my biggest smile. "Evening, Frederico."

His lip twitches up.

"Alessa."

"From where I'm standing, you have two options," I claim boldly.

Fredster's eyebrow lifts up, the expression on his face curious.

"Help me get out of here and back before Dante wakes up."

"Or?"

I sigh. "I haven't gotten that far yet, but, Freddie, it's my only chance. I'm not running away. No one knows where I'm going, and we'll be back before anyone even realises I was gone. Please, please, please."

"Oh, I'm going with you now?"

Chewing my lip, I look into his eyes. "I don't know where the local high school is."

"You want to go to Blackwood High?" He shudders.

"Just to the library."

"I'm sure Dante would take you if you'd ask him."

I hold back the tears threatening to break free. "You know how protective he is. Please, Freddie. He'll never even know we were gone. I just need five minutes."

"He'll kill me if he finds out."

"Please." A tear born of desperation slips past my lashes.

"Fuck," Fred curses. "Fine, but we have to be back within an hour."

I quietly squeal with delight. "Thank you, thank you, thank you!"

"I really need to get my head checked," Fred mutters as he opens the garage door.

I make a beeline for the Maserati and slide into the driver's seat.

"No way." Fred shakes his head.

"Come on, pretty please," I make puppy eyes at him.

"What the fuck is wrong with me?" He looks up to heaven, making me grin. "I suppose I'm most likely already dead."

"I'm driving."

Sighing, he opens the passenger door before making a spectacle of buckling his seatbelt.

"Ready?" I ask, not waiting for a reply before speeding out of the garage, down the driveway and through the now miraculously open gate.

Fred directs me, and we're in front of a school building within fifteen minutes.

"Do you know how to pick locks?" I ask Freddie as we get out of the car and look at the closed school gate—I don't want him to find out all my secrets just yet.

He sighs. "Follow me."

I do as directed, walking along the fenced area until we get to the back of the building. Standing in front of the metal bars holding the fence together, Fred kicks one three times until it pops from its hinges, swinging aside to let us in.

"Sweet." I rub my hands with glee before sliding through the small space and walking up to the stone wall of the building. "What are the chances they left one of the windows open?"

Fred shakes his head. "Were you seriously trying to get here on your own, completely unprepared?"

I shrug, "I've got my bobby pins. They haven't failed me yet."

"Let's see what you got, then." He gestures at a metal door to the right of where we're standing. I give the rusty lock a once over before pulling out the bobby pins from my pocket. Before I even start to make a fool out of myself and pretend that I know what I'm doing Freddie chuckles, pushing me aside and opening the door with a fucking key he had all along.

I decide not to give him shit for messing with me since he's the reason I'm even here.

"Which way to the library?" I ask as we slip inside, the metal door closing behind us with a dull thud.

With his warm hand on the small of my back, Freddie guides us until we're in front of large double doors. Pushing them open, I lift my phone in front of me and flick the flashlight on, illuminating the large room around us. There are shelves upon shelves filled with books, and normally, I'd be skipping from one to another, trying to find hidden gems. But right now, my eyes don't stop on any of the spines for longer than a second, hyperfocused on what I'm searching for.

Finally, I spot the shelf that houses yearbooks and break into a run until I'm in front of it, fingering the spines and whispering the dates on them, looking for the one that could hold answers. By my calculation of how old Dante and his mum were when she passed away, I narrowed it down to three books.

The first one comes up empty. I don't know Elena's maiden name, so I have to look through every photo, trying to find her. The second one doesn't have her either. My heart thudding behind my rib cage, I pick up the third book, partly worried I completely miscalculated and partly excited to find out more.

Fred grumbles from beside the entrance for me to hurry up, just as I lift the cover open to a landscape picture of the whole class standing in front of the building. Scanning the faces—not that I'd recognise Elena, having never seen a picture of her—my eyes snag on something I equally was and wasn't expecting.

*I am* in the photo. Grinning widely, I have my arm around another woman who's got a mischievous smile on her face. The same smile Dante gave me when I told him I was all orgasmed out last night before he proceeded to prove me wrong. Swallowing a lump in my throat, I turn the pages, looking for the familiar face, until I find it once again. Standing in front of an archway made out of flowers with a handsome, older-looking guy. My finger traces her face down her dress to the text below the photo.

*Prom night - Rosa Mancini with her date Alessandro Carusso.*

My heart stops in my chest, the breath I was about to exhale locked in my lungs as I try to process what I'm seeing. *Rosa. Rosalita.* All the names I've been called by strangers. I look exactly like her. Then I look at the guy again. Alessandro Carusso. His face is familiar, too. Like I should know him from somewhere, yet can't quite place him. But it's the surname that catches my attention. *Carusso.*

*Little caruso*—is what the bus station guy called me, except maybe it wasn't a nickname. Maybe he meant Carusso.

Clutching the book close to my chest, I glance around, but there is no one here to witness the monumental discovery I have just made. With a heavy sigh, I reluctantly peel the book away, tearing away the page that immortalises the love so clearly captured in the photograph. Gently, I tuck the image into my bra before leafing through the remaining pages of the album. Several more snapshots of Rosa with Elena surface before I turn to the portrait page.

*Rosa Mancini - voted most likely to save the world.*

A hushed sob wracks my body, resonating with sorrow for never knowing the woman in the photographs. Never even having a chance to find out what sort of person she is. Closing the yearbook, I gingerly return it back to its place on the shelf. Has she truly been out there, changing the world? Did the prospect of motherhood hinder her path to greatness? And what about Alessandro, the man whose first name echoes mine so closely—it can't be a coincidence. Is he with her wherever she is, looking at her as if she was the world's greatest wonder, just as he did the moment the picture was taken?

Dusting my jeans off, I get up, my heart lodged in my throat, a cacophony of unanswered questions swirling around in my head. It's time to tell Freddie I'm ready to head back.

Except, as I approach the door he last stood next to, unease settles in. He's not there. Silently, I walk past the rows of shelves and push the door ajar, encountering an obstacle. Something is blocking the door. I shove at it more forcefully pushing at whatever's obstructing my exit on the other side.

"Fred?" I whisper, my eyes scanning the dark corridor in both directions. It's only when I look all the way down and whatever is in my way, I spot it.

The leg of a body lying on the floor.

Gasping, I cover my mouth with my shaking hands, recoiling a step back only to collide with something hard.

"Hello, little Carusso," a menacing growl reverberates, sending a shiver of fear coursing through my entire being. "You should be dead."

Before I can even comprehend the threat hanging in the air, something heavy hits the back of my head, and the world plunges into darkness.

# 42

## ALESSA

I have a splitting headache and my right arm is dead. But I don't make a sound when I come to. Lying on a dusty hardwood floor, my hands and legs tied behind me I keep my eyes closed and try to breathe steady, listening for any sounds.

Once I'm satisfied I'm alone, I peer around me from underneath my lashes. The room I'm in seems empty. The furniture around me is covered in white sheets and the floor has a thick layer of dust disturbed with footprints and a large track going from the door to where I'm lying. Nice. The kidnappers couldn't even carry me to the middle of the room dragging me on the floor instead; I swear if they snagged my jacket on anything I'll be livid.

This is not the first time I find myself in a precarious situation, with my hands tied behind my back. I've stolen things from powerful people who don't appreciate thieves, I counted cards, lied and made enemies, and I always managed to come out the other side unscathed. It's why I was always on the move. But this is the first time I have no idea why I've been taken hostage. I'm sure I'll find out soon enough, though, so, instead of wasting time, I should be trying to get myself out of these binds before anyone comes back into the room.

Bending backwards I get to work on the chaotic mess of knots securing my feet together, my tied hands working swiftly. The kidnapper must really have me mistaken for some kind of damsel in distress, who wouldn't even think of escaping because it takes me less than a minute to undo the sad excuse for restraints. As soon as the rope is untied, I wiggle my arms over my bent legs and get to work on the knots around my wrists. They are a lot tighter than the ones around my feet were. With a resourceful twist, I clasp the rope between my teeth, leveraging every ounce of determination to get free within me. I pull at the strands, taking care to loosen the knots, until finally there is enough give in them I can wriggle my wrists free.

Sitting up, I take the time to look around, taking in the space around me. Judging by the glimpses of the sky and the tree peeking from between the window covering I'm on higher ground. First or second floor maybe, which means escape via that route is most likely out of the question. Listening for any sounds of movement from behind the door I get up, the rope which bound me firmly in my hands as I quietly creep to the window, moving the curtain slightly to figure out my next steps. To my dismay, I find the window boarded up, one of the nails must have rusted over, as the slither of sky I saw before is coming from a space where a wooden board must have fallen off. I'm also definitely not on ground level.

Just as I make my way back to where I woke up I hear footsteps outside. Without a thought, I drop to the ground wrapping the rope around my legs and wrists, my heart hammering in my chest as I try to steady my breathing and look unconscious.

The door creaks open and a slither of light falls on my face. I don't move a muscle.

"She's still out." I hear a man's voice.

"I'm not blind." The second voice is raspy, marred with wheezes in between each word, like whoever is speaking has just run a marathon.

I fight the urge to half open my eyes and see who I'm up against, the only thing stopping me—the knowledge that as soon as they realise I'm awake they'll need to do something about me. For now, I'm safer staying unconscious.

"I don't have all night to wait for her to wake up," the wheezy voice says.

"Do you want me to shoot her?"

Or maybe I'm not so safe. Fuck.

"No. Wake her up."

As footsteps draw near me, I keep my breathing steady despite the urge to hold my breath until the person stops right in front of me.

I pray they don't notice my shoddy attempt at pretending I'm still tied, but before I can even start worrying about it, pain shoots through my body as a heavy boot connects with my stomach.

I gasp in pain, the instinct to curl in on myself over-whelming as nausea takes over, yet I keep still, fighting the tears threatening to spill. The sole of the boot that kicked me rests against the side of my face, digging into my cheek and pressing my head into the cold hardwood floor. Panic settles beneath my ribcage. This is bad. Very, very bad.

"Wake up, little birdie, or I'll smoosh your pretty face until your brain pops out through your cracked skull," he menaces, pushing his boot harder into my face.

Heart hammering in my chest, I whimper, unable to stop myself, and fling my eyes open.

The man sighs, removing his foot from my face. "Such a

shame, I do think your brain would make a beautiful painting on the floor."

I'm definitely in and over my head with whatever I got myself into this time.

"Up," the wheezy man says, and I catch sight of him for the first time. He's short, heavily overweight and looks like he just walked off a set of a black and white gangster movie with his pin-stripe suit and the unlit cigar in his hand.

"Yes, boss." The other guy's menacing face nears mine, I hold onto my ankles and pray for the rope to stay in place. Grabbing me by my hair, he hauls me up until I'm kneeling in front of him, my hands still behind me, proud of myself for keeping my mouth shut while all I wanted to do was scream in pain. He must have broken a rib with his kick.

He steps away and stands behind the short guy he called boss. He's the one clearly in charge.

"Well, well, well," he wheezes as he steps towards me, his small eyes raking up and down my body, judging every inch of me. "You look just like her."

I want to ask who, but I have an idea of who he means, the picture I ripped from the yearbook still pressing against my boob inside my bra. I keep my mouth shut, hoping that like every villain in every story I ever read he'll start talking, just to fill the silence.

But he doesn't. He watches me instead, his bushy eyebrows draw together so closely they almost look like a monobrow. His lips twitch into a smirk as dread seeps into every pore of my being. I've miscalculated. He's not like every villain in every story because those are fictional. He doesn't care if I know why I'm here or who I look like.

"Should I kill you myself or should I leave you to Antonio? He does like to play with his food." Droplets of saliva spit out of his mouth as he speaks.

He chuckles when, once again I stay silent, a barrage of

Sun Tzu quotes I've ever laid eyes on flashing in my mind. I have no weapon, no way of getting past the two looming figures, and no idea why I'm even here. My phone lies forgotten on the library floor of Blackwood High where I dropped it before I was struck in the back of the head. And the only person even aware of my absence is blocking said library door, hopefully still alive.

Except, I know *one* thing. And if he isn't talking maybe he'll start if I ask the right questions.

"Rosa," I whisper, my eyes watching him for any tells. "Who is she?"

He laughs, a booming laugh that breaks when he goes into a coughing fit. The hand holding the cigar flies to his chest as he thumps it forcefully, dislodging something wet in his throat, which he proceeds to swallow. Nausea comes back in full force, and I have to hold in the gag that threatens to break free.

"She's funny, Tony," he wheezes, elbowing the burly man beside him in the ribs.

"I'm not trying to be."

Tony's in front of me in three steps, the back of his hand connecting with the left side of my face so hard I hurdle to the ground. The death grip I have on my ankles ensures the side of my head hits the floorboards. Tasting copper in my mouth, I groan, the pain is unbearable but I must remain strong. I rack my brain for any options on how the hell I am supposed to escape. But it's too muddled to come up with any solutions.

Tony grabs my hair and roughly shoves me up. "No one asked your opinion, *puttana*[1]."

I look down at the floor, all hope of trying to get out of this unscathed, leaving me. Tony stays beside me as the other man slowly waddles closer, a stench of cigars mixed with BO following him like a cloud of expensive cologne.

The tip of his polished shoe nudges my knee, making me look up at him, my head throbbing in the process.

"Rosa Carusso," he wheezes, "was your mother."

# 43

## ALESSA

My heart stutters in my chest as my mouth goes dry.

"Mother?" I croak.

Tony lifts his arm as if to strike me, but the boss shakes his head, making him drop it back down.

"Ye-e-e-e-s," he leers. "Your lying, cheating, useless cunt of a mother."

Digging my nails into the flesh of my ankles I stay silent, dropping my gaze back down in submission.

"Is—is she—"

"Dead?"

I nod, wincing as a dull ache shoots through my brain from the movement.

He chuckles. "Oh yes, she is. Killed by your own father, the fucking Carusso piece of shit." He spits at me, the glop of saliva hitting my jean-clad thigh. I try not to recoil, but a flinch escapes me nonetheless. "Once he got rid of her, he went after the lover your whore of a mother seduced. *My son.*"

I can't help but look up in disbelief. Would my mother really cheat on my father? They looked so in love. So happy.

322

And would he really kill her? Once again, I gain an unpleasant glimpse into the harsh world Dante Santoro is from. Why would my mother knowingly tie herself to someone as horrid as this guy? Or his son.

"Nico was going to be the next Don," the boss continues. "He had his whole future ahead of him. I had a plan. Santoros were going to fall, and Nico was going to lead the mafia into the Nicolosi era. Your cunt of a mother ruined it all."

My breath catches in my throat.

*Nico Nicolosi.* The man in front of me is the same man I've been trying to hack with Arrow for the past few weeks. I wonder if Arrow managed to find something? But that's a future Alessa problem. Right now I need to figure out how to stay alive, when Nico is determined to make me pay for what my family did to his.

"And you," Nico continues, oblivious to the turmoil in my head. "You were supposed to be dead."

I bite my lip.

"Tell me, how did Alessandro," he spits again, the saliva catching my shoulder this time, "manage to save your life?"

I swallow hard, my eyes darting to Tony, making sure he's not going to hit me for speaking again. "I don't know," I say the truth, while my heart picks up speed. Could this be? Was my father the one who saved me? Did he try to get me to safety and then join me later, but got caught in Nico's trap along the way?

"Lies!" he spits, furious. Tony grabs my hair and yanks my head back, the pain in my temple increasing tenfold.

"I swear," I plead, my whole body shaking. "I only remember waking up in front of an abandoned house. I had no idea who my parents were or what happened when I came to Blackwood."

Nico narrows his eyes. "You were what, five? Six, back then?"

"Just turned three."

He shrugs. "It doesn't matter. You were still supposed to be dead. Every Carusso was. And since you're not, you'll die now."

He motions to Tony as my heart stops.

"Why?" I ask, halting his move and drawing his attention back to me.

"He killed my son. I killed everyone he ever cared for."

"But he's dead now. He doesn't care anymore. Please just let me go. I'll leave town."

He smirks, "Even if I was a nice man and had it in my heart to forgive you for your father's sins—which I am not, and I don't—I wouldn't let you go."

It's on the tip of my tongue to ask why, but Tony's raised hand stops the words from escaping me mid-throat.

"I don't owe you an explanation," Nicolosi continues. "Carusso's fucked up my plans to take over once. They won't do it again."

I search his face for clues. What the hell is he on about? Then it hits me.

"Dante," I whisper.

"You're a distraction to him. A whore," he looks at me with disgust, "he occupies his time with until he can fulfil his contract and marry my daughter. There *will* be Nicolasi at the helm after all," he laughs. "And once Natalia is at the top... well, I'll leave that to your imagination."

"You're going to have him killed," I say in shock, searching his face for any signs I'm reading this wrong.

"You're not as dumb as your mother, I see," he tilts his head to the side. "I'd say it's a shame to lose a young, bright mind like yours," he smiles, showing his yellow teeth, "but I really don't care." Loathing pours off his body as he gives me one more once over before turning his back to me and walking out of the room. "Do with her what you want," he throws over his shoulder, stepping over the threshold, "as long as she's dead at the end."

The door closes behind him, leaving Tony and I in darkness. Shaking with a mix of disgust and fear I look up from my kneeling position, meeting Tony's eyes. His grip on my hair tightens as he wets his lips with his tongue, his cold eyes dropping to my cleavage.

Before I have the time to recoil, he drags me closer to him, his voice a menacing whisper. "Maybe I'll take my time with you. Find out exactly what it is about your cunt that has Santoro so wrapped up." He licks my cheek before pressing his lips against mine and pushing me down to the floor. Trying not to gag I struggle to pull away from him, but he doesn't let up.

Heart pounding in my chest, I shift the rope I've been clutching in between my hands just as he pushes his knee in between my thighs, spreading them open. Letting go of my hair he palms my breast roughly. "Tell me, how does it feel to be fucking the man who killed your dear old daddy?"

Freezing in place, I try to process his words. He takes the opportunity to grind against me.

"Please," I whimper, trying my hardest to chase away the scared thirteen-year-old girl within me. My brain at war with what's happening to me and the words it's trying to understand. His hand moves from my breast to the bottom of my hoodie, lifting it up and exposing my stomach.

"Did Dante ever tell you how he slit your father's throat? How, like a coward, he came in the night while your father was sleeping, defenceless."

No.

No, no, no, no.

Tears prick behind my eyes as my body sags. This can't

be true. Dante would never...why? A sob escapes me as Tony roughly pushes my hoodie up, pinching my nipple through my bra. It hurts, but I'm no longer in my body. Like the little girl I was when it first happened to me, I go into a space in my head where only happy thoughts exist. Except that space is now filled with memories of Dante. Dante, who killed my dad. Dante, who's the reason I was orphaned, alone and left to the system.

Anger races through my veins as Tony busies himself with undoing the buttons on my jeans, his fingers brutally ripping them off. He doesn't pay me any attention, too wrapped up in what's about to happen to notice my hands are no longer behind me or that my feet aren't bound. In a split second, hours of training with Dante kick in, and with my mind shut off to anything but escaping what's about to happen, I let my muscles take over, following the pattern of movements I practised over and over again. Relax, push, kick, flip, hold, tense, push. The next time I blink, I'm on top of Tony as he lies face down on the floor with my rope tight against his throat, one hand pushing his head down, the other pulling at the constraints tightening around his neck. My whole body shakes with fury as he tries to kick me off balance, but Dante trained me well, teaching me where to dig my knee in if I want to incapacitate a larger, much stronger opponent. Tony gurgles beneath me, his hands reaching for the rope, trying to purchase a grip, pull it away. He didn't expect the strength a girl can possess when she's about to be defiled. Bile rises in my throat as I squash down silent sobs. Too close, this was too close. And if it weren't for Dante, I'd not have had a chance of getting free.

Then again, if it wasn't for Dante, would I even be in this situation? I shake my head, focusing back on the man beneath me, squeezing the rope tighter until, finally, his jerks become softer and his whole body sags.

With my heart beating out of my chest, I get up shakily, taking a few steps away from the body on the floor, my eyes locked on the large, unmoving frame. My knees buckle, and I have to hold onto whatever piece of furniture is next to me, covered in a white sheet, just to avoid falling back down on the floor.

On unsteady legs, I back out all the way to the door, making sure Tony doesn't move. Jesus Christ, I killed a man. A bad man who was about to rape me, then kill me. But still. I killed someone. My hand flies to my mouth as I force a sob back down my throat, looking at Tony's body one last time before turning around and opening the door to the corridor. My eyes are assaulted with bright light, and for a second I can't breathe for fear I'll get caught, standing here like a blind mouse ready to be eaten by the fat cat. But then, by some miracle, my vision adjusts, and I take light steps on a plush carpet covering the floor, grateful for it as it cushions the sounds of my footsteps. My ears straining for any sounds, I slowly make my way down the corridor, trying to figure out if Tony and I were the only people left in here or if there are others I should be aware of.

A commotion coming from downstairs makes me halt my steps as I strain my ears to listen. Shouts, whispered orders and gunshots. Then my head turns back to where I came from as the sound of a loud crash and a pained groan reaches my ears. With my heart in my throat, I push the doors I've been leaning on open and close them behind me just as Tony barrels out of the room we were in.

# 44

## ALESSA

Flinching, I listen with my ear against the door as more gunshots are fired somewhere downstairs. Whatever is going on down there, every instinct in my body screams at me to stay as far away as possible. But staying upstairs is no longer an option either. Not when Zombie-Tony has risen and is definitely not going to be gentle with me when he finds me. Seriously, what does a girl have to do around here to keep a guy dead?

Breathing harshly, with my back blocking the door, I look around the room. It's bigger than the one Nicolosi originally put me in. There's a large bed in the middle, a couple of pieces of furniture covered in white sheets, and a door that most likely leads to an en suite bathroom. Rushing to the one which is as tall as a desk should be, I lift the covering and exhale with relief when I do, in fact, find a desk. There's a chance there's something inside I could use as a weapon.

And even though my heart is half convinced the whole ordeal is futile and everything will be empty, judging by the thick layer of dust around me, I'm shocked to find I am wrong. Opening the first drawer of the mahogany desk, I find it full of odds and ends, as if whoever lived here stepped out for just a minute and never returned. There are fountain pens, pencils, a ruler, and an old-school calculator, amongst other things. I grab the sharpened pencil, remembering all the ways I imagined I could stab a person with one, but then my eyes catch on the sharp letter opener and I quickly swap it, forgoing my pen-icide plans.

I quickly close the top drawer as quietly as I possibly can and check the one below. This one is filled with paperwork, all dated nearly two decades ago from what I can see. Sifting through the forgotten letters, newspaper clippings and bills, my eyes snag on a name and my heart flutters in my chest.

*Alessandro Carusso.*

Holy shit.

Holding my breath, I look through the rest of the contents, finding his name on almost every single one. Could this be Alessandro Carusso's house? Could this be the place where he lived with his wife? Did I spend my first three years of life here? It would make Nico Nicolosi one twisted asshole to bring me into my childhood home just to kill me. I wouldn't be surprised, though. From the little interaction I've had with him, I can tell he'd relish the idea.

Biting my bottom lip, I close the drawer and look around the room with fresh eyes. Could this have been my parents' bedroom? For a second, I forget why I'm here, who's outside and what's going to happen to me if anyone finds me. For a second, I choke on my own tears as I take in the space I probably came into often. Did I sleep in the huge bed with *them* when I had nightmares? My feet take me to the piece of furniture, and I can't help but sit on the cloth-covered mattress. A spring digs into my ass as I bounce up and down, wondering which side of the bed was my mother's and which my father's. Is this the bed Dante killed my dad in? Where was I?

Noticing the nightstands, I pry the door open and find it empty, except for an upturned picture frame. I slowly pull it out and flip it in my hands as a crash outside startles me. It's too near for comfort, but I couldn't care less as I stare at the faces of my mother and father smiling at each other on their wedding day. Rosa and Alessandro Carusso.

*I'm* a Carusso. Alessandra Carusso. Not Jones like I thought my whole life. I trace my finger over the simple white dress with laced sleeves and high neckline my mother adorned, a true reflection that you don't need an elaborate outfit to highlight one's beauty.

With a door smashing nearby, I flinch once again and get up, closing the door to the nightstand with my boot as I stuff the picture frame in the waistband of my jeans and cover it with my hoodie. There's no way I'm leaving it behind, and I don't have the time to fiddle with the frame.

"I will fucking find you, *puttana,*" comes a growl from right behind the bedroom door, and I shoot across the room to the one thing large enough to hide in.

Clutching the letter opener in one hand I lift the white covering up and stop, my breaths coming in shallow as my eyes take in the antique looking wardrobe in front of me.

Something in me screams, *get as far away from this thing as possible*, but I have no idea why. I still haven't moved, my body frozen in place as my brain urges my limbs to move.

*Reach the fuck out, Alessa and open the door*, it says. *Get the fuck inside and hide*, it screams at me. But no matter what I should be doing, the fact of the matter is I'm not doing it. In fact, cold sweat covers my body as my eyes take in the intricately carved details on the outside.

"There's a snaggy nail in the left corner," I whisper, dread pooling in my stomach. Seeing the exact space I'm thinking about in my mind like I've stared at it so long it was burned onto my memory. Light floods the room as the door to the corridor opens, but I ignore it. I ignore the loud roar from the man rushing toward me. I ignore his heavy footsteps as he gets closer and closer.

My world shattering around me while I *remember*.

# 45

## ALESSA

Time stretches like an endless abyss as my eyes stay glued to the wardrobe, each second feels like an eternity. The memories crash over me, pulling me back into the depths of confinement, hunger and unrelenting fear. Hours spent inside echo in my mind, the haunting question of 'why' tormenting me relentlessly. What had I done to warrant this?

Even more memories unravel as I remember the one face I trusted with my whole being—the architect of my torment, my own father.

A force crashes into me, hurling me to the floor. I barely notice the agony at my side as something pierces my skin. My mind is too busy transporting me back in time to my three-year-old self. A tear escapes my eye as Tony's enraged screams fill the air, his spittle landing across my cheek as my gaze remains fixed on the mahogany door. Flawless on the outside, scarred within detail etched in my memory from futile attempts to escape. How could I have forgotten this? How could I not remember the duct tape binding my wrists too tightly? Or the one placed over my mouth because I was crying too loudly.

Tony pushes onto his elbows and slaps me, hard, his aggression escalating at my blatant lack of response. Jerking my face to the side, I let him grind into me as he tells me the things he will do to me. But I don't hear his words, a metallic resonance drowning out everything around us. And I don't see his menacing face as I watch the bedroom door with unseeing eyes.

A tear slips past my eye as Tony rips the button of my jeans, the haunting memory of betrayal resurfacing.

*He* came for me. *He* hugged me and told me he'd make sure I was safe, and then he left me. Alone and terrified.

A pair of boots thunder past the open door, then comes back, halting in the open doorway like harbingers of an impending storm.

"Alessa," a voice roars, but I don't have the strength to reply, so I close my eyes instead, tears spilling down my cheeks as I remember falling asleep in *his* car and then waking up alone and scared, with the jacket he was wearing draped across my small frame.

Tony jerks on top of me, his full weight crushing into me as liquid sprays the side of my face, the pain in my side increasing. The boots draw nearer, and suddenly Tony is gone. His unmoving body pushed away as I'm being lifted into someone's arms. Orders are shouted and more rushed footsteps sound in the distance as the scent of wood and citrus envelopes me in a tight embrace. I should be able to say something. Move. But there's no more strength within me. My eyes slide past Tony and back onto the wardrobe.

"Alessa," his distressed voice pulls at my heartstrings, seeking reassurance. "Are you okay, baby?"

I want to shout back that, no, I'm not okay. How can I be, having remembered everything? But he doesn't let me answer anyway as he pulls me closer, crushing me into him even harder. The pain in my side is excruciating now, but I don't make a sound, powerless in the feeling of sadness.

"L-let's get you home," he chokes, and a hollow laugh bubbles within me. I am home. This is the house that belonged to my family. The house he killed my father in. The house my father killed my mother in. And the house he probably planned to kill me in, too.

"You saved me," I manage to whisper. How many times now?

"I'll always save you. I swear."

My head lols to the side as he carries me through a house I don't recognise. Breathing becomes a desperate struggle, with every door we pass and as we descend the stairs, I can't help the moan that escapes me.

Dante freezes, his concern etched with a gravity that matches the dire reality that was my childhood.

"Baby, are you hurt?" he asks.

But instead of an answer I want to give him, something metallic fills my mouth, choking me.

"Alessa, fuck!" he jolts me. "Aleeesaaaaa!" His panic screams echoing in the distance, a haunting symphony of despair.

## 46

# DANTE

I pace relentlessly around the cold, sterile confines of the hospital waiting area, each step echoing around the empty space. The seconds stretch into eternity, and I find myself raking my hands through my already dishevelled hair. The white walls seem to close in on me, mirroring the suffocating anxiety gripping my chest. Alessa is somewhere behind the set of double doors, grappling with a battle that I, for all my power, cannot fight for her.

Images of the blood trickling from the corner of her mouth flood my mind, and I freeze in place, trying not to roar with anguish. Trying not to rip this whole place apart. Not because thinking of the blood makes me feel sick. No.

Because remembering her limp body in my arms, her laboured breathing fills me with an anxiety I have never felt before.

Helplessness can be so crippling—but as long as she's still breathing, so will I. I can't lose her. Not now, when she finally came back into my life, dispersing the storm clouds around my soul. Her attitude, covered in sass despite everything she's been through. My *Fata*. My sorceress.

"Sit down. You're scaring the staff," Angelo sighs from

behind me. I whirl around to face him. How can he even ask me to be still when the woman I love is dyin—

Fuck.

My heart flutters in my chest, unsure of its movements as if it's afraid I'd get spooked if I got a hint of who it's beating for. But the joke is on my stupid heart because I knew already, even if I pretended it wasn't the case.

I need Alessa like she's the air that fills my lungs. I love her. I knew it when I told her she was mine. I knew it when I fucked her, and I knew it when I made plans to break the marriage contract despite the consequences. In fact, the engagement ring I got her is burning a hole in my pocket.

Clenching my fists, I resume my pacing because if I let myself think about not being able to slip that ring on her finger, I will combust, and anyone in my presence will be in danger. The uncertainty of the future is eating me alive, breaking my essence into tiny little pieces and chewing them leisurely before spitting them back out.

The door opens, and I stop, hopeful to see a doctor coming in with good news, but it's just Luca walking in. One look at me, and he gives me a wide berth, choosing to sit by Angelo instead.

"*Cazzo*." I dip my head into my hands, unable to hide the anguish in my voice. I cannot wait any longer. With purposeful steps, I walk towards the double door.

"Dante," Luca tries to stop me, but one sharp look over my shoulder is enough to make him close his mouth and sit back down. "Just remember they're already trying to help her," he calls after me.

I ignore him as I push the door open and walk in, startling the young nurse, who is noting something on her clipboard.

"You're not supposed to be back here." She narrows her eyes at me. On any other day, in any other situation, I'd admire her spirit because it takes balls to stand up to *me*, but right now, her stance means nothing to me. Well, except an obstacle between Alessa and I.

"Where is she?" I growl. "Take me to her."

"Look, I'm sure whoever you're talking about is fine. The doctor will come and find you as soon a—"

"Do you think I'm an idiot?" I boom. "This is a private wing. One that *I* fucking funded." Her face pales at the realisation. "Now, take me to her," I demand. "Ple-ase," my voice cracks as I whisper, "Take me to Alessa."

"Mr Santoro." I turn my head to face the male doctor speaking to me. "This way." He gestures down a corridor, then starts walking in the direction he pointed to. I follow him, unable to speak again for fear he's going to say something I won't be able to un-hear.

"She's lost a lot of blood," the doctor continues.

"She can have mine," I rush. He turns to look at me, his gaze dropping to my chest. I follow his gaze to the large patch of dark, dried blood. *Alessa's blood.* "It's not mine. I have way too much blood. She can have it. She can have it all," I blurt out, feeling like a hole has opened up in my chest.

"That's nice." I get a condescending look in return. It takes everything in me not to pull my gun out and shoot him. "But we don't know if you're a match." I open my mouth to speak, tell him, I know exactly what her blood type is and that I am, in fact, a match, but his hand flies up to stop me. "Besides, we have plenty of O negative in storage. We're good. But you can donate all that extra blood you have at some other time. We're always looking for donors."

I nearly stop at his words—he must have the information wrong. What fucking excuse for a hospital is this?

"You have two minutes." He gestures at the door in front of us.

Gingerly, I push it open. I won't tell him he can fuck right off with his two minutes just yet. I'll wait until I'm inside.

Then I see her, and all the air escapes my lungs as I rush to her side. Taking her hand in mine, I bring it to my lips, giving it a gentle kiss. She looks pale, her usually tanned complexion ashen and dull. Still beautiful, though, making my heart pick up in my chest at the sight of her face. Despite all the wires connecting her to various machines.

"Don't you dare fucking leave me, baby," I whisper against her knuckles before straightening them out and slipping the twelve-carat diamond onto her ring finger. "You said you're mine, and I intend to keep you, Alessa."

I pull my phone out and dial, placing the phone in between my shoulder and my ear while pulling Alessa's chart out of its holder. Something niggling at my subconscious.

"How is she?"

"She's in recovery. I'm with her now, but..."

"What is it? Is she going to be okay?"

"You know when you texted me her blood type...are you sure you had the right one?" I scan her chart—and there it is, at the very top, 'O negative' in bold letters.

"Don't insult me, Dante. You know I'm the best damn hacker in the United States. Do you really think I'd get something so simple wrong? I checked her parent's blood types on record. Her mother was an O, and her father was a B."

"That would make her a B just like me, except her chart says she's O negative," I murmur into the phone, disregarding all the self-love Arrow just spewed at me. Hiring them all those years ago was the best decision I made for my business. It was a cherry on top that Arrow and Alessa hit it off when Arrow was checking her out. A cherry that paid for itself tenfold when they woke me up in the middle of the night, ringing me to check why Alessa's phone and the bracelet they gave her with a nifty little tracker inside it were at two separate locations. Neither of which was my bed where she was supposed to be.

"Well, fuck," Arrow says. "Give me a second." I hear them tapping away before humming. "So there's no record of her blood type at birth, but...Yes! She sold her plasma a couple of times. Poor baby—must have been really hard for her." I growl with frustration at Arrow's tangent. "Fine, fine. Keep the anger in your pants. The hospital's records are right. She's 'O negative'."

"So you made a mistake." There's ice in my veins.

"No," I can practically hear the eye roll in their voice. "Rosa's and Alessandro's blood types are exactly what I told you they are."

"What the fuck then?"

Arrow tsks. "For someone so intelligent, you can be a real—"

"You better not finish that thought, Arrow," I growl.

"Please. Like you'd ever do anything to me. I'm indispensable. Plus, you love me." They finish, gloating. It's frustrating as fuck, but they're not wrong. Over the years, Arrow became like a third sibling to me—annoying, lovable, and someone I trust implicitly. "Anywhooo, have you ever thought Alessa might have been adopted?"

"I saw her mother pregnant," I snap.

"Okay. Then maybe, Carusso isn't her father?"

I want to snort at the absurdity of that statement because Rosa Carusso wouldn't dare...but then—they had tried for children for so many years with no luck until Alessa. "I don't know," I hesitate, but the more I think of it, the more I see Arrow's point.

"I mean, he killed her because she had an affair. Could

there have been another man before Nicolosi? One who—you know—got her pregnant."

"Or it could have been Nicolosi." A plan is forming in my head. "Can you—"

"On it. Let me run some checks and get back to you. It'll be difficult to prove anything without his DNA."

"I've got to go," I snap, letting my phone drop with a quiet thud onto Alessa's bed. Clutching her chart to my chest, I pace around the hospital room, my head filled with a million thoughts.

"Mr Santoro." The nurse pops her head through the door. "It's time to head back to the waiting area."

"I'm not leaving my fiancée's side," I snap, probably harsher than I meant to, but I need to get my point across.

"Mr. Santor—"

"What's your name?"

"Bri," she answers, her eyebrows scrunched in confusion.

"Have you ever been in love, Bri?"

She opens her mouth as if to answer but I stop her, raising my hand in the air.

"What I mean is—have you ever loved someone so much, your heart beat just for them? Have you ever loved someone so much every second spent away from them manifested as pain in your chest? Have you ever loved someone so much," I swallow, "that living without them was no living at all?"

Bri's mouth closes as she shakes her head from side to side.

"This here is my future wife, Bri. The woman I can't be apart from. I need to be here when she wakes up. She's my forever, do you understand?"

Bri opens her mouth again.

"Forever is a long time," Alessa croaks out and my head

340

snaps back to her beautiful face, my heart lodged in my throat.

"Alessa." In an instant, I'm by her bed, brushing a lock of brown hair off her forehead.

Bri rushes to her other side, performing checks, but my focus is solely on Alessa and the small smile spreading across her lips.

# 47

# ALESSA

"Hi," I rasp as Dante threads his fingers through mine, squeezing my hand.

"Hi, baby." His eyes are shining as his forehead touches mine, his thumb grazing my cheek.

"Future wife, eh?" I wince at how dry my throat is. Every word hurts.

"Was it me? Did I hurt you?" He lets go of my hand, jerking back, his eyes scanning my body for fresh injuries.

"No." I try to wet my lips, but my tongue feels like sandpaper. As if reading my mind, Dante reaches off to the side and comes up with a cup of water. I try to smile as he cautiously lifts it to my lips and watches me take a tentative sip. The cool water feels like heaven on my parched throat. It is also giving me the head space to figure out what exactly is going on.

"Mr Santoro. I need you to leave." My eyes bounce from Dante to the young woman in scrubs standing on the other side of the bed I'm in. Hospital bed. Dante growls something incoherent at her as I take stock of myself. The side of my face hurts, my ribs ache with a dull throb each time I take a breath, and there is something uncomfortable on the side of my stomach. Other than that, I don't feel too bad, but there are wires sticking out of my arm, and when I follow them, my gaze lands on the bags hanging from a hook. Shit. I don't think I'd be out of line in assuming that one of those has strong painkillers in it. Meaning, my situation is probably worse than I first assumed. My mind is hazy enough that I can't piece the last few hours of being awake together.

While Dante and the nurse argue in hushed tones, I try to remember what happened. I was going to go to the high school to find out more about Rosa. Fred was with me... I found the picture... I look down at my chest, scrunching my brows—I'm no longer wearing a bra, so someone must have taken it away. I'm about to open my mouth and ask where it is when memories flood me. Fred's body on the floor. Nicolosi. Tony. The house I grew up in.

The wardrobe.

I squeak as a tear spills down my cheek, unable to hold the pain in check. The memories I buried so deep inside resurfacing with renewed strength.

"*Fata*, are you in pain?"

I shake my head, despite being in agony over my lost childhood. The family I never had, and the father who was determined to make me pay for my mother's sins. It's not the sort of ache that painkillers can fix anyway.

"Is Fred okay?" I manage to ask, pushing everything else to the back of my mind. Dante's jaw tightens as a muscle in his vein starts to tick. I slide my hand across the bed to his, trying not to wince at the pain just the slight movement causes. "Dante," I soothe, squeezing his hand.

He squeezes mine back, his posture relaxing. "He's...fine. For now."

"Dante."

"He was shot."

I gasp, the movement making me wince.

"He's fine. My men got to him in time." The muscle in his vein ticks again.

"Please don't hurt him."

His eyes snap to mine. "Alessa," he says sharply.

"Please, Dante."

"He disobeyed my orders. You were kidnapped because *he* took you somewhere it wasn't safe," his voice raises. "You were almost killed, *Fata*."

"I asked him to take me there. Would you rather I've gone alone?"

"Baby—"

"No," I say sharply. "He got shot, trying to protect me. I was the one who snuck out. I was the one determined to find out the secrets *you* were hiding from me. It wasn't his fault."

"It was mine," he whispers and as much as I want to deny it, I can't, because if he told me the truth from the start I'd have never left to find it for myself.

"No secrets, remember?" I shake my head as the nurse huffs in frustration then leaves the room. "Why did you keep secrets from me?"

He's quiet again, his face downcast as his eyes focus on our joined hands.

"My empire is built on secrets, Alessa...I didn't want to keep them."

"But you did, anyway," I sigh. "From the very beginning."

Dante licks his lips. "I was afraid that if you found out the truth, you'd hate me. "

I chuckle. "Keeping the truth from me was the last thing you should have been worrying about. You were a total dick to me from the start." *Until he wasn't.* Until he was everything I didn't know I wanted and needed. "Truth about what, Dante?" I ask, squeezing his hand with mine. Something digs into the side of my finger, and if it didn't kill so

344

damn much, I'd have tried to investigate, but even the slightest movement hurts like a bitch.

"About everything." He lets go of my hands and buries his face in his hands.

"Like the fact I was born in Blackwood?" I ask. Dante freezes. "Or that my mother had an affair with Nico's son?" I continue, watching him for any sign of emotions. "Or that my father killed my mother and the-en," my voice breaks.

Dante's hands fall off his face revealing eyes full of anguish. "I killed your father."

"You saved me," I say at the same time.

He shakes his head "I thought I was saving you, but I made it worse. The things you went through...the shit that happened to y—"

"You saved me, Dante," I state firmly. "You were just a kid yourself. You couldn't know."

"I should have checked up on you. Made sure." He grips my hand and lifts it to his lips. "I will never forgive myself for abandoning you like that."

"Well, I—What the fuck is that?" I blink in shock at the huge diamond trying to blind me.

"What?" Dante asks in confusion, looking over his shoulder then back at me.

"That!" I motion with my eyes at the rock the size of a disco ball. "No wonder I can't lift my arm," I mutter.

"It's your engagement ring." Dante shrugs like he's not blowing my mind with his statement.

"My *what* now?"

"Engagement ring," he says patiently.

"What the hell, Dante? Shouldn't you like, ask me first?"

"I did, you said yes."

The hell? Were we having two different conversations? I remember us joking around, not him proposing. I'm about to open my mouth in protest, but he places a finger on my lips, stopping me.

"It's not like it matters anymore. You're mine, I'm yours. This ring is just a formality—I'm going to marry you."

"Dante," I whisper against his finger. "But—"

"No buts. As soon as you can walk, we can go get our licence. I had the application filed already. We can have a proper wedding later."

"What about the contract?"

"I don't give a fuck about the contract."

I try to shake my head, but the movement hurts too much. I guess I'm getting married?

## 48

## DANTE

It takes a week for Alessa to be discharged. Coincidentally, it is the exact amount of time it takes me to convince her there's no point in taking off her engagement ring—I'll only slip it back on at the next opportune moment. I'm not discouraged by her determination not to wear it. She knows as well as I do that we belong together, and as much of a fuss she's making about me being an 'obsessed mafia douche', I see her looking at the ring wistfully and smiling when she thinks I'm not watching.

"How are you feeling, baby?" I ask, placing a kiss on her knuckles as I help her out of the car, and grab the hospital bags from the backseat.

Alessa bites her bottom lip, trying to squelch the grin dancing threatening to break out. "I can't believe I'm finally out." She inhales deeply. "Aahhh, the smell of fresh air. The feel of gravel under my feet. This is what freedom feels like."

"You sound like you just got out of prison, not a luxury hospital suite."

"Well, Dante." She whirls to face me, a small grimace appearing on her face with the quick movement.

I'm by her side in an instant. "Are you hurting? Should I carry you?"

She rolls her eyes. "I'm fine, nurse Santoro."

Oh, I'll nurse her back to health, alright. Now that I've had the 'all clear' from her doctor, I've got plans for that delicious pussy of hers. It's been a week of torture not being able to sink into her, and the couple of times I licked her to orgasm in her hospital bed was nowhere near enough. Just the thought of how she screamed my name, causing poor Bri to run in and get an eyeful of my head between Alessa's legs, is making me smirk.

She blushes, her green eyes widening as if she knows exactly where my mind has gone. "Let's go," I growl, taking her hand in mine and guiding her up the steps to the front door.

"But...the bags," she mumbles.

"Someone will get them. There are important things we need to discuss." I lift her into my arms and kick open the door before making my way up the stairs.

"Y-you want to talk?" There's a note of disappointment in her voice, and I fight the smile that's trying to creep up.

I grunt a non-reply as we step through the threshold of our bedroom. Yes, *our* bedroom. While in the hospital, I had my men move all of Alessa's things into the master. There's no way I'd let her sleep anywhere else now that I have her, anyway. Placing her on the bed, I kneel and gently slip off her shoes one by one.

"I don't bow for anyone," I say, stroking the sole of her foot. "I don't kneel for anyone," I continue letting my hands slide up her legs and hook under the waistband of her leggings. "But you, *Fata*. For you, I'm on my knees. I have never been so scared in my entire life." I press my face against her stomach, trying to take control of my breathing.

Her fingers dig into my hair. "Scared of what?" Her voice is just above a whisper.

"Of losing *you*. You know, I never believed in love. I know now it's because no one else could make me feel the way you do. No one could lay claim to my heart because it has always been yours." I suck in a breath.

"Dante—"

"I love you, Alessa. Like a fool."

She chuckles, "Like a fool?"

I shake my head, looking up into her eyes. "I love you like a fool because every breath I take, I take for you. When you're not around, there's a storm inside, tearing my world apart, and all I can do is pray for your calm. You're my chaos, a mix of passion and pain I can't control, and I should be terrified because I crave control. But I crave you more, Alessa. I crave your smile, your touch, your taste..."

"Dant—"

"You are my reason for living, baby. Don't you ever put yourself in danger like that ever again." Hooking my finger into the waistband of her leggings, I pull them down her smooth legs. "People are terrified of me. They think I'm ruthless. And they're right, *Fata*, I'd burn this fucking world to the ground if you weren't in it. Do you understand?"

She nods

"So if you want the world to be a safe place. If you want peace, you better live a long and happy life."

"With you..." she whispers.

"Is that a question?"

"No, Dante. I want to live my life with you." She lifts her arms, letting me pull her loose sweater off.

"Good, because I'm not sure I'd be able to let you go if you didn't." I press a soft kiss over the bandage covering her wound.

"I love you, too," she whispers, making my heart soar. "But—" she bites her lip.

Standing up, I pull my t-shirt off and undo the buttons on my jeans. Alessa reaches out, her fingers tracing my taut muscles above the waist.

"No buts." I push my jeans down, freeing my already hard for her cock.

"I don't want to be the reason there's a rift between you and the other families," she gasps as I lean over her, gently laying her on the bed.

"*Fata.*" I pull off her panties. "Nicolosi declared war the minute he took you. Now, I'd rather not talk about it when you're naked under me," I continue, slowly moving up her body and placing small kisses on her skin.

"But...the contract," she shivers when I lick her hip.

"You're the only person I'm marrying." I close my mouth over her nipple, biting it gently, then licking the sting away.

"Dante," Alessa gasps.

"No more talking, *Fata*. Let me take care of my fiancée."

"What—" she moans when my fingers find her soaked pussy. "What about...dirty talking?"

My lips lift into a half smile. That sort of talking is always allowed. But I don't reply, finding her lips instead.

We kiss for so long that time seems to stretch, each languid stroke of our tongues an eternity in itself. Basking in the feel of her skin against mine, I let the moment take over as she moans into my lips, her kisses growing erratic with each movement of my fingers against her swollen clit. I can feel her need in the way her fingertips are digging into my shoulders, in the way her breathing shallows, and her thighs start to shake. It takes all my strength not to sink into her wet cunt and fuck her like the crazed man she makes me. Hard. Demanding. And with abandon. I know she wants that too, but she's still recovering, so it will have to wait.

But then Alessa does what she does best—she surprises me. Her hand wraps around my wrist as she pulls my fingers away from her pussy, guiding it up her body until I'm touching her lips. She closes her eyes as her tongue darts out, licking her taste off of my hand. I growl as my vision hazes. I'm on the verge of losing control. It's been too long since the last time I felt her tight cunt squeezing my cock. There's no time to contemplate that thought, as with a smile, she gives my fingers a small suck before moving my hand down, placing it on her neck then looking me straight in the eyes. Her green ones filled with lust as my fingers close around her throat.

"Fuck me, Dante," she breathes shakily.

My eyes flutter closed as I try to steady my breathing.

She doesn't wait for my reply, her small hand wrapping around my stiff cock as she guides it towards her entrance. I shudder as my tip, already leaking precum, nestles against her hot entrance.

"I need to be gentle," I say, reminding us both that she's not quite ready for what she's asking for. Not in the state she's still in. I sit on my haunches, trying to pull myself back in, but she just takes my dick into her hands once more and pumps it before guiding it to her pussy again. This time, the tip goes in, making me shudder at the feel of her warmth.

"Dante," she pleads, and my name on her lips undoes me. I push into her, one hand on her throat, the other on her stomach, to stop her from moving too much. I pump into her slowly, my thumb reaching down to her clit. She screams my name as I pinch it then trace circles around it.

"You're so fucking beautiful, stuffed full of my cock," I rasp, watching myself pump in and then out slowly, my whole body aflame with the sensation of being inside her. It's like she's in my every nerve ending, in my bloodstream— hot lava pumping straight into my heart. My chest squeezes as her eyes find mine, her mouth opening in a silent gasp. Her legs begin to shake as her fingers dig into the sheets beneath us. I drive into her over and over, an unrelenting slow pace, designed to drive her wild, take her to the edge. Each time I feel her getting too close, I slow down, my fingers leaving her clit determined to make this last. Not wanting it to stop. The need to feel her around me outweighing the need for release.

"Fuck, *Fata. Voglio restare dentro di te per sempre... No, per sempre non è abbastanza.*[1]"

"Dante," she moans.

"Not long enough, Alessa," I chant as a bead of sweat drips down my chest and lands on her bronze skin.

"Dante, please."

"I could listen to you beg for my cock all day long." I pick up my pace.

She squeezes her tight pussy around me, making me groan. Fuck it feels so good. Like she's been made just for me. I'm on the cusp of losing all my restraint. I circle inside her hips, grinding into her so that she knows every single bit inside her pussy belongs to me. She's mine. "Mine," I growl.

"Yours, Dante," she whispers on an exhale, trying to move her hips.

"Do you want to come, *Fata*?" I ask only because I'm no longer in control of my body. Even if I wanted to slow down, I wouldn't be able to.

"Yes, please."

"Yes, what?"

"Please..." she whimpers as I pump into her.

"Alessa," I growl.

"Please make me come."

My thumb finds her clit again as the fingers around her throat tighten. "Come, then," I demand as I pound into her.

"Come all over my cock, baby. Show me just how good I make you feel."

Her cunt squeezes around me as her eyes widen, her gaze never leaving mine. Trembling beneath me, Alessa explodes, screaming my name. I follow straight after, letting her pussy milk my dick as she keeps coming, wave after wave hitting her each time I move inside her.

"Oh my god," she gasps as last tremors wrack her body.

I smirk. "Just your average Saint, baby."

"Nothing average about what just happened, Dante. Nothing average about you." She nuzzles my neck as I pull us to the side, my cock still inside her. I help her lift her leg over my thigh for comfort.

"Are you okay? Did I hurt you?"

"I'm fine." I can hear the smile in her voice. "More than fine."

"And your side?" I gently trace the edge of her bandage.

She shrugs. "It was always going to be uncomfortable, but it wasn't too bad. You really need to stop babying me. I was fine days ago."

"Oh, yeah?" I ask, driving into her.

She gasps. "Okay, well, I do need a minute to recover."

I nip her earlobe. "Fifty-five seconds."

"What are you—" she sucks in a breath as I pinch her nipple. "Dante."

"Forty-five," I whisper before capturing her lips with mine.

Her arms instantly wrap around my neck, and I lose count of the seconds she's supposed to have left, but it doesn't seem to matter, as with a moan, Alessa starts rocking on my cock, making every coherent thought in my head disappear.

# 49

# ALESSA

"Hey, it's my hospital bag," I yawn as I settle myself on my favourite stool by the kitchen island while Dante puts the coffee machine on. Little sleeping has been done in the last few days, but you won't hear me complaining. I'm in two minds about getting up to get the bag and staying right where I am with my butt firmly placed on the comfy seat watching Dante's tattoo-covered back while he makes me a coffee.

Gracefully, Dante moves around the kitchen, captivating me with how at home he looks. My gaze roams over his body, noting the flex in his arms as he pulls breakfast ingredients out of the fridge before placing them next to the stove. It's a pleasant distraction from a subject I know I'll have to broach soon.

"I didn't realise you can cook," I muse, genuinely surprised as he places strips of bacon under the grill. Somehow I never imagined Dante as the cooking sort.

He shrugs, cracking eggs into a bowl. "We didn't always have a chef. After my mum passed away, Massimo was too busy with the Family to worry about minuscule things such as feeding his children. Someone had to step up."

I swallow. "Yeah, I guess we've got that in common—having to grow up at a young age."

Dante visibly stiffens, and too late, I realise my blunder. Of course, reminding him about how I grew up was not my best idea. "Where's your chef, anyway? Lorena was it?"

"I let her go."

My jaw opens, half in mourning for all the deliciousness I'll never taste, half in shock. "Why?"

"She disrespected my future wife in my house."

I blink. "But—that was weeks ago."

He looks at me pointedly. "Yes."

"So you fired her today?" I glance at the glinting diamond on my ring finger.

"No."

"While I was in the hospital?" I play with the band, twisting it side to side.

"No." He says from behind me, his breath making a strand of my hair flutter.

"When?" I lean into him as he nuzzles my neck.

"The minute Angelo told me what she implied. So probably about an hour after she said it."

I gasp. "But—"

"What part of 'you were always meant to be mine' don't you understand, *Fata*?"

A shaky breath escapes my lungs, my body lighting up just at his proximity, but as quickly as he appeared behind me, he is gone, leaving me cold, breathless, and buzzing with need.

Stunned into silence, I stay seated as the turmoil of emotions within me dies down. When I'm sure I'm no longer in danger of turning into putty, I clear my throat, pushing away the lingering thoughts about Lorena and focusing on Dante, who is now expertly mixing eggs.

When he notices me watching him, he smiles at me,

then turns to pass me a cup of coffee. I want to relax into this domestic scene, but there's a question that has been lingering in my subconscious for the past week.

"Dante," I start hesitantly, "how did you know where to find me?"

His movements halt as the smile on his face drops, the spatula in his hand suspended mid-air. *No more secrets*, I chant in my mind.

"There's a tracker in your bracelet," he replies, his eyes darting to my wrist. My gaze follows as I look at the unassuming gift from Arrow, confused.

"W-what? I don't understand." My mind is racing a million miles a minute trying to come up with a solution that won't collapse the carefully built world around me.

"I had Arrow put a tracker in your bracelet, just in case," Dante confesses, his voice a low murmur that sends shivers down my spine.

My chest tightens, his words carving hollow spaces within me as the conflicting emotions within start to churn —anger, hurt, confusion.

Dante's admission feels like a betrayal. A breach of trust we so carefully tried to build. My stomach revolts, the taste of coffee now sour in my mouth, as I try to process the betrayal. I could expect a move like this from Dante. He's always made clear he achieves his goals no matter the path of destruction. But Arrow? My Arrow, whom I've become so close with, has never been mine in the first place. They have worked for Dante all along. My gaze focuses on the bracelet once more, a supposed symbol of friendship and connection —which feels like a big fat joke now.

I look up, meeting Dante's eyes, a mixture of remorse and determination behind the dark brown of his irises.

"I needed to make sure you were safe at all times, Alessa." His words don't ease the absolute mess of emotions inside me. Releasing a breath I didn't realise I was holding, I let the disappointment consume me. I'm not angry at Dante. I'm not angry at Arrow. They were both trying to protect me in their twisted way. The betrayal I'm feeling is of my own doing. I knew both Dante and Arrow have low morals, I should have expected they were working together, should have expected a move like that. And in the end, the tracker is what saved me.

"So, what," I say bitterly, "you get an alert when I'm too far away?"

Dante reaches out over the island, his hand gently touching mine, there is a plea for understanding in his expression as I shrug my emotions away.

"Arrow must have been working late," Dante starts, and just a mention of their name is making me wince. "Alessa, they really care for you."

Swallowing, I try not to look away. Deep down inside, I know Arrow cares. Deep down, I know they'd never want to hurt me, yet the sense of betrayal lingers.

"They noticed your phone was in one place and the bracelet in another—"

"They were tracking my phone, too?" I shake my head, incredulous.

Dante bites his lip. "And neither location was my house, so they called me," Dante continues, "and when I realised you weren't beside me in bed. When I realised they weren't joking." His jaw tightens. "Baby, I nearly lost it." His voice breaks. There's pain and anguish on his face—like he's feeling the emotions of that night again. The hurt in my chest loosens. "I've never moved as quickly in my entire life as when Arrow told me the location of your bracelet. I knew. I just knew."

I squeeze Dante's hand as his eyes soften with wetness at the edges.

"When I got to the house, I had the worst sense of deja vu, except this time I didn't have to be quiet. I must have killed a dozen men before I managed to get upstairs. And you were—" he sucks in a breath. "I have never wanted to rip someone to shreds with my bare hands until I saw Nicolosi's man on top of you," he whispers. "You weren't moving, blankly staring at the wardrobe I found you in, and I nearly broke there and then. I was convinced this was my payment for all the sins I have committed. That Karma has finally come to collect, I wanted to die, too. But then when I picked you up into my arms, you were breathing and my world came into focus. I had one mission—get you out of that godforsaken house."

"Dante—"

"It was the same bedroom I killed your father in, Alessa. I did that. With my bare hands. A knife to his throat."

I climb on top of the island and throw myself into his arms, hugging him tightly. I can't be angry at him when he's just been trying to save me. And I can't be angry at Arrow, because if it weren't for them I'd have probably been dead by now.

"I can't promise you it's the last of my secrets," he murmurs into my hair. "But I will always tell you the truth when you ask." He lifts my chin to face him, his thumb stroking my cheek as he brushes his lips against mine, a promise he's determined not to break.

Hunger coils in my stomach as he deepens the kiss, his fingers digging into my hair. Then my stomach—the cock blocking bastard that it is—growls.

"Let me feed you breakfast, *Fata*," Dante murmurs as he pulls away.

I so wish this was a euphemism for him feeding his cock into my mouth, but as he turns to take the bacon off the grill my wish gets trashed. At least it gets trashed with something tasty.

With a sigh, I hop off the kitchen island and pad over to my hospital bag, curious to see if the pictures of my mum are somewhere inside. One of the nurses promised me she'd located the frame with my parents' wedding photo. I know Dante would have it destroyed if he knew it was here, blaming the little frame for my injury. But the photo inside had nothing to do with it, and it's the only thing I have left of my parents. With shaky fingers I pull out the frame, the glass that lodged into the side of my body missing. Miraculously the photo inside is intact, not even a spec of blood in the corner. I run my fingers down my mother's body, my mind in turmoil over whether I should cut my father out of the picture. Then I remember the things he did and with shaky fingers I pry the picture out of the frame.

A folded letter falls onto my lap.

# 50

# ROSA

**D**earest Alessandro,

   There's a weight in my chest that's been there for years, and if I carry it any longer, I won't survive. I don't want to hurt you, but the truth is this loveless marriage is unbearable and suffocating. What began with so much hope and love, has faded away to pain and mistrust. I tried to stop it from happening, but the tighter I held on, the faster our love slipped through my fingers.

   It's been so long since we've truly talked. I used to tell you everything, but now it feels like we're strangers passing in the night. Our conversations are shallow and guarded, and I can't remember the last time we shared a genuine laugh or moment of intimacy.

   I know I'm partly to blame for this distance between us. I let my hurt and resentment consume me, and it poisoned our relationship. But even when I tried to reach out and connect with you, it felt like you were always pulling away. I know there were expectations for our marriage, but did they have to take precedence over our own happiness? We've sacrificed so much for the Family's sake, but at what cost?

*You were my world once, my everything. I wanted so badly for this to be my happy ever after, to be the woman at the centre of your world, like you were the man I revolved around. That's why it cut so deep when you turned away, blaming me for not being able to bear your children. Every harsh word and accusation wounded me, as I, too, yearned for a child—someone to love unconditionally and who would love me back just as fiercely. I felt if I could give you this, it would bind us, overcome our rift and rekindle the bond we started out with.*

*But it's a yearning that you could never understand, couldn't see past our obligations to our families. So I tried to fill the void with other things—work, hobbies, friends—but nothing could replace the emptiness in my heart.*

*I know you didn't mean to push me away or hurt me intentionally. But your indifference felt like a constant rejection that chipped away at my self-worth until there was almost nothing left.*

*When I tried to talk to you about our failing marriage or my desire for a child, you shut down or changed the subject. It was like talking to a brick wall—frustrating and disheartening.*

*And so the silence between us grew deafening until it drowned out any shred of hope that things could ever get better between us.*

*In a moment of weakness, when I was starving for the affection you withheld, I met Nico. In one night, he made me feel alive again, the weight lifted and I could breathe and hope for something more.*

*At first, I didn't think much of him—he was handsome and charming, but so were many other men in your line of business. As the night went on and we talked, I found myself drawn to him in a way I hadn't felt in years.*

*He was a breath of fresh air. He listened to me—really listened—and made me feel seen and heard.*

*One night. That's all it took for the cracks in our marriage to deepen, for me to see that the flame that once burned between us had flickered out. I'm not trying to justify my actions. I'm simply trying to explain how things came to be.*

*When I discovered I was carrying a child, a part of me hoped it would bring us back together. Maybe this new life would rekindle the love we once had and help you see past the ruthless world of the Family. But as my pregnancy progressed and you became more consumed by your ambitions, I realised that our marriage was beyond repair. I held on for two and a half years, burying my longing for affection and pretending everything was fine. But when Nico resurfaced, all my suppressed emotions came crashing down, and I couldn't deny the emptiness in my heart any longer.*

*Nico has always been perceptive. He saw right through my facade and knew I was unhappy in our marriage despite my insistence to the contrary. In his eyes, I could see the same longing and loneliness I felt every day with you.*

*He knew the truth the moment he laid eyes on Alessa—she was his, not yours. He didn't react with anger or jealousy like I expected him to. Instead, he looked at me with such tenderness and understanding I was caught off guard. And while part of me wanted to deny it and keep up the charade, I couldn't ignore the overwhelming feeling of relief that washed over me when I finally let myself admit it.*

*Please understand I'm not writing this out of cruelty or malice. I'm doing it because we can't keep living this lie. The ache of what we have lost has gnawed at my soul for far too long, and I need to unburden myself.*

*You may never forgive me for what happened between Nico and me, but I hope someday you can find it in your heart to understand.*

*I'm sorry for how things turned out, for all the pain and*

*confusion this will bring. I want you to know that even after everything, there's a part of me that still cares for you. It pains me how things slipped through our fingers, how we let all the dreams we shared die.*

*Maybe this will be the beginning of a new chapter for both of us, where we can each find peace at last. I did not make this decision lightly, but I believe this is what is best for all of us. You, Alessa, Nico, and I. I don't want Alessa to grow up in our world. A world filled with hatred and power-hungry men. I want her to be able to live freely, laugh, love whom she wants to, and not have the threat of the Mafia over her head.*

*You might not believe it, but Nico never wanted to be a part of this world either. All he ever wanted was a loving family. Exactly what Alessa and I were looking for, too.*

*I don't know how else to say it, so here it is—we are running away. As far away from Blackwood as possible. Please don't look for us, it will only bring hurt and confusion, but will not change my mind.*

*If you find us and drag us back, I will fight you every step of the way for the future my daughter deserves, one not filled with treachery, lovelessness, and isolation. Let her be free, Alessandro, I won't hide from her how it began, her roots or what awaits her should she choose to step back into this life. But let it be exactly that, a choice.*

*Find peace and perhaps a woman to soften your heart and fill your dark world with light and hope. I am no longer that person, and we both deserve happiness that cannot be found in each other. Alessa deserves a childhood of warmth and love, something that would never be found growing up between two people who, on their best days, exude detachment and coldness, and on the worst hatred and anger.*

*I am doing what any good mother would—I am fighting for the best possible future for my daughter.*

*So, please, do the right thing, forget we exist, and live your life. Choose your happiness, and if you can't—choose happiness for Alessa—an innocent soul who is untainted by the treachery riff in your world.*

*Yours,*

*Rosa*

## 51

### DANTE

For a second, I'm taken right back to the worst moment of my life. For a second my heart stops, because when I look up to check on Alessa, she's on the floor, slouched over. All too quickly, my mind races back to when I found her in her childhood home.

She had the same expression she's wearing now—face pale, eyes glazed over. But although her posture is rigid, her lips are silently moving along with the words she is reading. With a deep breath, I stop myself from throwing the food I'm carrying onto the floor and rushing to her side. Instead, I place the plates on the counter and slowly walk to her, trying to figure out what has her so distraught.

With her hands trembling, she clutches a crumpled piece of paper so tightly that her knuckles turn white as the colour drains from her face.

"What is it?" I crouch beside her, my hand instinctively reaching over and stroking her arm in comfort. My gaze lands on the cursed photo frame I hoped would be burned or thrown into the ocean, but no luck—somehow, it has found its way back into our lives. The picture of Alessa's mother and father smiling at each other discarded on the floor right next to it.

"*Fata*?" I probe further, when she doesn't reply.

Silently, her eyes still focused on her lap, she hands me the paper she's been holding. It's a handwritten letter.

My breathing ragged, I scan the words Rosa must have penned nearly twenty years ago. A confession and a plea for forgiveness, for freedom. Everything I have suspected since Alessa's first day in the hospital is confirmed. Alessandro Carusso was not Alessa's real father. Nico Nicolosi's only son was.

I know I should feel something. I can see tears spilling from Alessa's eyes at the shocking revelation. The world she thought she finally pieced together shattered once more. But it's hard to look past the ever-expanding ball of happiness in my chest, so strong it nearly takes my breath away.

Because this is the best possible outcome I daren't have hoped for.

I pull her trembling frame onto my lap. "Hush now, *cuore mio*[1]," I murmur thickly, stroking her hair. "Everything will be alright..." The truth of that statement pierces my soul—Nicolosi can't fucking touch us now. His marriage contract will be fulfilled by the one person he wanted to get rid of—Alessa, his own blood. The darkness in me rejoices at the cruel twist of fate. I will marry a Nicolosi, after all.

She sniffles, hiding her face in the crook of my neck, and despite the happiness, my heart aches at the pain I know she must be feeling at this moment for the life she could have had. Except the ache is shallow because as much as I love her, I can't help the selfish thoughts—if she had that life, would she be here with me? Would I have ever found her? The possibility of a life without her—bleak and colour-less—cuts deeper than a sharp knife, leaving a searing pain in its wake.

Her hands dig into my t-shirt as I press my lips onto her temple. Pressing my fingers below her chin, I lift it up, turning her to meet my eyes. Eyes that flashed like lightning storms when we first met and made me yearn to kiss away their fury. Now they swim with hurt and questions that shred me deeper than any bullet or blade ever could.

"I know this—this letter shakes the foundation of who you thought you were," I say, brushing away a stray tear with my thumb. "But it does not change the person you are. The brave, stubborn, vulnerable woman who has completely bewitched me—body and tattered soul. The woman who saved me from the monster within."

She bites her lip. "You are still the same courageous. *maddening*," I give her a smile, "beautiful Alessa, who had me spellbound from the first moment. My *Fata*."

She lets out a shaky breath, but keeps her watery gaze locked with mine. Seeing the trust lingering there, I feel something loosen in my chest. My voice drops lower, rough with sincerity and promise. "This letter does not define you. What matters is here and now. You and I."

I take her face between my hands, drawing it closer and forcing her to truly listen—see the love I feel behind my eyes. "You hold my heart, baby, for all eternity. No vow I make to you will ever be broken. No one will ever come between us. Because, *Fata*, I am bound to you. Irrevocably bound to you."

"You're mine, and I'm yours," she whispers.

"Nothing will tear us apart, baby." I place a kiss on her nose. She came back to Blackwood looking for answers, but I know what she ended up finding goes beyond the truth.

I shift her around until she straddles me.

"I love you, Dante," she says, my name on her lips sounding like a prayer.

My phone buzzes in my pocket, reminding me there's a

world outside of our bubble. Ignoring it, I kiss her fiercely, desperately, knowing there are still storms on the horizon.

"We'll fly to Vegas this weekend," I murmur against her lips. "I don't want to wait any longer."

"Okay," she agrees, through a small smile. "Who's going to marry Nicolosi's daughter, then? Angelo? Luca?"

I grin. "Me, baby. Did you not read the letter? You're a Nicolosi."

She gasps. "Oh my god, does that mean—"

"Nico Nicolosi is your grandfather? Yes."

"Eeww," she makes a sour face, making me chuckle.

"He'll get what he deserves."

She bites her lip. "Shouldn't we—"

"No, he doesn't deserve mercy. Not from me, and especially not from you."

She sighs. "Shouldn't we at least tell him?"

I shrug. "I'll decide once he comes out of hiding. For now he's too big of a coward to face me head on."

"Or..." She bites her lip. "He's planning something."

"Whichever option it is, we'll face it head on. You and I, *Fata*."

"Together." She smiles.

"Forever."

My phone buzzes in my pocket again.

"You better take it." Alessa leans back as I decide to ignore my phone and kiss her instead.

With a roll of my eyes, I pull the phone out and mouth, "To be continued," at her before answering.

She wriggles in my lap then pulls her top off. Fuuuck. She's not wearing a bra, her tits bouncing freely as she moves off my lap and plays with the waistband of my sweatpants.

"You have three seconds," I growl into my phone as I watch my fiancée play with her nipples.

I shake my head in awe, a smile spreading across my face. I cannot believe how fucking lucky I got. Without even bothering to listen to the person on the end of the line I toss my phone aside, not caring if they are still able to hear or not. "Come here, baby," I say, my voice as thick as my cock. "Let me take care of my future wife."

*The End*

# EPILOGUE
## ANGELO

"He hung up," Luca chuckles. "Well, I'm hanging up, to be exact, but it's best for all the parties involved."

"For fuck's sake," I growl.

"I guess it's up to you guys to check it out," Arrow's voice is way too cheery on the other end of the line.

*Fuck. Fine.* I kick a stone across the pavement and watch it roll away, disappearing off the pier and into the ocean. Once again, I'm fucking left to deal with shit alone. I get my brother is in love, but come on! With Nicolosi in hiding, we really should be making a plan on how to get rid of him or at least on how to smoke him out.

I sigh. "Okay, tell me exactly what you found again." Luca steps beside me, giving me a goofy grin, and I have to squelch the urge to roll my eyes at him. I swear mum must have dropped him as a baby.

"I was only following Alessa's trail," I try not to growl at the name. I don't hate her, but I do resent the amount of attention she's getting from Dante, "and it seems like Nicolosi smuggled something he shouldn't have last week." The numbers are all out of whack.

"This would have been—"

"The same night he took Alessa, yes. I guess whatever he had delivered must not have been important enough to risk coming back for it after shit went down."

"He's a scared kitty cat in a pinstriped suit." I shrug, making my way to where empty containers are stored. "Stay on the line."

Arrow grumbles on the other side but doesn't disconnect the ten minutes it takes us to get to the fenced area.

"Do you have the number?"

They rattle off a string of letters and numbers, I repeat them to Luca as he opens the gate, and we walk in. Most of the sea-weathered containers in here should be empty, but there's still enough of them that it takes thirty minutes for me to spot the right one. Probably because two minutes into the search, the fog rolled in, clouding my vision and making it impossible to see anything farther than a few yards away.

Luca cuts the chain locking the door as I tap my foot impatiently, my suit getting soaked by the drizzle which just started. I fucking hate Blackwood's weather.

With a grunt, I yank the door open and look inside the dark container. Instantly, a rancid smell envelopes me, and I have to fight the coffee I had this morning, threatening to come back up.

"What did you find?" Arrow asks.

I cover my nose with the sleeve of my jacket and take a step inside.

"It stinks," I reply with a muffled voice taking another step. "But it seems empty. Could they have gotten to it already?"

"No, the surveillance cameras are all clear."

"Luca put the fucking torchlight on," I growl. He fumbles with his phone for a few seconds before, finally, the light comes on.

The hand with my phone in it drops to my side as I take the sight in front of me.

"*Cazzo*," Luca swears.

A woman. There's a body of a woman lying on the floor of the container. Empty bottles of water scattered around her.

I rush to her side, placing my fingers on her pulse—faint but still there.

"Call the hospital," I tell Luca as I put my arms under her frail body and lift her up. "And then call Dante. And keep fucking calling him until he picks up. Time for fucking around is over."

# BONUS EPILOGUE

Want more of Dante?
Scan the QR code to receive an EXCLUSIVE EPILOGUE
straight to your inbox.
There might be some spanking...

# GLOSSARY

## 3. Alessa

1. Good morning
2. Why are you still here?
3. Does your life mean so little to you?
4. I like her

## 11. Alessa

1. Errand boy
2. What the fuck?

## 12. Alessa

1. Shit

## 14. Dante

1. Fuck
2. Understood
3. Don't intervene in someone else's marriage

## 15. Alessa

1. Angry

## 21. Alessa

1. My sorceress
2. I'm sick and you are my medicine. Your taste, your body, is the only thing that can bring me back from this madness.

## 23. Alessa

1. The family

## 36. Alessa

1. Perfect. So damn perfect.
2. What, my beautiful sorceress?
3. This will be the sweetest torture, won't it?

## 37. Dante

1. Christ, so tight.

## 39. Alessa

1. Christ, Sorceress.

## 42. Alessa

1. bitch

## 48. Dante

1. I want to stay inside you forever... No, forever is not long enough.

## 51. Dante

1. My heart

# MORE BOOKS BY THE AUTHOR

**THE FALSE STARTS SERIES**

For Crying Out Loud

For What It's Worth

Forever and a Day

For Heaven's Sake

**THE HOLIDATES SERIES/ THE FALSE STARTS CROSSOVER**

The Sexiest Nerd Alive

**HEART OF A WOUNDED HERO/ THE FALSE STARTS CROSSOVER**

Nothing Left To Lose

**CURVES FOR CHRISTMAS/ THE FALSE STARTS CROSSOVER**

Frost My Cookie

# ACKNOWLEDGEMENTS

Firstly, I want to thank my readers. Thank you for picking up this book. If this is the first time we meet, I hope to see you gain. If you've read my books before, thank you from the bottom of my heart for continuing to support me. I love you all so much, and am incredibly grateful for each and every one of you.

Secondly, I have to thank my OG team, Bri, Kristina and Deb. You guys know I have struggled with burnout this year, and your words of encouragement and love for everything I teased meant the world to me. This book would not be what it is without you.

My newbie alpha readers, Sierra, Cara, Nichole, Sarah and Tiffanie. How the heck did I get so lucky? Props to Jasmine, my wonderful PA, for finding my new favourite group of people.

Special thanks to Adina, for helping me with the Italian, and Zoe-Amelia for her eagle eyes and amazing words.

Of course, I will always mention my rocks, KBWs, especially Maddison, Letty, Adeline, Amanda, Rosa and Keeley. I love you guys. Thanks for being you.

And thank you, Mr Jo, for all the night you spent alone, while I sat upstairs writing this book

THANK YOU! THANK YOU! THANK YOU!

# ABOUT THE AUTHOR

Jo Preston writes fun and sexy romance books.

She lives with her husband, son and a dog (that doubles as a teddy bear) in the UK, where she wraps up in warm clothes and hang out under umbrellas, dreaming of warm destinations.

When she's not writing, she enjoys a glass of wine (or two) with a good book or a favourite Netflix show and coming up with terms like #SmutCom.

Want to be a part of an exclusive smut-loving community? Come hang out in Jo's Facebook group *Jo Preston's Book Besties*

facebook.com/authorjpreston

instagram.com/authorjpreston

goodreads.com/jpreston

bookbub.com/authors/j-preston

Printed in Great Britain
by Amazon